"YOU'RE A FOREVER KIND OF WOMAN, ASH. You deserve a gold ring and promises in front of a preacher and a wedding dress all stitched in satin. I'll leave you, lady. I'll break your damn heart."

Desperate to drive the resolve from those beloved eyes, Ashleen succumbed to impulse, loosing her hold on the folds of wool clasped beneath her chin, shrugging the fabric free.

It was reckless, more wanton than anything she'd ever done before, yet as the wool glided down her slender form, it seemed as inevitable as the sea reaching for the shore. She heard Garret's sharp intake of breath, saw the raging hunger explode in those silvery eyes.

"Sweet Jesus, lady," he gritted between clenched teeth. "What are you trying to do to me?"

"Love you, Garret. Just love you." She ran her fingertips over his chest. . . .

Pain flitted across Garret's face, mingled with the most hopeless longing. "Please, Ashleen, don't do this."

"It's too late, Garret," she said, pressing a kiss against his racing heart. "I already have."

Books by Kimberly Cates

Crown of Mist
Restless is the Wind
To Catch a Flame
Only Forever

Published by POCKET BOOKS

Most Pocket Books are available at special quantity discounts for bulk purchases for sales promotions, premiums or fund raising. Special books or book excerpts can also be created to fit specific needs.

For details write the office of the Vice President of Special Markets, Pocket Books, 1230 Avenue of the Americas, New York, New York 10020.

ONLY FOREVER

KIMBERLY CATES

POCKET STAR BOOKS

New York   London   Toronto   Sydney   Tokyo   Singapore

A Pocket Star Book published by
POCKET BOOKS, a division of Simon & Schuster Inc.
1230 Avenue of the Americas, New York, NY 10020

ISBN: 0-671-74083-0

First Pocket Books printing April 1992

10 9 8 7 6 5 4 3 2 1

POCKET STAR BOOKS and colophon are registered
trademarks of Simon & Schuster Inc.

Printed in the U.S.A.

In memory of my grandmother, Elinor Millicent Swanson.

For lovely evenings of Tchaikovsky and sharing Little Women, Shakespeare and Laura Ingalls Wilder on your sunporch.

For giving me Dickens and the Brontes and saving every story I wrote through the years.

For listening—really listening—to a child's view of everything from Vietnam to Watergate to E.T.

And for crying with me when Bobby Kennedy died.

But most of all, for believing in my dream of becoming a writer long before I did.

Thank you, Gram.

I miss you so much.

1

*T*he glen was alive with dragons. Their greedy claws were disguised as wisps of twilight, their breath, plumes of mist, but Ashleen O'Shea knew they were there. She moved quietly along the burbling stream, her damp palms curling in the cloth of her novice's habit.

For as long as she could remember she had reveled in the tales about the dew-sweetened Irish hills. Legends reaching down from the days when druids glided silently through mystical woods. She had delighted in the stories of bold heroes and beasts a-haunting from the time she had run wild, an urchin with scraped knees and sun-gold hair, wielding a blackthorn-twig sword.

Yet today the games she had played so often held no allure. For now the monsters had faces—hideous features more terrifying than any even Ashleen's fertile imagination could have conjured. Masks that were the hunger, fever, despair whose shadows chained all of Ireland.

She had held them at bay for a year now—fended off the slashing of their talons, the snapping of their teeth. Now she could feel them closing in for the kill—eager, ruthless, relentless as death.

She caught her lower lip between her teeth, her blue eyes shifting to look at the distant stone walls silhouetted against the sky. The convent of St. Michael of the Angels had been a haven for the weary and the suffering for five hundred years. It had been as much a home to Ashleen as the tiny crofter's cottage on the mountainside where she had been born.

Still, as she peered across the glen to look at the ancient convent a cold sliver of dread slipped down Ash's spine, and her mind filled with images of small, beloved faces with wide, trusting eyes. No, she thought, crushing the sick churning in her stomach, surely even the horrors afflicting Ireland could not have stolen away the last wisps of faith that had been tended within the convent walls for so long. No famine, no fever could induce those within God's own house to turn away innocents who had sought shelter there. . . .

"Psst! Sister Ashleen!"

The high-pitched whisper a mere arm's length from where she stood sent Ash's heart bounding, a tiny cry rising from her throat as her gaze flashed to a gorse bush. Bright green eyes brimming with mischief peeked out at her from their shielding of brush.

"The dragon," eight-year-old Liam Fitzsimmons hissed eagerly, poking his crutch toward an outcropping of stone. "He's right over—"

"Liam's tattling, Renny!"

Ash gritted her teeth at the shrill, self-righteous cry as a blond-pigtailed girl of about twelve flounced into the open.

"He's telling Sister Ash where you are!"

"Shevonne," Ash chided, "Don't stir up tempests." But even before she spoke Ash knew the warning was futile—the girl delighted in sparking tempers, and the incorrigible Renny O'Manion was a painfully vulnerable target.

"Blast it, Liam! No fair!" A most undragonlike protest erupted from behind the boulders as a gangly boy with hair like fire and a temper to match burst from his hiding place. "You told her where I was! Three more steps and I could have devoured her right proper!"

"Consider me devoured, Renny." Ash felt some of the

tension of moments before drain away, her lips curving in affection as she remembered the boy's protests earlier that he was too big now to be playing at "baby games." Games he secretly adored as much as little Liam.

She ruffled the glowering Renny's hair. "In truth, Liam saved my life. You would have scared the soul right out of me if you'd leapt down from there."

"'Twas the best dragon lair yet!" Renny huffed, his chin thrust out at the pugnacious angle that had earned him more than his share of blackened eyes. "Liam's naught but a scare-baby. Jealous 'cause he wanted to be the dragon."

"Am not!" Liam cried, stumping out from behind the gorse bush. "Didn't care a pin if you were the dragon, 'cause I get to be the monster next. Sister Ashleen promised."

"Not for all the swells in Dublin! I'll be dragon again, I will, 'cause you spoilt my turn! And——"

Ash stepped between the boys and slipped an arm about each of them. "But if you are *both* dragons, who will be my handsome prince?" Ash inquired with a warm smile. "When we began this game you vowed I would win the hand of the Prince of the Night-wood if I were the fairy princess. And after the fright the lot of you gave me, letting me wander about waiting to be eaten, I full *expect* my just reward."

Both boys flushed, flustered, and Ash couldn't stifle a grin. "What? Neither of you is eager to carry me off to your castle?"

"It's just that it's more fun to growl and snarl and have claws, even if it's just pretend," Liam explained earnestly. "The prince has to go about being *noble*. It's boring."

"You think it tiresome to rescue fair maidens, do you?" Laughter bubbled upon Ashleen's lips as she hunkered down, catching the boy's face gently in her hands. "Come back to me in ten years, Liam Fitzsimmons, and I wager you will have changed your mind."

Liam pulled a face, raking the preening Shevonne with

a scorn-filled glare. "I shall *never* change my mind," he said with an eloquent shudder.

"Nor shall I!" Renny brandished a make-believe saber. "When I grow up I shall *always* be the villain! I'll dress in a black cape that swirls, and everyone will tremble when I ride past!"

Ash's smile faded but a whisper, the boy's words unconsciously echoing Sister Bridget's dire predictions for his future.

"You will be a right fine brigand, I am certain." Ash attempted to infuse her usual enthusiasm into her voice. "But now we have a more pressing difficulty. The prince you promised me. I should be pure fuming at the lot of you, leaving me thus abandoned! And I in my finest crown!" She touched the wreath of wildflowers they had placed upon her head earlier.

"You *should* be angry." Liam's lips quirked in an impish grin as he nestled closer. "But you never are. 'Cepting when Sister Bridget scolds 'bout Meggie."

Ash winced inwardly at the innocent words, cradling the precious weight of Liam closer as pain knotted about her heart. She glanced toward the base of a tree, unable to stifle a sigh as her eyes rested upon a small figure curled within the root's cradling arms.

The waning sun glistened upon four-year-old Meggie Kearny's dark hair, kissing features that seemed those of a lost little angel. Huge, haunted eyes, unutterably old and weary, peered warily out at the world, lips bowed soft and innocent, like the first fragile rose of spring. Lips that should have bubbled with little-girl giggles and shrieks of excitement. Lips that were agonizingly silent —as if a dark fairy had slipped between them and stolen the child's soul.

Releasing Liam, Ash straightened and walked over to where the little girl sat, oblivious as ever to the game going on around her. The child's skirt was filled with rocks she had been gathering, one arm clutching her raggedy doll against her thin chest.

How many times had Sister Bridget scolded that the

4

threadbare doll should be tossed away? Even Sister Agatha had offered to make the child a new one. Yet Ash had refused to hear of it, for it was that tiny bundle of rags and stuffing that gave her hope. Hope that one day Meggie's troubled eyes would clear, hope that someday the child might speak.

Every time Ashleen saw the plaything she remembered the day she had found little Meggie huddled beside her dying mother. The child had been half starved, her fever-stricken mother unable to care for her. The two had been alone, abandoned. Afraid. And when death had come, grief had torn cruelly through Meggie's small body, leaving nothing but a shell of the laughing, lively imp she had been. A grief Ashleen had shared as she gently closed Moira Kearny's eyes for eternity. Meggie's mother. Ashleen's most cherished friend. The woman who had married the man Ashleen had loved.

Ash crushed the thought and knelt beside the girl.

"What pretties have you found, Meggie-love?" Ash asked softly, stroking the child's silky raven curls. "Will they be our dragon's treasure?"

Eyes the hue of a rain-washed sky turned up to meet Ashleen's gaze, one tiny hand curling over the pebbles pillowed in the dove-gray cloth of the little girl's skirt.

"No? Well *you* shall be my treasure, then, Meggie-mine. The most wondrous treasure of all." Ash drifted a kiss onto the child's brow. She felt Meggie instinctively stiffen at the caress, but it no longer hurt Ash to feel the child's rejection. It only made her sad.

"Meggie, do you know that the gentlemen here refuse to play prince?"

"Gentlemen?" Shevonne sniggered. "Liam's no gentleman! And Sister Bridget says Renny's a reprobake."

"Reprobate," Ash corrected automatically.

"Does reprobate mean you're gonna hang someday?" Liam asked guilelessly. "When the Devons brought Renny back from adopting him the last time, Sister Bridget said—"

"I think we've had enough discussion about Sister

Bridget's opinions." Ash couldn't keep the edge from her voice as she glimpsed the shading of hurt crossing Renny's face.

Ash forced a smile, intent upon distracting Renny—and herself—from thoughts of the indomitable Sister Bridget. Thoughts that made Ashleen's stomach clench with wondering at what was transpiring, even now, in Sister Agatha's chamber.

Yet as Ash's gaze swept the brood of children she loved so much, fear slipped its insidious dagger into her breast, tormenting her with the unthinkable possibility that this might be the last time they were all together—the last time they played at dragons in their own enchanted glen.

Sudden tears stung Ashleen's eyes, and she turned away in an effort to conceal them. Nay. No one—not even God himself—would take these babes from her, these children who had filled her life with such laughter, such hope, such love. These children who gifted her with such absolute trust.

"Sister Ash? I don't much listen to what Sister Bridget says." There was such rare gentleness in Renny's voice it nearly undid her. Gritting her teeth, she resolved that no shadowy fears, no subtle cruelties would sully this day that was so precious to her, to them.

She spun around, catching the boy in a fierce hug. Renny grumbled at his dignity being thus assaulted, but his eyes sparkled with shy pleasure. "You see? I always knew you were a bright lad."

"I have an idea!" Liam's whoop of excitement made Ash jump, the rest of the children dissolving into gales of laughter.

"Well, I do!" Liam protested. "It's about the prince trouble."

"The prince?" Ash asked, aware that she had all but forgotten the game. "Oh, Liam, it doesn't matter. I was but teasing."

"I know, but just listen! It's perfect! Shevonne, give me your sash."

"My sash?" Ash expected Shevonne to balk, as ever, at

relinquishing any of her possessions for even a moment, but curiosity won out, and the girl slipped the dark blue swath of cloth from about her waist. "If you ruin it, Liam Fitzsimmons, I'll pull your ears right off, I will!"

"It won't be hurt a bit! Watch!" Liam leaned against the boulder, bracing himself to take all weight from his crooked leg. "I'll just tie it about my crutch—so—" Brow furrowing with concentration, he knotted it about the smoothed length of wood. "There." He presented his work, chest swelling with pride. "It's his majesty's cravat. Tied most ex-squeezitly, I must say."

"That's nothing but your crutch, and my sash getting all crumpled up with knots," Shevonne protested.

"I think it a fine prince." Renny shot her a killing glare and turned, stretching one hand out to Liam. "With your permission, me lord dragon?"

Balancing on his sound leg, Liam offered him the crutch.

Renny took it and faced Ashleen, sketching her a bow with most admirable solemnity. "Your most royal highness, princess of the fairies, may I present you this most majestical prince?"

Ashleen resisted the urge to catch both Renny and Liam in her arms and give in to the torrent of tears that the stress of waiting for the nuns' decision had built within her.

Instead she dropped into her most graceful curtsy, her voice a properly awed whisper. "My prince, I have been waiting a lifetime for you."

"Give me back my sash," Shevonne's voice intruded. "It's a silly game anyway. Nuns can't get married. Sister Ash—"

"Sister Ash isn't a *real* nun yet," Liam objected. "That's why Sister Bridget looks all sour when we call her Sister. And anyway, this is just pretend. You spoil everything, Shevonne."

"Do not! It *is* a silly game, and you're a—"

"Hush, children!" Ashleen snapped, her gaze locking upon a solitary dark-robed figure making its way up the

path to the glen. Her stomach lurched, her hands clenching together in a desperate prayer. Please, God
. . . please . . .

The children's silence closed about her, and she
glanced at their faces, suddenly so still, their eyes ques-
tioning.

"I—I have to run back and speak with Sister Agatha
now." Ash attempted to feign a lightness she did not feel.

"Why? Did . . . did we do something wrong?" Why
did she feel so guilty as she looked into Liam's trusting
face?

"No. It's nothing like that. Sister Magdalene is coming
to watch you, so you may keep playing."

Renny glanced from the approaching figure to Meggie,
who was making a circle with her stones. "I'm a bit tired.
I think I'll . . . just sit for a little." He slid down beside
the little girl, a protective light in his eyes.

"You . . . rest then," Ash said with a grateful smile.
"I'll be back as quickly as I can."

"An' then I get to be dragon," Liam piped up.

"Then you get to be dragon."

Ash swallowed hard, remembering the motley group
the children had made when she had brought them
together a year ago. Renny belligerent, his fists ever
flying, Liam constantly weeping for the parents he had
lost, Shevonne whining even more gratingly than she had
today, and Meggie . . . They had all been determined to
wall out the others, yet somehow during the past months
they had let go of their defenses enough to become
something akin to . . . to a family, she thought. Trusting
one another, depending, however reluctantly, upon one
another. Even protecting one another—bristling at any,
save themselves, who dared cast aspersions upon one of
their number.

And they would never lose that, never be alone again,
Ash promised herself.

She hastened down the winding dirt road, her eyes
fixed upon Sister Magdalene. The face that had been
apple-round and rosy when first Ashleen had come to St.

Michael's was gaunt now, gray, testament to the hardship the great hunger had wreaked upon even those within the convent's sheltering walls. Thin fingers were gripping the rosary beads that hung at the nun's waist. But it was Sister Magdalene's eyes that sent dread scrambling through Ash.

"Sister"—Ash fought to steady her voice—"have they—"

"You are to go to Sister Agatha at once, Mary Ashleen." Was there sorrow in the woman's voice, or was it but the reflection of Ashleen's greatest fear?

"What . . . what did they . . . decide? Please, you must tell me."

"They struggled to discover God's will. 'Tis difficult sometimes." Magdalene gave her hand a gentle squeeze. "Quickly now."

Ash nodded, prayers, promises roiling inside her as she scooped up her skirts and ran toward the convent gates.

The statue had stood within the tiny chamber for two hundred years, the face of Christ's own mother serene as she turned her gaze to the heavens, oblivious to the sufferings of the people below.

Always there had been something gentle in those carved features, something comforting to Ashleen's restless spirit. Yet now the statue seemed to mock her with its sorrowful acceptance, its sweet, sad smile doing nothing to soften the soul-crushing despair engulfing her.

"Please," Ashleen choked out, her gaze seeking out resigned, rheumy eyes in a face lined with a thousand sorrows. "Sister Agatha, there must be something we can do. Some way we can save them. They're just children . . . so small. Helpless." Her voice trembled, faded to a whisper. "They're so alone. I cannot believe you are willing to abandon them—"

"Ashleen, child, it's hardly as if we were drowning them like a litter of unwanted pups." The nun raised hands gnarled as aged oak to the edge of her wimple. "We've done everything we can. Sheltered them, fed them for nigh on a year now." Ash started to speak, but the older woman lifted a finger to stay her. "'Tis glad I am that you gathered these wee ones together. That you made us see their need. God will bless you a thousand-fold for what you have done. And the way you have loved them—their own poor dead mothers could not have given more of their hearts."

The flaccid skin webbing the old woman's throat shook as she swallowed. "Sister Magdelene, Sister Bridget, and I have left no stone unturned in our efforts to find families willing to adopt your foundlings these past months."

Ash grasped at the words, desperate, her eyes widening with a wild, faint hope. "I know how hard you've tried. But we've managed to place so many of the children. I'm certain if we are patient—if we have faith, we'll be able to find homes for the rest."

"For a child with a crippled leg? Or a boy who has blackened the eyes of half the lads in Wicklow town?" Sister Agatha sighed, shaking her head. "We might have a chance of finding a home for Shevonne. Truth to tell, I cannot fathom why she has not already been taken up by someone in need of a strong, willing girl. But as for the others—little Liam, or Renny or Meggie—"

Ash couldn't suppress a choked cry. "Meggie, too? Surely you couldn't send her away—from here. From me. She won't allow anyone but me to touch her. She'd be terrified if she was ripped away from me. She couldn't survive it. I know—"

Ash saw the old nun's eyes flicker away, the worry-creased face paling as Sister Agatha fumbled with the worn gold band upon her finger. "Ashleen, we have no choice. The poorhouse is the only alternative—"

"The poorhouse is no alternative at all! It's so filled with fever the babes wouldn't last a month there!" Ash cried out, banging her fist against a cherrywood prie dieu. "People die there by the score. You know it! How can you condemn innocent children to that—that hell-hole?"

"Enough, Mary Ashleen!" Sister Agatha's voice cracked through Ash's tirade. "My first responsibility is to this convent. This order. The sisters here in my charge. Five hundred years has this order served these hills. We kept the light of learning alive while barbarian hordes swept Europe. We dwelt in caves, a sword's breadth from death when devil Cromwell drenched Eire in blood. 'Tis my sacred trust to see that we remain within these walls, to do God's will even after the famine that afflicts our land is but a nightmare to be forgotten."

"And while you are preserving this hulk of stone, will you be able to forget? The children's faces? Their eyes? Their laughter? Will you be able to forget the way they cry out in the night when they're frightened? Only in the poorhouse there will be no one to comfort them! If that is God's will, I'll go joyfully to the devil."

"Mary Ashleen!" The voice that could be so gentle lashed out, hopeless. "Sixty years I have lived within this 'hulk of stone.' I was placed here when I was twelve years old—gave my life up to God gladly. Since then I have seen more suffering, more pain than I had ever imagined. I watched my brothers fall beneath English swords, four of them left thus in their graves. My father—a learned scholar—scarce dared teach us to read, for fear that the Sassenachs would confiscate what few possessions they had left him. I have watched our people fade from conquered yet proud warriors to beaten-down curs. Now we starve—quietly, miserably—unable to muster enough strength even to stop the English from shipping grain from our shores."

"And you would add to the power they hold?" Ash challenged. "You will allow them to so taint us that we would turn children out to die?"

Sister Agatha made her way wearily to a plain wood chair and sank down upon it. "I do not tell you these things to excuse myself for this decision. 'Tis just that you are so young, Mary Ashleen. Life is clear when you are young. 'Tis all bright colors, stark patterns. When you are old, child, the patterns blur, and the colors—

they blend as you look upon the years as you would an ancient tapestry. Even this, child. Even this horror that devastates our land will pass one day. And no one save you and I will remember the faces of these children."

"Sister Agatha, I'll do anything," Ash pleaded, her voice breaking. "Let—let *me* leave the convent in their stead. I—"

"So that you can starve as well?" The nun lowered her face into her hands. "My decision is final, Mary Ashleen. Sister Bridget has volunteered to escort the children to their . . . new quarters tomorrow morning."

"Sister Bridget?" Ash cried. "She—"

"And *you*—you shall go now, and pray. For the strength to accept God's will—and for the courage to leave your charges in His most merciful hands. While I"—the nun's voice fell to a whisper—"ask his forgiveness for what I am about to do."

"No . . . Sister Agatha . . ." A choked sob rose in Ash's throat as she went to the old nun, catching at the wrinkled hands in a desperate plea. But Agatha rose with majestic dignity, her eyes reflecting a resolve Ashleen knew would prove impossible to shake.

Withdrawing her withered hands, Agatha cupped Ashleen's cheek with one palm. "Go now."

The words were as final as a death knell.

Ash turned, running blindly from the room. By instinct she half stumbled down the narrow halls past faces of the other nuns, reflecting sympathy, regret. She wanted to bury herself in dark unconsciousness, wanted to convince herself the day had been nothing but the cruelest of dreams. But reality ground down upon her like a miller's stone, banishing hope, nigh robbing her of sanity.

Her children . . . *her* babes . . . they were taking them away.

Panic coiled wire-taut about Ash's chest, her slipper-toe catching in the hem of her habit. She tripped, her palms grating against harsh stone, but she scarcely felt the pain. Her eyes fixed upon a stone archway at the end of the corridor. Wooden doors were flung wide, welcoming, the chamber beyond beckoning Ash like a chill stream in a land of endless fire.

Hot tears flowing down her cheeks, Ash rushed into the convent's ancient chapel.

Always Ashleen had found succor in these hallowed walls, always she had found strength. When her father had died it was here she had come to grieve. And when Timothy Kearny had shattered her life, her faith, her trust, she had raged and railed, cried and mourned within this room.

It was as if she could ever feel God's presence here, as if Ashleen could feel the comforting touch of that gentle, sacred hand.

She reached for it now.

Falling to her knees upon the stone floor, she gazed up at the aged crucifix that graced the wall. A thousand prayers, a thousand pleas dashed madly through her mind, unintelligible, desperate. "I cannot let them go," she pleaded with the tortured figure upon the cross. "You championed the helpless as well—ransomed their lives with Your own. I would give my life for these children if it would save them. Would give my very soul. But I cannot, will not abandon—"

Meggie with her sad dark eyes. Renny, so fragile despite his belligerent facade. Liam, who had so guilelessly gifted her with his crutch. And Shevonne, with a myriad of hurts buried somewhere beneath her preening smile.

"Please, God, help me. Sister Agatha bade me come to You, to pray for the strength to accept—accept Your will in sending them away. But I cannot believe it is Your will that my babes die in that evil place."

Ash turned her tearstained face toward the altar, its fine linen cloth draped across the marble slab like a shroud, votive candles flickering at the feet of statues of the saints, each tiny tongue of flame bearing a petitioner's prayer up to heaven. A chair of rich-carved mahogany glowed in the multicolored fragments of light filtering through stained glass windows, drapings of crimson velvet fringed with gilt framing the gold crucifix nuns two centuries before had managed to keep hidden from devil Cromwell. Even the stone ledge upon the far wall glittered, bearing its treasure of a golden chalice encrusted with amethyst.

Ash struggled against the tears welling up inside her as her mind filled with images of the children that very morning, sitting next to her as old Father O'Hara celebrated Mass. Renny, as ever, had sat nearest the window, his whole body taut as he fought to keep from fidgeting, his eyes brimful with some wonderful adventure he was indulging somewhere within his rich imagination. Shevonne had perched upon the bench so primly, Ash had been tempted to nudge her off, wondering what mischief the girl was plotting.

Liam had snuggled close against Ash, his eyes resting upon the priest as if he could truly see angels, while Meggie had curled upon Ash's other side, clutching her doll, her gaze, as ever, upon the glittery chalice.

And Ashleen herself had sat beside the children, offering up the most fervent prayer of her life as she begged for intercession. Her stomach lurched, betrayal sluicing through her, her eyes burning accusingly as she glared at the scene that had ever been so comforting. She hated it suddenly, hated the tranquil rays of light blessing the pristine linen, setting the gold afire, oblivious to her pain.

"What kind of God would do this?" she demanded, as if the very walls could answer. "What kind of God would consecrate His Mass with gold and velvet while children starve? That chalice alone could carry all four of my babes away from Ireland—could see them safe. But nay. 'Twill sit upon that shelf another hundred years, gathering dust . . ."

The words trailed into silence, a terrible silence that seemed to clutch about Ashleen's throat, setting her hands atremble. It was as if the huge stone archways flung her words back to her, mocking, taunting, like the devil's own tempting.

. . . that chalice alone could carry all four . . . away from Ireland . . . see them safe . . . safe . . . if you but had it in your hands . . . Ash's heart thundered in her breast, her fingers clenching until the nails bit deep into the flesh of her palms. The gombeen men would pay a small fortune . . . enough to book passage on a ship, enough to gain them all a start in America's wildlands . . . an ocean away from famine and fever and poor-houses reeking of death.

All she had to do was walk up to the stone ledge and slip the chalice beneath the fall of her habit. Take it. There was no one to stop her, no one to know. Ash caught her lower lip between her teeth.

No one to know but God and her own gnawing conscience.

It would be stealing.

Aye, as if she were stealing from God Himself . . . and good Sister Agatha, Sister Magdalene . . . they loved her, trusted her in their way as implicitly as Renny and the others. And yet . . .

Ash stared at the glistening chalice, touched now by the sun's waning rays, glowing, beckoning, until she could nearly feel its smooth surface beneath her palms. Who was to say that this was not her miracle—the one she had prayed for? Who was to say that it was not God's own hand that had brought her to the chapel? That it was not His will that had enveloped the chalice in rays of sunlight—a beacon to guide her, to aid her in saving the children she so cherished.

It would be wrong to take it, a voice within her whispered. Mortal sin.

"Aye," Ash whispered, "yet would it not be the graver sin to allow four children to be carried off to their deaths?" Slowly she stood, her footsteps echoing upon the stone as she mounted the platform upon which the altar stood. She could hear laughter from outside the window, innocent, piercingly sweet laughter as Sister Magdalene herded the little ones back from the glen.

A rainbow of rays from the elegant glass window enveloped Ashleen, warming her as she stood in a pool of light. Her eyes fixed until the pattern of amethysts, the ornate engravings upon the chalice blurred. She reached up, her hand brushing gold heated from the sun.

"I'll send back money the instant I can." She choked out the vow as her fingers closed about the gold-swirled stem. "I promise to repay . . . repay You. Please"—her voice dropped to a whisper—"let this be my miracle . . ."

Holding her breath, Ashleen slid the vessel from its stone shelf. Yet instead of some invisible benediction, some ethereal comfort, a chill pierced through to the marrow of her bones.

Her heart seemed to cease beating, her breath catching in her throat as she whirled to face the window that had glowed so brightly moments before. But the sunlight that had caressed her had vanished, leaving her lost in cold, gray shadow.

The sails of the frigate *Windsong* snapped in the brisk breezes, surly, unwashed sailors swearing at the elements and at one another as they wrestled coarse lengths of hemp to heave the canvas squares aloft.

Ashleen leaned against the taffrail, the soft gray homespun of her dress billowing behind her as she watched the rim of Ireland's coastline drifting farther, ever farther into the mist-swirled distance. Her arm tightened about Liam's thin shoulders, Shevonne clutching her hand in a grip that belied the girl's unruffled expression.

Renny had already dashed off to watch the men scaling the rigging, the adventure of a sea voyage driving from his mind any thought of bidding farewell the land that had used him so cruelly. And Meggie—she had climbed into a huge coil of rope, as if using the wall of twisted hemp to block out sights and sounds that were strange to her.

It seemed as if an eternity had passed since the night Ashleen had awakened them upon their cots, stealing them away from the convent beneath night's dark cloak. They had stared up at her with huge, confused eyes but had followed her, would have followed her even if she had been leading them down to hell.

Was she?

Please, let me be doing the right thing . . . the plea echoed in Ashleen's mind as she stifled the urge to reach out over the crashing waves and catch the emerald-skirted hills of the land she so loved.

A tugging on Ashleen's skirt made her look down into Liam's upturned face, puckered now with worry. "When we were at St. Michael's Sister Agatha took care of us. Took care of you, too, Sister Ash," the child said slowly. "Who will take care of us now?"

Ash forced a reassuring light into her eyes as she stroked Liam's babe-smooth cheek. "God will," she said softly. But as Liam blessed her with a trusting grin she turned away, unable to meet his gaze.

God will, the winds seemed to jeer at her.

If He has not deserted you.

2

*A*sh sagged against the wall of the wheelwright's shop, her eyes sliding closed in an effort to block out the mayhem all around her. The shrieks of the children mingled with the clang of hammer against red-hot iron, the scraping of blade against wood rasping against her nerves until she wanted to scream.

A sick, gnawing fear had deepened and sharpened inside her with each mile she had traveled away from the convent. Until now she could hardly move, hardly breathe as she surveyed the disaster her recklessness had wrought.

What little money she had managed to hoard after landing in America had long since been spent, the rickety wagon standing out in the dusty street of St. Joe, Missouri holding everything they owned.

Dear God, what had she done? Ash thought numbly, catching her lip between her teeth as she glanced at the heavy wood wheel even now beneath the wheelwright's hands.

It would've been more merciful if the ship had sunk to the bottom of the sea, she thought, fighting back tears. Then she would have been spared the pain of realizing what an idiot she had been, believing the awe-touched tales spun out over peat fires in distant Ireland—stories of riches for the taking, oceans of verdant land fairly crying for the plow, and food—so much food one need never be hungry again.

America.

Heaven.

They had almost seemed one and the same.

But no one had mentioned that even in New York and Boston the Irish were starving—starving for a single taste of the prosperity America offered. Starving for a tiny snippet of the glorious plenty that flourished all around them. Barred from jobs, barred from the future they had risked their very lives for by signs that warned "No Irish Need Apply."

Refuge had become but another kind of hell—one into which she had plunged not only herself but the children as well.

And it seemed as though their suffering had only just begun.

"Ma'am?" the gruff voice of the wheelwright broke through Ash's despair, and she steadied herself, peering with faint hope into the broad, honest face. The fleshy cheeks reddened, this man of thick arms and burly chest obviously disconcerted by a decidedly weepy woman. He cleared his throat, unable to meet her eyes.

"I'm 'fraid I got bad news for you. The wheel—well, even patched, like I done, it might not make it to Oregon. The wood—it shrinks in the heat, see, and swells up in the water—and the rocks an' ruts beat the very devil—I mean blazes—out of it. Now, if there was a wheelwright every twenty miles from here to the Pacific, I'd tell you to chance it. But once you're on the trail . . ." He shrugged, holding scarred hands palms-up in surrender.

Ash gritted her teeth. She would not—*would not*—disgrace herself by bawling like Liam. "Mr. Logan, I . . . I have to get on the trail. As soon as possible. I've put all my money into outfitting this wagon. Buying food. Supplies. If we're delayed, the provisions will never last."

"'Scuse me for askin', ma'am, but how long do you think they'll last if you're stranded in the middle of the open prairie with hardly a scrap o' civilization for a hundred miles?"

Ash winced at the harsh picture Logan's words painted in her mind, icy fear trickling down her spine. As if he sensed her dread, Logan rushed on.

"Ma'am, I don't mean to frighten you, but I got me two young'uns of my own. When I think of my Sarah and the boys trapped in a broken-down wagon in the middle o' nowheres . . . well, it makes my blood run cold."

Ash's fingers clenched, the nails digging deep into her palms as the man echoed her worst fears. "Mr. Logan, we have no choice. I should have pulled out with the wagon train that left at dawn. I can't afford the time or the money to wait and hook up with another. As it is, I'll be lucky to catch up with the train before nightfall."

The thought of being alone in the wilderness made Ash shudder, visions of marauding cougars, grizzly bears, and warpainted Indians writhing in a macabre dance in her head. Impatient, she crushed the clamorings of a too-vivid imagination. For heaven's sake, she thought, she had bought an old Hawkin rifle to defend her and the babes—if she could just remember how to load it. And there would hardly be hostile war chiefs so close to St. Joe . . . would there?

Loathing herself for what she deemed cowardice, Ash stiffened her spine, her chin jutting out at a pugnacious angle. If the whole Comanche nation descended upon her, so be it. But they'd not find her trembling in fear, hiding in some little town in Missouri.

"Ma'am," Logan broke in, his voice touched with a wisp of condescension, "you're such a little slip of a thing. Plenty of full-growed men don't have it in 'em to make the westward passage. I don't see how you can—"

"Just fix the wagon!" Ashleen snapped, clinging to a sudden fearsome anger. "I managed to bring these children all the way from Ireland. Across the ocean. Halfway across the country. I'll see them settled in Oregon, by all the saints, I will. If the wagon should break down . . . well, the children are—are strong. We would get along somehow."

A low chuckle from behind her made Ash spin toward the door, the opening seemingly dwarfed by a giant of a man. Impossibly orange hair wreathed a face as craggy as a mountaintop, while a full beard blanketed a barrel-thick chest. But it was the eyes beneath that shaggy crop of hair that arrested Ashleen—dark as blackberries and shiny as beads, but holding such an innate kindness that Ash felt a sudden, unwelcome urge to go to the burly giant and cast her troubles into his capable hands.

"I think ye'd best surrender an' be done with it, Logan," the man chortled, smacking his belly in delight. "I've seen friendlier eyes in a Tonkawa war party."

Logan bristled. "Well, the lady'll be seein' plenty of those where she's headed, Kennisaw. That is, if she's bullheaded enough to charge out onto the prairie with a wagon that's fallin' apart."

"That wagon out yonder?" The man called Kennisaw scratched at his chin. "Aw, Logan, it ain't so bad as all that. Gave it a look-see 'fore I came in. Some little tyke on a crutch was showin' it to me. Right proud of it, he was."

"Liam," Ash muttered, glancing out the window once again to where the children clambered in and out of the wagon bed in some game. From the moment she had bought the rig in St. Louis Renny, Shevonne, and Liam had viewed the old wagon as if it were some magic carpet from a fairy story, sent to spirit them away to an enchanted kingdom. Even Meggie had burrowed into it like a tiny mouse in its nest. Ash had dreaded the day when they learned the stark realities of a wagon trek—dirt, heat, and backbreaking work.

"Them your young'uns, ma'am?"

Ashleen started, her eyes locking with Kennisaw's. "They're . . ." She almost said orphans, almost launched into an explanation of how she'd come to be in charge of the brood. But a sudden surge of possessiveness, a welling of soul-deep love washed through her. She smiled, unaware of how devastatingly vulnerable she looked at that instant, how disarmingly lovely. "They're mine," she said softly.

The bearded man's gaze rested on her face long moments, then he grinned, a gap-toothed grin that reminded Ash of sunlight after a storm. "You should be fair burstin' with pride over the lot of 'em."

"I am." Simple, it was so simple now, somehow the frustration, the grinding responsibility drifting away, leaving in its wake remembrances of Renny tending Meggie's skinned knee, Liam giving a pretty stone to Shevonne. The hope in their eyes, the love, the trust would have made a journey to hell worth the misery.

Kennisaw reached out, enfolding her small hand in callused paws. "If I was a bettin' man, I'd lay a year's trappin' pay that this gal's got enough grit to make it clear to Chiny if she's a mind to. You jest put that wheel back on the wagon, Logan. And when you're finished, take this package over home." Kennisaw dug in voluminous pockets, dragging out a doeskin-wrapped bundle. "Got some genuine Oglala Sioux moccasins for those ornery boys of yours—jest like I promised 'em last time I was in town."

The thunderous expression on the wheelwright's face faded, a reluctant grin tugging at the corner of his mouth. "Damn you, anyway, Kennisaw Jones! You spoil the pair of them rotten!"

"'Tween't no trouble a-tall." Jones winked at Ashleen, a conspiratorial light in his dark eyes. "Met up with this squaw named Sweetest One. Prettiest damn woman ye ever did see. An' she was . . . well, after a time, she was all a-flutter to please a fine figure of a man like me."

Logan guffawed, and even Ash couldn't stifle her laughter. She knew she should be shocked—Sister Agatha would have been in apoplexies over Kennisaw Jones's raw humor—and yet there was something delightful in the wicked amusement in the big man's smile. Something that warmed her. Calmed her. Made her believe in herself again. It was ridiculous. Absurd. But she thanked God for it.

"Now, Mrs.—" He arched a brow in question.

"Miss," Ashleen said. "Miss O'Shea." At the odd expression on the wheelwright's face Ash hurried to explain. "I'm a—was a novice at St. Michael of the Angels before—"

"Before you became a mother o' four? They're lucky ye scooped 'em up, Miss O'Shea. Now, if you'll permit me, I'll go take a look at that rattletrap wagon of yours an' see if Logan here's just bein' an old woman about it." Kennisaw offered her his arm in such a courtly manner that Ash curtsied, fluttering her lashes with mocking coquettishness. Jones's chest rumbled with laughter.

"Did ye learn that in the convent, girlie?"

"No. I learned it because it made Sister Bridget look like she'd swallowed a bug."

Kennisaw flung back his head and roared. Ash felt as if a huge stone had been rolled off her chest, and she let him lead her out into the street, aware of the wheelwright tsking quietly to himself behind them.

They had scarcely stepped into the street when she was deluged by a melee of racketing children, Renny firing questions, Liam regaling her with tales of strange sights, Shevonne tattling on everyone from Meggie to the barkeep across the way.

Ash answered Renny, chided Shevonne, and rumpled Liam's curls almost at the same time, while Kennisaw Jones beamed at her in approval.

"You found the bear man," Liam enthused, pink lips round with awe as he arched his head back to gaze up at Kennisaw's face. "He's wondrous nice, Sister Ash. And he knows 'bout wagons and such. He's even blood brother to a 'nindian chief."

"Named Sweetest One?" Ash couldn't resist teasing.

"Ugh! That's an awful name for an Indian!" Renny made a face. "Takes A Hundred Scalps, or Tomahawk Thrower, now *those* are names."

"My blood brother's name is Sneaks Up On Red-

Haired Boys And Carries 'Em Off In Their Sleep,"
Kennisaw said in a spooky voice. Ash heard Shevonne
give a little gasp, saw Liam's eyes widen. Even Renny's
expression showed the tinest hint of nervousness. Ash
could see the food for nightmare already wending its way
through their minds.

"I don't believe you," Renny said, thrusting out his
chest. Kennisaw leveled a look on the boy that would
have made most men blanch, but Renny met it with a
resolved belligerence that made Ash want to laugh.

After a moment Jones reached out to chuck the boy
under the chin. "Ye're a smart lad not to believe an old
coot like me. Make a fine man one day."

But Renny was not one who took to being made a fool
of, even in the spirit of fun, and he glared at Kennisaw
Jones as if the man sported horns and a tail.

Ash intervened hastily, hoping to avoid the sparking of
Renny's temper, but she had the sensation of dancing the
fling on a sheet of spring ice.

"Mr. Jones here has kindly offered to check out our
wagon. What with the spoke splitting, I thought it might
be best if—"

"The rest of the wheels are fine." Renny's face reddened, eyes glittering. "I looked them over real good this
morning."

"And I'm grateful for it, moppet. But Mr. Jones here is
worlds more experienced in all this than any of us is,
and—"

"How do you know that, Sister Ash? He already told a
lie."

"Renny!" Ashleen exclaimed, startled.

"Well, he did! About that Indian stuff! Even a baby like
Liam wouldn't believe him."

"Mr. Jones was just teasing, and you know it. Now
you'd best ask his pardon for being so rude."

"Don't fret, ma'am." There was a gentleness to Jones's
voice, a kind of wistfulness that hinted of secret pain.
"My own boy, he was full of the devil, just like this one of
yours. Always flyin' in the face of anyone who dared

tweak his pride. Turned out to be a fine man, my Garret did. Seen a whole raidin' party o' Sioux turn tail and run just at the sight o' him." Kennisaw pierced Renny with a keen glare. "And *that*, boy, ain't no bedtime story."

Renny snorted in disbelief, then stalked off to nurse his injured feelings amongst the horses tied to the hitching post nearby.

Kennisaw Jones began moving about the wagon, running his hands over wood, tugging on harness and canvas to the accompaniment of Liam's nonstop chatter. But Ash scarcely saw them, scarcely heard them as she watched Renny disappear among glossy flanks and withers.

She had handled the boy badly. Ash berated herself inwardly. He had taken such pride in being the man of their little family—doing a man's chores, seeing to the other children with a budding responsibility that had delighted Ashleen when it wasn't wrenching at her heart. She'd been wrong to undermine that, however unintentionally.

She'd talk to him later, Ash vowed, after they both had a chance for tempers to cool. After Renny had had some time to bury himself in the company of the animals he was devoted to.

She shook her head as she heard the soft whicker of greeting from the showy bay Renny had named Finn McCool after the ancient Irish hero.

From the moment she had purchased the animals Renny had shown a kind of kinship with them, lavishing them with affection, rubbing them down, combing mane and tail, making excuses for the equine foibles that had Ash near tearing her hair out before she had driven them ten miles from St. Louis.

But though he loved all the beasts, it was Cooley Renny stroked most often, Cooley who rubbed its soft muzzle against Renny's brow whenever the boy was near.

Even if the wagon was rickety, Ash thought with a grimace, at least she had managed to do one thing right in buying the stock that would pull it.

She was drawn from her thoughts by the weight of a sudden silence, aware that Kennisaw was standing behind her. She turned, looking up into those open, animated features, and what she saw there filled her with dread. Jones was staring off toward a cluster of buildings, his face pale beneath its leathery tan.

"Mr. Jones, what is it? The wagon?" Ash followed the path of his gaze and glimpsed two figures melting back into the shadows, the midmorning sun filling the place where they had been.

Kennisaw seemed to shake himself, but the smile he flashed her lacked sparkle. "No. No. The wagon's fine, ma'am. It's just for a moment there I thought I saw a ghost."

"Someone you know?"

"Someone I shoulda plugged with a bullet years ago." There was a deathly cold to the voice that had been so warm.

Ash regarded him quietly until at last his lips twisted into a mockery of a smile. "Don't worry, missy. I'm not some half-crazed, glory-hungry fool 'bout to go off in a hail o' gunfire. And those men I saw . . . well, couldn't be the ones I was speakin' on anyways. They've both been buried in some hellhole prison for passing twenty years. Probably dead by now. Hope they're roastin' on the devil's own spit."

Ash crossed herself, and Kennisaw seemed to drag himself out of dark thoughts by force of will.

"Pardon, ma'am. My mouth's always been a little too free, my wits a little too slow. Now, as for your wagon, I think it'll hold right enough. Logan's good with his mendin', and if you take care with the wheel, nurse it along a bit, you should be fine. But . . ." Jones drew out the word, his eyes tracking to where Renny stood amongst the horses. "Ma'am, those ain't—tell me those ain't yours."

"The horses? I bought them from the man who sold me the wagon. They're a little, er, restive now and again, but—what's wrong with them?" She groaned, weighed down with a kind of hopeless foreboding.

"Probably nothin'. 'Cept the chances of those horses pullin' this heavy wagon all the way to Oregon . . ." Kennisaw's voice trailed off. Ash couldn't bear to look at him, see one more disaster reflected in his eyes.

"Mr. Jones." She struggled to keep the quaver from her voice. But the confidence Kennisaw's humor had renewed in Ash minutes before had crumbled, doubts crashing down about her again with suffocating force.

"Oxen," Kennisaw muttered, but it was as if he didn't know what he was saying. "Now, that's what you . . . son of a bitch!" The virulence of the oath stunned Ash, and she looked up to see Jones's bead-bright eyes glittering with hate, disbelief, and a very real fear.

The world seemed to explode in a heartbeat. The two figures Ash had glimpsed between the buildings charged out from behind the corner of the saloon as Jones grabbed for the gun stuffed in his belt. Liam, engrossed in a game with Shevonne, darted into the line of fire.

The sight of the boy seemed to slam into Kennisaw with the force of a blow, and the man cursed, dodging behind the wheelwright's shop. Ash knew instinctively that he was trying to draw his pursuers away from her and the children. Knew, as well, that he had probably lost his best chance to face his attackers.

She had to do something . . . something to slow them . . . help . . .

The footfalls of the men cracked into the hard-packed earth as they bolted toward her, toward the place where Kennisaw had vanished.

She screamed—the terrified princess scream she had delighted the children with in countless make-believe games— and, with a dramatical skill that would have made Sarah Siddons proud, faked a stumble, flinging herself into the two running figures, entangling both in arms and legs and the folds of her skirts.

They tumbled over her, cursing, elbows and knees

slamming into her as they fell. Ash heard the children's shrieks as the impact drove the breath from her lungs, dust filling her nose and mouth until she couldn't see, couldn't breathe.

She struggled to pull herself upright as the men rolled off her, her fingers clawing the tangle of gold curls from her face. But as her eyes locked with those of the men she had duped she wished she had kept her face buried in the dirt.

Images burned into her mind, and she knew that as long as she lived, she would never forget them. A scarred visage with soulless eyes, the other face atop a giant of a man, features carved with a kind of bestial savagery, dull, yet no less frightening.

Evil.

The sensation jolted through her as if she were peering into the world of demons and devils and spirits that old Father O'Hara had told of. She tried to raise her fingers, cross herself, certain in that instant the men would kill her.

But the wiry, mean one only clenched his fist, cracking it into her face with a power that sent her careening backward. Pain shot through her, the world spinning crazily on its axis as she smacked back into the hub of a wagon wheel.

Black splotches swam before her eyes, dragging her toward unconsciousness, but the desperate cries of Liam and Shevonne, the panic in Renny's shouts made her drive back the whirling mists by force of will.

She struggled to open eyelids seemingly weighted with lead, the tear-streaked faces of the children spinning in sickening circles before her. Arms were helping her up—hands smelling of woodshavings and hot iron. The wheelwright . . . what had his name been? Logan . . .

"Ma'am? Are you all right, ma'am?" His anxious voice drove spikes of pain into her skull.

"I . . . yes . . . but those men," Ash stammered, "are they—"

"They knocked her right over!" Liam's high-pitched sobbing broke through her words.

"And then they hit her!" Shevonne's voice was indignant, shaky with tears.

"I'll rip their ears right off, Sister Ash!" Renny was vowing. "I'll chase 'em down and—"

"You'll do nothing of the kind!" Logan snapped. "Do you think she wants to bury you over a bruised eye, boy?"

"No, Renny." Ash groped to catch hold of the boy's hand, fearing that he would, indeed, rush forth to avenge her. "It's—it's nothing. I'm fine. Please don't—"

Her vision cleared enough to see the expression in the boy's face, and her heart broke for him.

"Sister Ash . . . your face . . ." His voice cracked, and he turned away. She knew he didn't want her to see his tears.

"Go get me a cloth, Renny, dipped in cool water. I'll be good as new in no time." Ash gave a wan smile.

Renny dashed off, and Ash felt something brush against her skirts. Meggie. She didn't touch Ash, only stared up at her, eyes huge with silent terror.

"It's all right now, Meggie, love." Ash attempted to infuse a lightness into her voice as she gave the child a hug. For once Meggie allowed the contact—a brief but infinitely precious moment.

Ash savored it, then released the little girl before she could draw away.

"Sister Ash?"

Ashleen looked into Liam's upturned face, the little boy's eyes filled with trouble.

"Do you think the Bear Man got away? Mr. Jones, I mean."

"I don't know, Liam. I hope so." Her eyes traced to where Kennisaw had disappeared, the men in hot pursuit.

"Do you think those men are gonna hurt him?"

"I hope not, sweeting."

"I liked the Bear Man, even if he did fib about the Indian stuff. I don't want him to be dead."

"Neither do I, Liam," Ash said softly.

But the eyes of his attackers rose up in her mind. Eyes cruel, lifeless, as soulless as those in a grave. And she whispered a desperate prayer for the man called Kennisaw Jones.

3

*D*arkness crowded about the campfire, shadows clawing at the wagon in eerie patterns. Lost souls, they seemed, trying to get in amongst the warmth of the sleeping children, away from the mournful sounds of night creatures, away from the chill whisperings of danger.

Ash sat near the rear wagon wheel, her back propped against the bumpy spokes as she mounted guard. She shivered despite the quilt flung around her shoulders, the cold that had settled over the countryside at sunset creeping beneath her meager covering. Her hands were numb where they gripped the barrel of the old Hawkin rifle, and she prayed incessantly to St. Jude, patron of hopeless causes, that she had managed to load the weapon correctly.

Why, oh why, hadn't she caught up with the string of wagons somewhere up ahead?

She should have been chatting with the other women by the cookfires, laughing softly with them as they mended little breeches and torn petticoats. There should have been the comforting camaraderie of dozens of families, each brimful of the dreams they sought in a new land. But instead there was only a suffocating quiet, an aloneness more profound than any Ashleen had ever known.

"There was nothing you could have done to get on the trail any sooner," she muttered to herself for the hundredth time. "You did your best."

She had—rushing about half-crazed as morning melted into noon, hitching the horses and trying to hustle out of town the moment Mr. Logan had reattached the mended wheel.

But Cooley had been in a particularly contrary mood, objecting even more than usual to being subjected to the indignity of the harness. Then Liam had tumbled off of the wagon seat and scraped his chin. And while Ashleen had been tending him Meggie had wandered off. It had taken them almost an hour to find her. Ash had been sick with panic by the time Renny had discovered the little girl, squirreled away in the back of Mr. Logan's shop, making necklaces for her raggedy doll from the wood shavings littering the floor.

Ashleen had wanted to delude herself that mishaps were to be expected, what with the confusion of making ready to leave. And yet in her heart she knew why she was so distracted.

Everywhere she looked it seemed that cold eyes peered back at her, the two men she had seen chasing Kennisaw Jones haunting her with a sense of wickedness so deep, so chilling, she could still feel the power of it seep through her very bones.

Had Kennisaw Jones managed to escape them? Even if he had, there had been something in his pursuers' faces that warned Ashleen the kind man could not elude them forever.

The thought made the hair at the nape of her neck prickle, and she clasped the Hawkin tighter in an effort to still the sudden tremor in her hands.

What would the outlaws do if they were robbed of their prize? Would they circle back? Attempt to find the woman who had stalled them in their chase? Would they hold her somehow responsible for their failure in finding Jones?

A sudden shifting sound behind Ash made her jump to

her feet, a croak of fear rising in her throat. But after a second she recognized the sound she had heard countless times since they had sailed away from Ireland—Renny, restless even in sleep, clunking one of his long limbs into a wall as he thrashed about in the throes of some dream.

She let out a shuddery sigh of relief, a rueful smile curving her lips as she shook her head in self-disgust. "You should be ashamed of yourself, Mary Ashleen O'Shea!" she scolded herself, sagging back against the wagon box. "You're worse than the children, spinning scare-stories in the darkness till the whole world seems crawling with monsters. There is nothing to be afraid of. Nothing."

She started to sit down again, but at that moment a sound out of synch with the night drifted to her, a kind of soft, rasping sound, as if someone or something was creeping.

Her heart froze as she wheeled around, the heavy Hawkin weighing her hands, her trembling fingers clutching the trigger.

Eyes glowed in the pools of inky blackness, reflecting the light of the flames. Ash dragged the rifle to her shoulder, trying to steady it, knowing she should shoot. But suddenly a faint moan rippled out.

Pain. Ash could sense it, feel it.

Terrified but unable to stop herself, she hurried toward the sound, the circle of light from the campfire waning until she, too, was swallowed up by the night.

Her hands were damp with sweat, her heart hammering against her ribs as she edged closer, closer to where she had heard the sound. The glittering she had judged to be the creature's eyes had vanished as though in a grimace of agony, even the moans fading into silence.

"Who—who is it?" She tried to keep her voice from shaking. "Who's there?"

No answer.

Visions of renegade Indians, marauding bears, and a dozen other terrifying possibilities filled her imagination. Mary, Mother of God, what was she doing? Trundling off into the darkness in the middle of nowhere, searching for who knew what? The children lay asleep in the wagon, so vulnerable it made Ash's stomach lurch. And even if she screamed to high heaven, there was no one else to hear her.

She should turn around, rush back to the relative safety of the campfire, and wait, gun in hand, until dawn revealed whatever had made those awful sounds. If something should happen to her, the little ones would be left alone in the middle of the wilderness, in a strange land. They would have nothing, no one. . . .

She took another step, deeper into the inky darkness.

"Sister Ashleen?" The wavering, fearful call tore a cry from her throat, made her spin toward the campfire. She lowered the Hawkin, horrified at her shaky fingers, as her gaze fixed upon the small figure silhouetted against the flames.

Liam leaned upon his crutch near the tailgate of the wagon, looking like a wandering ghost in his little nightshirt, his hair tousled about his small face. "S-Sister Ash?"

"Liam, I'm out—out here," she called softly. "I heard someth—"

Forever after Ash would remember the horrible sensation of something seeming to erupt from the bowels of the earth, clutching at her skirt as if to drag her into hell.

She screamed, attempting to pull away, the heavy rifle all but useless at such an angle. But as she whirled to face her assailant horror ripped through her.

Even in the meager light from the campfire she could make out the raggedy shape of a wild mane of hair, the burly shoulders and thick arms she recognized as those of Kennisaw Jones.

"Don't . . . shoot, girlie." The voice was faint, garbled. "I . . . surrender."

"Mr. Jones . . . what . . ." she dropped the rifle and sank to her knees beside him, her fingers closing about his hand—a hand that was wet, sticky. She recoiled inwardly, the sickly sweet stench of blood assailing her nostrils. "What are you doing here? Are you . . . You're hurt."

"Shoulda . . . seen the other . . . hombres." A weak laugh faded. An awful, watery-sounding cough rumbled deep in the man's chest, racking his big body.

"Liam! Get Renny!" Ash cried out. "It's Mr. Jones— hurt. I need help to get him into camp."

Ash cradled the big man's head in her lap, feeling the shudders of pain roiling through him.

She heard the commotion from the wagon behind, heard running feet pounding toward her. Renny's anxious, sleep-blurred eyes peered down into hers, his hunting knife gripped in one hand as if to defend her.

"Renny, put that thing away. We have to get Mr. Jones to the wagon."

"Mr. Jones? But why . . . how . . ."

"He's hurt."

"How bad—"

"Bad!" Ash hated the threading of tears in her voice. Yet Kennisaw Jones had been a glimpse of sunshine during those dark minutes in St. Joe. Shown her the first real kindness she had known in a bustling country where most were far too busy chasing after their own dreams to concern themselves with just one more Irish immigrant girl dragging along a bevy of children.

Another shuddering groan racked Kennisaw, the sound galvanizing Ashleen into action. "Mr. Jones, can you help us? If we try to support you, can you walk?"

The big man grunted his assent. Ash attempted to wedge her shoulder underneath his arm, Renny, on Jones's other side, struggling to keep his balance while doing the same. It was like trying to raise a mountain. Except mountains didn't feel pain.

Ash felt Kennisaw's muscles knot in agony as the man battled to get his feet beneath him. Twice he stumbled, his knee striking the earth in a jarring blow. Both times Ashleen and Renny managed to keep him from crashing to the ground.

But when the firelight enfolded them the horror Ash

had felt beneath the merciful blanket of darkness increased tenfold. The campfire exposed in gut-wrenching clarity how much courage, how much force of will it had taken for Kennisaw Jones to make it this far.

Ash heard Liam's tiny cry of fear and felt Renny's gasp as she lowered Kennisaw to the ground. His blood-caked features were so badly beaten they seemed barely human. One of Jones's hands was crushed, one ankle twisted at an impossible angle. But it was the welling of dark, sticky crimson stiffening the fabric of his shirtfront that filled Ashleen with the sick certainty that Kennisaw Jones was going to die.

"Renny, we need water, and—and that bottle of medicine we bought in St. Louis. And something—something to stop the bleeding . . . my petticoat." She raised her skirt, ripping at the hem of the garment with desperate fingers.

"Tide's goin' out, girlie. Ain't nothin' you can do to stop it," Jones said. "Seen enough death t' know when it's too late."

"No. It's not too late." Ash shoved the wad of material against the wound in an effort to staunch the flow of blood. But even as she said the words Ash knew Kennisaw spoke the truth.

"Only thing . . . important now is to—to ride . . . warn . . ." Something akin to a sob wrenched Kennisaw's chest. "Garret."

Garret? Ash searched her memory desperately as she grabbed up another scrap of fine lawn petticoat, dipping it in the bucket of water Renny had dashed over to thump down beside her.

"My boy. My . . ."

Ash gently swabbed at the grime and blood encrusting Kennisaw's face, recalling Kennisaw's 'boy,' the one who could stop a Sioux raiding party at twenty paces.

Ash heard the awful rattle in Kennisaw's chest and wondered if his Garret had the power to stop death.

"Garveys." Kennisaw was struggling to choke out. "Have to warn Garret they're free."

"As soon as you're . . . better, able to travel safely." Ash ripped off another band of cloth and wrapped it gently around his shattered hand.

She had a fleeting image of the wagon train somewhere up ahead, wending its way onward toward the distant horizon, farther, farther, like a will-o'-the-wisp, dancing out of her reach.

If she stayed here with Kennisaw Jones she would never catch up with the other wagons. The food she had stored away so carefully in barrels and crocks would never last. And yet she couldn't abandon the old man she held cradled in her arms.

"A horse. Please, God, just give me a horse to get to West Port. Get to Garret . . ."

"Mr. Jones, we can't move you until"—Ash hesitated but a heartbeat—"until you're well."

"I'm dying, girl!" The desperation in the old man's voice raked at Ashleen. "Have to warn him. May already be too late."

With agonizing effort Kennisaw tried to raise himself upright. Trickles of blood dripped from the countless scrapes that had broken open in his struggles. Ash grasped his shoulders as gently as she was able, pressing him back onto the feather tick. "No. Lie still. You could never ride that far in this condition."

"I'm . . . going, damn it. Don't you see? Have to."

Fear sluiced through Ash that he would do himself even graver harm if she tried to force him to stay.

In that instant she decided. "Renny," she said, "hitch the team. We're going to West Port."

"West Port?" Renny echoed. "But the wagon train. If we don't—"

"We can hardly leave him here to die," Ash snapped, then she loathed herself for the sharp edge to her voice.

Renny flinched back, and in the light from the campfire she could sense his confusion, see his pain.

"I—I didn't say we should. I just—I know you've been worried about the supplies lasting and all."

How like the boy to realize it and worry in silence.

"I'm sorry, Ren. I'm just . . ." Terrified that she was doing the wrong thing. Terrified she and the children would be stranded in Missouri, alone, friendless. Terrified she'd not be able to provide a decent life for them, no matter how desperately she loved them.

She felt a soft, shy touch upon her shoulder, the evidence of affection from one so steeped in adolescent dignity tugging at Ash's heart in a way that left her eyes stinging, her throat tight.

"Renny, I'm frightened." The admission was hushed as she caught his hand in her own.

She looked up into that child face, into the eyes that had known far too much pain.

"I know," Renny said softly. "Me, too."

Then he was sprinting across to where the horses grazed, hooked to their picket ropes. For once the animals went comparatively easily into their traces, led by the normally recalcitrant Cooley.

With the help of Shevonne and Liam Ash settled Kennisaw onto the feather tick where Liam and Renny had slept.

For a moment she thought Kennisaw was unconscious, and blind panic raced through her as she realized she had no idea which way West Port was, or how they were to find this Garret the old man loved so much.

But the craggy-featured frontiersman forced open his eyes, whispering faint directions Ashleen prayed they could follow in the darkness.

Crooning words of comfort to the wide-eyed Meggie, Ash brought out the lanterns and affixed them to iron hooks near the driver's seat where Liam and Renny now sat. She called to the red-haired boy, telling him which way to go. Telling him to be careful.

The wagon lurched into motion, and she saw the knuckles of Kennisaw's good hand whiten as his fingers clenched one of the wagon bows.

"Garret. Have to—to live long enough to find . . ."

Ash's throat tightened. It was as if the old man were pleading with the angel that had come to sweep him into the netherworld. His hand loosened, fell limp to the feather tick.

Shevonne's small voice came from the corner of the wagon. "Is he dead, Sister Ash?"

Ash lay her palm against his chest, relief washing through her as she felt the faint thrumming of his heart. "No, sweeting, he's just . . . sleeping now." Thank God, Ash thought numbly to herself, grateful that the old man had found surcease in the blessing of unconsciousness. The constant jolting of the wagon would have proved torture beyond bearing for a man so brutally battered.

She slipped her hand into Kennisaw Jones's good one, willing the old man's heart to keep beating, willing him to live. "I don't even know who your Garret is, Mr. Jones," she whispered, as if her voice alone could somehow keep him tied to the world of the living. "I don't know where to look in West Port Landing."

A sound came from Kennisaw's swollen lips, unintelligible yet somehow comforting. Ash clung to it as the piece of sky visible through circular opening in the back of the wagon's canvas washed red with the sunrise, then burned, blindingly blue, in the heat of day.

The children munched on bread and dried apples, Renny eating even as he drove. Much as Ashleen wanted to relieve the weary boy, she dared not leave the man who lay tossing, turning, clinging so tenuously to life in the wagon bed.

Twice she dumped the bucket's darkened contents out the back of the wagon, refilling the oaken container with fresh water from the barrels to cleanse Kennisaw's face. Only the cool cloths she used to swab the man's brutalized features seemed to bring him relief, make it easier for him to rest.

Three times she changed the wadding of cloth over the wound in Jones's belly, and though the blood had thickened and darkened, it continued to drain, slowly and relentlessly, from the injury.

Darkness had shrouded the world once more, and Liam, Shevonne, and Meggie were huddled together in sleep when Kennisaw opened his bleary eyes. Ash forced a smile to her lips, taking up a spoon in the dim lantern light to try to drizzle some water into his parched mouth. "Mr. Jones, try to drink. Take a little water."

With great effort Kennisaw did as she bid him, though most of the liquid trickled from the corner of his mouth. Ash spooned up some more, but Jones's hand closed over her wrist, staying her, as he struggled again to speak.

"My boy. Can't let . . . Garveys . . . hurt him again."

Ash felt a tugging in her heart, picturing Kennisaw Jones's boy—a young, blustery tintype likeness of his father with a quick smile, kind eyes.

"Got such a good heart in him," Kennisaw murmured. "Been hurt so much already."

Ashleen dabbed gingerly at an abrasion marring Kennisaw's forehead. "Of course he's a good boy." She squeezed the words through a throat choked with tears. "With a father as kind as you are—"

"N-not own blood. Born to . . . best friend. Tom MacQuade."

"Hush, now. Don't talk," Ash chided, rinsing the cloth in water darkened now with Jones's blood. "You need to save your strength."

The wagon lurched over a rut, and Jones dissolved into another fit of the awful-sounding coughing. Ashleen stiffened, willing him to stop, willing him to breathe. After a moment he did so, air wheezing between gritted teeth. His eyes found hers, but it was as if he didn't see her, as if they were glazed with some nightmare vision he alone could see.

"Sorry, Tom," the man almost sobbed. "Jesus, God, I'm sorry. If I had known . . . what . . . happen . . . would never . . ."

"Hush, Mr. Jones, hush," Ashleen soothed, her tone soft as if he had been one of the children. But she could feel the emotions racking the man's big frame, could feel an agony of the soul deeper even than the tearing pain that was clawing at his body. She groped for the words to bring him peace, prayed for them. "Whatever happened, whatever is troubling you, I know your friend MacQuade understood."

The laugh that breached Kennisaw's lips was ugly, bitter, filled with a self-loathing that made Ash draw back, her own breath catching in her throat.

"Understood?" Jones blazed with astonishing strength, as if confronting the cruel fates that tormented him. "Wife . . . murdered. Little Beth . . . Tom . . . dead. All dead. Because of me. And Garret . . . worse than dead. Heard it all . . . saw . . ."

Ash caught her lip between her teeth. Even the vague images Jones was revealing filled her with stark pity, for the man Kennisaw, for the child Garret, who had seen his family die. She recoiled at the picture of a boy facing such evil, helpless, while it consumed those he loved.

And yet loyalty to Kennisaw stirred within her heart, and she knew instinctively that this man was incapable of cruelty, incapable of betraying his best friend. Love, grief, guilt—they had tangled amongst Jones's garbled words until Ash couldn't bear it.

"It wasn't your fault. There was nothing you could have done."

"It was my doing! All of it!" Jones grasped at her skirts, his eyes twin pits of hell. "I put the gold on their land—brought the Garveys down on 'em. I didn't even warn Tom it was there . . . but I thought I could make it back in time. Bring help. I swear to God I did."

"Hush, now, Mr. Jones. It was all a long time ago," Ash murmured, trying to soothe him.

But it was as if the man were possessed by the demons that had tortured him so long. She listened as Kennisaw brought the MacQuade family to life with his words, the loving frontier family so real to her she could hear their laughter, taste their tears. But the simple beauty of Stormy Ridge, the farm they had carved from the midst of Texas wilderness, had disintegrated, descended into a hell more chilling than any Ashleen had ever known.

Bile rose in her throat, her hands shaking with the intensity of Jones's words as he spun out a tale of violence so brutal it seared into the very center of her being.

She could see the Garveys' savage faces, feel the stark panic of the little girl, the hopelessness, the grinding terror of the child's parents. And most devastating of all, she could feel the agony of the boy, Garret, caught up in that maelstrom of horror.

Sweet Savior, what scars had been left on that child's spirit that long-ago day? How had he ever survived? This little boy Kennisaw Jones's words had etched forever in Ashleen's heart—a child who had painted sunrises for his little sister with dyes made from roots and berries. A son who had fashioned a pendant in the shape of a wooden dove for the mother who so cherished him.

"Never . . . forgive myself." Kennisaw's voice was weak, so weak. "Never forgive . . ."

What little strength he possessed spent, Kennisaw drifted again into troubled sleep. But now Ashleen knew the visions that would give him no rest.

She wept for him.

And for the little boy who had lost everything on a blazing Texas day.

4

*D*usk trailed ribbons of purple and rose across the Missouri sky, the first tiny stars sprinkled like spangles on a dance-hall girl's gown. Ashleen peered with gritty eyes through the front opening in the canvas wagon top, past Renny's slumped shoulders to the distant splotch of gray-brown marring the horizon.

West Port.

She blinked back tears as she caught her first glimpse of the bustling town Kennisaw Jones had so hungered to see.

Ash choked out a sob, her fingers tightening their grasp upon Kennisaw's limp hand. She could feel the life ebbing out of him, feel him slipping away as inexorably as the setting sun.

"Hold on, Kennisaw, just a little longer. We're almost there."

She wanted desperately for him to reach the streets of West Port; she wanted the Garret who had lost so much at least to have the comfort of bidding Kennisaw goodbye. But it seemed as if even that faint solace was to be denied.

For Kennisaw Jones's eyes were glazing with death, the stubborn beat of his heart failing at last.

Behind her Ash heard Shevonne and Liam murmuring the rosary in their sweet, sad voices, felt Meggie's solemn, silent regard. They had all seen death before, in the misty Irish hills. Ash had hoped they would not witness it again so soon in this new land.

Her vision blurred, tears brimming over her lashes. She had known Kennisaw Jones but a few days, and yet the red-haired giant had tunneled his way into her very heart with his devotion to his boy, Garret MacQuade.

She could almost picture the sensitive, solemn young man Kennisaw's description had conjured in her imagination. Garret had lost so much already. He would be desolate, Kennisaw's death stealing away what little joy the serious youth had managed to wrench from life's tightfisted grasp.

And she would be the one to bring him the grim tidings, she would be the one to deliver him yet another brutal blow.

Ash caught the inside of her lip between her teeth in an effort to keep from dissolving into sobs. "It's not fair," she said fiercely. "It's not—"

The wagon bumped over a rut, and she saw Jones's lips tighten in pain. His lashes fluttered open. For an instant Ash felt a surge of hope, the black orbs startlingly lucid as he looked deep into her eyes.

"Life . . . not always fair . . . girlie." His voice was halting, faint, almost lost in the horrible rattling sound deep in his thick chest. "But sometimes . . . can be good. Sometimes find gold in . . . sea o' mud."

"Kennisaw," Ash whispered, smoothing the tangle of fire-red hair away from his bruised forehead. "Don't talk. Just rest."

"Have . . . eternity t' sleep. Precious little time t' say . . . what needs sayin'." He swallowed painfully, his grip tightening slightly about Ashleen's hand. "You're an angel . . . Sister. Runnin' off to help . . . man you barely know."

"Just hold on a few more miles," Ash urged him. "I can see West Port in the distance. We'll be there before you know it."

The corner of Kennisaw's mouth twisted up in a mockery of a smile. "Too late."

"No!" Ash's fingers clutched his, as if she could give him some of her strength.

Jones moved his head just a fraction in denial. "Not going to make it.... but you, girlie, you will. Find ... young'uns future. Keep 'em ... safe ... strong."

It was as if even with death tugging at his soul the old man had sensed her deepest, most secret fears, as if *he* were trying to comfort *her*.

Ash's throat felt swollen shut.

"Pocket ... look in ... my pocket."

She barely caught the old man's whisper.

Turning back the quilt, she did as he asked her, withdrawing a beautifully crafted doeskin bag, its beaded design obviously worked by loving hands. A hint of light flickered in Jones's eyes as he looked upon it for what he must know was the last time. Ash remembered his story about the Sioux woman who had made moccasins for John Logan's boys and wondered if Sweetest One had fashioned this pouch as well, filling it with simple treasures for the man she loved.

"Open it," Kennisaw bade Ashleen.

She fumbled with the soft leather thong knotted about its top, tugging it free. She slipped her fingers into the mouth of the bag, but it was not the polished shells or herb medicines she would have expected as gifts from an Indian maiden. Rather, the bag contained something thin, flat, bound up carefully in a small piece of canvas, no doubt to keep out the dampness of rainstorms and creek fordings as Kennisaw Jones wandered the prairies.

Carefully Ash unfolded the canvas, withdrawing two sheets of age-yellowed paper. In the dim light filtering through the opening at the back of the wagon top she was able to make out a bold, official-looking scrawl upon the first sheet, a heavy wax seal, cracked, yet still clinging to the paper's edge.

"Land," Kennisaw wheezed. "Deed to Stormy Ridge."

The piece of wilderness Tom MacQuade had carved into a farm. The place where Garret MacQuade's dreams had died.

"I'll give it to Garret when I find him," Ash said.

"Garret won't want it. Vowed never go back. Want you to . . . have it."

Ash's mind filled with images of her most cherished dream: land to work, a home, fields for the children to run wild in. But she shook her head, disbelieving. "I couldn't."

"Missed wagon train . . . 'cause of me."

"You don't owe me anything. We'll manage fine."

"Know you would. But it pleases me . . . to think of you . . . and young'uns there."

Grief tore through Ashleen, mingled with gratitude for this old man who had again placed hope in her hands. At last she nodded, unable to speak.

"Garret'll . . . take you there. Tell him I said he would."

"I will."

"And this." Kennisaw's weak fingers grasped the edge of the second piece of paper, a page so old its creases were fragile, worn. "Give him . . . this. Tell him I saved it . . . all this time."

Ash spread the page open, holding it in the light. And what she saw broke her heart.

It was only a drawing, a child's picture of a log house, a starry night sky overhead. Yet there was a magic about it; a magic about the images of the people outlined in the glow of a fire in front of the structure.

A woman, laughing, dancing, her hands clasping those of a sweet-faced little girl. A man, his features unyielding as granite, leaning against the cabin wall. And Kennisaw —yes, a younger, vital Kennisaw, with a fiddle tucked under his bearded chin, the bow rollicking over the instrument's strings.

It was as if the child artist had plucked a single moment out of eternity, captured it forever with his small hand.

Ashleen knew who had drawn the picture even before she looked down at the note scribed carefully in the bottom corner.

To Kennisaw from Garret.

Ash forced her gaze away from the picture, feeling as if she had somehow intruded on something too precious, too private to share. It was as if Jones had tried to save for Garret some scrap of the life he had known, as if the old man had tried to drag from the ashes of Garret MacQuade's childhood one tiny ember of hope.

"You'll give it to him." Kennisaw's voice drifted to her.

"I will."

"Tell him . . . about the Garveys. Tell him . . . I'm sorry."

Tears rolled freely down Ash's cheeks as she promised. Kennisaw's lips twisted into a hint of a smile. "Angel . . . be his . . . angel," Kennisaw whispered.

And then he was gone.

Night blanketed West Port, the air thick with the threat of a coming storm. Ash peered down the dirt road, the grimy windows that lined the narrow streets filtering bits of gold light out into the darkness. But even those snippets of light seemed to mock her with the knowledge that somewhere, hidden in this maze of shadowy buildings, Garret MacQuade was waiting, not knowing that she was about to break his heart.

She braced one hand on the top of a hitching post and tugged at the woolen stocking that had bunched up in the heel of her high-button shoe. An hour ago she had felt a blister forming. Now, as she pulled the stocking into its proper place, the damp spot on the wool told her the bubble had long since popped, leaving a raw, red sore.

It seemed she had been walking an eternity, knocking on the doors of any who would listen to her. She had gone to all the places she had imagined a serious-minded man like Garret MacQuade might be. The church. The mercantile. The feed store. Though the establishments were closed, she had gone to the back doors, pounded on them until she had roused the proprietors.

She had even trundled off to the doorstep of a Mrs. Magillicuddy, where someone had informed her there was a literary society meeting at her home that evening. The sour-faced matron had been most distressed at having to interrupt her dramatic reading of Longfellow and had all but run Ashleen off of her property with a broomstick.

And yet at least she had gotten some response from the witch of a woman. God knew most of those she had talked to had scarcely looked at her, let alone given her aid.

Ash caught a glimpse of her reflection in a barbershop's window and grimaced. Little wonder people had been looking at her so strangely. She had changed out of the bloodstained dress in which she had tended Kennisaw, not wanting the sensitive Garret to have to endure such tangible proof of the old man's sufferings. But the gown she now had on—the only other one she owned—was questionable at best, embarrassing at worst. Still Ash had had no time to be choosy when she had made her wild dash to the Irish coast. She had bought a few lengths of fabric after she had reached America, but first there had been petticoats to stitch for Meggie, shirts for Liam, pants to cover Renny's long legs. For the time being this secondhand gown had been the best she could do for herself.

Ash grimaced. At least she had been the same height as the first owner of the dress, but her figure was distressingly more curved than the other woman's. Ash's breasts strained so at the tiny silver buttons that she had taken up her needle at the first opportunity, restitching and tightening the fastenings until her fingers had ached.

The bodice's neckline had been cut just high enough to dance upon the edge of respectability, just low enough to give tantalizing peeks of the soft, pale swells of the tops of Ashleen's breasts.

She had nearly died of shame the first time she had

donned the gown. Now she could not even muster a blush. She was too exhausted, too drained, too weighed down with grief to care.

"It hardly matters anyway," she said to herself, giving her reflection a hopeless glare, "with your hair tumbled all about your face."

Her crop of sun-gold tresses had shed its confining pins days ago, the strands wisping about her bared throat, clinging to her cheeks. And as if that wasn't bad enough, the delicate skin beneath her left eye was still shadowed a light purple, courtesy of Garvey's angry fist.

Discouraged, Ash leaned her face against the pane of glass, letting the coolness seep through her. She should just turn around and walk back to the campsite she had made for the wagon on the outskirts of town, she thought. Renny had been as exhausted as she was, and the little ones had been subdued by their first taste of the swift brutality to be found on the open trail.

They would need her. And yet she couldn't forget the fear, the desperation that had been on Kennisaw's face as he had pleaded with her to warn Garret that the Garveys were out to kill him.

If she could only gather up the whole blasted town, demand the information she sought one time, and be done with it. Surely someone must have seen Garret MacQuade and knew where he was.

The throbbing of a headache made Ashleen raise her fingertips to her temples, the night sounds of the raw, rowdy frontier town making her want to cover her ears.

Crude shouts from a group of men at the livery mingled with the racketing clank of a badly tuned piano. The questionable music flowed from the swinging doors of the Double Eagle Saloon with the same meandering quality as that of the drunken patrons weaving in and out, intent upon a night's revel before hitting the trail.

It seemed as if the whole of Missouri was jammed in that one building.

Ashleen stiffened, an idea striking her like a splash of icy water. But her mind had scarcely formed it before she dashed it away. Enter a saloon? It would be madness. Shameful. A lone woman—a decent woman—plunging into such a den of iniquity.

Ravening wolves could not have dragged Sister Bridget into such a place, and even Sister Agatha would have been horrified at the thought of Ashleen being exposed to such wickedness as must lurk beyond the Double Eagle's doors. If Ash was not already traipsing along the path to hell, such rash actions would most certainly nudge her toward the devil's domain.

Still, what other choice did she have? She couldn't wander aimlessly about the town all night. Couldn't leave the children alone much longer. Neither could she break her promise to the old man who had given her so much.

She looked at the slice of room visible over the swinging doors, revealing a melee of inebriated men and the feather-plumed headdresses of women of ill repute, both wreathed in whirlings of smoke from dozens of cheroots.

How much harm could it really do if she just slipped into the establishment and asked one simple question? She'd not darken the saloon's door for more than a few moments, and she might learn where to search for the elusive Garret.

She nibbled at a fingernail, uncertain. What would Garret MacQuade's reaction be if he ever discovered that she had sought news of him in such a place? No doubt he would be filled with well-bred disgust. But there was no help for it.

Mustering all her courage, Ash thrust her chin at a defiant angle, stalking across the street with as much dignity as her burning heel would allow her.

Steeling herself inwardly, she shoved the swinging door with such force that it careened wildly on its hinges, the crash of it against the inner wall sounding like cannon fire. Not that anyone within the stifling room would have noticed if the whole Mexican army held the saloon under seige.

Ash thought she had prepared herself for what would be revealed within, but as the stench of whiskey and cheap perfume assailed her the reality of what she was doing struck her with daunting force.

It was as if she had stepped into another world. A world she had never even suspected could exist.

Men sprawled on chairs, playing cards held lazily in their hands, enough money to feed and clothe the children for a year being wagered on a turn of the cards.

Ladies—only in the loosest of terms—clung to the men's muscled arms, their feminine charms all but poured into tawdry garments so tight every line, every curve was displayed to shocking advantage. Feathery trim accented necklines that plunged scandalously low, and Ashleen's cheeks fired when she glimpsed the rosy crest of one girl's nipple as a spindly youth sporting his first set of whiskers ogled it hungrily.

The woman beckoned him with a carnelian-painted smile, leading him up a steep staircase.

Ashleen cringed with a sudden sharp perception of what must be transpiring in the chambers above her head.

But at least the youth and his . . . partner were seeking some semblance of privacy, Ash thought as her gaze turned to a man sitting at the end of the highly polished bar. Obviously he didn't care if all of West Port witnessed his debaucheries. The man was all but obscured from Ashleen's view by not one, not two, but *four* fawning women—women who, even to Ashleen's innocent eyes, were obviously the most beauteous the Double Eagle had to offer.

One woman was perched upon each knee, one draped against his side, feathering kisses along his neck, while the fourth brushed full breasts against his back, her fingers threading in erotic patterns through hair black as sin.

Ash tried to swallow, tried to tear her gaze away from the decadent wretch, but at that moment he turned to look at her. And in that frozen instant she was assailed by the same dizzy sensation that had swept through her when she had been eight years old and had fallen off the ridgepole of the convent's stable.

Features rugged yet almost agonizingly sensual were set against the foil of longish dark hair. A wide, firm mouth seemingly shaped for secret pleasures twisted in a smile that screamed of lazy arrogance. While the man's square jaw jutted in a line of such pure stubbornness, Ashleen was certain he'd had countless people try to break it for him.

A small scar upon the curve of his chin attested to the validity of Ashleen's insight into the despicable rogue's character.

But it was his eyes that made her forget to breathe. Eyes hard as gunmetal, burning with a raw animal intensity that made her take a step back, her whole body seeming afire at his bold appraisal.

"Enjoying the show, darlin'?" His voice was like black velvet, seductive, tempting, yet concealing a jagged edge of cynicism that surprised her.

Ash looked away hastily, certain her face must be redder than the dance-hall girl's gown. "Yes—I mean no! I—"

"Don't worry, honey, you still have plenty of time to impress the hell out of me. I haven't made up my mind yet."

"Mr.—whoever you are," Ash sputtered, indignant, "I couldn't care less who you . . . you . . . well, do whatever you're going to do with! I—I've come here on—on business, and—"

"I just bet you have," he drawled, words only slightly slurred from the contents of the empty bottle of whiskey in front of him as he shed his layer of women like a buckskin jacket and walked unsteadily toward her. "I'm real interested in any, er, business proposition you might want to make me, pretty lady." He stopped bare inches from where she stood, blocking her path.

Ash squirmed inwardly, knowing how a rabbit must feel when cornered by a badger.

"I've been a long time without a woman." The man's breath heated her skin, the smell of his whiskey mingling with the heady scent of leather and the unmistakable tang of danger. "But be warned," his voice rasped, beguiling in her ear, one beautifully shaped hand rising to trace her cheek. "I plan to examine all my options real closely before I take my lucky acquisition upstairs."

"Of all the—the pompous, arrogant—"

"Not arrogance, honey. Just fact."

"Leave me alone," Ash choked out, desperate to break whatever spell the man had woven about her. "I—I'm looking for—for someone."

"Honey, you've already found him."

At that instant Ashleen knew she should have kicked, screamed, dived across the bar, anything to avoid the arms that flashed out and crushed her to a body lean and tough as storm-battered oak.

One big hand drove through the curls at her nape, forcing her to tip her head back to a dizzying degree. For a heartbeat Ashleen feared she would faint; then in the next moment she wished that she had. For she knew if she lived to be a hundred, she would never forget the way the tall man's mouth closed over hers, all hot desire and wild promise.

Her bones were melting, her pulse racing, her breath catching in short, terrified gasps—a terror not of the man's kiss, but of her own violent reaction to its power.

For the briefest of moments she melted against him, her lips parting in a gasp of surprise. With a groan of raw hunger the man ground his lips against hers.

It was as if he had possessed her in that single kiss more thoroughly than Timothy Kearny had in an entire stolen night of lovemaking. That sudden certainty, mingled with the memory of the trauma that had followed that single indiscretion, rocked Ashleen to her very core.

Panicked, she flattened her palms against the man's chest, shoving with all her might. But if the drink had befuddled his brain, it had done nothing to weaken the tensile strength of muscles as unyielding as steel. It was as if he didn't even notice her struggle, so lost was he in the pleasure that made his heartbeat crash erratically against her breasts, his hands seek the bare, fevered skin of her shoulders.

"Baby," the man was murmuring into her mouth as he kissed her. "Christ, you're sweet. You're . . . the lucky . . . winner."

With a cry of outrage Ash made one last desperate attempt to free herself. She slammed one sharp heel down onto the man's instep with all the force she could muster, at that same instant sinking her teeth deep into her tormentor's lower lip.

A yelp of surprised pain erupted from the man as he pushed her away, clapping one big hand to his bleeding lip. "What the hell—"

She half expected him to strike her, scream at her, shake her. What she would never have imagined was the hurt confusion in his voice as he rubbed at his injured mouth. "What the hell'd you do that for?" he demanded, gray eyes as shocked as if a pampered kitten had just flown, clawing into his face. But whatever stirring of sympathy or regret Ash might have felt vanished at his next words.

"I told you, you won. But lady, if you begged me on your knees now, I wouldn't take you upstairs."

"You despicable clod! You touch me again and . . . and I'll . . ." She searched for some threat awful enough to give the man pause, sensed that he was not one to be daunted at the ravings of a mere woman—or, most likely, a man. But she had to think of something.

She fixed upon a scene she had once read in one of the forbidden novels she had hidden beneath her bed ropes at the convent. "If you accost me again, I'll set my protector upon you, sir, and—and he'll demand pistols at dawn!"

"Pistols at what?" There was a strange sound to the man's voice.

"At dawn." Ash stuck her chin up, infusing her voice with as much confidence as possible. "I suppose a ruffian the likes of you has never heard of the way gentlemen settle questions of—of honor. My—my protector is a deadly shot with a pistol. He's killed scores of scoundrels like you."

"Oooh," one of the saloon girls trilled, "you'd best watch your back, handsome."

The corner of the man's mouth was twitching, a distressing light burning deep in his eyes. He didn't believe her. Ash could see it in the way he looked at her, as if he was waiting, watching with an unforgivable amusement as she dug herself a hole so deep she would never be able to scramble out.

And to appear the fool before this man after all that had happened since she entered this accursed saloon was more than Ashleen could stand. Her temper snapped, and with it, what little sense of caution she yet possessed.

"You may expect to hear from my protector directly," she said, scooping up her skirts and starting to plunge past him.

But his fingers swept out, catching her arm, stopping her.

"Take your hand off me," Ash said with as much dignity as she could manage.

"Gladly, you bloodthirsty little monster, but first, why don't you tell me who this terrifying protector of yours is? I like to know who's going to shoot me in the back."

"Unlike you, a gentleman like Mr. MacQuade would never shoot a man in the back."

The man looked as if he had swallowed an anvil. Ash took the fiercest of pleasure in the way his eyes bugged out, even the hazings of drunkenness seeming to fade. Garret MacQuade must have a reputation to rival Davy Crockett's if even this man blanched in fear.

"M-MacQuade?" he choked out.

"Mr. Garret MacQuade." It was as if, now that she had the man retreating, she couldn't stop from torturing him as he had her. She shoved past his broad shoulder, sweeping out the door.

The moment the night air struck her face she had an

urge to bolt and run, but she'd not give the man the satisfaction of knowing how badly he had shaken her.

It was to prove a fatal error.

She'd not even made it to the squat silhouette of the horse trough before he cut her off, perching with one hip upon the trough's low edge.

She paused, unable to stop herself.

"Ever thought of a career on the stage?" he inquired with a lazy superiority that made her glad she'd bitten him. "That was some performance in there, darlin'."

"It was no performance, I assure you."

"Then maybe you wouldn't mind telling me more about this Mr.—what was his name again?"

"MacQuade. Garret MacQuade."

"Mmmm." The man drew a wicked-looking gun from the holster slung low on his hips, a thong at the bottom of the leather casing tied about one long thigh.

Ash's heart skipped a beat. Even she knew what a tied-down gun signified—a man who took his target practice in deadly earnest. What in heaven's name was she getting Kennisaw's poor boy into?

She swallowed hard as the dark-haired man tugged a bandanna from his pocket and began polishing his gun.

If only she could find some way to frighten this beast—cure him of any desire to press this confrontation. She searched her imagination, groping for snippets of the countless hero tales she'd spun for the children.

"Go on," the lout urged her. "I'm waiting with baited breath."

"I . . . he . . . he's a giant of a man, with . . . hands big as bear paws, and—and he wears a knife as long as . . . as my arm."

One night-black brow arched disbelievingly, and Ash's cheeks flamed. "As long as your arm, eh?" the man echoed. "And how does this MacQuade manage to sit down with a knife that size strapped to his middle?"

"He—he doesn't wear it strapped to his middle. He has it shoved in his boot."

"Sounds painful."

Ash loathed the man for mocking her. And she would have sold her soul to the devil himself just to be able to put the lout in his place. "He wears his guns around his waist. Two of them. And a rifle—"

"I can't wait to hear where he keeps his rifle."

"Well, you'll find out soon enough, mister! He can shoot a gnat off of a squirrel's eyelash a mile away."

"Really!"

"But that's nothing in comparison to what he can do with—"

"Don't tell me," the man interrupted. "He pulls a cannon along behind his horse. You really should inform the army about this one-man brigade. Think of the rations they could save."

Ash sensed that somehow she was being badly outdueled in this battle of wits, knew full well when it was time to beat a hasty retreat. If only she could have the pleasure of smacking him clear into next Tuesday before she did so!

"I have nothing more to say to you." She turned her back on him and started to move away with an icy hauteur.

"Oh, but I think you do, darlin'. See, there's just one problem with your little story here."

His next words struck her with the force of a gale.

"I *am* Garret MacQuade."

5

*A*shleen prayed that the earth would split open and swallow her, but it seemed God wasn't disposed to be that merciful. She gaped at the man before her, struggling and failing to reconcile the conceited, lecherous oaf with the sensitive artist who had drawn the picture even now tucked deep within her skirt's pocket.

It was impossible.

"You—you can't be," she stammered. "Kennisaw said—"

"Kennisaw?" The man was grinning at her with the devil's own smile. "Ah, so that explains it. You're one of the old buzzard's harem. Never knew him to pluck 'em so young before."

"How dare you?" Her voice shook.

But the loathsome Garret went on, laughing at her. "Ah, well, I must admit you've got a look to you—all ripe and sweet, begging to be tasted."

Ash blanched with fury, remembering how Jones had clung to her hand, begging her, from the edge of death, to find the boy he loved so much. God's blood, she'd even been weeping for Garret MacQuade, grieving for him.

Now she wanted to kill him.

She settled for the next best alternative. With a strength born of anger she slammed open palms into Garret MacQuade's broad chest. For the barest of heartbeats he teetered upon the edge of the horse trough, fighting to regain his balance, but it was too late.

He let out a stunned shout as he tumbled backward, crashing into the water with a horrendous splash. Pleasure, sharp and sweet, ripped through Ashleen at the sight of him as his head broke the surface. He came up cursing, clawing the wet, dark hair from his face. And Ash thought she had never seen anything so infinitely satisfying.

"You little wildcat!" MacQuade roared. "No wonder you've got a damned black eye—whoever gave it to you must've been acting in self-defense!"

Ash's fists knotted at her sides, and she felt betrayal slice through her—betrayal of Kennisaw Jones's love, betrayal of her own soft heart. She wanted to hurt Garret MacQuade—hurt him as deeply as the wounds that he had dealt.

"I got this black eye from a man named Garvey," she hissed between gritted teeth, "a few hours before he killed Kennisaw Jones."

Her voice caught, tore on a ragged sob. Hating herself for showing even that weakness, she spun on her heel and ran into the night.

Garret sat in the trough, feeling as if someone had driven an axe into his chest. He couldn't breathe, couldn't move, blind horror tearing at him like ravening wolves.

Kennisaw . . . dead . . .

The words roiled wildly through his head until he wanted to retch.

No. Kennisaw Jones had survived more perils than any man living—he was like the huge oak that had been on Garret's father's land, the towering tree that had been twice struck by lightning yet, despite its broken branches, refused to die.

"Liar," Garret choked out, feeling for all the world like the child he had been, battling desperately to deny that which was too painful, too horrible to contemplate.

That was it. The woman was lying.

She had to be.

Damn it, he'd shake the truth out of her once and for all. But even now the slender figure in the tight blue dress was vanishing in the shadows, only her pale hair visible in the faint moonlight.

With an oath Garret sloshed to his feet. Clambering out to the street, he snatched up his gun from where it had fallen in the dirt an arm's length from the trough's edge and ran after her. His jaw clenched until it ached, his throat seemingly crushed in some brutal noose of raw fear and soul-deep, searing anger.

Even so, she had reached the outskirts of town before he closed in on her, her slight frame silhouetted against the backdrop of a dilapidated wagon, limned in the light of a waning cookfire.

"Stop, damn you!" Garret bellowed.

But she ignored him until he grabbed her arm in a bruising grip and spun her to face him.

"You lying witch!" Garret saw her face pale, eyes widen in fear. He wanted her to be afraid. He wanted her damn well quivering in her boots.

"What the hell do you mean, Kennisaw's dead? The whole Comanche nation couldn't kill that stubborn jackass! And God knows they've tried. If this is a goddamned joke you and he brewed up between you, I'll break your blasted necks!"

"Sister Ashleen? Sister Ash?"

A child's voice, thin, frightened, pierced through Garret, and he glanced at the wagon to see a spindly, red-haired boy charging toward them, a knife clutched in one skinny hand.

"You take your hands off her!" Garret heard stark terror in the boy's voice and saw fierce protectiveness in his eyes.

If there was a hell, Garret thought numbly, then he was in it—hurtled back twenty-odd years into a hideous nightmare that mocked him, jeered at him.

It was like looking into his own face the night death

had rained down on Stormy Ridge. Seeing his own terror mercilessly exposed.

A terror as sharp, as devastating as the one now slashing through Garret's taut belly.

He released the woman. Holding his hands palms up, his voice low, soothing, Garret spoke to the distraught boy. "Easy, son. Easy, now. I won't hurt her."

The knife glinted in the firelight. Garret didn't want to have to take it from him, to risk hurting him in the resultant struggle.

God knew Cain Garvey couldn't have taken Garret's knife from him that night at Stormy Ridge unless the outlaw had severed Garret's own hand.

"You—you *were* hurting her. I saw you," the boy accused, his voice touched, like the woman's was, with the strange, sweet lilt of Ireland.

"No, Renny, love. It's all right. Mr. MacQuade here is just upset—"

"Well, so are you!" the boy flung out defensively, edging to her side, eyes never leaving Garret. "You cried the whole time we made camp."

"Renny!" the woman chided, petal-soft cheeks still whisker-burned from Garret's fierce kiss, reddening.

"You did! And I never—never saw you cry before." There was confusion in the boy's voice, and so much love it made Garret ache.

He looked up to see three more child-shadows huddled near the wagon regarding him as if he were the devil himself.

Love, sincerity, sorrow. It wreathed this tiny campsite as certainly as the Missouri night sky.

He didn't want to look into the woman's upturned face, didn't want to see the truth that was written in the cherry-sweet, trembling lips, the sky-blue eyes brimful of hurt and grief and tears. Blast it, she was looking at him as if she hated him, blamed him. . . .

In that one soul-crushing instant, he knew.

What the woman had told him was true.

Garret felt the anger drain from him, leaving in its

wake a stark barrenness as parched and empty as any desert.

Dead. Kennisaw dead.

Never to roar out his bellowing laugh. Never to sing bawdy songs tunelessly before a campfire. Never again to look at Garret with that glow of pride that had made him want to be everything the old man had imagined him to be.

"How?" Garret faltered. "How the devil could it have happened?"

"Mr. Jones was shot. I couldn't stop the bleeding. We tried to make it to West Port before he died, but . . ." Her voice trailed off; she shook her head. "He wanted so much to see you, Mr. MacQuade."

Garret felt as though she'd rammed her fist into his gut.

Eyes soft with compassion flicked to the wagon, and Garret knew then that the old man was there. That he was not even to be spared seeing that craggy, animated face lifeless, dead.

Garret turned away, away from the boy, away from the woman, the grief tearing through him too raw, too deep to expose to anyone.

He staggered to a scraggly cottonwood like a wounded animal burrowing away to hide its pain. Covering his eyes with his forearm, he leaned against the tree's trunk, forcing himself to suck in deep breaths. His chest burned, his eyes stung, his fists knotted against the rush of loss, emptiness driving deep into his soul.

He wanted so much to see you . . . The soft, aching words raked at Garret's heart.

Sweet God, for ten years he and Kennisaw had looked forward to their annual Rendezvous—meeting in Santa Fe, Sacramento, once even the bustling town of St. Louis.

Garret had been anticipating this meeting at West Port Landing for months now, packing away stories to tell the old man as carefully as he preserved the sheaf of drawings stored in his saddlebags.

There had been the one about the two Kiowa women

who had slipped into Garret's blankets outside Santa Fe, and the tale about the Comanche youth who had stolen Garret's horse—stolen it only to have his father force him to return it once the brave learned the animal belonged to the dreaded white man Indians had named Spirit Stalker.

Kennisaw would have laughed until tears ran down his cheeks at the image of the fearsome Comanche eyeing Garret as though Garret were about to devour him.

Not his body, but rather his spirit. Imprisoning it forever upon a bit of paper.

It had been Kennisaw himself who had saddled Garret with that mystical aura one night when they had been surrounded by a dozen Tonkawa braves and were about to become the cannibalistic tribe's dinner.

Kennisaw had told them that if they killed Garret, they would kill the spirits of all Garret had entrapped in his drawings. Drawings so lifelike that when the Tonkawas had looked upon them they had been like fearful children confronting some creature spawned of night terrors.

Garret had never suspected, when he had sketched the band's leader from a hiding place in a jagged cliff the day before, that it would save his life. Save it many times over from more hostile tribes than he could count.

Nor had he ever suspected how much pleasure Kennisaw Jones would take in the hilarity of it all, feeding into the growing legend with his own tall tales.

But Kennisaw Jones would never laugh again.

A soft sound behind Garret made him stiffen. He could feel her—the woman, watching him with those wide blue eyes. He could smell the wild rose scent that he'd buried himself in when he'd crushed her in his arms, kissed the hell out of her.

Well, he'd already paid a hundredfold for the churlishness of that kiss—paid with the loss of the one person in the world Garret MacQuade gave a damn about.

He turned and raised dull eyes to hers. "I want to see him."

Nodding her assent, she led the way toward the wagon.

The faces of the children huddled there were clearer in the moonlight, and Garret felt as if he were running an Apache gauntlet when he saw the loathing in their eyes.

The flaxen-haired girl of twelve looked as if she could cheerfully have slit him from stem to stern, the lame boy as if he were contemplating wielding his crutch like a sword; and the littlest one, the girl with masses of dark hair, only peered up at him in a condemning silence that pierced even Garret's killing grief.

"Damn it, I'm not going to hurt"—Garret hesitated, groping for what the boy Renny had said—"I'm not going to hurt your sister. So you can quit looking at me like—"

"She's not our sister." The lame boy bristled. "She's Sister Mary Ashleen."

At what must have been his look of total bewilderment the older girl tipped up her nose in utter contempt. "She's a nun sister, not a sister sister."

A nun, sister? Judas Priest, he'd been mauling a goddamn *nun*?

"An' I know you won't hurt her"—the boy brandished his crutch—"'cause if you do, I—I'll shoot you dead! We got a Hawkin, and—"

Garret dragged a weary hand through his hair, the children's ragings making his head throb unmercifully. "Don't make threats you can't make good on, boy," he snapped. "You couldn't even lift a Hawkin, let alone use it, and any man who's been in the west three days would know it."

The child flinched, but he stuck out his chin, defiant. "You're mean. If the Bear Man was still alive, he'd eat you right up! He wouldn't let you yell like that!"

The Bear Man . . . there could be no doubt in Garret's mind whom the belligerent brat meant. Kennisaw, with his stories of wrestling grizzlys. Kennisaw, with the huge, pawlike hands that could wield an axe and then, miraculously deft, dance a bow across fiddle strings with so much skill no one's feet could keep from tapping.

Kennisaw who had always had time for children. In every town, in every settlement, in every Indian village there had been a bevy of the greedy little creatures hanging on the old man, digging into his pockets for horehound drops or pennies or shiny rocks he had saved for them.

He had remembered all of their names, remembered their favorite trinkets. Hell, he'd even remembered the colors of their dogs!

Garret had tried to forget.

He turned away from the boy and strode the last steps to the wagon.

Bracing one hand on the tailgate, he swung up into the box. Light from a lantern suspended from an iron hook at the top of a bow shed a soft, homey glow about the canvas-roofed interior.

Garret heard the swish of the woman's skirts as she climbed in beside him. With a delicate hand she gestured to where a plump feather tick was wedged in the corner of the wagon, a faded patchwork quilt spread with the tenderest of care over the bulky figure pillowed upon it.

Slowly Garret made his way toward the shrouded form, one hand grasping the edge of the covering. He hesitated for a pulse beat, as if by not looking into Jones's death-masked face he could somehow delude himself into believing Kennisaw was yet alive.

But at last Garret steeled himself, drawing back the quilt as carefully as if he were afraid of waking the old man from sleep.

Light spilled across features battered yet strangely serene in a way that the living Kennisaw Jones had never been.

Lacerations and bruises marred a face more savaged than Garret had seen in a half-dozen saloon brawls, but this time they had been cleansed and tended by loving hands. His barrel chest was naked, stripped no doubt of a shirt badly bloodied in whatever altercation had led Kennisaw to his death. A wadding of white cloth bandage covered the wound in the old man's belly. Unable to help himself, Garret lifted the pad of cloth and stared at the small hole beneath.

Countless scars had crisscrossed Kennisaw's flesh for as long as Garret could remember—scars from battles with Indians and outlaws, grizzlys and panthers and jealous husbands. It seemed ludicrous that this one tiny mark could have sent Kennisaw Jones to his grave.

"Damn you, you old bastard," Garret gritted, his eyes stinging, "what the hell did you have to go and do this for?" Garret's jaw clenched as the reality, the merciless finality of Kennisaw's death swept over him.

"Goddam it!" Dropping the quilt, he swung around, slamming one fist into the bumpy tin lid of an old trunk. The woman started at the sound as the raggedy metal and half-splintered wood scraped his hand, but Garret barely felt it, the pain raged through his soul so deeply.

He sucked in a steadying breath, wishing he were somewhere else—anywhere but in this cozy wagon with its quilts, its lantern glow, and its few handmade toys tucked lovingly in the nooks and crannies left by boxes and barrels.

And yet, if Kennisaw had had to die, Garret was glad it had been in such a place, with someone kind to tend him, and not alone on some barren wasteland with the scavengers circling, waiting with fiendish patience for the time when he'd be too weak to fend them off.

He glanced up uncertainly at the woman who stood there so quiet. Damn, he'd never known one before that could keep her mouth shut this long—especially when confronting a man who deserved a real tongue-lashing.

What had the sniping little cat with the pigtails said? That the woman—Sister Ashleen?—was a nun. That explained her saintlike silence. Wasn't there a rule that kept 'em from talking in those convent places?

What it didn't explain was why she looked so damned vulnerable and sweet, and why, despite everything he'd said and done, her eyes were shadowed pools of compassion, soft with a sudden understanding so clear, so deep, it seemed to Garret as if she could touch the very depths of his soul.

Secret places. Hidden places that he had almost forgotten existed.

He cleared his throat, driven at last to break the silence himself. "I suppose I should thank you," he said, the gruff edge to his voice more fitting for an epithet.

Roses stole into her cheeks. "For what? Ruining your night's entertainment? Biting your lip? Or shoving you in the horse trough?"

Humor. He hadn't expected it from her. Didn't deserve it. Or was she trying to bait him into an apology? She'd see him in hell first.

"You know damn well what for, lady. For taking Kennisaw in. For being there when he died."

She looked down into Kennisaw's still face, and Garret could have sworn those indecently long lashes of hers were damp with tears. Tenderly she drew the quilt up beneath the red whiskers.

"I didn't do it for you."

She raised one hand to shove a wayward golden curl from her forehead, and Garret was suddenly aware of how exhausted she appeared, how fragile. Blast, it was a bloody miracle he hadn't broken her in half, the way he'd crushed her in his arms, the way he'd ground his kiss down on those winsome wood-sprite lips.

He regarded her, wary.

"The children and I would like to be there when—well, when you have Mr. Jones's wake," she said. "When I was walking about the town tonight I saw a church. I could talk to the priest."

Garret shook his head, his voice harsh even to his own ears. "The only god Kennisaw believed in was the mountains and an eagle soaring. He wouldn't want some hypocrite spouting lies over him."

She winced, and Garret knew he'd hurt her. Again. He wondered why it should matter.

"I'll get my horse, get Kennisaw out of your wagon quick as possible," Garret bit out. "You're probably anxious to get on with . . . well, whatever you were doing before."

"We were going to Oregon," she said in that lilting, sweet voice. "But we're not anymore."

"Thank God Kennisaw shook some sense into you before he died." Garret felt an unexpected surge of relief. "It's pure hell on the trail. No place for a woman."

Was there defiance in the tilt of the chin suddenly jutting toward him, a certain belligerence in the eyes that had been filled with sorrow?

"I assure you, Mr. MacQuade, in the last months I've been countless places that could have been labeled pure . . . whatever blasphemous rot you were spewing. And as for Mr. Jones shaking sense into me, his reaction was quite the opposite of yours. He encouraged me, told me—told me I was strong enough to carve out a life for the children. He even offered me a place of my own."

Garret gave a hollow laugh. "Kennisaw Jones never owned anything but his fiddle, his gun, and the clothes on his back."

"That's why I couldn't take it." She went to where a bit of weathered canvas was tucked carefully upon a small wood table, then turned, unwrapping what the fabric contained. "The land he tried to give me—it belongs to you." She extended a piece of paper toward Garret, and he stared at the lumpy official seal, so faded, so battered, like the dreams his father had dreamed the day he'd shown them the land grant for Stormy Ridge.

The sight of it after all these years was like a knife thrust, the memory of Tom MacQuade's usually stoic face beaming with rare pleasure filling Garret's mind. His father had clapped Garret on the shoulder as if the boy had been a man, and there had been wonder in his eyes.

Someday your sons will work Stormy Ridge land, boy, Tom MacQuade had said. For a hundred generations there will be MacQuades on this land.

But Tom MacQuade's plans of rich fields and seas of

livestock had crumbled into nothing—nothing save a vast emptiness yawning, still, in Garret's heart.

Driving back the painful musings, Garret glared at Sister Ashleen. "That land is worthless. No good to anyone anymore. The whole place has probably gone back to scrub timber—even what fields we had managed to clear."

"I'm not afraid of hard work, Mr. MacQuade."

"Well, how do you feel about bears, Miss—I mean Sister Mary Ashleen?" He sneered, wanting to infuse a healthy fear in this dreamy-eyed little waif. "The house —whatever's left of it—is probably full of God knows what kind of animals. That's if you're lucky and bush-whackers or outlaws haven't found it and taken it over."

"Mr. MacQuade, the land is yours. I've already said—"

"I don't want it!" Garret fairly bellowed.

It was as if, in that instant, something snapped in the woman's sea-sprite face. The delicate, soft gold angel transformed before his eyes into a steely-eyed tigress. "Then I do."

"For Christ's sake, woman, it took you half the night to find me in the Double Eagle. How the hell do you expect to find some little patch of dirt farm in the middle of goddam Texas?"

That impudent chin rose another notch. "Mr. Jones said that you would take us."

"*I* would—son of a bitch!" If he wasn't so furious, he'd be laughing his head off. "Listen, lady, I've done a helluva lot of stupid things in my life. But saddling myself with a woman and a pack of whining kids in the middle of the wilderness isn't one of them." He snarled the words, hating the crawling sense of fear for her and the children that he couldn't keep from stirring inside him.

She paled, her eyes blue fire. "Then we'll just have to trust to God and find the land ourselves."

"That simple, eh? Well, that shows just how ignorant

you are! It's no damn church social out there, Sister. And the Comanche wouldn't care if you were the Virgin Mary herself when it came time for 'em to lift your scalp."

"At this point, Mr. MacQuade, I'd like to see them try!"

The words cracked out whiplash fast, hard.

"I should take that damn deed and feed it to the fire!" Garret raged.

He saw her wince, her eyes cloud, but the determination never left that soft, kissable mouth.

"You do what you have to do, Mr. MacQuade."

He stared at her, seeing the challenge there, the fear. "Oh, I get it. Do what I have to, but it won't make any difference, will it? If I burned the deed, you'd just hare off on some other brainless goose chase. Find another way to get the lot of you killed."

"I managed to make it all the way from Ireland on my own. Brought the children this far."

"Maybe there is a God after all. 'Cause lady, from what I've seen the last few minutes, your getting clear to West Port Landing is a cursed miracle."

"I believe in miracles, Mr. MacQuade."

Garret took a step toward her, his face a bare whisper from hers, her rapid breath warm on his skin. "Where the hell was the angel that was supposed to be watching out for Kennisaw when he was shot, Sister Mary Ashleen? Huh? Where the devil was your miracle then?"

He felt the urge to kiss her fire through him again, a fierce need deep in his loins. It was as if he needed to show her how brutal real life was, how little hope existed, how little good—starting with Garret MacQuade's own jaded soul.

But she already knew what a bastard he was. Had known it from that first moment in the Double Eagle.

With an oath Garret turned away. "The hell with it, lady. The hell with you. You want to get yourself killed, courtesy of that crazy old coot, far be it from me to stop you. Just get the hell out of my way. The hell out of my life."

Garret started to shove past her toward the wagon's tailgate, but her hand flashed out, gripping his steel-tense arm. "Wait."

He wheeled on her as if he'd like to take her damn head off. Glared at her.

"There was something else Mr. Jones wanted you to have. And a message he wanted me to give you."

She was holding something toward him—the rattiest-looking scrap of paper Garret had ever seen. He snatched it away from her, one corner of the sheet tearing. He shook it open, eyes locking upon the image inscribed there.

He had thought he'd known what grief was.

He hadn't even suspected how devastating it could be.

His mother smiled out at him, so real he could hear her laughter. His father stood alert as ever, watching them all frolicking to the tune of Kennisaw's fiddle. Little Beth had been singing that night, breathless as she'd danced, the new dress Mama had made out of one of her old ball gowns from back east swirling about the little girl's delighted form.

Beth had begged Garret to dance with her that night, but he had been buried too deep in his sketching to succumb to her wish.

He still saw her, still heard her lispy voice pleading with him in his most anguished nightmares.

Garret crumpled the paper in his fist and dropped it as if it had burned him.

"You said there was a message." His voice was dead. Dead like Beth. Dead like his soul.

The nun's hand had gentled on his arm until it seemed almost a caress, her voice low. "Mr. Jones wanted me to warn you that there are some men loose from prison. The men who shot him. I think Mr. Jones was afraid that they would come after you."

Garret raised his eyes to hers and felt hunger race through him. The hunger to ride long and hard, to face Kennisaw's murderers in a blaze of gunfire and killing fury. The hunger to get away from eyes too probing, too beautiful, too filled with an innocence Garret MacQuade could never know again.

"These men—who were they?"

"Mr. Jones said they were named Garvey. Cain and Eli Garvey."

Rage. White-hot. It swept through Garret with the fury of a flood-choked river, raking away all other emotions in its path.

"I'll kill the murdering bastards." Garret's fingers clenched over the butt of his Colt, as if the feel of the weapon against his palm could bring his quarry closer. "Damn it to hell, I'll kill them."

He stalked to the end of the wagon and leapt out of it with the killing grace of a stalking panther.

The children crowded around, scattered like a flock of frightened birds, their eyes still steeped with dislike, distrust.

"Sister Ash," the lame one squeaked, "is he gonna kill—"

"Quit asking questions, boy, before I decide to kill you!" Garret snapped.

The boy hopped back, taking shelter behind the red-haired lad's shoulder.

"Mr. MacQuade."

He expected the woman to squawk at him, dared her to with his eyes. But she only looked at him, her slender body silhouetted in the lantern glow, framed by the oval opening in the back of the wagon top.

"About Mr. Jones . . . and about the land . . ."

"I'll bury Kennisaw before I send the Garveys to their graves. And as for the land—lady, if you and these brats are so eager to die, feel free to do it at Stormy Ridge. God knows there are enough graves there already."

He wheeled and stalked into the night.

6

Garret slumped in the slat-backed chair, oblivious to the racket of the Double Eagle's more festive patrons as he drained the last of a bottle of whiskey and thumped it down on the spur-scarred table.

"Dead soldiers," Kennisaw had called the empty containers during the countless nights of carousing he and Garret had shared. The old man had lined them up with the precision of a general, taking inordinate pride in the fact that he could outdrink any man west of the Missouri.

It had been a vanity Garret had allowed him to keep, always surrendering the contest when Kennisaw's eyes had that unmistakable glazed look that warned him the old man was about to pass out.

Garret had always excused his actions, grumbling to himself that the reason he capitulated to Kennisaw was that if the old man did ever hit the floor dead drunk, it'd take a team of six oxen to move him.

But now, as Garret stared at the empty bottle, at his empty life, he knew that seeing the blustery pride in Kennisaw and hearing his delighted bragging had been one of the few shreds of enjoyment Garret had ever allowed himself.

It had seemed fitting to send the old man off to the devil this way.

Far more fitting than that nun's suggestion of listening to some dour-faced preacher extolling the beauties of heaven.

His mother had always looked a bit wistful when she told him and Beth about the wondrous church she'd gone to back east. But Garret had never understood the allure of stone and stained glass when there were mountains and skies filled with thunder. She had tried to keep him from being a heathen, but between his father's cynicism and Kennisaw's tales of the Great Spirit, Garret had early woven his own strange mix of beliefs. Lily MacQuade's Catholic upbringing had seemed as far removed from him as the heaven she spoke of.

He grimaced at the memory of the picture of heaven he'd seen in her Bible. People running around in their nightshirts playing golden harps and looking about as exciting as milk-sopped bread.

Kennisaw would've gone mad as a rabid bear in a place like that—if it did exist. Far better for him to be kicking up a ruckus with the rest of the hell-raisers in the devil's saloon.

But that woman—Sister Mary Ashleen—she'd never understand. Life to her was all good or bad, black or white, evil or godly. No shades of gray a soul could get lost in. She would probably have made the sign of the cross and sent up some petition to a saint or something if he had been so foolish as to tell her that heaven could be hell. A subtle hell that burned a man's soul just the same.

He closed his eyes, seeing her as she had been hours earlier in the dusk-shrouded cemetery as he had lowered the pine coffin that was to be Kennisaw's final resting place into the freshly turned soil.

She had stood some distance away, the four children clustered around her. All starched and pressed they had been, the girls' hair plaited in stiff braids tied up in ribbons, crisp gingham pinafores covering dresses Garret had known instinctively to be their Sunday best. The boys had squirmed, uncomfortable in pantaloons and white shirts, their unruly hair slicked down with a wet comb. Even then wisps had stuck up at both boys' cowlicks, giving them a flyaway, mischievous appearance that made Garret wonder what scrapes they were planning.

But it was the woman whose image was clearest in Garret's mind, dressed in a gown of soft gray-blue that made him think of dawn high in the mountains. Her hair had been pinned in a loose knot atop her crown, short, curling wisps escaping the pins to curl in a nimbus of sunshine gold about a face lovely even in its sadness. In her hand had been a bunch of prairie flowers, their riotous colors spilling over her fingers like jeweled velvet.

He had wanted her to feel as if she were intruding, pushing her pious little nose into his private grief. But she had stood a little away from the gravesite, hovering, uncertain, until, with an inward curse, he'd motioned her to come forward.

With a grateful smile that could have melted the heart of Beelzebub himself she had knelt down beside the grave, laying the blossoms upon the brown dirt.

"It's so peaceful here," she had said, gazing over the tree-spangled hillock. "I wish . . ." Her voice had faded, soft. "If we were going to stay here, I'd visit often. Bring flowers and—" She stopped and looked up at him with a shy smile that laid Garret out as thoroughly as the Kiowa lance he'd taken in the shoulder fifteen years ago. "You probably think I'm foolish," she had said, a hue more engaging than the wild rose in her bouquet staining her cheekbones.

Garret couldn't remember what he'd said in answer, only that it had been gruff and grating. More so than usual, because the picture of her trailing up the hill to Kennisaw's grave in the springtime, or in the first glittering frost, wrenched at something deep inside Garret, pleased him in a way that at once stunned him and terrified him.

After a moment he had turned on her, snapping out

that if she had any brains she *would* stay in West Port Landing—or better yet take herself back east, where a lone woman with a batch of children belonged.

Hard—yes, he'd been hard on her—but dammit, the thought of any woman alone on the trail, alone in the vast emptiness of Texas made Garret's gut churn. And the thought of this woman thus was a thousand times worse—this fairy-waif, her vulnerable angel eyes filled with dreams that would be ground to dust a hundred miles out of Missouri, when a reality more ruthlessly brutal, more grindingly cruel than any she could have imagined would crash down upon her.

At least he would damn well not be there to see it.

He dragged the makings from his pocket and rolled himself a smoke with unsteady hands. No, some other idiot could stand by and watch the sun sear her delicate skin, watch her grow exhausted, disillusioned, sick with unrelenting heat and despair.

He lit the cigarette and drew in a soothing lungful of smoke. The hell with it. The hell with her. She wasn't his blasted responsibility, no matter what that crazy old coot had promised her.

Kennisaw said you would take us to Stormy Ridge, her voice seemed to echo in his memory.

Well, Kennisaw Jones had said a hell of a lot of things in his time—a good portion of them half-truths, the rest downright lies. And Garret was in no way obligated to follow through on one of the old man's harebrained schemes, especially when it included dragging a tenderfoot woman and four smart-mouthed kids halfway across the country to a place Garret had vowed he'd never return to.

What the devil could have possessed the man to promise something like that, when Kennisaw knew— *knew,* goddamm it—that Garret would never willingly go back to the site of the home he'd loved, the site of his family's deaths?

The truth struck Garret in that instant, and he reeled inwardly. A ripe oath tore from his lips, and he would have sold his soul to the devil himself to have Kennisaw alive just long enough so Garret could flatten him.

"That bastard! That son of a bitching, scheming old bastard!"

One of the dance-hall girls that had been crawling all over Garret the night before skittered back a step as she passed, eyeing him with a wariness usually reserved for customers not averse to taking hostilities out on softer, feminine bodies.

She hesitated, as if trying to get up the courage to solicit his attentions. Cursing, Garret gestured her to leave him. Alone.

The way he damn well liked it.

No, he was not responsible for Sister Mary Ashleen. Or for those children of hers. Hell, he'd never even seen her before he had kissed her in the Double Eagle.

Garret had the grace to shift, uneasy, upon the hard seat of his chair, remembering the nun's quiet explanation of how she had ended up with the dying Kennisaw. She had not known the old man, either, before she had put both herself and the children at risk helping him.

From what she had said, the woman had already had one confrontation with Eli and Cain Garvey on Kennisaw's behalf. Garret's skin crawled at the thought. Had she any idea how stupid she had been? Dancing beneath the fangs of creatures more deadly than any snake? Though twenty years had passed, Garret could still see the Garveys' faces as clearly as if the horror at Stormy Ridge had happened yesterday. And in all the countless miles he'd traveled, in all the innumerable battles with hostile Indians, savage outlaws, and merciless elements he had never experienced such a sense of demonic, chilling evil as he had while staring into Cain Garvey's soulless eyes.

Had Sister Mary Ashleen known that she had been courting a hell worse than anything her fire-and-brimstone priests could have imagined? Even now, did she realize that Cain and Eli Garvey were not men disposed to forgive and forget interference in their plans?

Mad with blood lust, they would turn and attack whoever happened to be nearest them, whoever was so foolhardy as to draw their attention for even the briefest of heartbeats.

Had the woman known that when she had stepped in to aid a man she'd never seen before? Had she realized that when she had dragged Kennisaw into her wagon and made a desperate flight to West Port Landing?

She must have. Even newborn lambs instinctively knew the snarl of a wolf. But then Sister Mary Ashleen was, no doubt, a saint. Steeped in tales of martyrdom from the cradle. She'd deem it a privilege to sacrifice herself—she'd sacrificed her womanhood already, hadn't she? Embraced the cold marble of an altar instead of the body of a man when she'd taken whatever vows nuns had to take.

If there was sin, Garret thought wryly, Sister Mary Ashleen was guilty of a heinous one. She had felt so pliant, so giving, so right in his arms. It had to be a sin not to let a man taste such warmth, such perfection. A sin to tempt with lips so full and sweet. Her eyes had been smoky dark with confusion and a kind of wonder for those brief, dizzying moments. . . .

Before she bit you.

A wry grin tugged at one corner of Garret's mouth, his fingers rising to touch his still-tender lip. What the devil would Kennisaw have said if he'd seen that? The old man would've laughed till he couldn't breathe.

For as long as Garret could remember, women had flocked around him, hungry, fascinated, in the same way a skittering mouse was fascinated with a soaring hawk— waiting for the bird to swoop down on it, afraid, yet tempted by even the briefest glimpse of flying.

Never before had his attentions been met with outrage. But then, he usually had more sense than to kiss a decent woman as if she were a dance-hall girl—usually had more finesse than to maul her as if he were starving for the taste of her.

The thought gave Garret pause, and he swallowed hard at the threading of unease that niggled at him.

Maybe he had been starving, desperate to bury himself in the innocence, the infinite loveliness Mary Ashleen had radiated.

But he'd seen men driven by thirst to drink from an alkali pond, had heard their screams as death throes overtook them.

And to Garret, a woman like Mary Ashleen O'Shea was a wine-sweet draught of poison.

Garret shrugged, signaling for another bottle of whiskey. By tomorrow he'd be miles away from the temptation, all his attention focussed on bringing down the murdering Garveys. The woman's face would fade, blur with time. He'd quit hearing the lilting magic of her voice in his dreams. Quit remembering what it felt like to crush her slender frame against his hard one.

A disturbance at the front of the saloon made Garret glance up. A slack-jawed buzzard of a man who looked as if he hadn't bathed in years was weaving through the swinging doors, his lanky frame supported by a couple of no-account drifters that made up the Double Eagle's less-than-savory clientele.

Despite the ever-present din of the saloon, the man's shrill laughter pierced Garret's eardrums, setting his teeth on edge as the trio moved to the end of the bar that was a mere arm's length from where Garret sat.

A girl in a feathered headdress plunked whiskey in front of Garret, and he drank deep, hoping to dull his senses enough so that he'd not have to listen to the man's blatherings or smell the stench of year-old sweat and grime emanating from him in waves.

"Yep, boys, it's my lucky day," the drunken sot slurred, smacking his lips. "By t'morrow night I'll be buryin' myself in the choicest piece o' female flesh I've seen since that whore in Mexico."

Garret grimaced. He hoped the man would at least bathe before confronting the unfortunate lady. Garret understood the desperation that drove women to provide services to men for coin, but there wasn't enough money in the whole west territory to compensate for having to touch that vermin-infested skin.

"Spader, that high-nosed little filly wouldn't let you ride 'er in a million years, an' you know it," the drifter with the scraggly blond beard jeered.

A woman of discerning tastes, Garret thought wryly, almost glad of the distraction the three men were providing.

"Yeah," the other drifter chortled. "From the look o' her, she's kept that tup o' hers bottled up tight. You'd have t' pry 'er legs open with a damn axe handle."

Garret stiffened, his vague amusement dissipating into simmering anger.

The lascivious Spader rubbed his crotch suggestively with one grimy hand. "I'm not opposed t' using a little force t' give that gal the treat o' her life. Even if she be buck-shy, she'll be pure howlin' with pleasure once I spend a night pumpin' her." The man cackled, pulling his baggy trousers tight to display his erection. "Besides," he said, stroking himself one more time, "even if she screams herself hoarse, there'll be no one t' hear her once we're on the trail."

Garret leveled a killing glare at the boasting Spader. "You'd be surprised how many men listen while riding the plains," he said in a deadly quiet voice. "Listen for Indians, listen for predators, listen for bastards like you. And most of 'em get real touchy when they hear a lady scream."

Garret drew his Colt, checking the cylinder with deceptive calm.

Spader glanced at the weapon, his jaundiced eyes widening. "Hey, mister, it ain't like I'm gonna be kidnappin' her or anything. She's goin' with me willing-like. I mean, she's the one who hired me. I didn't go pokin' around after her!"

"Hired you?" Garret let a feral smile play about his

lips. "For what? Emptying the outhouse? It's the only thing I can see you're fit for."

Despite Garret's gun, Spader bristled, thrusting out his chest. "I be a trail guide, mister. I'm leavin' at daybreak to take that woman clear down t' Texas."

A sick suspicion stirred in Garret. His stomach heaved. He remembered the resolved look in Sister Ashleen's eyes, remembered her vow that she'd find Stormy Ridge by herself if need be.

She and the children had nowhere else to go.

Slowly Garret stood, pacing toward Spader. One wrong word, one wrong move, and Garret knew he'd wring the horny little weasel's throat. "This woman," Garret said, leaning up against the bar. "She wouldn't happen to have a bunch of children, would she?"

Spader took a gulp of the beer the barkeep had just poured him. "Yessiree. A whole slew of 'em. But they look so different, musta had four different pas." He made a clicking noise with his tongue. "Mebbe come next summer she'll be lucky enough t' be swelled out with a brat that has my good looks."

Rage exploded inside Garret, and in a heartbeat his fist flashed out, the frustration, fury, and pain of the past two days infusing the blow with bone-cracking power. His knuckles connected solidly with Spader's grizzled chin, a sickening, garbled sound coming from the man's throat. Garret knew the instant his fist made contact that the man's jaw was broken. It was bent at a strange angle, his howls of agony strangled as he clutched his face.

In that split second Garret brought his gun to bear, making Spader's cohorts freeze, their own weapons half drawn. "I wouldn't." Two words, ice cold.

The men released the butts of their pistols, letting them fall back into their holsters.

"He b'oke my 'amn 'aw," Spader was wailing.

"Consider yourself lucky," Garret warned. "You ever go near that lady or those kids again, and I'll make sure you can never—what was the ignorant way you put it?—pump another woman as long as you live."

"Can't th'eaten me," Spader gurgled.

"It's not a threat, Spader. It's a promise. And I can assure you, I'm a man of my word."

Garret saw one of the drifters make the slightest move toward his gun. Lightning fast, Garret had his own weapon aimed at the man's chest. "Before you do anything stupid, mister, you'd better ask yourself whether this slimy piece of garbage is worth getting killed over." The scraggly bearded one swallowed hard, looking at Garret's gun—a gun held with the ease of one who had used it so often, so skillfully, it was almost an extension of his hand.

After a moment the drifter shook his head.

"You're real smart," Garret said softly. "I might just let you live."

"Crathy. He'th bloomin' crathy," the injured man moaned.

"That's right, Spader. And don't you forget it." Garret holstered his gun and started to turn away. He glanced over one shoulder, his voice low. "You know, four men have tried to shoot me in the back. They're all dead. Dead like any one of you will be if I ever lay eyes on you again."

Garret tossed a crumpled bill on his table, then strode from the saloon.

Hands on hips he stalked down the dark street to where the buildings thinned, giving way to open country. To where Sister Mary Ashleen's wagon sat, serene, peaceful under the stars.

Garret's jaw clenched. He'd like to make that little fool see stars! Shake some sense into her, for God's sake! How could she have been so foolish as to hire someone like that vermin Spader to be her guide?

Or so desperate, his conscience whispered.

"Son of a bitch!" Garret snarled, slamming his fist against the wall of the livery stable. He muffled another oath as knuckles, yet tender from connecting with Spader's jaw, throbbed.

"Damn Kennisaw. Damn her. Damn me!"

As if he had summoned her up by his words, Garret saw a figure in a sheer white nightgown climb down from the wagon. Hair soft as cornsilk tumbled loose about her shoulders, the moonglow casting her slender body into relief beneath the fragile white cloth. She bent down to retrieve something, but Garret never knew what it was.

He stared transfixed at the graceful line of a slim leg, the indentation of a waist so narrow he could span it with his hands, breasts full, yet so dainty that the sight of them made sweat bead his upper lip.

His loins tightened, and he ached with need—the need to reach out, to touch, to worship, to plunder.

If Kennisaw Jones had wanted to deal one last hand in the infernal game of wits he loved to play with Garret, he couldn't have devised anything more agonizing than this—this untouchable angel with a temptress's own body—this trek back to Texas, back to Garret's own private nightmare. Kennisaw must've known Garret would be trapped by his own conscience, by the clamorings of his body, by the haunted innocence in Ashleen's sea-blue eyes.

Garret cursed. He should've known better than to try to best the old buzzard at one of his damn games.

Kennisaw Jones was an incorrigible cheater.

There was only one thing to do.

He would take the woman to Texas and then—then try to pick up the Garveys' trail. God knew that shouldn't be too hard. Garret's jaw tightened. Scum like them always left a trail of garbage in their wake.

But before he did either of those things there was something else he had damned well better take care of.

With an oath Garret turned, striding back toward the saloon, making an effort to drive the hardness from his face. He entered the door, scanning the chamber until he found the girl he'd frightened earlier.

He'd be gentle as hell with her now. Please her until she moaned with it. He had to. Had to drive back the savage needs the golden-haired nun spawned in him, had to loose them on another, more willing lady.

Otherwise the weeks ahead would be pure holy hell. Endless weeks seeing Ashleen, eating with her, sleeping a few yards from where she lay as he guided that infernal wagon to the home he'd left behind.

7

Ashleen shifted, restless, beneath the faded quilts, trapped in a hazy half world between wakefulness and sleep.

He was kissing her again, his mouth unlocking secrets deep inside her soul. She reveled in the dream, threading her fingers through long, dark hair, feeling it slip like silk against her skin as he cradled her closer in his arms.

She knew she should protest, knew she should push him away, but the corded muscles of his body were so hard, so hot, imprinted against her. He was hungry, with groans of pleasure, of need rumbling from that broad masculine chest as he loosed the ties of the velvet cloak that draped about her like liquid midnight.

"Beautiful," he whispered, his voice gritty with desire, gentle with a kind of reverence. "Sweet Jesus, you're so beautiful."

She gasped as he reached out to touch her, grazing her nipple with a rein-callused palm. And she drowned in eyes, not hard and cold as steel, but a silvery wolf gray that shimmered with love.

"Ash . . . ah, Ash," Garret MacQuade breathed into her mouth, "I've been waiting for you forever."

"Forever," Ash murmured, losing herself in the feel of him, the taste of him. Her heart thundered in her breast, the whole world seeming to whirl away into magic. A magic sweet with the sounds of wind whispering through the trees, crystal brooks burbling over stones like polished gems, birdsong pure as the finest crystal.

And something heavy banging against wood . . .

Ash's brow furrowed at the disturbing sound intruding into the most delightful dream she'd ever known. She tugged the covers over her head, trying to recapture the soul-searing kiss, but old Sister Michael, who was stone deaf, could not have blotted out the crashing and banging, the cursing and shouting somewhere outside the wagon.

The misty dream world disappeared, and she opened her eyes to see the dim pattern of quilt patches over her head, hear the sleepy grousing of the children.

Embarrassment surged through Ashleen, as potent as the imagined kisses had been, and she was agonizingly aware that her very skin seemed to be humming with the sensations the image of Garret MacQuade's loving had provoked.

Loving? Ash berated herself, scrambling into a dressing gown as reality crashed down around her. Far better to label his kisses as a display of his many talents to—how had he put it?—some lucky winner.

"Sister Ash . . . who's making that noise?" Shevonne asked, scooting up to a sitting position.

"It sounds like a dragon fight, or a cyclops, or—"

"Well, whoever it is, I'm going to tell them to go about their marauding more quietly," Ash began.

But at that moment the whole wagon rocked on its springs, a tall, buckskin-clad figure pulling himself up onto the seat. A broad-brimmed black hat with a beaded band was jammed low over features Ash couldn't quite see, deep fringe accenting shoulders dauntingly broad, set with a pugnacious stubbornness that made Ash stare. But it was the dark hair spilling past his collar in rich ebony waves that sent recognition jolting through her.

"Mr. MacQuade," Ash stammered, her cheeks firing as if he could see in excruciatingly sensual detail what she had been dreaming. "What are you doing?"

The man slanted her a glance seething with impatience, irritation, and a resignation that made her think of Renny those times he'd almost managed to escape going to Mass. "What the hell does it look like I'm doing, Sister?"

His hands closed about the small wood table stashed in the wagon. With a grunt he jerked it through the opening in the canvas, then, under Ash's stunned gaze, flung it to the ground below.

A splintering sound cracked the air, outrage racing through Ash. "That's my table!"

"Wrong, Sister, that *was* your table. Now it's kindling." Was there a certain smug satisfaction in that whiskey-warm voice?

"You have no right to—"

"To what?" Garret pushed his way past her. "To lighten up your load so this wreck of a wagon might have some chance of making it to Texas?" Amid the squeals of the children Garret dredged up the rocking chair Ashleen had tucked lovingly in one corner of the wagon box.

"This wagon is none of your concern!" Ash blustered. "You're not responsible for it, or for us—"

Garret spat a crude expletive.

Stiffening, Ash barred his path to the back of the wagon. "And as for my furnishings, Mr. MacQuade, I'll haul whatever I please. My guide, Mr. Spader, examined the wagon last night and found nothing amiss."

"Damn right he found nothing amiss." MacQuade's lip curled, his eyes raking her. "Unfortunately, your guide, Mr. Spader, has had an accident. He ran in to my fist."

"Your—"

"Yeah." Garret's eyes blazed silver fire. *"After* he told everyone in the Double Eagle Saloon what he intended to do to that sweet little body of yours once you were on the trail."

Ash raised one hand involuntarily to where the neck of her dressing gown hung open. "I didn't give him the least encouragement," she said faintly.

"You didn't have to. Most men don't have my willpower, Sister. They see lips like those, all red and ripe, and hair all gold like sunshine, and they want to bury their hands in it."

Their gazes locked, and Ash could see in the turbulent gray eyes of Garret MacQuade a reflection of her own too-vivid memory of how their lips had melded. For the briefest of instants a fever hotter and more virulent than anything she'd ever experienced had swept through her.

Something wild, unexpected.

Something a man like Garret had doubtless indulged in so many times he could not even remember the women's faces.

She saw his hands knot upon the smooth wood of the chair.

"Bloody hell, woman!" he roared, flinging the rocker out inches over her head. "Quit looking at me like that, or I'll be as bad as that damn Spader! I'm not a blasted saint! Unlike you, denying myself the pleasures of the flesh is not my idea of a good time."

"Don't you shout at Sister Ash that way," Liam shrilled. "Go away!"

"I wish the hell I could," Garret said, digging through a barrel, then tossing it the way of the chair. "We're going to get goddamn sick of each other by the time this torture is over."

He swung down from the wagon box, every muscle taut with dangerous power.

Clutching at her dressing gown, Ash moved to follow him, her temper blazing. "I don't know who you think you are—"

"I think I'm a damn fool."

He stalked to where the horses were tethered, yanking their lead ropes free. With a cry Renny ran, flinging his arms around Cooley's glossy neck, the other horses skittering back as if they, too, sensed the menace in MacQuade.

It was then Ash saw the oxen—huge, ugly beasts with wicked-looking horns, tied to a hitch rail.

Garret motioned to the man standing beside them.

Realizing MacQuade's intent, Ashleen dodged in front of him, barring his path, hands on hips. "Keep your hands off my horses, Mr. MacQuade, or I'll call the sheriff."

"If these are your horses, lady, you got cheated but good. You're lucky they made it this far."

"They're fine horses. Sound."

"Sound enough to pull a buggy to Sunday meeting, or to take a leisurely ride around town. But there is no way these horses would be strong enough to drag that hulk of a wagon of yours halfway across the country."

"S-Sister Ash." Renny's voice was quavering, pleading, his eyes desperate upon her as he clung to his beloved horse. "Don't—you can't let him . . . him take . . ."

"The horses go, or I won't guide this wagon as far as the next street. It's your choice." Garret crossed muscled arms over his blatantly masculine chest and glowered from beneath lowered brows.

"Guide our wagon? Did you say you would take us to Texas?"

"Yes, God help me. Unless, of course, you want to look around and find another fine, upstanding pillar of the community like Mr. Spader to take you."

Torn between astonished relief that MacQuade would guide them and fury at the insufferable man's arrogance, Ashleen loathed him, hating the helplessness weighing her down. Regarding his decree about the horses, she really had no choice, and Garret MacQuade knew it.

She'd never forgive him for the touch of smugness about that wide, sensual mouth. "I should've drowned you in the horse trough."

"Too late now. Well, what's it gonna be, Sister? It's your hand to play."

Ashleen felt tears of frustration burn her eyelids, but she held her jaw rigid. She wanted to tell him to go dive in the stream. Wanted to tell him to leap from the nearest precipice. But she glanced over to see three small, frightened faces clustered at the back of the wagon. She turned to see Renny clutching at Cooley with raw anguish, his eyes on her, filled with blind faith.

It was a choice that was no choice at all.

She hated MacQuade for it.

"Have it your way, then," Ashleen bit out. "But you'll not take Cooley."

"Cooley?"

"The bay. He belongs with Renny."

"You got enough feed and enough stamina to take care of an extra piece of livestock?"

Ashleen stepped close, her face but a few inches from MacQuade's own, her voice so low no one else could hear it. But in spite of its whispered tone it was shored up with words, whiplash tough.

"I know you don't much care, Mr. MacQuade, but that boy over there has lost more than enough already. He lost his parents, his home, his country. He's not going to lose that horse."

Something unreadable flashed into those wolf-gray eyes, but his voice was unyielding as stone. "Fine. Maybe if you get hungry enough on the trail, you can eat it."

Ash knew the oaf was trying to rattle her. He succeeded. Her stomach lurched at the picture his words conjured. She was tired, so blasted weary of traveling, of fighting for every scrap of food for herself and the children. The responsibility seemed to grind her down like a giant boulder, and each mistake she had made— exposed by arrogant men like Garret MacQuade— chipped away at her faith in herself. Her faith that she had done the right thing sweeping the little ones away from Ireland, away from the horrors of the poorhouse, into what seemed a hostile, unforgiving land.

"Mr. MacQuade," she said between gritted teeth, "I'd eat you first, except you'd probably give me indigestion."

The tiniest hint of a smile played about the corner of MacQuade's mouth, a twinkle of raw amusement glinting in his eyes. "There'll be plenty of time for that, Sister, once we get on the trail," he said in a voice saturated with mocking seduction.

With a shiver of awareness that made her skin burn Ash spun away, stomping through the wreckage of the things Garret MacQuade had tossed from the wagon.

It doesn't matter, she said inwardly, turning her gaze away from the remains of the meager possessions she had managed to gather since her arrival in America. Nothing matters except getting the children safely to Texas.

Her grim thoughts were cut off by MacQuade's hard voice. "Just one more thing, your holiness."

She wheeled to glare at him.

"I'm not a goddam nursemaid. One episode of whining or weeping or complaining about the work, the heat, or the hardship, and I dump the lot of you in the middle of nowhere. We do things *my* way. *Mine.* If I tell you to drive that wagon off a blasted cliff, you'll do it and won't bat an eye. Understood?"

It was the outside of enough. Ashleen stalked over to him, her whole body shaking with fury. "You burst in here, breaking my possessions—"

"You can build a new table in Texas," he snarled.

"Trade my horses—"

He snorted a crude oath.

"And stomp around, roaring like—like a wounded lion, and then you expect total obedience? Who do you think you are, Mr. MacQuade? *God?*"

She disliked the narrowing of quicksilver eyes, disliked the danger in the harsh planes of that devastatingly sensual face.

"Yeah. Come to think of it, as long as we're on the trail, Sister Mary Ashleen, I am God. That ought to make things simpler all around."

Ash started to say something but was suddenly aware of a small hand clutching at her dressing gown, a tiny body pressed against her leg. She looked down into Meggie's wide, dark eyes.

"It's all right, Meggie, love." With agonizing effort she

softened her voice. "Mr. MacQuade and I were—were just having a little disagreement."

But the eyes that had been so achingly blank for so long were fixed upon Garret's face, Meggie's baby-pink lips parted in awe and more than a little trepidation. It was the same odd expression with which the child had been regarding MacQuade since the first time he had blazed up to the wagon.

It seemed that innocent stare pierced MacQuade, somehow chafed at him.

He glared down at the little girl, and there was something in his face, some lurking of pain so swiftly hidden, Ashleen was sure she'd imagined it.

"You've been staring at me for two days, girl," he snapped. "If you've got something to say, spit it out."

Meggie dived behind Ashleen's dressing gown like a frightened fawn, and Ash could feel the child trembling.

"Leave her alone!" Renny blazed. "You leave Meggie alone!"

"What the—"

"She can't talk," Ashleen cut in with frigid accents.

The expression that had been so arrogant, so smug, wavered into confusion. "What the devil do you mean, she can't talk?"

"She hasn't spoken a word since I found her. Huddled on a cot beside her dying mother."

Ash saw something akin to regret flit across Garret's face, a deep crimson staining his high cheekbones. She could almost have felt sorry for him in that moment—if he hadn't been a mule-stubborn, pompous, intolerant oaf.

"I—I didn't know," MacQuade said stiffly, those disturbingly unreadable eyes flicking again to the child's upturned face.

"Well, maybe when you're arranging things tonight, *God,* you could give her the power of speech. Heaven knows, I've been trying to long enough."

She saw MacQuade's flush deepen. She wanted to sweep the little girl into her arms, hold her, soothe her, but she knew Meggie would pull away. Her throat constricted with tears, Ashleen took the little girl's hand and guided her back to the wagon.

They would only be on the trail a little while, Ash tried to tell herself. She would only have to endure MacQuade's surly temper a short time.

Why did it suddenly seem as if that time would be more grueling than any penance old Father O'Hara could have devised?

A fleeting memory of her dream taunted her—silver eyes, warm, vulnerable, words so sweet they had pierced her very heart.

The lump in Ash's throat knotted tighter still, hated tears clinging to her lashes.

Even in a dream she should have known better than to succumb to seductive words, to eyes burning with need, lips warm, persuasive.

Hadn't she done so with Timothy Kearny many years ago? A lifetime ago, filled with dreams long surrendered. Of a man's arms cradling her, a man's deep, loving laughter, a future filled with a home and children.

She winced inwardly at the remembered pain, the scar from that disastrous night in the dew-sweet Irish hills burning afresh.

She had lost so much, hurling herself heart-first into passions she had not understood. She had lost her innocence, lost that wild freedom with which she had lavished the world with her affections.

In some ways, she had lost herself.

But she had the children now, a precious, miraculous gift. It was more than she had dared hope for in those desolate days after she had been battered by Kearny's duplicity.

More than she dared dream of.

It was enough.

Why then did she keep remembering the fire in Garret's kiss, the yearning? Her skin burning beneath hard, callused hands. The man had been drunk, for heaven's sake! An insolent, inebriated oaf. And yet his touch, his mouth upon hers had stirred her in a way Timothy Kearny's awkward gropings never had.

He was an enigma, Garret MacQuade. An intriguing one.

And perhaps the most dangerous temptation Ashleen had ever known.

8

*T*he wagon swayed monotonously in the blazing heat, waves of light shimmering upward toward a blindingly blue sky. Ash held the bullwhip loosely in one hand, cracking it at intervals above the plodding animals' heads. Her palms no longer blistered, toughened at last as they were with calluses beneath the leather's constant friction. And she rarely managed to clip herself with the lash any more.

She wished that her emotions regarding Garret MacQuade were as easy to master. But they flashed out at odd times, stinging her as unexpectedly as the bite of the whip had during those first awkward days after the wagon had left West Port.

Ash peered beneath the brim of her blue-sprigged sunbonnet and strained to see him, a dark silhouette at the crest of a hill some three hundred yards away. He sat astride a paint gelding. Solitary. Silent. As closed off from the world in his way as little Meggie Kearny was in hers.

If someone had told Ash that it was possible for a man to travel alone while guiding a wagonful of children, she would have laughed at the mere thought. But the two weeks they had spent on the trail had changed her view.

Garret MacQuade had spoken more words in their

disastrous five-minute interlude in the Double Eagle than he had in the past weeks. His only communication had been gruff syllables snapped out in those rare times he deigned to draw near the wagon—usually to criticize her driving, her care of the oxen, or the grindingly slow pace.

The man had been nothing save consistent in his obnoxious behavior. She should have been glad that he was keeping his distance, glad he wasn't spoiling the children's appetites by glowering at them over dinner.

She would have been.

Except for those rare moments when he thought no one was looking. Those times when she would catch him watching Renny with a kind of understanding, or regarding the plucky Liam with empathy, or following Meggie's dark head with an almost palpable pain.

A hot breeze blew gritty dust across Ashleen's face. She swiped it away, her eyes still fixed on that distant figure who was engrossed in what looked to be a piece of paper propped before him in the saddle.

"You gettin' tired, Sister Ash?"

The voice behind her shoulder made Ashleen start, and she turned to see Renny, his face shaded with concern as he climbed from the back of the wagon onto the seat beside her. "Thought I might spell you for a while up here. Let you climb down and stretch your legs with the others."

Ash flashed him a grateful smile, her gaze turning to where Shevonne and Liam gamboled like frolicksome puppies, oblivious to the heat, the dust, and Garret MacQuade's foul disposition. Meggie wandered even further ahead than the other two, poring over the faint wagon tracks as if in search of treasure.

Ash felt the familiar stirring of depression at the sight of the wisp of a child in sunflower yellow, a perfect angel with a stunningly beautiful face and empty, empty eyes—eyes that seemed to fix upon Garret MacQuade almost as often as Ashleen's own. It was strange, the little girl's fascination with the rough-talking, ill-tempered MacQuade. Always before Meggie had flinched and cowered when confronted with loud voices or anger. But she seemed to regard Garret with a kind of quiet acceptance tinged with puzzlement, and more than a little awe. An odd combination, but one that Ashleen would capitalize upon, if only she could think how.

"Well, do you want to?" Renny interrupted her musings. "Want to walk awhile, I mean?"

"Actually, kind sir, I would *love* to get away from these lumbering beefsteaks." Arching her back to work out the kinks, Ashleen surrendered the bullwhip to Renny. "Between you and me, Renny me darlin', the only use I can see for oxen is dinner."

"We should've kept the horses." Renny's lip thrust out, his eyes sullen. "They would've been fine. I know it."

Ash tucked a wispy curl beneath her bonnet and lay a hand on Renny's thin one. His nails were bitten to the quick, a dozen scratches crisscrossing his skin from his forays through the brush.

"I wish we could have kept the horses, too, Ren," she said with a sigh. "But now that we've been on the trail awhile, I have to admit that Mr. MacQuade was right. The trail is too rough for them, the wagon too heavy. They would've broken their hearts lugging this big hulk of a thing all the way to Texas."

Renny gave a snort of disbelief, but Ashleen rushed on. "At least we got to keep Cooley," she said, waving her hand to where the horse was tied to the wagon, its velvety muzzle turned pointedly away from the milch cow trudging alongside. "I don't know what we'd have done without that horse of yours."

"*I* do. I wouldn't've gone! I would've—would've told that Mr. MacQuade to—to go to hell."

"Renny!"

The boy flushed, but his eyes were narrowed with defiance. "Well, *he* says it all the time, and you never tell *him* not to."

"I am not responsible for Mr. MacQuade's language, Renny O'Manion. But I *am* responsible for yours. 'Heck' is a perfectly acceptable substitute—"

"It's not half as good as hell. Babies like Liam say heck, and—"

"So will you, unless you want me to scrub your mouth out with a prickly pear."

The threat seemed dastardly, but immediately Renny's stubborn-set lips began to twitch. They split into a reluctant, pouting grin.

"Now, try to keep control of these high-spirited beasts while I'm away," Ashleen teased him, tweaking his nose. "I know they race at terrifying speed, but I have faith that you'll manage to keep 'em from running away."

"If only they *would* run," Renny groaned.

"Well, Mr. MacQuade insists it's possible for them to get restive—especially if they're thirsty. But I have a hard time believing it."

"I think a whole tribe of Indians could come whoopin' down on 'em, and they wouldn't even blink," Renny said sullenly.

Ashleen's laughter rang on the air as she leapt lightly down from the wagon. "I certainly hope we never have the opportunity to find out."

For a while she wandered along beside the vehicle, glad of the opportunity to work the kinks out of stiff muscles. But before long her gaze tracked again from the dark-braided hair of Meggie to Garret MacQuade, her mind drifting back to her earlier musings.

No, she had not imagined Meggie's fascination with the glowering man who served as their guide. If there were just some way to bring them together—she grimaced—for longer than three seconds of snapping out commands, was it possible that the child might actually respond? It was the faintest of hopes. And yet with each week, each day, each hour Meggie spent in her silent world, Ashleen feared it would be harder and harder to break the child free of whatever bonds entrapped her.

If MacQuade could stir even the slightest of reactions from the little girl, Ashleen had to try.

How? Ash thought wryly. By inviting the man to a banquet in his honor? The smile faded, and she caught her lip between her teeth. No. A simple plate of roast prairie chicken and a dried-apple pie. A half hour, maybe more, for Meggie to be close to Garret MacQuade . . . listen to him talk . . . and, pray God, to talk herself.

Ashleen sucked in a bracing breath. She paced back to the side of the wagon, laying one hand on the rough wood as she angled her face up toward Renny. "You watch the younger ones for me, Ren. I—I think I'm going to walk ahead and talk to Mr. MacQuade."

"Why? He'll just yell at you."

"Probably. But I'm going to invite him to dinner anyway."

"What?" Renny exploded. "You can't—can't—the way he's always scowlin', he'll make the milk go sour."

"Then you'd best be prepared to drink water." Ash looked up into the boy's face, high above her on the wagon seat. Lines of disgust furrowed Renny's brow, his mouth puckered as if he'd just had a gulp of milk as distasteful as he'd predicted. "Renny," she explained gently, "in spite of all Mr. MacQuade's shouting, he is being very kind. He didn't have to guide us."

"I wish he hadn't."

"Be that as it may, if he does come this evening, I'm depending on you to be polite."

"Not to him, I won't! After the way he treated you, and the way he yelled at Meggie, and—"

"Renny, I'm asking you to be polite as a favor to me. Please." Ash glanced again to the solitary horseman. "He probably won't come anyway," she said, more to herself than the boy.

"Humph. He'll come. He does everything else he can to make me mad."

"Renny, enough!" she said more sharply than she meant to. The boy stared at her with surprised, hurt eyes.

"Renny," Ash attempted to begin again. "I understand how you feel about the horses, and about . . . well, Mr. MacQuade's temper. But this hostility between you can only make a difficult situation worse."

She looked up at the boy, saw his face turned pointedly away from her.

Surrendering to the knowledge that it was futile to discuss it further until Renny simmered down, Ashleen attempted to shed her own gnawing irritation and started with long strides up the hill toward MacQuade.

The high prairie grasses brushed against her skirt, sweet-smelling blossoms rippling in gusts of wind that swept down the hillside.

Ash shoved her sunbonnet back until it dangled by its strings against her shoulders, letting the sunshine warm her face, wishing it could melt away the unpleasantness with Renny, the stiffness of muscles cramped from sitting in one position too long, and her gnawing dread of speaking to Garret MacQuade.

Sister Agatha had often told Ashleen a strong will was the best cure for almost everything. Ash resolved to will into herself the brightness, the warmth of the meadow around her.

Her hand swept out to pluck a fragile wild rose, tucking it behind one ear. The scent filled her, soothed her, and she gathered more of the blossoms that sprinkled the rise. Blue and butter-yellow, purple and orange, tiny white flowerets and garish red ones, each more perfectly beautiful than the last one.

A flock of birds darted up nearly beneath her nose, taking wing in high dudgeon, scolding in their cackling voices.

Shielding her eyes against the glare, Ash watched the bright-hued birds scatter up into the vast cerulean sky like jewels spilled from a duchess's trunk, and she wished for but a moment that she could fly with them.

Garret watched her from his perch atop the paint gelding, his eyes hungry, a dull twisting in his chest. His fingers tightened their grip about the bit of charcoal he held, but for once he couldn't make it whisk across paper, couldn't seem to capture the outlines of the image he would labor to finish later.

He had painted majestic mountains garbed in mantles of snow, had done portraits of Indian maidens far more beautiful than the child-woman wandering toward him, knee-deep in flowers. But never before had he felt this trembling of inadequacy deep in his gut, this strange certainty that if he worked the rest of his life, he could never catch the perfection, the magic of Ashleen O'Shea drenched in sunshine.

There was something fey and innocent about the wide blue eyes that delighted in every beauty the prairie had to offer, something so tender in lips that parted with pleasure and ready laughter while she observed the antics of her brood.

She seemed scarce older than Shevonne sometimes, seemed to have all of Liam's dreamy-eyed wonder, and yet was possessed of an inner strength far greater than anything Garret had ever known.

A devastating combination. An enchanting one.

She confused him. Unsettled him. Made the endless nights pure holy hell, tormented as he was by the memory of how she had looked with moonlight turning her nightdress into shimmering silver, the most fragile of veilings over coral-tipped breasts so lush they would fill his hands, legs so long, so supple, even now he could imagine their soft, silky lengths twining with his, drawing him deeper, insistently deeper.

Garret cursed at the painfully clear image, shifting uncomfortably in his saddle as his loins hardened with fearsome need.

"Sweet Christ, MacQuade," he ground out, dragging his gaze away from her by force of will. "The woman's a nun, and you're not a man to be riding around defiling virgins. Women like Five-dollar Nell are more your sort—women who know what they want and aren't afraid to take it."

Garret tried again to picture Nell's lush body, powdered and scented to perfection, her lips and hands so skillful they could make a man break out in sweat even before she'd unbuttoned his shirt. He'd shared her bed a dozen times in the past five years, anticipated their liaisons with pleasure during those long stretches when he had roamed about the west, immersed in his art.

They had always understood each other, he and Nell. Understood that life was often bitter, that people could be cunning, cruel, and that surrendering one's heart left one vulnerable to a torture more merciless than anything the Comanches could devise.

Yet when he had gone to the room above the Double Eagle the night before the wagon had left West Port—the night he had stood in the shadows and seen Ashleen O'Shea wreathed in moonlight—Nell's hands upon his skin had seemed as detached as those of the sawbones who had set his broken leg when he was eight. Her lips had seemed too wet, too hot, as if still warmed by the last man who had kissed her. And her eyes had seemed so hard, empty—lifeless as Garret's own.

Quick. Hurried. They had assuaged the needs of their bodies, emptied themselves of inconvenient passions as expediently as possible. But with every practiced movement of her hands upon his skin Garret imagined the achingly sweet, hesitant touch that would be Ashleen O'Shea's. And with each of Nell's groans of pleasure, each of her explicit sexual urgings, Garret's mind filled with the whisperings of surprised, awe-filled gasps, words vibrating with wonder in the musical lilt of Ashleen's voice as he initiated her into a magic she'd never known existed.

It had sickened Garret, unsettled him, that the Irish woodsprite of a woman could insinuate herself so deep into his consciousness that he could not escape her, even in the arms of another.

And though Nell had urged Garret to stay, indulge again, he'd left her. He'd spent what remained of that endless night sitting on the cold ground beside the mound of Kennisaw's grave, feeling a chill stirring in the pit of his belly that was something akin to fear.

He had soothed himself by latching on to the certainty that Ashleen would be wailing and whining by the time they were two days on the trail. That the moment things got dirty or hot or the work gruelingly hard she would lose that enticing, sunshiny optimism, and her eyes would haze with gritty, hard acceptance of the ugliness of life.

She would be raging at the children, drooping about exhausted, blaming him for everything from the bugs to the weather to the unforgiving terrain.

But he'd never been so damned wrong in his entire life.

Garret couldn't stop his eyes from seeking her out yet again, drinking in the sight of her, as refreshing to the spirit as ice-cold mountain water in the midst of hellish heat.

Not a word of complaint had he heard from her, or from any of her brood. They seemed to revel in the adventure, exploring each new facet of the journey with an enthusiasm that made Garret tempted sometimes to swing down out of the saddle, point out to them the dust griming their clothes, the sunburn and windburn searing their skin, or the fact that he was rousing them from bed at an hour that would make most sane people blanch.

Christ, even now, as Ashleen plucked a riot of flowers, he felt an urge to go to her, warn her of stinging nettles and poison ivy and thorns.

"You're losing your mind, MacQuade," Garret grated to himself. "No one—*no one*—could really be all that woman appears to be."

Why, then, did she seem almost to shimmer with innocence, an innate goodness spiced by just enough mischievous humor to keep her from being priggishly pious? Why did he watch her whenever she wasn't looking? A gnawing sense of emptiness, of need grew within him until he wanted to go to her, bury himself in the dreamy-sweet world in her eyes.

For two weeks he had been fighting to ignore her, to

keep from speaking to her, from listening to the loving banter between her and the children. Their familial love was a deceptive cocoon of security whose fragility Garret knew only too well.

And now here she was, trailing about in a sea of wildflowers, laughing at birds, her face shining with a beauty so heart-wrenching Garret could hardly breathe.

Well, she could damn well get back to the wagon, get far enough away so that he didn't have to see her smile, didn't have to see the bright gold of her hair, didn't have to hear her laugh.

"Bloody hell," he bit out. He'd agreed to guide her blasted wagon; he hadn't agreed to lay himself open to this kind of torture.

Jamming the charcoal and his half-finished drawing into a saddlebag, he turned and spurred his horse toward her, the thundering of the animal's hooves giving him some small relief. She looked up, surprised, a little alarmed, the flowers dropping from her fingers.

He reined in an arm's breadth from where she stood, her eyes suddenly wide, cheeks paled.

"M-Mr. MacQuade . . . is there something wrong?"

"What the devil are you doing out here?" he snapped, swinging down from the gelding's back.

Her mouth dropped open at his harsh words, then her lips firmed into a line, and her eyes narrowed as she realized that no imminent peril was threatening.

No peril, Garret thought grimly, except the clamoring in his loins.

Her eyes were strangely clouded, uncertain as she looked up at him. "I'm out here because . . . well"—she hesitated—"I wanted to invite you to supper."

"Supper." Garret was damned if he'd make this any easier after the miserable nights filled with fantasies that he'd suffered because of her.

"Supper," she said tartly. "You know, Mr. MacQuade. You open your mouth, but instead of spewing out swear words, you stuff in food."

"There's enough jerky packed in my saddlebags to take

me to Santa Fe, if need be. And I hardly think you can be eager for my charming company. You'll have to find someone else to play martyr to."

Her face flushed and her eyes blazed, but Garret was distressingly aware of a sheen of moisture clouding the enchanting blue with something that might be tears.

"Blast you, anyway! Why do you have to be so—so ox-headed? I just thought . . . well . . . I might not be eager for your—what did you call it?—charming company, but I think . . ." She faltered.

Garret followed Ashleen's gaze to the wagon tracks baking in the sun and the lone little figure wandering there, her yellow dress making her seem almost as much a splash of blossom as the flowers Ashleen had been plucking moments before.

"I think maybe Meggie is."

Her words made Garret's hands clench on the reins, a sudden whirling of dizziness overtaking him as he stared at the little girl who, despite her difficulty, reminded him soul-crushingly of his own small sister, lost an eternity ago.

"I've been trying ever since I found her to get her to speak," Ashleen went on in a rush. "Tried to get her to pour out the terror, the grief, the fear that keeps her silent. I've tried everything. Anything. But she won't—maybe can't—respond. Even with me she's withdrawn. And with most other people—especially strangers—it's as if she looks right through them. As if they don't exist."

Garret cleared his throat, feeling off-balance. "I'm sorry. About the girl, I mean. But I don't see what I have to do with—"

His words choked off as a hand drifted feather-light onto his rigid arm, the contact jolting him to his core.

"She sees you, Mr. MacQuade. I don't know how or why, or what it means. I only know that she looks at you. Really looks at you. Often."

"And that means something?"

A wistful half smile tipped those lips he was aching to kiss. "I pray so." She turned toward him, taking his hands in her soft, warm ones. "I know we've not been on the best of terms since—well, since the beginning."

He could see by the delicate flush along her cheekbones that she was remembering the moment she spent in his arms.

"And I know I've no right to impose upon your kindness any more than I already have. But if you would consider coming to dinner tonight . . . being close enough to Meggie so that she might . . ." Her words trailed off, and Garret saw the fragile hope. And if she'd asked him to impale himself on a Sioux war lance, he knew that in that moment he would do so.

It might have been more merciful if she had.

He dragged his hat from his head and ran his fingers through tousled hair while he watched, mesmerized, that beautiful angel face.

"All right."

She smiled—a smile so dazzling Garret felt the earth shudder beneath him.

"I'll make it worth your while. Dried-apple pie, and the best prairie-chicken stew you've ever eaten."

"Don't use up your apples. You'll be hungry as hell—I mean heck—for something sweet before we cross the border. I might be able to come up with something instead."

"All right. If it's not too much trouble."

Garret couldn't suppress a smile. "Lady, you've been nothing but trouble from the first moment I met you."

Her eyes widened a little, and he was aware of her gaze flicking to his lips, her own smile wavering as if, even in her innocence, she could sense the currents sizzling between them.

"I—I was a lot of trouble at the convent, too," she stammered. "Always in the middle of . . . of some kind of mischief."

"I'd just bet you were. You can tell me all about it tonight. Consider it my price for enduring your chicken stew."

She nodded, then started away down the hill. Suddenly

Garret couldn't bear for her to go just yet. He stooped down, swooping up her handful of flowers. "Sister!"

She wheeled to face him, something shy, engaging, enticing in those cornflower-blue eyes.

Feeling suddenly unnerved himself, he extended the bouquet toward her. "You forgot these. They'd look mighty pretty in your hair."

He couldn't stop himself from reaching out, touching the delicate rosebud tucked behind her ear. Her breath caught in her throat, her golden curls clinging to his fingers in a silken, sweet-scented web, her skin softer than the blossom's petals.

He stood thus for long seconds, unwilling, unable to draw his hand away, drowning in her dark-lashed eyes.

The sensation was exquisite, agonizing, and he knew —damn well knew—that she felt its magic, too.

Then, suddenly, she was sweeping the blossoms from his numbed fingers and running lightly down the hill, taking all of the sunshine with her.

9

A lone coyote howled in the distance, its mournful cry at one with the gnawing emptiness in Garret's heart. He lingered far from the warm circle of the cookfire, listening to the laughter of the children, Ashleen's lilting voice as she bantered with them, cajoled them, guided them through the countless tasks that filled the end of day.

The crippled boy was tossing potato skins at Shevonne from the big crockery bowl on his lap. Renny was adjusting the picket line on which the horse—what had its ridiculous name been? Cooley?—was tethered. Meggie, a sad little waif with huge dark eyes, sat in the shadow of the wagon, tucking what looked to be a bundle of rags into a bed fashioned of the flowers Ashleen had picked earlier.

It could have been a scene from a fairy tale, some idyllic easterner's notion of the grand adventure of taming the west. The courageous woman with her brood of pink-cheeked children. Except that this woman had no strapping husband to deal with stubborn oxen or cracked wagon wheels, or to bring in fresh game to bolster what meager supplies the wagon could hold.

And the little girl playing with a rainbow of flowers couldn't exclaim over the colors, wouldn't run up to the woman who had given them to her, flinging small arms about her in childish glee.

Garret's fingers clenched around the bulging leather pouch he held, struggling desperately to wall away feelings he'd kept in check for so long. He wanted to view Ashleen O'Shea and her pack of orphans with the same practiced detachment he held for Logan's sons in St. Joe, and Sweetest One's nephews in the Oglala Sioux village. Looking through them almost as skillfully as little Meggie did.

Because it hurt too much.

Scared the living hell out of him to face how helpless, how small they truly were, how vulnerable to the cruel blasts the capricious fates might deal them.

Damn, what had possessed him to agree to put himself through this? To be drawn, however unwillingly, into the cozy circle Ashleen had woven about the campsite? He glanced down at the leather pouch he held, his mouth twisting in wry confusion. What had ever goaded him into spending part of the afternoon gathering wild berries clinging to the bushes near a stream bank?

At first he had only meant to take a quick bath in the burbling rill, to scrub the grime of the trail from his hair, his clothes. It had had nothing at all to do with Ashleen O'Shea, Garret had assured himself, or with the supper to come. He'd only wanted to feel clean again, and he had reasoned that it would have been folly to deny himself the chance to become so only to prove to himself that he didn't care about a woman.

He'd been lying on his back, letting the sun dry his naked body, when he had seen the ripe berries weighing the branches of a nearby bush and had remembered his promise to Ashleen.

He winced at the memory of how carefully he had selected each bit of fruit, grimaced as he recalled the unbidden need he had felt to please this woman who so disarmed him.

And now, standing just outside the golden glow of the fire, he felt for all the world like a green lad taking his first girl to a church social, stomach aflutter as he hovered on her parents' front porch.

It aggravated him. Terrified him.

Muttering an oath, he stomped into the ring of light.

He had resolved to be distant, to be so prickly Ashleen would never be so foolhardy as to invite him to join them again. But at that moment one of Liam's potato peels struck her skirts, and she turned from where she had stood, stirring the contents of a black iron pot over the fire, to call out a laughing admonition.

Her face was flushed from the heat of the fire, her hair caught back so primly in a chignon that Garret's hands burned to pull out the pins that held it, letting it cascade, liquid gold, through his hands.

Then she saw him, and her eyes, glowing with welcome, made Garret's heart plunge to his toes.

"Mr. MacQuade!" she cried, hastening toward him with a dazzling smile. "We were just wondering if you'd ridden off to the stream again."

Garret choked, his face flaming as he remembered how he had dozed in that protected clump of bushes, buck naked, oblivious to anyone who might have strayed by. "You—you were at the creek?"

Twin imps danced in eyes so blue he could drown in them. A dimple appeared at the corner of her lips. "No. Renny was, when he watered the oxen. I heard the . . . um . . . scenery down there was interesting."

Garret tried to think of something to say, but for once in his life no ready rejoinder sprang to his lips. Jesus, had the boy seen him picking the damn berries, too? What the hell, she'd have to know they hadn't dropped from the sky into the bag.

He felt an urge to stuff the pouch into the pocket of his denims. Instead he thrust the leather bag toward her in an effort to do something, anything, to distract himself from the image his unruly imagination was conjuring— Ashleen trailing down by those rippling waters, finding him there . . .

But not scurrying away, offended in her innocence. Rather coming toward him, shy, beautiful, letting him drift her back onto a bed of fragrant grasses, to touch her . . . taste . . .

"What is that?" Her voice made Garret suddenly, excruciatingly aware of the rigid evidence of his sex.

"W-what?" he stammered, instinctively grabbing his hat, ripping it off to shield that part of himself so embarrassingly revealed.

She looked at him as if he'd waxed mad. "The bag," she said, innocent as a babe. "What's in it?"

Garret followed her gaze to the leather pouch, gaping at it as if he'd never seen it before. Then, with blessed swiftness, his head cleared enough for him to speak. "Told you I'd bring something," he said shortly. "Found 'em by the creek." He could feel heat rising from his freshly washed collar and knew that color was suffusing his face.

She slipped loose the thong that bound the leather pouch, the children coming to crowd around her to peek at the surprise.

"Mmmm! Berries!" Liam enthused. "Can we have 'em with cream, Sister Ash?"

"And sugar!" Shevonne begged, licking her lips. "Please, Sister Ash!"

"I suppose we might spare a little. Just a little, Shevonne!" Ashleen said, popping one of the berries into the child's mouth.

Only Renny stared down his nose, disdainful, muttering, "They're probably full of bugs."

"Renny," Ashleen chided as Shevonne's face washed green.

"Don't worry. I washed 'em," Garret snapped, incredulous that he should feel the necessity of defending himself to a mere stripling.

"Humph," was all the boy said, stomping off to scoop up a bit of harness in need of mending.

As if to fill the awkward silence the boy had left, Ashleen turned, shooing the children toward an array of upended crates and kegs.

"Shevonne, fetch the bowls. The stew is ready."

"Been ready for an hour," Renny grumbled just loud enough to be heard. But it seemed Ashleen had chosen to ignore him.

"Liam, get Meggie to wash her hands," she said. "Mr. MacQuade, if you'd like to sit down . . ."

She gestured to the boxes like a duchess in a grand dining hall.

Clenching his teeth, Garret crossed to the keg farthest away from the others. Under the guise of moving it to more even ground he managed to draw it even farther from those Ashleen and the children would be sitting on, separating himself from them as much as possible.

If anyone noticed, no one said anything. That little firebrand Renny would probably have been just as happy if he'd moved the keg clear to the next territory.

Within moments Shevonne came to him, a steaming bowl in her hands. "Your stew, Mr. MacQuade," she said with a preening smile that would've done a southern belle proud. He took the container, tempted to reach up and give her white-blond plait a teasing tug. The very thought was enough to quash any thought of doing so.

Garret muttered his thanks, then, fixing his attention upon the meal, took up a bent spoon, shoveling in mouthfuls of the savory mixture in hopes of escaping as quickly as possible.

He had just filled his mouth with another heaping spoonful when a reverent feminine voice made his spoon freeze midway to the bowl. His eyes darted up to see Ashleen and the children, hands clasped, heads bent in prayer. Even little Meggie's fingers were laced together over what Garret could now distinguish was a worn doll as she stood in the wagon's shadow.

The piece of prairie chicken in Garret's mouth seemed to swell to five times its size, his mother's long-ago admonitions about thanking the Lord making it impossible to swallow.

"Bless us, O Lord . . ." Hushed, earnest, their voices blended into a sound Garret had not heard since the last night he had squirmed at his parents' table at Stormy Ridge, waiting impatiently for his father to finish with prayers so they could all dive into his mother's crusty turkey pie.

There had been a time he had believed that the violence that had followed that horrendous night had been his fault—God's vengeance because he had neglected his prayers, not learned the Bible verses his mother had assigned to him and Beth to memorize each Sunday.

But now he knew better.

The vengeful, angry God his pa had read about in the Old Testament didn't really exist.

No God did.

Garret forced himself to swallow the chunk of meat, but it was as if the tender morsel had grown spikes, tearing at his throat with the painful memories.

Shaking himself inwardly, he struggled to focus on the fire, the night wind, the whickering of Cooley grazing nearby. But it was Renny's sullen voice that jerked him back to the present. Garret looked up, aware that the formal prayer was over, but that each of the children apparently were now free to offer up their own petitions.

". . . get to Texas. *Soon,"* Renny was saying.

But whatever else the boy might have wanted to add was lost as Liam jumped in, eager. "God bless Meggie an' Shevonne, an' help Renny not draw my cork, an'"— the boy paused to take a deep breath—"an' please, God, don't throw Mr. MacQuade into hell, even if he does take Your name in vain."

Garret thought things couldn't possibly get worse.

Then Shevonne snickered.

"Yeah," she added, "and even if he keeps lookin' at Sister Ashleen like he wants to gobble her up. Amen."

"Amen," the other children chorused.

Ashleen's voice sounded strangled, and Garret jerked his gaze away from her, feeling guilty as a schoolboy caught gawking at the teacher.

Still obviously flustered, Ashleen swiveled to beckon to

Meggie, offering the child a bowl. "It's hot, Meggie, treasure. Hot stew."

The child regarded her with solemn eyes for long moments, and Garret almost thought she was not going to take it. But after a moment, the little girl tucked the raggedy doll beneath one arm and came shyly forward to retrieve her supper.

"C'mon, Meggie, sit by me," Renny called out, his voice more gentle than Garret had ever heard it. "I found you a pretty stone today."

But even the offer of such a prize did not entice the little girl to Renny's side. She stood for long minutes just staring at the boy. Then, as if in a trance, she turned slowly, and before the astonished gaze of them all she paced over to the keg where Garret sat.

Silence settled in a suffocating blanket over the campsite, and Garret could feel a barrage of hostility crackling from Renny's stormy gaze, could feel the fragile hope in Ashleen, the astonishment in Liam and Shevonne.

Yet all Garret could see was Meggie Kearny's lost-angel face, achingly old eyes beneath lushly curled little-girl lashes peering up at him with some emotion he could not name.

He cleared his throat, trying to think of something to say to her, not wanting to frighten her away. It had been a long time since Garret had made an effort to be gentle. He did so now.

"Sister Ashleen tells me your name is Meggie," he said tentatively. "My name is Garret."

The child solemnly shook her head in dissent.

Garret glanced over at Ashleen, unsure whether to correct the child or not, but the woman only shrugged, her eyes hopeful. So damn hopeful.

Garret swallowed, his throat raw. "That's a real nice doll you've got there," he said, reaching out a finger to touch yarn hair that must once have been bright as Renny's, but which had faded through time to a nondescript orangish gray.

As Garret's finger touched the plaything he heard an audible gasp from the others around the fire, heard Ashleen softly hushing them. The moment seemed to stretch out forever, the tension so thick he couldn't seem to draw breath.

Then, as suddenly as the exchange had begun, it ended, the little girl merely turning around and sinking to the ground beside him, the stew bowl pillowed on her lap.

Out of the corner of his eye Garret glimpsed Renny dumping his bowl onto a crate and stalking off, a wounded expression on his face. Liam clambered to his feet and, tucking his crutch beneath one arm, limped after him, a worried frown puckering the crippled child's features.

More disturbed than he cared to admit, Garret shifted his gaze back to the little girl beside him, watching as she took up the spoon in a dimpled hand and began nibbling at the hot food, a smattering of brown gravy rimming her pink lips. She licked the gravy off, looking for all the world like any other four-year-old girl. Looking for all the world as Beth had before the Garveys had cut her down.

Then it struck him, swift, unmerciful. The emotion he had seen in Meggie's dark eyes. Trust. She had regarded him with the same absolute faith that had always danced in his sister's eyes.

Why? A voice cried deep inside him. She doesn't even know you, MacQuade . . . doesn't know the truth . . . that in the end you couldn't help Beth. You won't be able to help her, either.

The feeling of helplessness he had barred from his heart twenty years ago ripped through him, leaving him devastated, stunned.

Garret forced himself to look away from the child, as if that could diffuse some of the pain. He tried to eat more himself, but he couldn't squeeze anything past the knot in his throat.

After what seemed forever the meal was finished. He started to rise, needing more than ever to get away from Ashleen and the little girl with the haunting dark eyes.

"Have to go now." Was his voice somehow betraying how shaken he really was? He wouldn't meet Ashleen's eyes. "Got some things to do before tomorrow."

"No!" There was a quiet desperation in Ashleen's voice as she hastened toward him. "We haven't even eaten your berries yet, and—"

"Everything was real good, Sister." He forced his lips into a stiff smile. "It beat that jerky all to he—" He stopped and swallowed hard, fingering the brim of his hat. "Thanks."

He started to stride away. A pleading hand on his arm stopped him. He didn't turn around. If he had, he wasn't certain he would ever be able to leave.

"Mr. MacQuade . . . please . . . if you could come back for a little while after the children have had their stories, after they're all tucked up in bed . . ."

"I don't think that's a good idea, Sister Ashleen." His voice was hoarse, low.

"Please! I just . . . I need to talk to you. About Meggie."

The child's name was like a razor-sharp blade, slicing deep.

"She's never done that before," Ashleen was rushing on. "I mean gone to a stranger, sat by him. And her doll . . . even I am not allowed to touch it. Please, Mr. MacQuade."

"Damn it to hell!" Garret grated. But even he knew when his back was against the wall. Resigned, he said, "I've some things to tend to first."

Most women he knew would have been all bundled up in wounded pride, sullen or teary-eyed with reproach over his harsh words.

Ashleen O'Shea beamed at him.

10

Garret retreated to where his gear was stashed, his gut clenching as he tugged his supplies from his worn leather saddlebags. Lighting a lantern, he took up his charcoal and paper, trying to lose himself in a world of his own creation. A world of line and shadow, of time forever frozen, where the flick of his hand could smudge away anything that brought him pain.

Yet though he battled to concentrate, he found himself pulled, not into his drawings, but into the web of words drifting upon the night wind from the campfire.

He had sometimes caught glimpses of the end-of-evening ritual Ashleen and the children indulged in, vaguely wondering what it was that brought the excited glow to the children's faces, sometimes letting their laughter ring out into the darkness, sometimes shouts of denial or encouragement or pleasure.

Yet with distance blurring the sound of their voices he had always had the power to blot out their words before. Tonight at the cookfire it seemed as if Ashleen had somehow snarled silken threads about him, drawing him into that charmed circle even now, with all the mystical magic of a siren.

Snippets of phrases reached out to taunt him, scraps of images created by words as vivid and varied as the colors on an artist's palette. When her voice dropped low he found himself straining to hear her, felt the muscles in his shoulders coil as she hurled her bold knight-hero, Sir Alibad, into countless fantastic perils. Evil villains plotted and poisoned, fierce monsters stalked and snarled; even the hero's own past rose up like some living beast to torment him.

Now Garret knew why the children clustered so close around her, devouring every word. He was almost tempted to draw closer himself, anxious that he not miss any of the grand adventure being spun out by the golden-tressed fairy who sat enthroned upon a crate.

She drew out the tension, honing it until Garret could hardly stand it, surrounding the beleaguered knight with not one but three slavering dragons, their teeth red with his blood. Yet just as a dragon claw knocked the sword from the wounded Sir Alibad's fingers the knight heard a cry of denial behind the brutal beasts. He looked past them and saw, in the shadowy entrance to the magic cave, a figure robed in purest white, hair like spun silver draping a woman.

She stood peering at the knight with eyes of violet, her arms cradling a golden harp.

Alibad screamed a warning to her, bade her run as the dragons turned upon her, snarling with venomous glee.

"And then . . ." Ashleen bent forward, her face mysterious, unearthly in the firelight.

Garret strained to hear, abashed to realize his pulse was racing.

"And then," Ashleen's clear voice rippled out, "the woman cast a spell on four small children and made them all fall into a deep, deep sleep."

Garret swore, his fingers clenching so tightly about his bit of charcoal that it snapped in his hand. He wanted to bellow at her to finish the damn story, joining the clamorings of Renny and Liam and Shevonne that she go on just a little longer.

But he clenched his teeth and, gripping one of the bits of charcoal, set to work with a vengeance. Even so,

Ashleen O'Shea's story held him spellbound, seeping into his consciousness until it seemed there was no room for anything else.

It was much later that he was startled by a footfall beside him. In an instinctive movement that had saved his life countless times he grabbed for his pistol, whipping it from his holster.

He half expected to see a purple-scaled dragon with claws as long as a church spire and fangs like a rapier. Instead his gaze fell upon a delicate enchantress's features, and he knew how poor Alibad must have felt when he had first seen the harp maiden in the cave.

Though apparently a little shaken by finding a six-gun aimed at her chest, Ashleen gave a wobbly laugh, raising her hands skyward. "I surrender, Mr. MacQuade."

It was tempting to join her good-natured amusement, but Garret felt as if he'd been running on a knife blade of tension since the moment she had stormed into his life.

"Do you know how damned dangerous it is to sneak up on a man with a gun?" Garret snarled, reholstering his weapon. "Chrissakes, I could've killed you."

"You didn't kill me. And I didn't sneak up on you." Her voice was laced with that infuriating calm she used when dealing with Renny's snapping temper. "I called out to you once, but you were so engrossed in your work that you must not have heard . . . oh, my!"

Her pleased cry made the rest of Garret's tirade fly out of his head. She plunked down on the ground beside him, leaning so close he could smell the scent of his berries still on her lips, could feel the excitement bubbling through her.

Her fingers strayed out, touching the piece of paper that lay forgotten upon his drawing board.

Garret made a move to shield it from her gaze, but it was too late. He looked down at what was supposed to be a picture of eagles soaring in a cloudless sky and was astonished to find the birds had somehow developed scales and giant claws, bulging dragon eyes fixed upon the small figure of a slender woman.

Embarrassment blazed a path through him, leaving him flustered, defensive, and totally speechless.

"It's Princess Niamh!" Ashleen enthused, holding up the lantern so the light spilled more brightly onto the page. "And look! I can just see Alibad behind Gobmora's legs."

"Gob—who?"

"The dragon, of course."

"Of course," Garret echoed wryly.

As if spurred by his show of interest, she raced on. "Gobmora is the mother dragon, you see, and these"— she pointed to the other sketchy figures—"these two are her sons, Macedon and Ripannia. They're not really evil—the sons, I mean. It's just that the mother has lied to them, told them that Alibad slew their father. But really it was Gobmora who killed him when he joined Alibad in his quest for peace between the Underworld and the World Above."

Garret allowed himself a reluctant laugh, his earlier irritation fading as he reveled in the sparkling delight in her eyes, the loveliness of her animated features. "This time *I* surrender! All I want to know is whether or not Gobmora here is going to have Princess Niamh for supper."

"A herd of wild horses couldn't drag that information out of me before tomorrow night, my fine sir." Ashleen tipped her head at a mischeivous angle, exposing the graceful line of her throat. Four buttons at the prim collar were open, baring a V of lily-pale skin to the cool breezes. He would have given a fortune just to press one kiss on that throbbing pulse beat.

Garret moistened his lips, feeling a sharp stab of desire. He made an effort to divert his attention with a heroism that would have made Sir Alibad proud. "Where do you come up with—with these things?" Garret asked. "Dragons and princesses and harps—"

"Enchanted harps," Ashleen corrected with obvious relish. She shrugged. "I don't know. It began when we were at sea. There was a storm—waves crashing, tossing the ship about until I almost thought . . ." She hesitated, shaking herself, and Garret could almost feel the fear that must have coursed through her that night, and the terror that must have gripped the four children.

"Anyway," Ashleen continued, her voice soft with reminiscence, "that was when I first began tormenting poor Sir Alibad. I must confess I used him ill that night. He was pitted against a cyclops then, as I remember, who gave him a potion to make him blind. That was when he met Gobmora's mate, Illitar, who restored his sight and"—with a self-conscious wave of her hand, she laughed—"at any rate, the children so loved Alibad that I've been making him miserable ever since."

Simple, so simple and unassuming the words were, free of any sense of the wonder she had wrought. Squeezed between the lines were innumerable pictures of children scared out of their wits, clinging to the single bit of security in their small world, and Ashleen . . . alone, little more than a child herself, cocooning them with her love.

Garret sucked in a shuddering breath, unable to tear his gaze away from her.

Did she see the look in his eyes? Sense the need jolting through him as the loosened strands of her hair were tossed on the fingers of the breeze to brush against his jaw? Did she know how badly he wanted to bury his hands in her hair? How much he wanted to crush those laughing, ripe lips with his own?

How could she know? With her innocence, that openness of heart that embraced everyone around her?

She's had enough trouble, MacQuade, without you adding to it, he warned himself inwardly, but he savored the delicate brush of her hair a moment more before he drew away.

"So," he said, his voice aggravatingly unsteady, "you said you needed to talk to me about something."

Setting the lantern back on the ground, Ashleen tucked her legs beneath her, sitting there in a pool of soft gray skirts. "It's about Meggie."

Garret winced, feeling memories dig deep in his chest.

"Mr. MacQuade, you were wonderful with her tonight. I can't thank you enough for—for coming."

"Don't thank me. I've been a horse's ass ever since West Port Landing. It was the least I could do. I'm just sorry you were disappointed."

"Disappointed?" Incredulous eyes met his.

Damn, he was pointing out thorns to the woman again. "That she didn't talk."

"What she did with you tonight—choosing to sit by you, letting you touch her doll—that was enough for me." She arched back her head, smiling up into the heavens as if she saw angels. "Sometimes miracles require patience. And this one . . . with Meggie, I've been waiting a long time."

Miracles . . . had Garret ever believed in them?

He regarded her, silent for a moment. "That first day, when I hollered at the child, you said something about finding her . . . with her mother."

"Yes." Ashleen's face was shaded softly with sorrow. "Meggie's mother was my dearest friend from the time we could both toddle through our front gates. For years we told each other everything, shared all our dreams, hopes, all our secrets."

Garret knew he should draw back from that musical, alluring voice, not encourage confidences borne of the starlit night. Instead he heard himself asking, "What kind of secrets, Mary Ashleen?"

"The delicious kind all little girls share. For months Moira and I plotted to run away and be gypsys, to dance wildly around campfires while people threw coins. Then we were going to take to the High Toby, like highwaymen of old. But neither of us could find a gun or a sword, so we decided to become opera dancers."

"The next best thing to being a gypsy?" Garret asked, recalling his own long-buried childhood dreams, woven in the sprawling tree branches that had ever been his special refuge.

"Exactly." She shot him a blinding smile. "Father

O'Hara was fit to be hanged the day Moira and I told him in confession."

There was so much life in her, so much devilish delight, that despite his better judgment Garret smiled. He could imagine Ashleen O'Shea in a whirlwind of adventure such as she'd described far more easily than he could picture her locked away in some musty old abbey.

Though Garret tried, he couldn't imagine that a woman who loved so openly, so eagerly, everything from recalcitrant horses and wilted roses to castoff children would choose a life walled off from the world.

It's none of your concern, MacQuade, he warned himself roughly. Why the hell should you even care?

But he couldn't stop himself from wondering why she had chosen a life she was so unsuited for. Had she been forced by her parents? This priest, O'Hara? Had she been so poor that she'd had to choose between life as a nun and starvation? Or had there been something—some*one* —who had taken the love she offered so freely and shattered her, so that she had fled to the only haven she had known?

Garret's jaw clenched, and he resolved that he would not—*would not*—ask any more damn fool questions or learn anything more that would make this ethereal angel seem real to him. Maybe then she would go away, back to her wagon, serene in the moonlight.

Leave him alone . . . so damn alone.

But she only sat there silent, her eyes a million dreams away. For a gut-wrenching instant Garret wished he could travel there with her.

The longing welled, expanded, filling the silence until he groped for something to drown out the echoes of his own secret need.

He busied himself stowing his drawing gear in his saddlebags, his voice edged with a subtle touch of something akin to panic as he grasped Ashleen's last words. "So what did this Father O'Hara do when he discovered you were plotting to run off? Lock you in the convent and force you to be a nun?"

"Force me? No." Was there pain about the tender corners of her mouth? Clouds of remembrance in eyes that had been wistful blue?

For all his inner turmoil, Garret couldn't bring himself to seek refuge in something that so obviously hurt her.

"It's none of my business, I know," he said gruffly. "It's just that you look so right in the middle of all those kids, teasing them, telling them stories, tucking them into bed. I would've thought that . . ."

He let his sentence trail off, unable to form his thoughts into words.

The idea of Ashleen tucked away in some cozy cottage filled with babies pleased him mightily, but the thought of her sharing it with some mule-stubborn man who didn't appreciate her set Garret's teeth on edge.

"You would've thought that I'd have found my own Sir Alibad a long time ago?" Ashleen supplied.

Garret shrugged, uncomfortable. "I suppose so. It's no secret that you're damn beautiful. And the way you're always laughing, your eyes sparkling . . . I can't believe some man didn't plunge heart over heels for you."

She flushed. "When my eyes were sparkling in Wicklow, most of the men were too busy checking their pipe-stuffings for pepper or their pockets for frogs to notice what I looked like. I was incorrigible. Sometimes I think that even then I was trying to get all the mischief out of me before I took my vows."

"You knew even then that you would be a nun?"

"I was lisping out my Hail Marys almost before I said da." She laughed, shaking her head. Pins loosened by the night's work slipped their grasp, the chignon threatening to tumble down. Garret's mouth went dry, and he wondered what she would say if he reached up, tugging the last of the ivory anchors free.

"You see, my mother married late and was afraid she would be barren," Ashleen's voice drifted on. "So Mam promised St. Gerard that her firstborn would be dedicated to God. I guess she should have stipulated that there be a secondborn and a thirdborn, as well, to keep me out of trouble. But unfortunately, I was all the angels brought her. And I was worlds different from the saintly little creature she'd imagined.''

With insight borne of the artist in him, Garret could see the babe Ashleen must've been, a tiny fairy princess of a child, all blue and gold and sweet, sweet laughter. "No matter what your mother imagined before you were born, she must've loved you very much.''

With a heavy sigh Ashleen plucked a grass stem, twirling it between her fingers. "I suppose she did in her way. It's just that all the years she had waited for a child, I think she had planned and dreamed exactly what this son or daughter should be. Everything from the color of its hair to how politely it would say 'yes, sir' and 'no, ma'am.' I'd catch her watching me, resigned, her fingers telling off her rosary beads whenever she wasn't busy baking or cleaning or mending. I think she was praying for my redemption till the moment she died.''

Garret recognized the sense of inadequacy reflected in those words, felt the same subtle sting of rejection that had marked his own first ten years. His father's impatient voice echoed in his head: "Makin' pictures is worthless, boy. Can't eat 'em, can't wear 'em, can't shoot 'em. Takes all the strength a man has just to make the crops grow.''

Garret toyed with the buckle on his saddlebag, his voice low, hoarse. "After she died, where did you go? What did you do?''

"Da tried to manage me on his own for a while. He really tried. But he was too free with the poteen even before my mother died. And after, he grieved for her so deeply, the bottom of a jug seemed to be the only place he could find peace. If I'd been wild before, I was a hundred times worse by the time Father O'Hara stepped in, reminding Da of my mother's wishes regarding my future. That very day I was bundled up, all scrawny and dirty and full of defiance, and taken off to St. Michael's.''

Garret bristled at the thought of the little girl she must

have been, frightened, grieving, alone, her father so far gone in drink she had no one to care for her. "So this priest just stormed in and took you."

"Yes, thank God. And he put me into the arms of the kindest woman I've ever known." A shadow crossed her features, and Garret could have sworn he saw her lips quiver, her voice thick with unshed tears as she whispered, "I wonder what Sister Agatha is doing now."

The blisterings of outrage he had felt on her behalf were suddenly diffused, and he could only bite out a grudging "Humph." Christ, he was sounding as sulky as Renny.

"Ah, I see. You think all nuns are crusty, crotchety, switch-wielding harridans holding small children in dungeons." Ashleen scooted around until she faced him, locking her arms about her bent knees. She pillowed her chin upon them. "Sister Agatha Augustine Murphy was the most understanding, most intelligent, most trusting person who ever . . ." The words ended with a watery sound, and Garret watched as Ashleen turned her face away from him, hiding what he knew to be tears.

Garret clenched his fists, at a loss as to what one did to comfort a crying nun.

If Kennisaw had been there he would've known what to do. God knew the old buzzard had soothed more feminine tears than any man west of the Missouri. Commiserating kisses, fervent embraces, expensive trinkets. Garret had seen Kennisaw lavish them all upon the weeping women that had comprised the man's harem. But even if Garret had had some pretty bauble to tempt her with, he was certain a mere present could not ease Ashleen O'Shea's pain. And as for kissing her, holding her—

Hell, once he had her in his arms, would he be able to hold on to what few notions of honor he had left? Be able to let her go without easing the fierce hunger she spawned in him? Once in an Indian village a chief had offered him a sacred herb called peyote. It had been as intoxicating as a keg full of whiskey, whirling up visions of dream worlds beyond the reaches of imagination.

Garret sensed that one taste of Ashleen O'Shea would hurl him further still.

A muffled snuffling sound from the tumbled golden head made something break inside him. And for the first time in his life his mind wasn't scrambling for some way to escape a woman's tears.

"Damn it to hell!" He reached out, awkwardly cradling Ashleen in his arms as if she were no older than Meggie. She pressed close against him as if seeking warmth, strength, not knowing that Garret MacQuade possessed nothing but barrenness.

The shudders racking her slender body pierced him. His eyes clenched tightly, his mouth a tense line as he stroked her hair with trembling fingers.

"Here, now, what the devil is this?" he demanded. His voice was rough with emotion; every place where the softness of her, the heat of her was pressed against his skin thrummed with pain and need and confusion.

"I'm sorry," she choked out, burrowing her tear-wet face in his throat. "I—I don't—don't mean to go all weepy. It's just thinking of Sister Agatha, and the convent, and Ireland, and . . ." The tremor that gripped her this time was so deep, it drove into Garret's soul.

Hell, had she been homesick the whole damn time they'd been on the trail? The whole time he'd been yelling at her, grumbling at her, stomping around in a temper? Had she been crying herself to sleep in that blasted wagon, her smile fading into secret tears once the children were in bed and he was off sulking in his own bedroll?

His arms strained tighter around her, and he lay a beard-stubbled cheek on the soft crown of her head. "Cry all you want, Sister," he said. "There's nobody out here to hear you."

"Nobody ex-except you. And I p-promised I wouldn't—"

Garret winced at the memory of how he'd laid down the law to her, bellowing that he didn't want to hear a word of whining, complaining . . . but now, holding Ashleen in his arms, he only wanted to be there for her, to listen as she poured out whatever grief seared her heart.

"Hell, if I'd had to put up with me these past weeks, I'd be hollering to high heaven."

She lifted her face from his chest, scrubbing at those wet cornflower eyes. Her lashes were lush, spiky from her tears, her eyes pools of such inner anguish Garret almost turned away, unable to bear it.

"I-It's not be-because of you that I'm . . . being such a cry-babe. It's just . . . thinking they'll never forgive me at St. Michael's. Thinking how hurt Sister Agatha must be after all her—her kindness. She trusted me, and I . . . oh, sweet Jesus, forgive me." She buried her face in those slender, expressive hands, crying as if her heart would break.

Garret felt something shatter inside him, flooding him with hot, branding anguish, emotion so fierce it was as if all the tears, all the grieving he had held at bay raged like a river over its banks, merging with that of the woman in his arms.

"Damn it, girl, what could you have done that was so blasted terrible? Christ, you're an angel of a woman. So damn good . . ."

"No . . . no, I'm not." There was a fierce self-loathing in those eyes that could be so tender, the tracks of her impassioned tears glistening in the light of the lantern. "I'm a liar, Mr. MacQuade. And worse. A-a thief. I stole . . . from people who loved me, trusted me. People who took care of me from the time I was Shevonne's age."

Garret knew he should be stunned, more than a little stung with righteous anger at this confession that showed what he had believed to be true—that no one could be everything Ashleen O'Shea had seemed. But instead he bristled like a damn mother grizzly, and at that moment he suspected Ashleen could confess to murder, and he would not believe ill of her.

"Whatever you did, whatever happened, there must've been a good reason for it," he said. "Sometimes people do things they're ashamed of. Even good people. Because they can't see any other way."

Hopeless resignation washed over those angel features, and she shivered, not from the chill creeping about the edges of night. "Th-that's the horrible thing. As awful as I feel, I'd do it again. There was no other way to—to save them."

"Save who?"

Her gaze strayed back to the wagon, the depths of her eyes stark with love.

And Garret knew in that moment. "The children," he said slowly. "You stole something to save the children."

Catching her lip between her teeth, she nodded, tears welling afresh. "I would've sold my soul to do so. Maybe I have."

"Tell me."

Garret listened as the woman in his arms poured out a tale more gripping than any she had spun by a campfire, a story laced with courage, with love, with pain, but also with such shining hope that Garret felt strangely humbled, fearsomely protective, not only of Ashleen, but of the little ones bundled safely in the wagon fifty yards away.

"This Sister Agatha," Garret said when Ashleen had lapsed into a heavy silence. "She sounds like a woman of sense. Don't you think she must understand about the chalice? About the children? I mean, for Chrissakes, you pawned some gold mug to save the lives of four children. I don't know much about the God people like your Sister Agatha believe in so fiercely. But if He does exist, I can't believe He'd want some bauble gathering dust on a window ledge when the thing could've been used to feed innocent children."

Ashleen pulled far enough away to look into his face, yet she stayed in the circle of his arms. It was a gesture wrenchingly childlike, and she reminded him painfully of Beth those times his sister had been confessing some childhood transgression.

"Even so," she reasoned, "I should have been honest with Sister Agatha. Told her—well, told her my plan instead of sneaking out in the dead of night. Who knows? She might have given me the chalice freely."

"And she might've told you no. Then what would you have done? Helped them cart the children off to that poorhouse you were talking about? No. You did the right thing. The only thing you could have done, under the circumstances."

"Do you really think so?" She asked with such hopefulness, Garret brushed her petal-soft cheek with his fingertips.

"Damn right, Sister."

Relief spread over those angel features, mingled with resolve. "The night before we left West Port I wrote to Sister Agatha and explained as much as possible. I promised to send money back to Ireland as soon as we reach Stormy Ridge, to cover the cost of the chalice. The hotelkeeper should have sent it off by now. So soon everyone at—at the convent will know I intend to make amends, if I can."

Garret thought of the nuggets he had stashed under the clean clothes in his saddlebags—gold he had found in a stream in the mountains. He had taken just enough to buy whatever necessities he might need for the next few months—a few new clothes, more drawing supplies, a pack horse.

Maybe he didn't need those things after all.

No, a voice taunted inside him, all you need is to bury yourself in this woman, kiss her, draw life from her, laughter . . ..

He peered down at those berry-red lips, so soft, so innocent, so sweet. The need that had tormented him ever since he'd ground his mouth down on them in the Double Eagle seemed somehow sacrilege, a defilement, in the wake of the longings that surged through him now.

He wanted to kiss her—hell, yes, he still did—but gently, thoroughly, introducing her to the depths of his passion as tenderly and patiently as if she were a fragile rose opening its petals to the sun.

Garret's heart seemed to cease beating, his whole body thrumming with a need so deep he could scarcely deny it. He lowered his mouth just a whisper toward hers. Saw her lips part, a tiny breath wisping, hot, moist, to caress his mouth.

His gaze darted to her eyes, and he saw a kind of tremulous expectation, as if she were waiting on the brink of something wonderful.

He wanted to give it to her.

Of its own volition his hand came up to thread through the golden strands of her hair, cupping her cheek, her skin burning his palm as he guided her mouth to his.

Garret closed his eyes, jolted to the core at that first soul-staggering contact, soft as a night breeze, sweeter than anything he had ever known.

He brushed her lips with his, back and forth, slowly, savoring, half afraid that she would pull away, half afraid that he would never find the strength to do so again.

"You taste so good . . . so damn good," he murmured against her mouth, tracing the crease of her lips with the tip of his tongue. "Ah . . . Ashleen . . ."

He clenched his eyes shut at her tiny gasp of surprise, of pleasure, every muscle in his body going rigid as her lips slid open, allowing his tongue entry into the mysteries within, her soft fingertips gliding uncertainly up the cords of his throat, to curve about his nape. Kissing her, still kissing her, he eased them both down upon the fragrant grasses, crushing her breasts against the thundering beat of his heart.

She felt so small, cradled there beneath him, felt so fragile he was almost afraid she would shatter like a thousand dreams long forgotten.

But her hands were smoothing over his shoulders, his back; her mouth was innocent, but so eager it turned his loins to flame.

Her nipples thrust impudently against his chest despite their shielding of fabric, a silent testimony that she was feeling the same dizzying need.

She wanted him. Damn it all, even if she didn't know it, she wanted him as much as he wanted her.

With a groan Garret eased his hand between their bodies, smoothing his palm up her rib cage to cup her breast in his hand. She whimpered, arching her back to press the mound deeper into his palm.

He could feel her shaking, sense the restlessness in her, the wanting. And he knew he would take her—here, now.

Fighting to hold raging passions in check, he rained kisses across her cheeks, her eyelids, blazing a path down the delicate skin of her throat to the patch of skin bared beneath. His fingers worked at the tiny buttons of her bodice, laying them open, kissing the fine lawn of her chemise.

He could already taste that pure coral crest he had dreamed of since that night in West Port, knew how infinitely sweet it would be to kiss it, suckle it, taunt it with his tongue.

He slid the fabric aside, skimming his thumb over the taut, delicate bud, lowering his lips to whisper against it.

"Ashleen . . . ah . . . you're so beautiful. Sweet God . . ."

The word slammed into Garret like a kick in the stomach, sending him reeling back, away from her, as if she'd turned to white-hot flame. Holy hell, what was he doing? Seducing a goddamn nun?

"Sonofabitch!" He yanked the cloth over her breast, but the image of her nipple, glistening wet from his kisses, seared itself into his mind.

She scrambled to a sitting position, grasping the edges of her bodice together, her hair a nimbus of gold framing eyes still hazed with passion, confusion.

"W-what . . . is it? Did I do . . . something wrong?"

Hell, she'd been doing everything too goddamn right!

She was the nun, damn it! Why the devil hadn't she stopped him?

He started to say so, roughly, but stopped as the lantern illuminated the vulnerable curves of her face. What the blazes did a woman like that know of a man's passions anyway? Of how far a single kiss could lead—how deep a single touch could carve into a man's body?

He dragged his hand through his hair, trying to quell the fire in his blood—a fire he knew now could be quenched only in the arms of this child-woman, with her dreams and her innocence. Dreams he could never share.

He sucked in a steadying breath, trying to force words through a constricted throat. "Ashleen . . . *Sister* Ashleen." He emphasized the word as if to brand it indelibly in his mind. "I shouldn't have . . . have . . . well, what we were just . . ." He sounded like a stammering idiot. Furious with himself, he stormed on.

"Damn it, I had no right. To kiss you. Touch you. You're a nun, for Chrissakes, and I was pawing you like—"

"No." That single, tremulous word stopped him. He stared at her, confused.

"Hell, yes, I was. My hands were all over you." He clenched his fists to keep from reaching out to her again.

"I don't—don't mean you weren't . . . touching me," she said, her cheeks flushed crimson. Her gaze darted away from his, and she fumbled with one tiny jet button. "I mean"—she hesitated, her eyes flicking back to his—"I'm not a nun."

Garret felt as if she'd poleaxed him. "What the hell do you mean you're not a nun? The kids call you Sister. You lived in a convent."

"I was going to be a nun, but I never took my vows. I'm not really . . . really Sister Ash. The children just always called me that, no matter how much I tried to correct them. So I finally just . . . let them."

"All this time I've been thinking I've been on fire for a damn nun, you—"

She nodded, and he didn't know whether to yell at her or tumble her back to finish what they'd started. Instead he just sat there, frozen, staring into her face.

"I'm glad now," she whispered. "Glad I never took my vows." She traced his numb lips with the tips of her fingers. "Because tonight, Garret MacQuade, when you were kissing me . . . touching me . . . you would've made me want to break them."

11

Cain Garvey stalked down the stairway of the Double Eagle Saloon, adjusting the crotch of his trail-stained buckskins. The woman in the room he had just left was still whimpering, her pale, perfumed skin darkening with bruises left by his fists. The white line of her throat was nicked by the knife blade he'd held there to prevent her from calling for aid, and lying on the coverlet was enough money to keep her mouth shut now that he was gone.

She had been a pretty one, all buxom and yellow-haired, reminding Cain vaguely of the woman in St. Joe who had thwarted the capture of Kennisaw Jones weeks ago. That resemblance had been the whore's crime. But she had paid for it in blood.

Paid like the prisoners and guards who had perished in the flames he had set before he and Eli had escaped from the prison that had been a living death for twenty years.

His lips curled in an ugly smile as he remembered how carefully he'd arranged the blaze so it would seem all within had perished, the Garvey brothers included. He and Eli were probably even now on the death roster—forgotten. *Free.*

Yes, the whore was real lucky he hadn't wanted to draw the attention of the law down upon him. He had wanted to kill her, slow and lingering-like. Had wanted to wring screams out of her with delicate, excruciating tortures learned in the depths of the prison where he'd spent so long. But he'd save those little pleasures for the real object of his hatred, once he found her.

And he would find her. After he tracked down that bastard MacQuade.

MacQuade. The only survivor of that bloody day at Stormy Ridge. The only remaining link to wealth beyond imagining, now that Kennisaw Jones was roasting on the devil's spit.

Stomping over to the bar, Cain shoved a frightened saloon girl out of his way and grabbed a bottle of rotgut.

The old man shouldn't have died. Not before Cain had had the pleasure of flaying the skin off him one knife-length at a time for each year spent in that hellhole of a prison. But it was like that old bastard to elude his just punishment and die laughing. Making the Garvey brothers look the fool for a second deadly time.

Cain guzzled the whiskey, trying to burn away the half-crazed rage that had eaten in his gut since the moment he'd awakened to find their dying captive riding away from their camp outside of St. Joe. A rage fired hotter still by the fact that Jones had managed to get off a shot from his rifle before Eli's six-gun had filled him with lead.

Cain flexed the muscles in his shoulder, feeling still the tightness that marked the path the bullet had blazed in his flesh.

That bullet had effectively quashed any thought of pursuit—for the time being. But Cain had known that Jones was injured himself and would have to hole up somewhere until he gained enough strength to travel. They'd thought that they'd have no trouble picking up the man's trail long before then, no trouble beating the truth out of him regarding Santa Ana's gold.

Yet although in the weeks that followed Eli and the rapidly mending Cain had scoured the countryside trying to find some trace of the man, there had been none. Until the day they had ridden into West Port only to find that Kennisaw Jones had escaped them forever in death.

Disbelieving, Cain had gone to Cemetery Hill and seen Jones's body buried real proper, a marker at its head. Garvey had kicked the wooden slab down, half tempted to claw away the dirt and search the rotting body for any clues Jones might have kept hidden on his person.

But in the end Cain had had to face the truth.

They had lost in this deadly gamble with the cunning Kennisaw Jones. There was only one chance left.

Garret MacQuade.

A man grown, no longer the terrified boy who had shrieked and clawed at Cain like a wolf cub, trying to save his dying father.

Cain flexed his scarred left hand, the throbbing that hadn't left it for twenty-odd years burning afresh. Maybe there was a kind of twisted justice in that—that in the end it would be MacQuade who screamed out the truth beneath the cut of Cain's knife, spilled the whereabouts of the treasure. MacQuade—the boy who had shown a man's courage that day in the clearing, and a man's deadly fury.

This way, Cain thought grimly, he could repay the one who had cost him so much—the slash across his hand, the scar twisting one side of his face, and the loss of bulging chests of gold.

Gold he should've been wallowing in when he was young—with a face so handsome he'd rutted with the preacher's daughters in three different towns.

Gold that should've bought him enough whiskey to drown in, a fancy house up on a hill with rooms upstairs even richer than the ones in this damn saloon, draped in red satins with mirrors on the ceilings, and enough women to sate even his darker sexual drives.

A commotion at the top of the stairs made Cain cast a surly glance upward, his lips curling in disgust as his gaze alighted on the coarse-featured face of his brother. Staggering drunk, Eli looked like even more of a blubbering idiot than usual, his eyes showing only the vaguest sense of awareness, his mammoth, loose-limbed body all but collapsing as he wove down the risers.

Cain's stomach turned at the sight of him, Eli's mouth gaping open, dribbles of whiskey and chewing tobacco running down his chin to stain the shirt beneath. But those dull dog eyes lit up, that mouth stretching into a disgustingly wide grin when Eli caught sight of him.

"Cain! Gimme some more whiskey!" Eli bellowed across the room, stumbling over to grab the bottle from Cain's hand. He gulped it down, slobbering over the glass rim.

"Yer th' besht brother inna whole world." Eli flung one heavy arm around Cain's shoulder. "The besht—"

"Shut up, you damn fool!" Cain snarled, shoving the arm away.

Hurt flickered in Eli's face, and he shoved the whiskey bottle back toward Cain. "Shorry, didn't mean . . . to make ye mad at me. Are ye mad at me, Cain?"

"Take the damn bottle! You ruined it!"

"Jesht . . . jesht took a drink," Eli said, his lower lip trembling in the way that always made Cain want to backhand him. "I'll buy ye 'nother bottle, Cain."

"Son of a bitch!" Cain wheeled on Eli, grabbing him by the shirtfront. "I don't want any more damn whiskey! I told you that as soon as I was finished with that woman upstairs we were going after MacQuade. We have to pick up that bastard's trail before—"

"You lookin' fer Garret MacQuade?"

The deep voice made Cain release his brother, turning narrowed eyes to a grimy-looking man who had just bellied up to the bar. "Could be. What business is it of yours?"

The man scratched at the gray skin of his neck with filthy fingernails. His eyes narrowed, a sneer curling his lips. "None at all, I guess. Jest that I wouldn't mind seein' that bastard slit belly t' chin with that knife o' yers, friend."

"Is that so, friend?" Cain said with a silky smile. "Well, me an' my brother here would like nothing better than to accommodate you."

The man guffawed, slugging down the remains of a warm beer.

"Name's Cain Garvey. What's yours?"

"Charlie Spader. Best damn trail guide east o' the Great Divide. Woulda been on a job right now if it hadn't been for MacQuade." Spader spat a stream of tobacco juice onto the wood floor. "Was gonna take some pretty gal all the way t' Texas afore that bastard stuck 'is nose in. Would even 'a' tolerated those brats o' hers jest t' get a chance t' give 'er a ride on my pistol, if'n ye know what I mean."

Suspicion stirred in Cain, and he motioned to the barkeep for another bottle. Taking the questionably clean glass from the man, he poured Spader a shot. "If you'd be willin' t' help my brother and me, Mr. Spader, you could have any whore in the house, on me." Cain reached into his pocket, pulling out a clump of bills. "Would you like that, Spader?"

The man eyed the bills with contempt. "If I had money like that, mister, wouldn't waste it on no whore. Naw. Get my women willin'-like, I do. But if ye got that many greenbacks to throw around, well, you could damn well throw a wad more of 'em my way, if ye want any more in-for-mation."

Cain's lips froze in a grin, only the crowded room keeping his knife from Spader's throat. Garvey forced a laugh. "Well, friend, I'm always ready to deal— providing a man's playing with an honest deck."

Spader guzzled down the whiskey, then belched. "I don't think you've ever touched an honest deck in your life. But then, I admire that in a man."

"Do you?"

"Yep. I do. And that's why I'm gonna tell you everything I know for"—his gaze flicked to the money—"say, double that."

"Li' hell!" Eli roared. "Cain, lemme wring th' li'l weasel's neck! We're not gonna—"

"Eli, Eli, break his neck and he can't talk, can he? No.

Mr. Spader here is a businessman. Can't fault him for driving a hard bargain. Only problem is . . . well, Eli an' me don't keep that kinda money on us. Keep it hid away so nobody gets the idea t' roll us for it, *comprende?"*

Spader sneered. "If you think I'm gonna spill my guts without that money, you're sadly mistaken. Naw, Mama Spader didn't raise no fools."

Cain chuckled, trying to keep his mounting fury from his eyes. "This much I promise you, Mr. Spader. You give us the information we need, and you'll get exactly what you deserve."

Eli gave a snort of disgust, but Cain ignored it. Slowly Cain drew his pistol, holding it up to the light. Spader's eyes widened a trifle, wary. "Don't worry, I'm not gonna put a bullet in you. Like I told Eli, dead men don't talk. I want you to take this as an assurance that you'll get the rest of your payment. It's inlaid with silver. Finest weapon made."

Spader took the gun, his fingers smudging its shiny surface. But his eyes lit up with approval.

"You keep that, Spader, until we go to get the rest of your money. Oughta make Mama Spader right proud o' how smart you've been."

After a moment Spader nodded, shoving the barrel into the waist of his pants. "Seems fair enough. What'd ye want to know?"

"Tell me about this woman. Where she was going."

"Goin' t' Texas. Thought she was plumb crazy, but you know them damn foreigners. Cain't tell 'em nothing."

"Foreigners?"

"The woman. She was one o' them Irishers. Talked real odd. Had the deed to some little patch o' dirt. An old man give it to her afore he died."

Cain's muscles tensed, as if he could already scent blood. It had to be her—the yellow-haired slut who had interfered in their pursuit of Kennisaw Jones. That was how the old bastard had made it this far, wounded as he was. That was how he had managed not only to escape, but most likely to have warned MacQuade as well.

MacQuade would be looking for them, be alert, ready. But that was just fine with Cain Garvey. He always liked a challenge.

Spader's grumbling drew Cain out of his musings. "I had jest been in here, braggin' on the job, the night afore we was to leave when that bastard MacQuade, he hit me. Broke my damn jaw."

Cain could understand MacQuade's temptation.

"And then what happened, Mr. Spader?"

"Next morning saw him ride out with that Irish lady. Now, let's see, when she hired me she said we was goin' to a place called . . . Crested Ridge . . . naw, Glory Ridge . . . or was it—Stormy Ridge. That was it! Yessiree!"

"And how long ago did MacQuade and this woman— what was her name?"

"Some foreign name—Ash-a-linn, Asheen, I dunno. Last name, though, I 'member right enough. O'Shea, it was. Yep. I'm certain sure of it."

The pompous idiot, Cain thought with a sneer. He'd be doing Spader a favor when he slit the babbling man's throat.

"How long ago did they leave town?"

"Three weeks now, maybe more. I was in a bad way after they left—doc kept me drunk most o' the time t' ease the pain. Medicinal purposes."

Cain chuckled. "You've been darned helpful, Mr. Spader. Darned helpful. If you'd come along with us, my brother and I'd like to settle our account with you."

Spader's lips pulled tight over his teeth as he shoved away from the bar, starting toward the swinging door. He pulled out the gun Cain had given him, finger looping around the trigger.

Cain glanced down at it, then back into the man's eyes.

"Like I told ye," Spader said, "my mama didn't raise up no fools."

"Can't blame a man for being cautious." Cain made his way out the door. "Might just save your life some-time, eh, Spader?"

He directed Spader toward the gap between two buildings.

The man chortled his agreement, but as his eyes met Cain's Spader's smile faded, his hand tightening convulsively on the pistol butt.

Cain's lips twisted into a sneer of raw pleasure and sadistic glee. He'd been able to elicit that reaction from people from the time he'd been nine years old. The year he'd first felt that staggering surge of power as he'd slashed his knife deep. Killed . . .

"I jest wanna . . . wanna get this over peaceable-like," Spader said, the slightest tremor in his voice letting Cain know that the man had suddenly become aware of the shadows pooling all around them, the unnatural quiet that had closed about them like a grave. "Jest wanna get what's comin' t' me."

"You will, Spader. That you will."

In that instant Cain's knife flashed out, glinting blue in the meager light. Spader's eyes bulged as he squeezed the trigger and heard a sickeningly hollow click.

Cain laughed as his knife drove deep into Spader's belly, blood wetting Garvey's hand as he jerked the blade upward beneath the man's rib cage.

The repulsive gurgling sounds of death rose from the man's throat as he collapsed to the ground, eyes bulging, hands flailing.

Then he lay still.

Cain reached down, pulling out his blade, wiping the blood on Spader's filthy pants.

A smack on the shoulder jarred him, and he looked up into Eli's eager face. "Ye did tha' real good, Cain. Shkewered 'im like a pig. Mebbe now 'at ye got in a good killin', ye won't be so tetchy 'bout everythin'."

"This'll do me for the time bein'." Cain rummaged through Spader's pockets, taking not only the greenbacks exchanged in the saloon but the rest of the man's money as well. "But I'll not be satisfied until it's MacQuade's blood wettin' my knife. MacQuade's belly laid open t' the maggots.

"Time, Eli. Now it's only a matter o' time afore we have everything just like I promised you in that there prison. Only a matter o' time before you can roast Garret MacQuade over a damn firepit if you want to, for what you've suffered."

Eli rubbed his groin with one hand, licking his lips. "That'll be right fine, Cain. But—well, I been meanin' t' ask ye . . . there's shomethin' elsh I'd like 'bout as much, I'm thinkin'."

"What, Eli? Ye know I always take care o' my brother."

"That woman Spader 'uz talkin' about. The one with the yaller hair. Ain't she the one 'at we saw outside that wheelwright's place in St. Joe?"

Cain grimaced, resheathing his knife. He bent to retrieve his pistol, tucking it away as well. "I s'pose she's the same one."

Eli's Adam's apple bobbed, that lust-filled animal light coming into his dull eyes. "I wan' 'er, Cain. I wanna pound 'er 'til she cain't even walk. She 'uz real pretty. Like a flower."

Cain had thought of a hundred different tortures to put the woman through in the weeks he'd been battling to find Kennisaw's trail. But as he stared into the slack, repulsive face of his brother and imagined Eli's rough paws mauling the woman's breasts, pleasure surged through him.

For a woman like that O'Shea bitch, rape at Eli's hands might be the most devastating torture of all. Especially if those brats Spader had talked about were there to watch it.

Cain looped one arm around Eli's shoulder as they turned back toward the saloon.

"The woman's yours as soon as we find her, Eli," Cain said with a malevolent smile. "And we will find her—and Garret MacQuade—before another month is out."

12

*T*he dawn burst over the horizon; a blaze of colors spilled across the palette of the sky. Ashleen stood by the creek bank, water pail forgotten in her hand as she watched the beauty unfolding.

She knew she should feel battered this morn by emotions too volatile to hold. Knew she should feel shame at the way she had allowed Garret MacQuade to kiss her, touch her—shame at the heat that had raced wildly through her body as she had returned those caresses.

Maybe she was not a nun, but that should not negate all the teachings she had learned at Sister Agatha's knee, or make what had happened between her and Garret excusable.

Had she truly been fool enough to forget in those too-brief, fiery moments what succumbing to such desires had once cost her? All she believed in, all she trusted, almost all of who she was. Had she forgotten what it felt like to weep alone in the chapel after Timothy Kearny had shattered her illusions about love?

She should be angry with herself, angry with Garret. She should be humiliated, disgusted, resolved never to let such madness overtake her again.

Instead she felt only wistful, and maybe a little sad, because she had felt the promise of wonder springing between them, and then she had seen the wariness, the stark vulnerability that had been in Garret's quicksilver eyes.

Who was he, this man who had made her forget oaths sworn to herself five years back? This man who had opened to her worlds of possibilities? Was he truly the hard-edged, snarling man whose temper seemed constantly honed to sharp-tongued anger? Was he the hide-tough trail guide who rode, confident, oblivious to dangers of hostile Indians, wild animals, the unforgiving terrain? Or was he the man Ashleen had glimpsed when they had kissed in the moonlight, the tormented artist, so beautiful, so excruciatingly sensitive that he had built unbreachable bastions around his heart?

"It doesn't matter," she whispered to the fluffy mauve-tipped clouds scudding overhead. "I can't let it matter to me. I have four children I'm responsible for, and even— even if I didn't, I doubt Garret would thank me for probing into things that are none of my concern."

She knew that it was true, abominably reasonable. She could ill afford complicating her affairs when they were already so hopelessly tangled. And yet she couldn't erase from her memory the unbearable hunger that had been in Garret's wondrously formed face, the longing that had burned through his palms, seeping deep into her skin.

If the stories Kennisaw had told her about 'his boy' on the nightmarish road to West Port had been true, then Garret MacQuade had been needing someone for a very long time.

And once he surrendered to the clamorings inside him, Ashleen sensed that no man would love more fiercely, more completely.

It made her ache inside to know that she could never be the woman to loose such feelings in him. That she could not be the one to break through the layers shielding the real Garret MacQuade from the pain of the outside world.

Ashleen grimaced at her reflection in the rippling clear water. At least she'd not have to worry about avoiding the temptation Garret posed. No doubt the man would now be dodging her as if she were infected with the plague.

She thought of him as he had been the night before, with Meggie curled at his feet. His sun-bronzed face had held the same quiet belligerence that had been on the features of the children when first she had brought them into the circle of family at St. Michael's. He had been painfully aware that he did not belong. But there had been something in his face—just the slightest twist to that full, firm mouth that had betrayed how much he had wanted to.

Wanted to? Ash thought, mentally shaking herself as she stooped down to fill the bucket. If that wasn't the most insane fantasy she'd ever entertained. The mere idea that Garret would want to involve himself with four squabbling children was absurd.

No, that was one facet of Garret MacQuade's personality that Ashleen knew she could not deny—the man was patently uncomfortable around children. Not with the irritation and impatience inherent in so many other men—men who could not be bothered to waste their time upon those younger and, therefore, much less important than they.

In Garret it was almost as if the mere sight of them opened old wounds, chipped away at his inner defenses, leaving him raw. She had seen the way he had looked at Meggie, had seen his eyes roving to Liam, Shevonne, even the surly Renny. And despite Garret's temper, Ashleen had seen some measure of enjoyment in his face as he had watched the little ones scatter about the campsite, playing at hoodman blind.

He had tried not to watch them. Tried not to watch her. But those efforts only infused the times he could no longer resist it with more power, more unwanted longing, more niggling aggravation.

She wanted to tease him, to hold him, to comfort him, as if he were no bigger than Liam. She wanted to lay with

Garret garbed in nothing but spun moonlight, wanted to delve deep into the passions she had tasted upon his lips.

Yet all she could really do was to get through their time on the trail as uneventfully as possible, focusing all her hopes, all her dreams on the children.

And from what she had been able to tell from Renny's reactions to her this morning, that task was going to take every ounce of patience she possessed. The boy had seemed a bit subdued, but somewhat better during the hour she had spun Sir Alibad's tale the night before. She had even wrenched a smile out of him when she'd tucked him up in bed.

But this morning Renny had been worse than she'd ever seen him. She had tried to talk to him, to discover what was upsetting him so, but the boy would scarcely talk to her, scarcely look at her. His eyes had been brimful of hurt in a peaked face, yet they had snapped with such temper that she had set him to doing tasks as far away from Liam's nose as possible.

But in the end she had simply not had the energy to probe into whatever was ailing Renny—had in truth felt a growing sense of aggravation and impatience with a temper that—even she was beginning to agree with Sister Bridget—had gotten out of hand.

That irritation, above all, was indelible proof that she had to sever this fascination she had for Garret MacQuade and turn her attentions to things not wrapped up in a haze of impossible dreams.

With a sigh she retrieved the bucket and started back toward the wagon, with its inevitable realities of washing faces, buttoning pinafores, yoking oxen.

She had left johnnycakes baking on their board beside the fire, the scent of the cornbread and a little precious coffee wafting on the morning air. There was salt pork to be fried, prayers to be heard, and ahead, another long day of heat and dust and trying to keep Garret MacQuade out of her mind.

Yet as she walked toward the campsite she couldn't

stop remembering the sweet reason in his voice as he'd approved of her taking the chalice; could not stop remembering the fever that had been in hands, burning with desire. And some part of her, some tiny part, wished he had not pulled away.

Renny raked the brush across Cooley's glistening coat, trying valiantly to resist burying his face in the horse's glossy neck and dissolving into a fit of most unmanly sobs. It wasn't fair, he thought, angrily, wasn't fair that just when he and Sister Ash, Liam and Meggie, and even that sniping Shevonne were starting to feel like—well, like almost a family—something had to barge in and ruin it.

The whole time he'd been at St. Michael's he'd been waiting to be ripped away from the only person who had ever believed he could be something—anything but a thief or a drunk or a liar like his da. He'd had nightmare after nightmare about being carried off in John Langan's jaunting car to some farm miles away from Sister Ash, where he was expected to work like a horse and be treated worse than the foxes that sucked up the eggs.

Twice those nightmares had come true, and he would never forget the clawing, sick feeling that had been in the pit of his stomach as he had watched Sister Ash bid him a tearful good-bye. He had wanted to cling to her skirts those times, as shamelessly as Shevonne and Liam. He had wanted to beg her not to let them take him away. And once he was at the farm he had nearly dared his new masters to thrash him, wanting them to get so mad they would send him packing back to the convent.

He had been glad when they hit him, glad when they hated him. Even the time Seamus MacFee had used a riding crop on his legs, beating him so hard that he could barely climb out of the cart that took him back to St. Michael's.

Because he had known he'd be back with *her* soon. That she'd smile at him, and tell him he was bright and funny, and she'd mess up his hair with that look in her eyes that made him know she cared about him. Really cared.

Yet even then he had known he had only bought a little bit of time. He had known his stay at the convent was temporary, that someday he would lose Sister Ashleen forever.

Renny scrubbed his rough sleeve across cheeks damp from what he fiercely told himself was sweat, remembering the elation that had swept through him the night she had crept up into the nursery where the children all slept. In that soft voice that always made his stomach feel like jelly she had told them her plan, that she was going to take them to America. That they would stay together always.

Renny would have trailed uncomplaining in her wake if she'd been leading them off of a cliff, so it had seemed impossibly wonderful when she had taken them on an adventure as exciting as any story she had ever told them.

He should have known better than to trust in anyone, in anything, Renny thought, plucking a burr from Cooley's withers. To think something that good could last forever.

"Hey, Ren." At the sound of Shevonne's voice Renny made his eyes go fierce. He glared at her as she sashayed up, all crisp starched pinafore and perfectly braided hair. "Sister Ash says to tell you breakfast's about ready."

"Not hungry."

Shevonne watched him, her eyes so bright that he wanted to slug her. "Well, you don't have to eat if you don't want to. But you got to come for prayers, and to talk and stuff, or she'll get all worried."

"No, she won't. She won't even care. So I won't either."

"She will too care, Renny O'Manion! She's been lookin' at you all sad ever since we left town." Shevonne waggled a finger at him. "I think you've been pure hateful. Yelling at people and punching 'em, and stomping around like a thunderstorm."

"Everyone's been snapping at *me!* Sister Ash, you, even Liam—"

"Liam didn't squawk at you until you boxed his ears last night! And you're bigger than him. It wasn't fair—"

Stung by guilt, but darned if he'd let Shevonne know it, Renny stomped over to begin combing out Cooley's tail. "I wouldn't have punched him if he'd 'a' shut up like I told him to."

Renny cast a fulminating glare at the place where Garret MacQuade had disappeared an hour before astride that paint gelding. "It's all that MacQuade man's fault. All of it. Meggie wouldn't even sit by me last night 'cause of him. And Sister Ashleen gettin' all blushed in the face and flustery, looking at him like . . . like he was peppermint drops in a jar, and she was real hungry. Made me sick at my stomach. And then Liam gushing over him in the wagon. 'Do you think Mr. MacQuade has killed outlaws with that gun?' " Renny mocked, inwardly wincing at the memory of the younger boy's ecstasies over everything from the way MacQuade sat his horse to the gun he'd had strapped on his hip. " 'Do you think he's fought wild Indians?' I wisht they woulda skewered MacQuade with a hundred million arrows."

"It's wicked to wish somebody dead. Sister Ash always says be careful what you wish for, or it might come true."

"Wish that one would come true, but it won't. Nothin' ever happens that I want. Only baby Liam and perfect Shevonne get wishes."

Shevonne got that cat-face look Renny hated, her lips all prissy, her nose crinkling as if the rest of the world was beneath her. "Is that what you were trying to do last night? Find a wishing star?"

"What ya mean by that?" Renny's fingers clenched in Cooley's tail, a sick suspicion stirring in his belly.

"Last night after you thought we were all asleep I saw you sneak out."

"I was going to check on the oxen. Thought I heard something."

"Yeah, and I'm Queen Victoria." Shevonne laughed.

She dodged out of the way just as he tried to pinch her. "You wouldn't care if the ground split wide open and those oxen fell right in. You went to see where Sister Ash was. What she was doing. 'Cause you were afraid she might be off somewhere with Mr. MacQuade."

Renny flinched at the memory of what he had found in his search—Sister Ash and that MacQuade man together. Even from beside the wagon he could see their shadows melting into each other, had known MacQuade must have been kissing her.

Renny had fled to where Cooley had been picketed, feeling a fear more devastating than any he'd ever known jolt through him until he had stood there shaking like a baby, like Liam would have, while Sister Ash and that horrible man kept on kissing.

He had stolen back to the wagon just before she had returned, and in the moonlight Renny had seen her face all flustery, her eyes all shiny, and then he had known that what he had most feared had happened.

Sister Ashleen loved that mean, ugly-tempered, kid-hating Garret MacQuade who had yelled at Meggie, thrown out their rocking chair, and sold their horses without even asking.

A choked sound came out of Renny's throat, his eyes burning. He wheeled away from Shevonne and scrubbed at them with one fist. She was quiet all of a sudden. And Shevonne never shut up.

"What happened, Ren?" she almost whispered, and he could hear fear threading through her voice. But wasn't it better if she knew the truth, so she had time to prepare before . . . before what? Renny thought, an awful lump clogging his throat.

Before Sister Ash dumped them all at some orphanage in Texas and rode off with Garret MacQuade?

"I saw him kissing her," Renny said at last. "And she . . . she was kissing him back."

"Sister Ash kisses us good night all the time. Maybe it was like that."

"You're so stupid, Shevonne! It wasn't anything like

that! It was like sweethearts kiss afore they run off to get married."

Shevonne nibbled at her lip, uncertain. "Well, Mr. MacQuade doesn't seem too terrible. It might not be so bad if he came with us."

Renny gave a hoarse laugh. "Do you think a man like him would want a passel o' kids nobody else'd bother with? No, sir, he wouldn't take us if his life depended on it. He'd want just Sister Ash, all to himself."

Shevonne's hands balled on her hips. "Well, that's the silliest thing I ever heard. What do you think she'd do? Dump us all out here in the middle of the prairie like we were the leavings from dinner?"

"No, but she might just dump us at a foundling home in Texas. She might—"

"She would never! You just—just quit sayin' things like that, Renny! Just stop it, or I—I'll tell!"

"Go ahead! Ask her if she's been kissin' him. Ask her what they were doin' last night! You just ask her!"

Tears sprang into Shevonne's eyes, her lips quivering as if she were trying to say something. But she was trying so hard to hold her crying inside, she couldn't get it out.

Renny glared at her, wanting to cry himself. He was glad when she slapped him, because it gave him an excuse to let his tears fall free.

He should've stayed in the damn horse trough, Garret thought, glaring blearily at the wagon nestled in the valley. It would've been more merciful if he'd just let himself sink under the water's surface and drown. But no, he'd had to follow after Ashleen O'Shea, had to lose himself in those incredibly blue eyes, that winsome fairy smile. Had to want her in his bed so badly that he had lain awake night after night, those brief wisps of sleep he'd managed to capture tormented with dreams of her warm, willing, wanting him—only him—in a way that even made his hands tremble.

But the reality of last night, the reality of Ashleen's wonder-filled eyes, her hands, so tentative in their innocence, and yet so excruciatingly sensual on his skin, far surpassed any erotic dream he'd ever indulged in—had made even his interludes with the most skilled of prostitutes seem tawdry and dull and distasteful.

She had made him quiver, made him ache, made him feel things he had not even imagined existed. And sometime between the moment she had sunk her teeth into his lip in the Double Eagle Saloon and the moment he'd watched her run back to the wagon last night, her hair aglow with moonfire, he had done the unthinkable.

He had fallen in love with her.

Garret knuckled eyes gritty from lack of sleep and stared at the drawing board he had cast aside minutes before, the half-finished picture he'd worked on through the night allowing him no quarter.

It was all there—in the woman captured on the paper—the laughing, vulnerable mouth with just a touch of hidden sorrow, the eyes that could look at ugliness and see only shadings of beauty, the courage caught in the curve of her chin, the hints of a child's mischief still hiding in the dimples dancing upon soft, smooth cheeks.

Garret squirmed inwardly at the image, feeling vulnerable, exposed, wary, as a hundred well-tended walls around his heart cracked like glaze ice, plunging him into rivers of emotion more dangerous than any he had ever dared before.

How the hell had it happened?

He'd been so damn careful in those first years after the massacre at Stormy Ridge not to get attached to anything, anyone. Only his friendship with Kennisaw Jones had managed to survive the wasteland that had become Garret's heart.

After a while he hadn't even had to try to keep a distance between himself and those he met. It had come naturally, chilling him inside little by little until he hadn't even noticed any longer how alone he was.

He had liked it that way. Yes, by damn, he had.

Until now.

"Well, what the devil are you going to do about it,

MacQuade?" he bit out aloud, giving the drawing board a shove. "What in God's holy hell are you going to do about *her?*"

What the blazes *could* he do?

He scowled. He could hardly desert the lot of them in the middle of the prairie, and what explanation could he give if he were to cut and run when they reached the next town?

Hell, no, Ashleen, I'm not going to guide you the rest of the way to Texas because I was fool enough to fall in love with you.

Yet wouldn't that be the best for all of them? If he were to exit their lives as quickly, as cleanly as possible, excising himself as thoroughly as Kennisaw had once done with the lance a Kiowa had buried in Garret's shoulder?

He was no man for a woman the like of Ashleen O'Shea—a woman who wanted roots so damn desperately for herself and those four children that she had made a journey most men would flinch from.

He hadn't stayed in one place for more than two weeks since he'd left his father's farm. But even if he had never moved from the cabin on the cliff's edge, it wouldn't have mattered.

Truth of it was, he was a bastard to live with—had a helluva temper on the best of days, and when he was buried in his work, and someone interrupted him—

Garret grimaced, remembering how he'd almost leveled Kennisaw with his fist the day the older man had charged up to him and frightened away a clump of deer Garret had been drawing.

It hadn't mattered that a dozen Apaches had been scouting nearby, or that their faces had been smeared with war paint. And if the cause of the interruption had been anything so trivial as a lost doll, or a butterfly caught in tiny hands, Garret didn't know how badly he might have reacted.

No. Ashleen needed a man like his father had been— wed to the land as certainly as he had been to his woman.

Stoic, patient, strong and tough as oak, and just as dependable. She needed a father for those children, and Garret had never even thought he would manage to be a decent one for a child of his own blood, let alone those of another man.

Garret raked his fingers through the longish dark strands of his hair, feeling that old familiar ache at the niggling wish that he could be the man his father had been. That he could be that man for *her*.

But he couldn't be. Couldn't ever be. And it would be cruel to himself, and crueler still to her, to pretend that he could.

Yes. He would take them all to the next town, then ride off. Say good-bye to Ashleen O'Shea forever. But even now he realized if he rode to the other side of the world, he would never be able to forget her.

Leaving was the only thing he could do. As soon as blasted well possible.

Yet at that very moment all his resolve vanished, borne away on the last mistings of dawn as a figure garbed in pink-sprigged calico came out of the brush, a bucket in her hand, her face turned up to the newborn day.

A sunbonnet as blue as her eyes hung by its strings down her back, letting the first fingers of sunlight thread through the golden tresses. And the sight of it made Garret burn with the memory of how those silken strands had felt, clinging to his fingers.

She was probably singing. Blast it, she always did, in that sweet Irish brogue that made him think of angels. And soon she would be laughing, tugging playfully at Shevonne's braids when the girl acted too dignified, or skimming her finger down Liam's freckled nose, or looking at Meggie with that sad, solemn hopefulness that never ceased to wrench his heart.

Longing raged inside him, making him agonizingly aware of an emptiness too great to be borne—a barrenness as wide as any desert he had ever traveled, and thrice as bleak.

Would it be such a crime to drink in just a little of the

life Ashleen O'Shea offered with those gentle, innocent hands? Would it be so terrible to bury himself in her smiles, her laughter, even her tears?

His own throat tightened as he remembered the way she had wept in his arms and the desperate need he had felt to soothe away her pain.

In her way, she had needed him as much as he had needed her last night. She had needed the reassurance that what she had done was right. Had needed to speak of things she had borne alone for too long.

Garret's lashes drifted shut as he heard Kennisaw's voice echo in his memory.

"Everyone needs someone, boy. To talk at, t' cry with, even t' holler at when the spirit moves 'em. Cain't keep your hurts buried inside ye forever—festers there, like a cancer eating away at all what is good, till it poisons everythin' ye do."

It was too late to rid himself of his own ghosts, Garret knew, but would it be so awful if he helped Ashleen bury her hauntings and gathered up in return snippets of her joy in life, like honey to pack away for the dismal days ahead without her?

Days that would be spent on the vengeance trail, tracking the men who had murdered his family, murdered Kennisaw. His mouth set, grim, as he pictured the Garveys as they had been that day at Stormy Ridge—Cain sneering, satanically evil; Eli a hulking giant with dull eyes, laughing at the MacQuade family's struggles with the benign cruelty of a boy watching a moth stuck on a pin, beating its wings to shreds as it struggled to live.

Garret's fist clenched, eyes narrowed. Yes. There would be time enough to kill them both once he had gotten Ashleen and the children as far as the town of Three Forks, twenty miles from Stormy Ridge. There would be time to be eaten alive again with hate. To feel the acid searings of memories so agonizing still, they haunted his dreams.

Just this one tiny space of time, that's all I want, he

reasoned numbly, to watch her smile, to listen to her laughter—to feel what it's like to be warm again. . . .

Stiff from sitting in one position for so long, he levered himself to his feet and stowed away his drawing materials.

He had just tied off the final leather thong on his saddlebags when he espied a splash of blue pinafore half concealed behind a boulder, and he was surprised to find dark, solemn eyes peering up at him from Meggie Kearny's pale little face.

"Shouldn't you be eating breakfast, girl? I can smell those johnnycakes from clear up here."

The little girl glanced back at the campsite, catching one pink baby lip between small white teeth in indecision. Garret expected her to dart away like a startled mouse, but she didn't. She only looked at him with eyes far too old in a child's innocent face. Then slowly, ever so slowly, the little girl held out her hand.

Garret looked at it a long minute, then carefully took it in his own.

Small, so small and fragile, her fingers felt in his, so damn tiny and helpless. He wanted to snatch her up in a crushing hug, to dare anything to try to hurt her. He wanted to jerk his hand away and ride hell for leather as far away as a horse could carry him.

Instead he let her lead him down the flower-starred hill to where Ashleen was waiting.

13

*T*he sky dragons were locked in combat, slashing at the night with talons of tempered lightning, their battle cries the distant echoings of thunder. Freshly awakened from troubled dreams, Ashleen huddled under the quilt listening to the storm buffet the wagon, the canvas snapping with the same sharp sound as the sails on the frigate *Windsong*.

Prickles of unease ran down her spine, not entirely from the knowledge of how flimsy was the shelter the wagon offered.

Even if she had been tucked away in her cell in the convent, with thick stone walls that had withstood the rage of kings, she would have felt the shameful urge to bury her head beneath the pillow, her fear of storms one last shadow from her childhood she had never quite been able to conquer.

Her only source of comfort the past two years had been that when the heavens thundered a terrified Meggie would allow Ashleen to stroke her brow, smooth her glossy dark hair, and whisper words to soothe them both.

Tonight more than ever before Ashleen needed that familiar ritual. Not only to ease her dread of the storm outside, but to calm the tempest Garret MacQuade had loosed within her from the moment he had walked into camp this morning, his sensitive artist's hand engulfing Meggie's smaller one.

He had seemed so achingly embarrassed, disarmingly vulnerable standing there, staring at the toes of his scuffed boots. His voice was gruff but whiskey-warm as he said, "Don't mean to intrude. Meggie here seemed to want me"—his eyes had flashed up to meet Ashleen's, a dull red staining his cheekbones—"I mean she wanted me to come down here and . . ."

Ashleen had tried to laugh, to tease him, but her own awareness of the passion that had jolted them the night before had been too intense, too bitingly real to be denied. Feeling every bit as uncomfortable as he was, she turned to slosh hot coffee into a tin mug, thrusting it into his hands as she hustled him to an upended box.

Their fingers had brushed for a heartbeat, but the sensation of that callus-roughened skin against hers had made Ash's heart slam against her ribs, made her fingers shake so badly a splash of the coffee had dampened his denims, bare inches away from that part of him that had been so hard, so intriguing, pressed against her in the dew-sweet grass.

With a distressed cry she had scooped up the edge of her apron, hastily moving to swab up the spill. Garret's hand had flashed out, roughly circling her wrist, yanking her hand away. But even in her innocence Ashleen sensed that the groan rumbling low in his throat had little to do with the coffee, and much to do with the feel of her hand brushing so intimately against him.

Even now, tucked beneath the coverlets, surrounded by sleeping children, heat sluiced through her at the memory of how that hard-muscled thigh had felt beneath her hand, the stricken, fiery expression that had pierced her from Garret's eyes.

A crash of thunder made her jump, and she looked out at the raging sky through the small hole in the end of the tight-drawn canvas. Maybe this was God's way of showing his disapproval of such wanton thoughts, as thoroughly as any scowl from Sister Bridget's keen eyes ever had.

But at least Sister Bridget had never battered anyone's eardrums with tantrums that shook the very heavens.

A stirring sound from the other end of the wagon made Ash sit up, draping the quilt around her. With an instinct gained in countless nights of walking the length of the wagon in the darkness to tuck little bare feet back under coverlets or straighten small bodies hanging half off of the feather ticks, she made her way to the corner where Shevonne and Meggie slept.

Carefully Ash smoothed her hand over Shevonne's shoulder, tugging the covers beneath that firm chin. Then, ever so carefully, she reached past the older girl, fully expecting to feel Meggie's tiny form rigid with terror, her eyes pools of tears reflecting images of monsters more horrible, more fierce than anything a mere adult could imagine.

Instead Ashleen's hand connected only with heart-stopping emptiness—a tangle of covers already cold with the night's damp chill.

Desperate, Ashleen searched the narrow tick with her hands, her heart sinking when she jammed her finger against the wagon's side board.

God in heaven, where could she have gone? Stumbling over trunks and crates, raking her shins through the thin fabric of her nightdress, Ashleen made a hasty search of the wagon. Her hands quaked as she hurriedly lit a candle and held it aloft. The glow played over Liam, his lashes resting on his cheeks, his thumb stuck securely in his mouth in that most secret vice the little boy hid so valiantly from Renny. Beside the younger boy Renny slept, arms flung hither and yon, eyes suspiciously swollen, as if from crying.

Shevonne was patently oblivious to the storm, a crown princess never stooping to take notice of such vulgar goings-on.

Only shadows lurked in the rest of the wagon, their dark forms dancing on the canvas like a demon band.

They seemed to jeer at Ashleen, as if they had leapt out of some nightmare to snatch Meggie from her very bed.

"Sweet Mary, Mother of God, where could she have gone?" Ash whispered, her imagination running wild. It was then that she noticed a flap of the canvas loosened, the tugging of the wind revealing a narrow slice of the night beyond it.

Instinctively she tied it off, her fingers numb. But at that instant her heart froze, a sudden, gut-wrenching possibility asserting itself in her mind.

God himself couldn't have induced Meggie to willingly leave the wagon in the midst of such a gale. But could something . . . someone really have dragged the child through that opening in the canvas and off into the storm she so feared?

With a cry of denial Ash scrambled to the end of the wagon. Hot wax dripped on her fingers, but she scarcely felt its burning as she tore at the canvas's drawstring with her other hand. Abandoning the quilt, she clambered out into the rain, the downpour soaking her to the skin before her bare feet even hit the ground. The candle gave a sick fizzling sound as the torrent extinguished it, and Ashleen cast it to the ground.

Help . . . she had to get help . . . find Meggie . . . the thoughts roiled in her mind. The little girl must be so frightened . . . alone . . .

"Garret!" Ash cried, running toward the lean-to he'd set up for himself a few dozen yards away. "Sweet God, Garret, help me—"

Lightning ripped across the sky, and she stumbled, her foot cracking into a stone, her ankle twisting painfully. But she kept running, panic tearing at her with ruthless claws.

"Ashleen! What the hell—"

She almost sobbed with relief when she heard his voice and saw him wrench out a lantern that had been obscured by the saddle leaning upright beneath the lean-to's shelter.

He jammed himself to his feet, coming out into the rain to catch her in his arms.

"Ash, what's the matter? For God's sake—"

"It's Meggie! I woke—woke up and she was gone. She hates storms . . . is more—more scared of them than I am, and—"

"Hush, now." His voice was soothing, his arms so warm. "She's fine, Ash, Meggie's—"

"No! You don't understand. She's not in the wagon—"

"Ash, stop this. Look." His voice was low, gravelly as he pulled her toward the lean-to and shoved her, resisting, beneath its slanted roof.

She dashed the rain and tears from her eyes, her knees buckling beneath her as she looked down into Garret's blankets.

There Meggie lay, curled up as snug as a baby squirrel in its nest, her doll cuddled close to her chest, her face so unearthly, so serene that for an instant Ashleen thought her worst fears might have come true. But at that moment the child sighed, shifting toward where another crushed blanket lay, as if even in sleep she were seeking something.

"Thank God." Ash breathed a shuddery sob as Garret swept that coverlet up and draped it about her shoulders. "Thank God she's all right!"

He cleared his throat, bunching the heavy wool tight beneath her chin. "I—I was sitting with her awhile. She came out so scared."

"Meggie . . . wandered out here? I don't—I can't believe it."

"Neither could I. She looked like a little ghost, and she was shaking so bad, I didn't know what to do. I was going to come and get you, but she hung onto me real tight—I didn't . . . couldn't . . ." He shrugged, looking incredibly guilty. "Hell, I dried her all off, put her in one of my old shirts. And figured—figured I'd just let her fall back to sleep and then carry her over to the wagon."

Ash felt an absurd sting of anger at Meggie for doing something so foolish, at Garret for being the one the child had run to. "She *is* asleep," Ash snapped, ashamed to feel tears again burning at her eyelids.

"I know." Garret turned his back on her, bracing his hand against one of the lean-to's support poles.

"Do you know how terrified I was, waking up? Finding her gone? I was half crazed by the time I ran out here."

"I'm sorry. It's just that she looked so peaceful. Like she wasn't afraid. Wasn't thinking about whatever makes her so sad all the time. And"—he turned, his voice edged with a kind of defiance—"well, she kept holding onto my hand."

He glowered at her from beneath dark brows, and Ash could have sworn she saw his lips tremble. He hunkered down beside the little girl, his fingers feathering over her cheek as if astonished by its softness.

Ashleen didn't want her anger to wane, but there was something about the look in those gray eyes, something so painful, something that left Garret so vulnerable, she couldn't lash out at him again.

And when he spoke, his words thick with grieving, she wanted only to wrap her arms around him, pull his head down on her breasts, and let his anguish pour free.

"Beth was Meggie's age when she was killed," he all but whispered. "My sister. She had the same dark hair, same big eyes. She always wanted to hold my hand, too. Sometimes I let her. But most of the time I was too busy to be bothered."

He lifted Meggie's fingers into his own, and Ashleen watched the lantern light play across his narrow, sensitive hand and Meggie's helpless one. And all Ashleen could think of was the hellish story Kennisaw Jones had spun out on the journey to West Port, the tale that had made Ashleen's heart reach out to Garret MacQuade's long before she had even looked upon that beautifully chiseled face.

He put the child's hand back onto the coverlet and pressed his fingers to his eyes. "I hated it when Beth was afraid."

Ash couldn't squeeze a sound past the lump in her

throat, his simple words raking her as no cursing of the fates could have.

She reached out, tentative, laying her hand on the tense muscles of his arm, realizing for the first time that he was wet, too. "Garret," she managed at last, "I'm sorry I—"

He shook his head. "It's all right. I'll carry her back for you."

"No." Ash raised her fingertips and laid them gently along the stubbled curve of his cheek. She felt a blush heat her face and leaned it against the hard wall of his chest, the warmth of him seeping into her very core. "I think Meggie would rather be with you now. And so . . . so would I."

Ashleen's arms went around his taut waist, and he enveloped her in his embrace. He held her, silent, a long time. Until the rain ceased and the whole world glistened new.

It was two hours before dawn when Garret reluctantly bestirred himself, ever so gently lifting his cheek from the pillow of soft gold tresses tucked in the lee of his shoulder.

His back ached, even the thick wool blanket draped about both him and Ashleen failing to cushion his spine where it was pressed against a knot in the lean-to's support. His leg prickled with a thousand needles whenever he moved it, and there was a cramp in one shoulder, but he didn't care; he was hardly aware of anything except the fingers curled, limp with sleep, in his shirtfront, the soft swell of a breast against his ribs.

Garret peered down at the face half-hidden in his shadow, the thick, dark lashes spread like the most delicate of fans, the pert little nose buried against his chest, her lips dampening his skin through the thin chambray with every breath she exhaled.

It felt so right holding her this way in the darkness, feeling her shuddery sighs, warming her in the circle of his arms. He wanted it to last forever. But in two hours the edge of the sky would begin to wash silver, revealing the damage left in the storm's wake, exposing mud, torn branches, flooded creeks, and the hopelessness of the love he bore her.

Garret traced one finger down the curve of her ear, tucking a wayward gold strand behind it. Odd. He had awakened with more women than he could remember, after nights of wild lustings and animal passions. Had awakened with "ladies" in St. Louis who, despite their laces and satins, had devoured him with carnal hungers so mad that he had been exhausted in their wake. Yet never once had he been so reluctant to have a night end. Never once had he been so depressed by the thought of releasing a woman from his arms as he was now with Ashleen.

Garret grimaced. He hadn't even kissed her. Hadn't caressed her. Hadn't made love to her. Hell, he doubted he could've even if he'd wanted to stoop so low, what with a four-year-old drowsing a few feet away. Why, then, did he feel so strangely . . . well, complete? Why was his restless spirit touched with a tranquility he had never felt before?

If Kennisaw could have lived to see this, the old man would've smiled that wide smile of his, his red beard rippling as he nodded his head. What do ye think I've been tellin' you all these years, boy? You always been waitin' for somethin', waitin' for her. . . .

Had he known? Kennisaw? Had those cunning dark eyes recognized Ashleen as the one from the moment Jones had seen her?

From the first time she had shown Garret the deed to Stormy Ridge and confided in him Kennisaw's promise that Garret would guide them, he had thought the whole thing a plot on Jones's part to get him to face the past. Yet had the old man really been attempting to give him a future?

A future he could never dream of? Never hope for?

Something small and cold seemed to lodge in Garret's chest, and he instinctively tightened his arms about

Ashleen. If things had been different, he would have hewn her a bedstead of oak, big enough for a brood of rowdy children to pile into when the night was filled with thunder.

He would have loved her there so fiercely, she'd never again notice the lightning slashing the sky, the rain sheeting down. She would feel safe, protected, as much by the strength of his love as by the thick cabin walls he would raise for her.

The picture his mind painted would have been more beautiful than any image he had ever captured with paint and brush, except that he would know that the ring of security would be an illusion. A mirage that could be swept away by one blow of the unfeeling fates' hand.

He felt a shudder rack him at memories he could no longer hold at bay—his father's agonized face as with his dying breath he struggled to get to the woman he loved. Lily MacQuade's shrieks as she tried vainly to staunch the flow of blood from his wound as his life ebbed into the dirt. Cain Garvey, his lips twisted in satanic glee as he tangled his fingers in Lily's long, dark tresses, tearing her brutally away.

Garret's fist clenched as if he could still feel his birthday knife in his hand, could still feel the sensation of its blade biting deep into Garvey's flesh. But it hadn't mattered—his desperate struggles or his father's courage. It hadn't changed the bloodbath that followed. The horror. The grief.

It hadn't changed the hopelessness that had ever after eaten at Garret's soul, or the vow he had made that he would never allow himself to love that much, to hurt that much, to fear that much again.

And now, with Ashleen in his arms, destroying his defenses, with Meggie's dark eyes glowing at him with such innate trust, he would have to be damn careful . . . never to forget that.

No, this was all they would ever have. He would make it be enough. And yet even now dawn was creeping inexorably closer, shaving away at this little bit of time they had shared. In just a few precious hours the other children would be stirring, readying themselves for the long day ahead.

He sighed, allowing his chin to rest lightly upon the crown of Ashleen's head. He should wake her now. Get her and Meggie back to the wagon long before there was any chance the others might know they'd been gone. That little firebrand, Renny, had been making Ashleen's life miserable for days with his sulking and snapping, and Garret had never been one to feed marauding Comanches fresh ammunition.

"Ashleen." He whispered her name, the sound of it, first thing in the morning, as sweet as the sound of her singing. She nuzzled her face deeper into his chest, a mumbled protest drawing from him a most reluctant smile.

So she was grouchy when she awoke. It was nice to know she had some damn flaws. His lips pressed a bit of smooth white brow barely visible beneath the fall of her curls, then traveled down to her temple. He wished his mouth could linger there always.

"Ashleen, time to wake up." He gave her a gentle shake. "Come on, lady. I can't carry both of you."

"Garret?" The sleepy sound of his name upon her lips wrenched at him as she struggled to focus eyes hazed with confusion. He watched her come awake by degrees, knew he would always remember the moment her gaze cleared and fixed upon him. She smiled. An angel's smile. It stole his soul.

He tried to steady his voice and failed. "Better get you back to the wagon, sweetheart, before . . ." He paused. "Well, we'd just better get you back. You don't want the kids after wondering . . ."

"Oh. Oh, no." One slender hand brushed a fine web of gold hair from her flushed face, and she looked from the slightly fading darkness to the wagon, basking in the last thin rays of moonlight. "Renny's cantankerous enough without—" She stopped suddenly, fully awake, her brow puckered as worry and embarrassment warred. Ash struggled to think of a way to explain the boy's hot temper, but also that innate goodness of heart he had hidden from all save her. But before she could finish, Garret's full mouth curved with something akin to tenderness.

"I know, Mary Ashleen," he said in a voice that made her think of satin slipping over warm skin. "The boy— he's just damned jealous of your attention. Can't say I blame him."

He touched her, running his fingertips over her cheek as reverently as if she were the most delicate of porcelain, the rarest of treasures.

"Hell," he grated. "When I was first with Kennisaw, after my ma and pa were killed, I could've cheerfully poleaxed anyone who even talked to the old buzzard. He was all I had to hold on to. Renny . . ." Garret swallowed, and there was a hunger, not of the body, but of the spirit, deep in those silvery eyes. "Renny's damn lucky he has you." Garret's voice dropped low, so soft she could barely believe she heard the words as he whispered, "I wish to hell I did."

Her breath caught, heart fluttering wildly as Garret leaned toward her, and Ashleen was suddenly, achingly aware that she was clad in nothing but the finest of lawn, the fabric as meager a barrier to the fierce heat of Garret MacQuade as a wisp of silver-spun cloud.

His lips brushed against her trembling ones with agonizing softness, the feel of them, moist, warm, setting her middle all aquiver. One callused thumb skimmed the pulsebeat at her throat, circling it in a way that made Ash melt inside. Her whole body tingling, Ashleen slid her palms up the muscled plane of his chest to those rock-hard, broad shoulders, pulling him deeper into the kiss. Wanting to lure him deeper still.

With a shuddering groan he drew away, his lips clinging as if loath to lose something Ashleen could not name.

She shivered when their mouths parted, wanting so much more. More than she'd ever foolishly sought in

Timothy Kearny's practiced embraces, more than she'd ever dared dream of. Something that bored deep into the very core of her and left her needing . . .

But Garret was already levering himself stiffly to a standing position, the side of the blanket that had shielded him sliding off his broad shoulders to pool upon the ground. Ash clutched the woolen edges beneath her chin with one trembling hand, her eyes yet wide with the heady power of their kiss, threadings of despair and impatience niggling at her as she saw the steely resolve in the ruggedly hewn planes Garret's face.

He swiped his palms on his denims as if to drive away the feel of her, his lips compressed in a hard line worlds away from the yearning softness that had wooed hers moments before.

Only the slight unsteadiness of his voice when he spoke revealed that he had been shaken as deeply as she. "I'll get Meggie into the wagon for you," he said, tugging at the collar of his chambray shirt. "Then you should both have a good hour or more to sleep before the others start stirring. I know you didn't—didn't get much rest."

His gaze flickered down to the bare skin of her throat, his mouth hardening into a line of iron restraint. And suddenly Ash knew that Garret had not slept at all—had spent the hours holding her in his arms, wanting her, denying his needs like some knight errant upon a temptation-laden quest.

Tearing his gaze away, he hunkered down beside Meggie, easing the drowsing child into his arms as if to use her as a barrier between them, and the thought flitted through Ashleen's mind that no enchanted shield could have served him better.

He turned, pacing down toward the wagon, to where the other children lay—a veritable army of reasons to resist the tide of passion sluicing through them both.

Ash's jaw clenched. He expected her to follow him back to the wagon, to a day that would be like all the others since they had left civilization. And yet even if she obliged him and struggled to pretend the link between them didn't exist, she knew that things would never be the same again.

She glared at his rigid shoulders, the longish dark hair spilling well past his collar, waves of tension seeming to ripple out from his taut body to taunt her own.

And in spite of her own raging emotions Ash felt a sudden urge to hasten up behind him, smooth her fingers over that silky dark hair, tell him everything would be all right. But it wouldn't be all right. It would never be all right while these wild, undeniable needs roiled between them, lashing them with the same awesome power as the storm that had racked the heavens the night before. And a thousand children standing between them would not change that single fact.

A shiver arced through her. Maybe it was time to prove that to Garret as well.

She caught up with him just as he reached the wagon. Bracing one hand against the tailgate, she climbed awkwardly into the vehicle, swathed as she was in the blanket's clinging folds. She reached out her arms, and Garret lifted Meggie into them, but he didn't release the child for long moments as he peered solemnly over the little girl's wispy dark hair. "Ashleen . . . thank you for coming out to the lean-to last night, sitting with me . . . talking. It was"—he faltered, then gave her a wistful smile—"almost made me glad of the storm. Made me wish—"

Pain flooded those silvery eyes, haunting them with an expression she had seen often in distant Ireland—in the faces of those who were starving, yet who would not take even the slightest crumb offered them for fear they would be robbing someone weaker, more deserving than they.

His gaze roved longingly past her into the dark coziness of the wagon—more of a home than any of the scattered campfires where he had made his bed. And suddenly she wanted, needed him to know how deeply he had touched her heart, how he had filled her with longings as fearsome as his own.

"Garret, I have to tell you . . . tell you I love—"

"Don't, Ash." He cut her off, his mouth twisting in anguish as he drew his arms away from Meggie. "Don't love me. I'd only hurt you if I . . . we . . ." As if of its own volition, his hand reached up to caress her shoulder, slide up the fragile cords of her throat. His fist knotted against her skin, eyes closed as if in an agony too devastating to bear, then he turned and stalked away.

Despair washed over Ashleen in waves of dismal gray as she watched him walk off. After a moment she turned to tuck Meggie into the bed beside Shevonne. Ash blinked tears from her lashes as she drew the patchwork quilt up to the little girl's chin, wishing she could as easily shut out all of Garret's pain as well.

But she felt lost—even more so than when she had crested the Dragon Hill above the convent and had turned to drink in one final look at the beloved old building that had been her home for so long.

She loved him. Loved him so much it raked her deep inside, the pain of it the greatest pleasure she'd ever experienced. Yet was loving him the cruelest thing she could do—to them both?

Don't, Ash, his strained plea echoed in her mind. I'd only hurt you if I . . . we . . .

Still, could anything cause more pain than this agonizing barrier he seemed determined to keep between them? Could anything make her ache more than the longing ever present in those eyes that had seen too much pain?

He thought he was sparing her, being as pigheaded as Sir Alibad in the tales she had woven. But she didn't want a hero carved out of stone, as boringly noble as the princes Renny and Liam had squawked about that last day they had played Dragon's Lair.

She wanted a flesh-and-blood man. Garret, with his foul temper softened by that wonderful wry humor, his fierce independence laced with grudging sensitivity, that rare combination more beguiling than any grand chivalrous posturings could be.

Her eyes narrowed with determination. Well, Garret MacQuade could take his damned notions of protecting

her from herself and shove them into the nearest rattle-
snake hole. She'd had enough of that lost look in his eyes,
enough of the tremor in him when he fought the need to
kiss her.

Enough of wanting him so badly she ached with it.

With a quick glance around the quiet wagon Ash thrust
her chin out at a stubborn angle and made her way to the
tailgate. Still wrapped in Garret's blanket, she climbed
out. Her bare feet chilled upon the still-wet grass, yet
deep inside her fires burned hotter than any flame, fed by
love, desperation, and the most fragile of hope.

The slanted roof of the lean-to was limned in silvery
light, and she could just make out the faint outline of
Garret pacing beneath its shelter—an animal caged by
its own savage pain, trapped in brutal jaws of loneliness.

Clutching the blanket closed above her breasts,
Ashleen marched up the hill, feeling for all the world as if
she were going to war—to fight for something far more
treasured than a mere patch of land or cherished ideal.

She knew the instant he saw her, for he stilled, every
line of his lean body whipcord taut. And when she drew
close enough to see his face the sight made her heart
clutch in her throat, her hands tremble.

"Go back, Ashleen," he said, his voice snagged, low,
rough, yet raw with stark need. "This isn't one of your
damn fairy stories. And I'm sure as hell not one of those
honor-bound knights whose tales you love to spin. I'm no
good for a woman like you. I'm a loner. A drifter. I've
done more than my share of things I'm not proud of. But
touching you . . . making love to you here, now . . . that
would be the most unforgivable thing of all."

"Why? Because I was almost a nun? Because . . .
because you feel responsible for me? Or because I won't
know how to please you like that dance-hall girl with her
dress split down to her middle?"

"Hell, no! It's not because you . . . you're not . . ." He
swore, slamming the flat of his hand against the support.
The roof shook, bits of bark and leaves falling from the
bunches of branches tied overhead.

"Damn it, Ashleen, if we make love now, how are you going to feel when we reach Stormy Ridge and I ride out of your life? How are you going to feel months later, a year later, when you don't hear from me, don't see me? I know you, damn it. I know you and your damn ways. You'd be talking to angels, asking them for miracles. Expecting them from me. And I don't want to think of you night after night, watching and waiting for someone who's never going to come."

Ash swallowed the lump that had welled in her throat, her eyes stinging at the bleak picture his words had painted. They were ruthless, close enough to the truth to make her chafe inwardly, and to build the desperation inside her until she quivered with it.

But she only met his gaze levelly, all her love glowing fiercely in her eyes. "Is that any worse than someone who always watches for the earth to crumble away beneath him? Who won't even look at a sunrise because he knows the nighttime will come?"

A harsh, hurting laugh rose from Garret's throat, and he lifted a trembling hand to curve along her cheek. "What would you know of nighttime, Ashleen O'Shea— you, who seem woven of light, of rainbows, of everything that is beautiful? Christ, sometimes I think you're one of your wood sprites come to life. But life—real life—isn't made of the magic kingdoms you wove locked away in your convent. There's more ugliness, more pain than an angel like you can imagine."

Ash turned her face to plant a soft kiss in his rein-scarred palm, lifting tear-bright eyes to his anguished ones. "I'm not the naïve angel you imagine me to be, Garret. I'm not blind to the ugliness you speak of. I held my best friend's hand while she died. I held her child in my arms and cried—cried because I had betrayed them both."

"Ashleen—"

"No." She lay her fingertips upon his lips, her eyes clinging to his, pleading. "I should have known Moira was starving. Should have known how desperate she was.

But I went to see her as seldom as possible because it reminded me . . . reminded me of *him,* and it hurt too much."

"Him?" There was a darkening in Garret's eyes. Jealousy. Yet also so much tenderness, Ashleen ached with it.

"Moira's husband. Meggie's father." Ash steeled herself, knowing she was laying open wounds she'd never allowed anyone to see, laying them open in hopes that they might somehow heal Garret's own.

"His name was Timothy Kearny. Handsome as the devil and thrice as daring. Every girl in Wicklow was half in love with him, and I was just as foolish as the rest of them."

She drew in a steadying breath before she could continue. "He said that he loved me. Wanted to marry me. But that we had to keep our betrothal a secret, because his raidings against wicked landlords might endanger me."

She let her hand fall from Garret's lips, shaking her head at the gullible child she had been. "I believed him."

Ash felt the warmth of Garret's fingers as they enfolded her own, chafing gently at her skin as if to warm it. "You don't have to tell me any more, Ash. You don't need to—"

"Oh, but I do. I need you to hear, to understand. It's just hard . . . hard to admit how foolish I was. But then I was only sixteen, even more full of romantic notions than I am now. The secrecy, the stolen kisses, the trysts when I could sneak away from the convent—they all seemed so deliciously romantic, like some hero tale of old. Until . . ."

She drew her hands away from Garret, closing her fingers again in the scratchy wool of the blanket draped about her shoulders. "It was harvest time. He and the other Young Irelanders were supposedly going on some dangerous raid. When we met in the glade he told me that as soon as he came back he would carry me off to

America. Make me his bride. If he lived through the attack."

Ash felt her cheeks burn, surprised that even now the thought of those hours could fill her with shame. "He pleaded for one night . . . one night to carry with him in his memory. Said he couldn't bear to face death without making me his own."

She could feel waves of tension roiling off of Garret's stiff frame. Feel his anger, his compassion, an almost feral protectiveness that touched her.

"You . . . you made love with him?" Garret asked, his voice grating with shared pain.

Ash nodded, lifting her face to meet his gaze. "I would have been glad of it, Garret. Glad. Except that when I stole away from the convent to meet him two weeks later, it was to find him wed to my best friend, his babe already growing in her belly."

"Goddamn that bastard to hell—"

Ash held up her hand to stop his tirade and gave a weak laugh. "The worst of it was that Moira didn't know. About Timothy and me. He had been feeding her the same lies—only when her brothers discovered that Moira was with child they made certain he did right by her."

"They should've broken the lying bastard's neck!" Garret's voice shook with fury. "I would have—son of a bitch!" He wheeled away, jamming his fingers through his hair.

"I don't know what happened to him. Only that he disappeared from Moira's life a year after Meggie was born. No one . . . no one ever heard from him again."

Garret turned back to face her, his eyes overly bright, his hands unsteady as he reached out to thread his fingers through her hair, cradling her face in his hard palms. "I'm sorry, Ashleen. So damn sorry. About him. About . . . about what happened."

"But don't you see? I'm not. Not anymore." She leaned against him, reveling in the warmth in him, the compassion. "If it hadn't been for Timothy, I wouldn't be here now. With you. You say I expect miracles, and maybe . . . maybe I do. While you look for emptiness. Would it be so wrong, such a heinous sin for us both— just this once—to reach out and take something that is precious, real, and maybe ours for only the briefest of moments?"

"You're a forever kind of woman, Ash. You deserve a gold ring and promises in front of a preacher and a wedding dress all stitched in satin. I'm no better than Kearny was, Ashleen. I'll leave you, lady. I'll break your damn heart."

"You're nothing like Timothy Kearny, Garret MacQuade. You're honest, and sensitive, and tender. I want you. I want this more than I've ever wanted anything in my life."

Desperate to drive the resolve from those beloved gray eyes, Ashleen succumbed to impulse, loosing her hold on the folds of wool clasped beneath her chin, shrugging the fabric free.

It was reckless, more wanton than anything she'd ever done before, yet as the wool glided down her slender form it seemed as inevitable as the sea reaching for the shore.

She heard Garret's sharp intake of breath, saw the raging hunger explode in those silvery eyes. "Sweet Jesus, lady," he gritted between clenched teeth, "have you heard anything I said? What are you trying to do to me?"

"Love you, Garret. Just love you. You don't even have to love me back. Just let me . . ." She ran her fingertips over his chest, seeing the hunger in his eyes spark with hauntings of fear. She knew he wanted to run from the emotions raging inside him, knew that some small part of her wanted to flee as well.

But it was too late.

Too late for Garret.

Too late for her.

She had always believed in fate, but never more strongly than she did at that moment.

His gaze fell away from hers but flicked in an excruciating path downward to where the curves of her breasts were glossed with the dainty fabric, the rosy crests of her nipples just visible in the faint light. Pain flitted across Garret's face, mingled with the most hopeless of longing. "Please, Ashleen, don't do this."

Catching her lip between her teeth, she moved to the small buttons beneath the V of bronzed flesh at his throat. Slowly she slid one little disk through its hole. "It's too late, Garret," she said, pressing a kiss against his racing heart. "I already have."

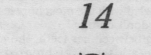

14

*H*eaven. Hell. Garret stood rigid, hands clenched at his sides as he was swept away into both. Ashleen's fingertips were tiny flames licking at his skin. The cool night air wafted over the flesh that she bared, her rapid breath stirring the dusting of dark hair spanning his chest, her tumbled curls taunting him with silken whispers where they brushed against him.

He wanted her. He'd known it since the moment she'd walked into that damned saloon. Yet he'd never known a man could need a woman so much until now, never known a man could need to bury himself inside her body, yet deeper still inside her very soul.

It was dangerous.

He knew it was.

He knew drinking of her sweetness would only leave him more barren than before. Yet he thirsted like a man lost in an endless desert—and he knew that God Himself couldn't turn him away from the magic Ashleen O'Shea offered in her soft angel hands.

He couldn't breathe, couldn't speak, reveling in the kisses she trailed along his ribs, her hands tugging his shirt from the waistband of his denims. Her palms slid beneath the fabric, easing it from the rippling muscles of his shoulders, letting the garment float to the lean-to's floor.

She made a tiny sound as she glimpsed the scars marring his flesh. The slash marks from a cougar that had objected to having its portrait done, a knife cut from a saloon brawl, the indentation of an old bullet wound gained in a fight with the jealous lover of one of Kennisaw's women.

"So much pain," she whispered, and there were tears in her voice.

Her finger traced the scar where the Kiowa lance had wounded him, and it was as if Garret could feel the force of her loving pierce him far deeper.

Then she was kissing him again, brushing her lips across each old wound as if her mouth alone could heal him, loving him in a way that stirred him beyond all imaginings.

Garret gritted his teeth against a groan as her mouth skimmed upward, grazing the tingling point of one dark nipple. Desire speared through him. White hot. Raw. Leaving him gasping.

"Ashleen." He moaned her name, grasping her arms and dragging her upward. "Sweet God, Ash . . ." He crushed her breasts against his chest as his mouth crashed down on hers. She opened for him, whimpering as his tongue plunged deep into her mouth, greedy with the need for her.

His hands roved up and down her back, over the delectable curve of her buttocks, his touch restless, devouring, hating even the wisp of lawn nightgown that separated them. He planted hot, openmouthed kisses down her throat, allowed just enough space between their bodies to fumble with the prim white ribbon at her breasts. He untied it with fingers that trembled, the backs of his knuckles brushing against supple skin soft as springtime, smelling of milk and cinnamon and honey. He was starving for the taste of her, terrified that he would frighten her with the raging depth of his passions.

But she gave a soft, soul-searing moan as he touched her, circled erotic patterns just above the swell of her breast, pressed a kiss on that dainty, lovely mound.

"Beautiful," he breathed against her fevered skin. "Ah . . . Ash, you're so damned . . . beautiful. I've lain awake night after night, imagining you like this, in my arms, imagining how you would look. How you would feel." With a reverence that stunned him he eased the nightgown down the pale curves of her shoulders, letting it wisp down her body to pool in a puddle of white at her feet. He took a step back, his gaze trailing down her slender, naked form, his mouth going dry.

She looked like the fairy princess he had named her, ethereal, enchanted, for no mere mortal could hold such mystical beauty.

In all his fantasies he'd never imagined such perfection, the small, dainty breasts crowned with impudent rose nipples, the delicate rib cage, the waist so small he could span it in his big hands. Womanly hips curved delectably below, giving way to long, slim legs Garret ached to feel twined around him. At their apex downy dark-gold curls caught the moonlight, sparklings of light seeming trapped there like morning dew, beckoning him, welcoming him.

Slowly Garret raised his eyes to her face, searching for the words to express how lovely he found her, how wondrously beautiful. But he had never had Kennisaw's gift for casting out blithe phrases, poetical speeches designed to make women swoon. Garret had only his art, and he knew full well that no master who had ever lived could have captured the wonder of Ashleen O'Shea garbed in nothing save a veil of moonlight.

He reached out and took her hand, guiding her down onto the tumbled softness of his bedroll, but when he moved to follow her she stopped him, pressing one warm palm to the flat plane of his belly.

"Wait." The plea was tremulous, yet it vibrated with such longing Garret felt its fire deep in his loins. "I want—want to see you, too. All of you." Her fingertips trailed down the rough denim encasing his leg. "You're so beautiful, Garret MacQuade."

Struggling to swallow, Garret moved his hands to the

fly of his denims, but small, warm fingers closed over his, moving his hands away. When her fingers brushed him, feather-light, through the worn cloth, he felt he would explode, just that tiniest of caresses driving him to a madness so swirling deep, he thought he might die of it. Gritting his teeth, he steeled himself for the sweet, sweet torment to come.

He watched her, loving her so much he burned with it, as she caught her bottom lip between small white teeth, the gesture bewitchingly childlike as her hands worked the fastenings of his trousers. He was hard, so damn hard with wanting her, and it was as if she had gazed into some fairy pond, unlocked some sorceress's secrets on how to make a man her slave.

Garret's mouth twisted, anguished with a pleasure so sharp he couldn't bear it when she worked the last button free, laying open the folds of fabric to reveal the underdrawers beneath.

Just the tips of her fingers whispered over his rigid flesh, learning the length of him, the feel of him through the thin layer of muslin. Then she tugged on the drawstring caught low beneath his navel, and the night air curled cool around his white-hot, aching flesh.

She hooked her fingers in the waistband, working both his denims and the drawers beneath them down the taut curve of his buttocks, the lean planes of his hips, until she bared that which deemed him a man. Then, with agonizing slowness, she leaned forward, pressing the softest of kisses against him there.

His breath hissed through his teeth, the feel of her mouth branding him forever as he caught her face in his hands and eased her away. With lightning-swift movements he rid himself of the rest of his clothes, casting them aside.

Then he was lying beside her on the rough wool blankets, kissing her, plundering that excruciatingly sweet mouth with his own.

He had thought he'd known what passion was, but he'd never suspected the power it could wield as his hands moved hungrily over her supple flesh. She was everything that was good, everything that was beautiful in a world that had shown him only pain. But even the agonies he had suffered were worth it if they allowed him to make love to Ashleen O'Shea for just one glorious night.

He shuddered, his tongue mating with hers in a primitive rhythm that presaged the mating of their bodies. She met him stroke for stroke, her hands so eager yet so innocent as she sculpted the sinews and cords of his muscles, the taut plane of his hip. "You feel . . . feel so good," she murmured as he pulled away to blaze a trail of hungry kisses to the fragile skin between her breasts. "So hard, so strong . . . like velvet and steel. I love you, Garret, love you so much."

Her words snapped something deep inside Garret, emotions he'd never even known he'd possessed rushing through him with the force of a flash flood, tearing away the last vestiges of control. He tried to cling to the knowledge of how small she was, how fragile, but her hands were urging him with incredible strength, her body crying out to him for the most wild of possessions.

He had to be inside her, had to be one with this woman who had stolen away his very soul.

In one swift movement he was between her thighs, pressing the pale lengths apart. There had been no gentle probings readying her for that part of him that seemed to pulse with searing flame. But he staked his arms on either side of her, staring deep into those glowing blue eyes as he thrust his hips forward, sheathing himself in the moist welcome of her.

Sensation jolted through him, her whimper of pleasure heating his flesh, her head arching back, her hands wild with need. He wanted to be everything she needed. Wanted to be good for her. But he was beyond thinking, beyond reason, beyond anything but sating the relentless desires she had loosed in him.

He thrust once, twice, arching his head back with a cry

of stark animal pleasure as his whole body convulsed, spilling his seed deep within her. Shudder after shudder rocked him, tore at him, until at last he buried his face in the tumbled waves of her hair, his eyes burning, his throat thick with words he could never say.

Then the shame came, washing over him with the most searing of regrets in the certainty that somehow he had failed the woman even now stroking the nape of his neck.

"Damn it, Ash, I . . . I'm sorry," he grated into the fragrant torrent of curls. "It was too . . . too fast."

"It was the most wonderful thing I've ever known."

Her words were soft, tender, and he couldn't stop himself from lifting his head to stare into that winsome wood-sprite face. His heart lurched as the moonglow tangled in the crystal droplets clinging to her cheeks, lips still reddened by the fury of his kisses trembling.

"You're crying." Garret swore. "Damn it, I deserve to be horsewhipped for—for taking you like that."

"You foolish, foolish man," Ashleen whispered, caressing his cheek with her fingers. "Don't you know why I'm crying? Because you wanted me, Garret. Wanted me so much that you . . . you . . ." A raw little sob rippled from her throat, mingled with the sweetest of laughter. "What greater gift could a man give a woman than this?" She drew her fingertips away from his skin and lay them softly on his lips.

Garret felt something clench in his gut as he tasted the salt of his own hidden tears.

"Make love to me again, Garret," Ashleen breathed, taking his hand in hers, guiding it to her breast. "I want . . . want to feel you inside me again. As if I can carry you with me always."

Ashleen held her breath long moments as Garret's hand warmed her flesh, unmoving, those gunmetal eyes gazing into hers as if he were seeing angels.

Then he moved, his palm grazing the throbbing crest of her nipple, his mouth trailing languorous, mind-numbing kisses down to brush back and forth across the pebble-hard flesh. "It'll be better this time for you, Ash," he vowed as his tongue stole out to wet her skin. He blew softly on the dampened flesh, taunting her, tormenting her. "I swear it will."

A shiver worked through Ashleen, her body shaking at his tender assault. Then he drew her straining nipple into his mouth, suckling her slowly, sweetly, the drawing of his lips tugging deep inside her.

She felt something stir in her womb, something wonderful, something frightening. Some secret, long-buried questing that seemed to rend her with velvet claws as Garret's roughened fingertips charted a path to the silky, damp curls that covered that part of her still throbbing from his earlier possession.

"Open for me, Ashleen." Garret's voice was hoarse, strained as he stroked the impossibly sensitive skin of her inner thigh. "I won't hurt you."

Ash's fingers curled into the blankets, her heart seeming to stop beating as she slowly let him ease her legs apart. Somehow in the fierce heat of his passion she had lost the sensation he was creating in her now, this slow simmering centered deep in the pit of her belly.

He was torturing her with this delicate savoring as he explored every part of her, those intense gray eyes seeming to burn her skin. She caught her lip between her teeth, trying to stifle the cry bubbling inside her as he touched the fragile petals that shielded that most private part of her. Then he was easing his way past them, to the hidden center that pulsed with a desire hotter than anything Ashleen had ever imagined.

Fire. Tenderness. They were both in his touch. The feel of him was sweetened further still by the desperation lurking beneath the thick fall of his lashes. It was as if he were worshiping her in the most primal way possible, a way as old as the first woman, the first man, the wonder of the first magical mating.

"You're so damn beautiful, Ash," he breathed, the velvet-rough tip of his finger caressing her. "So damn beautiful."

With a whimper half pleasure, half pain, Ashleen arched herself against the probing sweetness of his fingers, a hollow, aching emptiness seeming to yawn inside her, screaming to be filled. He slipped a finger down into the delicate opening, toying with her, loving her.

"G-Garret," she choked out, her head tossing, restless as she tugged at his arms. "I—I need . . . need . . . something."

"Hush, lady . . . hush. Let me give it to you." He pulled his hand away, and Ashleen whimpered at the loss of his touch. But then he was stretching that long, muscled body atop her, bracing himself above her as his lips found hers. He gazed into her eyes with a piercing despair, his face twisted in pain, in joy. "I love you, Ashleen O'Shea," he grated. "I don't know what the hell that means for you . . . for me. But damn it to hell, I do."

Ash gave a glad cry, her fingers digging into the hard curves of his buttocks, urging him forward. This time he entered by slow inches, as if he wanted this loving to last forever.

He loved her.

It was in every movement as his body wove its spell more tightly around her, filling her to bursting with her love for him. The fire he had stirred with his hand raged now, wild, wondrous as he thrust inside her, his mouth hungry on hers.

Her legs quivered as they tangled with the hair-roughened sinews of his, his hard palms bracketing her hips, guiding her to peak after peak of pleasure. She moaned, writhed, something she couldn't name dancing just out of her reach, like the stars she had tried to pluck from the sky as a child.

She heard a low groan tear from Garret's throat, the sweat-dampened satin of his skin abrading hers, his raw-silk hair warm, wonderful on her shoulder.

"Reach for it, Ashleen," he bit out, "reach for it—"

A low moan racked her as she arched her head back

into the blankets, a shivery feeling building, building where their bodies were joined.

Garret thrust deeper, faster, harder, his breath labored, his heart seeming to beat its way into her breast. She closed her eyes as the tremors rocked them both, and the heavens burst above her, showering her with a waterfall of shimmering stars the hue of Garret's gray eyes.

The first rays of sun were peeping over the horizon when Garret led her down the hill toward the wagon. He had slipped her nightgown over her head himself, tying up the bows with a tenderness that had made tears spring again to Ashleen's eyes.

"What the hell are we going to do now, lady?" he asked her as his fingers fell away from the bow at her breast.

She had struggled to smile, reaching up to touch his cheek. "I don't know," she said in a small voice.

"Well, neither the hell do I." The rough edge to his voice would have unsettled her, except that he turned his face to kiss her fingertips, then linked her hand tightly with his own.

They stopped a few feet from the wooden tailgate, Garret appearing suddenly endearingly shy, almost boyish as he chafed at her fingers with his thumb. "Ash," he almost whispered. "What happened between us . . . I want you to know it was never that way for me before. Never so . . ." He faltered, his eyes uncertain as they sought hers.

She smiled. "I know. Not for me either."

She started at her words, almost expecting to see some spark of jealousy, or maybe even the slightest tinge of condemnation in Garret's face for her allusion to that other, disastrous tryst she had suffered in far-off Ireland.

But Garret's eyes only warmed with such compassion, such love, Ash's throat constricted at the beauty of it.

"You're a hell of a woman, Ashleen O'Shea. A hell of a woman."

He turned and strode back up the hill. She watched

him. Smiled when he stopped halfway and turned to look at her. She kissed her fingertips, flinging a kiss to him upon the soft morning breezes. After a moment he raised his hand in a silent salute, and she knew, even though she couldn't see him, that his cheekbones were darkening with pleasure and the slightest hint of embarrassment.

Ash hugged herself, still feeling the heat of Garret's hands beneath her nightgown, still feeling the power of his loving, the anguish still racking his soul. He had warned her that he would leave her, break her heart. He had fought with everything in him to deny the passion ever raging between them. And even more, he had tried to block out the love that had crept so insidiously to envelop both their hearts.

But in the end even he had been swept away by something so rare, so precious he'd had no choice but to lose himself within it.

I love you . . . damn it to hell, I do.

He might not like it, but maybe with time—time and patience—he'd come to know how right they were together, how much he needed her. How much she loved him.

He had accused her of believing in miracles. Maybe it was time that Garret did as well.

With a happy sigh Ash climbed quietly into the wagon, finding by sense of touch the narrow path between the crates and pallets piled in the wagon box. The interior was silent, dark, the first faint glimmerings of dawn failing to penetrate the heavy canvas overhead. She wanted to go to her own soft pallet, to bask but a little longer in a reality that had outstripped her most magical dreams. Yet even before she had taken a step she sensed that something was very, very wrong.

She turned, her eyes adjusting to the deeper darkness until she was just able to make out the silhouette of a figure perched on a crate near the wagon seat. Her pulse leapt, a thrumming of dread dragging her down.

"Renny." She was glad of the darkness as she felt her cheeks flame.

"Mr. MacQuade tucked up all nice and dry?" Bitter, cruel, Renny's voice lashed out at her, leaving her raw. "Or are you goin' back out there in your nightgown t' make sure?"

Ashleen bit her lip until she tasted blood, her cheeks burning with embarrassment as she battled to keep from making the already unbearable situation between her and the boy any worse. A sick churning started in the pit of her stomach, her mind raking her with countless images this child might have seen, the sounds of pleasure he might have heard.

He was already violently jealous of Garret. If Renny even suspected . . .

Playing for time, Ashleen moved to where her pallet was tucked a few feet from Renny's perch and bent to straighten the rumpled quilt. Battling to steady her voice, she said, "I went to the lean-to late last night to check on Meggie. She had gone out into the storm, and—"

"Well, Meggie's in the wagon sleepin' now! And if she was too stupid to stay inside last night, you should've let her get sopped!" Renny blazed.

"Renny," Ash said levelly, "you don't mean that."

"Darned right I do! You're always pamperin' her, coddlin' her. A drenchin' woulda served her right, the little half-wit—"

It was that single word that did it. It snapped something inside Ashleen, and she reeled with the pain of it. She lunged across the small space that separated them, her hand flashing out with an instinct borne of her own stark despair. She grabbed him by the arm, giving him a fierce shake.

"Don't you ever, ever call her that again, Renny O'Manion! Don't you ever!"

"She *is* a half-wit!" The boy flung it into her face. "But that's better'n what MacQuade's makin' you! A two-bit—"

In that instant Ash's palm arced out, connecting

solidly with Renny's cheek. His cry of surprise mingled with her own shuddering sob, the stinging sensation on her skin filling her with guilt.

Ash heard the rustle of the other children shoving themselves upright amongst their coverlets, heard Shevonne's gasp, Liam's tiny cry. Their eyes seemed to burn into her back, hot with reproach, laced with confusion.

"Go back to sleep! Back to sleep!" Ashleen shouted, tears flooding her cheeks. They dived for their coverlets like frightened prairie chickens, burrowing their heads beneath the faded patchwork as if they were afraid of her.

Afraid.

In all the time she had cared for them, loved them, teased them, cajoled them, and comforted them, never once had she seen on their faces the slightest shadow of fear.

And Renny . . . the expression on his face was the most mercilessly cruel of all. Wisps of grayish light stole in through the opening at the back of the wagon, painting his edgy countenance in hues of such raw betrayal, Ashleen knew the image would haunt her forever.

"Renny," she began in a shaky voice, "I'm sorry—"

"No, you're not! You're not sorry at all! You don't care about nothin' anymore 'cept Mr. MacQuade. Fine! You just dump us all at some orphanage in Texas or somethin', then, and quit pretendin' like you love us an' want . . . want t' be our ma! That's mean, Sister Ash! The meanest—"

"Renny!" Ashleen cried. "I do love you! All of you! How can you think such—such ridiculous—"

"Sister Bridget always said I was the stupid one, remember?" Renny cried, wiping his streaming eyes with his forearm. "B-but even I'm not so stupid I don't know what it means when he looks at you that way. When he's kissin' you and—"

"Renny, I'd never leave you! Never leave any of you!"

"Why shouldn't you? My ma did when some fancy

man come callin'. She didn't even look back when she was walkin' away."

Ash reached out her arms, catching the boy in a fierce hug. "I'm not going to leave you, any of you, Renny! I swear it!"

"Swear it?" The boy gave a brittle, agonized laugh as he struggled and broke free. "Like you sweared you were goin' to be a nun, Sister Ash?"

Ashleen felt as if he'd kicked her in the stomach. She staggered back, bracing herself against a barrel. With a racking sob Renny shoved past her, clambering across the wagon seat to the ground.

Ashleen heard the soft pounding of his bare feet against the grass, heard Cooley's welcoming whicker from where the horse was picketed nearby.

Ash stood frozen in shock, feeling as if the world had suddenly crumbled from beneath her. Oh, God, there had been such pain in the boy's voice, such stark devastation in those belligerent eyes.

Had he suspected . . . realized what had happened beneath the shelter of the lean-to?

Did he know . . .

Bile rose in Ashleen's throat, and she pressed her hand to her mouth.

What in God's name had she done?

"S-Sister Ash."

Shevonne's voice. Timid. Tentative in a way it had never been before. Guilt boiled deep inside Ashleen. She tried to keep from crying, tried to keep her distress from showing in her voice and frightening the children further.

"What is it, Shevonne?"

"Meggie, Sister Ash. She . . . well, she just wet the bed."

Ash fought the urge to break into hysterical laughter. "Get her out of her wet things. I'll go heat up some water from the stream to wash her."

"I think maybe you should leave the water cool, Sister Ash. Meggie's hot already. Real hot."

Ash dragged a hand wearily across her eyes. "That's impossible. It's so cool in here I'm chilled . . ."

Chilled.

Ash stilled, then turned, her heart thudding crazily. She made her way to the bed, reaching past Shevonne to touch the child beside her.

The instant Ashleen's fingers skimmed Meggie's soft cheek, needles of dread shot through Ash. She had done battle with a half-dozen childhood ailments since she had gathered these children together. Dealt with them calmly, competently.

Why then was her stomach suddenly lurching as panic thrummed through her veins? Why was she drowning in memories of those hellish hours she had spent in the Kearny cottier's hut, with Moira's sweet face bloating with fever, her cries growing weaker and weaker until they were lost altogether in her tiny daughter's sobs?

No, those terrible hours had nothing to do with whatever was ailing the child now. A few hours ago Meggie had lain asleep on Garret's bedroll, wrapped up so cozily, so serenely, an ocean away from the horror of road fever, starvation, death.

Ash had tucked the girl back into the wagon herself. Meggie had been fine. Fine.

But there was so much heat radiating from the child's small body, and she lay listless.

"Mary, Mother of God." Ash swept Meggie up into her arms, fighting to quell the raw terror roiling up inside her. "Shevonne, run and get Mr. MacQuade. Hurry now, for the love of heaven."

Ash caught a glimpse of Liam's fear-white face as Shevonne scrambled from beneath the covers, eyes wide as she darted to the end of the wagon. Shevonne leapt out into the first rays of dawn, her high-pitched cries exacerbating Ashleen's own abounding panic.

It seemed an eternity before she heard the heavy thud of boot soles coming near, Garret's worried face appearing at the back of the wagon. Ash wanted to run to him, cling to him, beg him to make it right.

"Ash? What the devil's wrong?" He was shaken, too; she could feel it, his unease feeding her own blazing terror.

"It's Meggie," she choked out, a dozen prayers racing through her mind. "Sweet God in heaven, Garret, she's burning up with fever."

15

*I*n one swift movement Garret swung up into the wagon, taking Meggie into his arms. His large, long-fingered hands moved over the child, examining her with a gentle capability that Ashleen had never suspected he possessed. He spoke softly, soothingly to the tiny, fever-hazed girl, a hooded expression in those wolf-gray eyes.

"What is it?" she demanded, talons of terror ripping deep. "Garret, what's wrong with my little girl?"

"Don't know. Could be anything—a chill, one of those child fevers that come and go, or . . ." His eyes flickered away from hers as he settled the little girl on Ashleen's bed. "There's just no way to know this soon."

Ash swallowed hard, eyes afire with challenge, as if daring Garret even to hint at her darkest fears. "It's not—not anything serious—please, God, don't let it be anything serious."

"A hundred miles from towns and doctors and medicine any sickness is serious. So serious everyone is going to have to stay damned calm if we're going to help her. *You* have to stay calm, lady."

He lay a reassuring hand on her arm, only the slightest of tremors in those strong fingers betraying to Ashleen that he was as unnerved as she was.

"It may be nothing. Over before nightfall. We'll"—he

sucked in a deep breath, unable to meet her gaze—
"you'll have to pray that it is. In the meantime we'll need
to do everything we can to make sure the other children
don't get sick, too. Kennisaw—he always held with the
notion of keeping someone down with fever as far away
from everyone else as possible."

"No! You're not—not taking her away from me! She's
sick, Garret, she can't travel—"

"We're not going anywhere, lady, and I'm not going to
take her away from you." He hugged her hard, burying
his lips against her temple. "We're just going to have to
think what to do."

Ash leaned for one more moment against that hard,
strong shoulder, feeling Garret's inner strength melt into
her, easing the knots of terror in her stomach. *You have
to stay calm, lady . . . only way we can help her.*

He was right. Absolutely right. Meggie's fever was just
one of those childhood scares little ones had been stirring
up nurseries with since the beginning of time. But there
was no point in endangering the other children, just in
case . . .

"The lean-to." Garret's voice broke into Ashleen's
musings. "We could move you and Meggie up into the
lean-to. It's sturdy enough, and with a little more work I
can make it damn cozy. I'll carry over whatever you need
from the wagon. Even the damn feather tick, so she'll be
as comfortable as we can make her."

"But the others." Ash glanced at the children's frightened faces. "How can I leave—"

"I'll see to 'em."

Ash could imagine the expression that must have been
on her face, because Garret's lips quirked in the slightest
of wry smiles. "Don't worry, lady, I'll try not to hogtie
'em. We'll all live through it."

Garret faltered as his gaze fell on Meggie's fever-
flushed face, his smile dying, and Ash could feel the
sudden swift embarrassment jagging through him. "I
mean we'll—we'll get along well enough while you're
seeing to Meggie."

Liam's voice piped up, the tones a little wobbly. "I don't—don't want you an' Meggie to stay away, Sister Ash. I don't care if I get sick—"

"Don't be a baby, Liam," Shevonne cut in, her voice firm. "You'd be hollerin' to high heaven if you were wettin' the bed all over the place. An' then Sister Ash 'n' I'd have t' wash sheets forever."

Yet even as Shevonne glared down her nose at the little boy Ash noticed the girl slipping her hand into his.

"It'll only be for a little while, sweeting." Ash tried to infuse her voice with its usual soothing tones. "Maybe . . . maybe you could get Mr. MacQuade to show you his drawings . . . ones of Sir Alibad and the dragons."

She heard Garret start to protest, saw him flush, but he nodded, gruff. "I don't eat little boys, Liam. I promise." Garret reached toward Liam's curls, hesitated, then rumpled them with his hand. "I'm going to need lots of help getting the lean-to ready for Meggie. I could use a strong young man like yourself."

Liam regarded him for long moments with those gentle, infinitely wise eyes. He snuffled once into the sleeve of his nightshirt, scrubbing tears from his cheeks. "Better get Renny. I can't carry much, with my crutch an' all."

"I've seen you helping around camp. You do just fine, boy."

Despite her worry, Ash felt a lump form in her throat at Garret's words. She wondered if he had any idea what they meant to the child. But Garret was already moving over to Meggie's bedding, tugging it from where it was wedged into the wagon box.

"Garret," Ash warned, "I wouldn't—"

"No wonder the kid's sick!" Garret said, his hands stilling. "The damn mattress is soaked."

"She peed in it," Shevonne informed him loftily.

"Oh." To his credit, Garret didn't miss a beat. "Then we'll just have to take another one."

"Take mine," Ash said, kicking at it with her toe. "Once we get Meggie settled I'll clean up the other."

Garret cast a dubious glance at the tumbled, damp covers. "No. I'll . . . we'll handle it." He turned to gather up the fat feather tick and muttered, "somehow."

Within minutes he had squeezed the bulky tick out the rear of the wagon and, with Liam and Shevonne, had caravanned whatever supplies would be needed to the little shelter upon the rise.

It was when Ashleen at last climbed out, Meggie in her arms, that Renny emerged from amid the livestock, his face blotchy from crying, his eyes glittering with hurt and defiance.

"Movin' up with MacQuade altogether?" he challenged.

Ashleen met the boy's gaze levelly, her voice quiet. "I'm taking Meggie up to the lean-to for a while. She's sick."

His face whitened. "S-sick?"

Ash's heart went out to the boy. "She has a bit of a fever."

"So leave her in her bed." Dartings of terror and guilt were in Renny's eyes as he glanced up at the bustling of Shevonne, Liam, and Garret. "She—she'll get scared up there without me. Won't—won't you Meggie?" Renny reached out shaky fingers, awkwardly stroking at Meggie's dark hair.

Ash's eyes stung. "I'll be with her, Renny. I promise she won't be . . . afraid."

"Then let me stay up there, too! I'll tell her stories an'—an' sponge her off, an'—an' I can go fetch whatever you need, Sister Ash."

Tears trembled on Ashleen's lashes, the earnest, guilt-ridden expression on Renny's features driving like a fist into her stomach. "I can't have you getting sick, too. We all depend on you, Renny. And I'll need you to—to help Mr. MacQuade with the others."

At the mention of Garret's name Renny stiffened, his eyes swimming with betrayal. "I won't, Sister Ash! Won't help that no-good—"

Ashleen heard the crunching of boot soles and looked

up to see Garret approaching, his mouth set, firm with what she sensed was a shading of hurt. But when he spoke his voice brooked no argument. "You'll do whatever needs to be done, boy. Like the rest of us. And you won't make this any harder on Sister—er—on Ashleen by going into one of your temper fits."

Renny's chin jutted up, hands knotted in fists. "You can't tell me what to do! Only Sister Ashleen can."

"Renny, please," Ashleen put in. "I need you to be strong now. Meggie needs you to be strong. Shevonne and Liam are scared to death. And Mr. MacQuade isn't going to know how to help them. You have to."

Renny's face twisted. "I don't care! I'm goin' up there with Meggie an'—"

In a sudden, swift movement Garret had the boy by the shirt, those daunting gray eyes boring into Renny's belligerent ones. "Enough, boy."

Ash started to object, but neither of the two heard her as Garret went on.

"I know damn well you'd just as soon cut me down with that Hawkin as look at me. Truth to tell, I don't much like you either. Specially when you're acting like a damn wolf with his foot in a trap. But we're both just going to have to get hold of our tempers and do what has to be done here, like it or not. Understood?"

Renny didn't speak, but it seemed that his silence was answer enough for Garret. "Now, boy, you go to the creek and fill up a bucket. Then run and fetch some brushwood. Build up a nice hot fire by the shelter, and put a pot of coffee on to warm for Sister Ash."

"I know enough to heat up the water. I'm not stupid."

"I'd say your problem is you're too smart by a damn sight," Garret grated.

With a parting scowl Renny turned and dashed for the bucket.

Garret reached out, taking Meggie in his arms, his jaw knotting in an expression so like Renny's that Ashleen ached.

She rubbed her arms, overwarm still from the heat of

Meggie's body, but a shiver of apprehension worked its way through her. She felt gnawing fears, not only for the feverish child being borne up to the lean-to in Garret's strong arms, but also for the man, so surprisingly vulnerable as he stomped up the hillside, and for the boy, even now dashing to the creek bank, his narrow shoulders bearing a lifetime of rejection.

They were so much alike, Garret and Renny, Ash thought, her heart wrenching. Both hating that softer, more vulnerable part of themselves, both fighting to hide it behind an exterior so crusty no one would ever dare to slip past. Yet each in his own way had allowed her inside, trusted her to see the beauty in them, the potential for loving.

She only wished they could trust each other. But she knew instinctively they never would. Their animosity was an unbreachable gulf. And because of that, any dreams she dared dream of a life in Garret MacQuade's arms were as ephemeral as the fantastical tales of love she had woven for the children in the still of the night.

Bewitching. Bedazzling.

Impossible.

Ash rubbed at eyes burning from lack of sleep, bone-numbing exhaustion dragging at her senses until she felt as if her whole body was weighted down with lead. How many days had it been? Five? Six? She had lost track in the endless hours Meggie's tiny body was racked with shivering so awful her teeth rattled, her throat swollen with hoarse, pitiful moanings. The few times the fever had allowed her the slightest ease had been cruelly brief, only waking the little girl to more grueling hours of torment.

Ash dragged a cloth from the tepid water in the bowl at her side and, wringing out the excess moisture, smoothed it over Meggie's brow. With each day that had passed it seemed that the little girl's skin became paler, more translucent, until Ashleen could see the fragile blue veins that carried the child's lifeblood.

Fingers that had ever been ready to pluck up pretty stones lay lifeless on the coverlet. Still, there had been times the small bow-shaped lips had seemed to struggle to form the words that grief had stolen from the child for so long.

Yet though Ash had driven herself nearly insane trying to make out what the child was saying, she could discern nothing but whimpers and groans and pathetic, choked sobs.

Ash crooned to her, bits of stories, every lullaby she had ever known, humming snippets of tunes when her own mind was too bleary to remember the words. She had spooned countless dribbles of broth between the child's pale lips, pleading with the steadily weakening girl to swallow.

And during those rare moments when Meggie slipped into a heavy, fever-tortured sleep Ashleen had turned to stare wearily down at the wagon, feeling for all the world as if she and Meggie were marooned upon some vast deserted island.

At first there had been nothing but an ominous quiet clinging to what had been the most boisterous of campsites. Even the children's voices had been so hushed, Ash had been able to hear nothing except the rumblings of her own self-reproach. She had been fairly eaten alive with guilt—guilt at having been twined, naked in Garret's arms while Meggie had lain sick, guilt at leaving the other children, guilt at thrusting her responsibilities on Garret.

Yet after a while she had caught the barest hints of Liam's piping voice, then Shevonne's mingling with Garret's gruff one. And when at long last she had heard something that might well have been a strained laugh, the coils of guilt choking her eased a little.

Eased until she had glanced down at where the livestock was picketed and had seen Renny perched there on a boulder, the waves of sullenness rippling off of him as palpable as the feel of a coming storm.

She had gritted her teeth, knowing that there was

nothing she could do—not for Renny, not for Garret or the others, not even for Meggie, save wait and pray.

Her only contact with the others had been through Garret's brief visits—those times he brought up kettles full of broth, fresh water for Meggie, or platefuls of food that Ashleen had no will to eat.

After the first time he had discovered her plate untouched he had made it a habit to stand over her like some palace guard, making certain each forkful of food disappeared into her mouth.

When she had been so foolhardy as to object he had gotten that stubborn look in his eyes. "Who the hell do you think is going to take care of everything if you go and get sick, too?" he had demanded. "You're pale as a goddamned ghost yourself."

Then he had softened his words by touching her cheek gently, so gently, and she had seen the very real fear in his eyes.

I love you . . . what the hell are we going to do about it?

The words he had spoken after their loving had echoed through her, wrenchingly bittersweet. She had wanted to bury her face against his chest, to feel him hold her, to cry out all her terror, all her hurt, the despair suffocating her.

But she had only torn her gaze away from that worry-lined, handsome face and the belligerent, painfully vulnerable love in those wolf-gray eyes. And for the first time in her life Ashleen O'Shea tasted the dregs of despair. There was nothing they could do about the love that had sprung so rich, so wondrous between them. Nothing they could do to catch it, hold it forever.

For even if some miracle enabled them to work through the pain in Garret's heart, there would be the children yet to deal with—Liam, Shevonne, Meggie, but most of all Renny, with his anguish and his temper, teetering on the brink of what he deemed her betrayal.

Meggie whimpered, restless, her arms tightening about

the raggedy doll she held tucked beneath her small chin, and for once Ash was grateful for the distraction.

She ran her fingertips over the beloved toy, her throat swelling with unshed tears. Pain. Why did there have to be so much pain? Ireland, America, it all seemed the same suddenly, lost in whirlings of fates that were more often cruel than kind.

She blinked back tears, Garret and Renny's faces fading into thoughts of the last time she had battled fever beside this small child—how then, too, the little girl had clung to the single small well of security bundled up in the faded cloth plaything.

Wasn't that what Renny was doing as well? Clinging to her—Ashleen—with the same possessiveness, the same ferocity as Meggie did her doll?

He had had so little in his life, had been so often swept up by things that were not his fault, things he didn't understand, couldn't understand.

Like the love between a man and a woman. And how that could never change the love Ashleen had for him.

"You look like hell." The voice at her shoulder made Ashleen start, and she angled a glance up to find Garret standing near her, his lips compressed, lines carving between his brows.

Trying to muster a smile and failing, Ash brushed the straggly web of her hair from her face. "No wonder all the women you know shove you into horse troughs."

No flicker of amusement lightened his eyes as he hunkered down, not checking Meggie, but rather skimming his palm over Ashleen's own forehead.

"No fever. Yet. A goddamn miracle." He turned, leaning over Meggie, caressing her small cheek. "How's half-pint doing?"

"I don't know." Ash heard the quaver in her own voice. "Nothing seems to help. It's as if I can see her—her very life ebbing away, and there's nothing I can do to stop it."

The misery that had tormented Ashleen for days

welled up inside her until the words came out in a choked little sob. "Garret, I'm so afraid."

He curled long legs beneath him, taking her into his arms. And when his big hand urged her head against the wall of his chest, she hadn't the will to resist. His lips were against her hair, warm, comforting, his voice like rough velvet. "I'm goddamned terrified, too, lady. But we're not going to lose her. Damn it to hell, we're not."

Ash clung to him, shameful tears dampening his shirt as sobs shook her, and she hated herself for not being certain if she cried because of the child she so adored, or for the man who would one day slip from her life forever.

16

*M*eggie was going to die.

Garret buried his face in one shaking hand, fighting back the sick fear building inside him as he leaned against the wagon and peered up at the coming dawn.

Three more days had crept by, the path of sunrise and sunset excruciatingly slow, leaving him haunted by memories of another small, innocent face framed in a pinewood coffin, dark braids so neatly plaited, lashes dusting pale cheeks as if in slumber.

Beth.

Sweet Jesus, Garret thought, exhaustion and grief eating away at his nerves. It was as if he were losing her again. Losing her in the guise of this little girl who had silently, stealthily worked her way straight into his soul.

He pressed his fist against his chest, as if the pain there were a tangible thing, as though he should be able to feel something broken there, shattered by the woman with the anguished blue eyes and the child whose life lay in the balance.

It hurt. Worse than anything he'd ever experienced. Worse than Kennisaw's death. Worse than the first terrible shock of his parents' murders. For he'd been too damn young when disaster had struck at Stormy Ridge. And though he'd loved Kennisaw, they had both stared reality square in the eye, knowing, with the lives they led, that one day there would be a bullet too swift, an arrow too true, a bear whose claws might rip life away in one greedy swipe.

This vigil with Meggie Kearny was infinitely different, for Garret had damned well known better than to let the child burrow in so close to his heart, had known the hole she'd leave when she was inevitably ripped away.

It would be soon now. Soon. He was certain.

And he had not only his own searing torement to endure, but the suffering that was wasting away the face of the woman he loved.

He sagged against the wagon box, fighting down the emotions tearing within him, trying to muster the strength to return to the lean-to, to sit with Ashleen during these last precious hours.

He'd always been best at good-byes. But this was one that would tear his damn heart out.

"Mr. MacQuade?" Liam's voice made him peer down into the little boy's face. "I thought if you were going up to Meggie, well, that you could bring her this." The child extended a piece of paper. Garret took it and swore under his breath as he recognized the boy's rendition of Meggie's rag doll as seen with the rosy vision of a child's eye. Liam had drawn the plaything as it might have been long ago, before Meggie's small hands had loved its newness away.

It was sitting amid a spray of lopsided daisies, no smudges where the dirt was, its yarn hair smooth and untangled.

"That's real good, Liam," Garret managed to squeeze out.

"Shaded it just like you showed me," the boy said, coloring with pleasure at the praise, a light of hero worship in those open, honest eyes. "My hand got a little wobbly here," he said, pointing with a grubby finger, "an' I couldn't remember where the light hit on her shoulders, so I had to just guess."

"Meggie'll like it right fine." Garret couldn't tell the

boy the little girl no longer had the strength to open her eyes and see it at all.

"You can put it up there with the other ones I sent. The dragons an' the princesses, an' the magical rocks with wings. Meggie always listened real close when Sister Ash told us stories. I know she heard 'em, 'cause her eyes'd get this real misty-like look, like she was right there with the evil dragons an' stuff."

Garret ground his fingertips into his eyes, the image rising in his mind of the pages he had pegged up on the lean-to's slanted wall, messages sent up by Shevonne, pictures by Liam. It had seemed to comfort Ashleen to know that the others were thinking of Meggie, praying for her, and so Garret had whiled away the huge gaps of time, caring for the restless children by teaching them to draw or helping them create stories they grudgingly acknowledged were almost as good as Sister Ashleen's.

He had expected to be bored out of his mind, had intended to merely grit his teeth and do his duty by Liam and Shevonne—and Renny, if the stubborn little cuss would let him. But he hadn't expected to be touched by their concern for the little girl on the hillside, hadn't expected the thoughtfulness that was mingled with the usual childish squabbles. And he damn well hadn't expected the little snippets of enjoyment he had found while in their company—even when things in the lean-to were growing grim.

Yet of everything that had touched Garret or hurt him in the past week, nothing had cut more deeply than the flowers. A fresh bunch to tuck on Meggie's pillow, supposedly given each day by Shevonne's hand.

Yet despite the children's attempt at deception, it hadn't taken Garret long to discern who had really spent hours combing the prairies for the sweetest blossoms.

Garret sensed Renny would find the loss of Meggie the most devastating of them all.

Garret hazarded a glance down to the creek bank where the boy sat, trailing his toes in the water. The siege between the two of them had been as relentless as that of the Alamo, the boy speaking to him as seldom as possible, and then only with unmistakable loathing.

Three times Garret had gone to the boy, wanting to offer him some comfort, or at least to listen. But each time the child had closed him out with a cold effectiveness Garret knew only too well.

Garret wondered just how much pain, just how much emotion the boy kept closed away, and when it would break free, tearing out everything in its path. God help anyone in its way, Garret thought. And God help the boy when it happened, for there would most likely be nothing left of him.

Something small and warm slipped into Garret's hand, and he looked down, surprised to find Liam still standing there, his little fingers clinging to Garret's own.

The boy had followed the path of Garret's gaze, and he peered over at Renny, a look of perplexity crossing Liam's usually tranquil features. "Renny gets mad a lot. He likes to crack me in my nose."

Liam stopped to touch his finger to that much-offended part of his anatomy. "Right now, though, Renny's real mad at himself. He was terrible bad the night Meggie got sick. Was yellin' at Sister Ash an' makin' her cry. She hit him."

"Hit him?" Garret gaped, stunned.

"Yep. Never saw her do that before, even when Renny was being the most try—annical spalpeen in the world."

Garret didn't even try to understand the outlandish label; he was still reeling from the knowledge the boy had so guilelessly imparted.

"You're telling me Ashl—I mean Sister Ash—struck Renny?"

"Didn't give him a bloody nose, though. He deserved one, after everything he said about you an' her."

Garret got a sick feeling in the pit of his stomach as he remembered the wondrous abandon he had found in Ashleen's arms only a stone's throw away from the wagon and Renny O'Manion's glowering eyes.

"Renny said she was gonna run off with you an' leave us in an orphanage again, 'cause you don't like kids. An' Sister Ash cried, but Renny wouldn't listen."

"Damn it to hell." They had fought over him? Garret could envision the scene far too clearly.

"Don't worry, Mr. MacQuade," Liam's earnest voice cut in. "I don't think she hit 'im cause of you anyway. It was what he called Meggie that did it. 'Bout her bein' a half-wit."

Son of a bitch, Garret thought, no wonder the boy was being eaten alive with guilt.

He glared up at the lean-to on the rise. If Meggie Kearny died, there was no God. For only a deity spawned of hell would put a boy like Renny through such agonies, would heedlessly crush a woman as loving as Ashleen, would end the life of the little dark-haired child who had given Garret his first sweet taste of hope renewed.

Garret's jaw clenched. It was as if Liam's innocent confession had infused him with newfound strength. "I'm going up to the lean-to," he said in something much like his old firm voice. "You run over by Renny. Sit there a while, all quiet, for me, Liam. Even if he doesn't want to talk to you."

The child looked like a soldier going into battle, but he gave a gap-toothed grin. "Renny'll have to give me two bloody noses to get me to go away." Liam scratched at his chin. "'Course, I only got one. . . ."

Garret's lips twitched, and he wanted in that instant to draw the little boy into an embrace, to feel the warmth in him, the bubbling of optimism Garret had sacrificed to life's hardships long ago. He satisfied himself by squeezing the little boy's hand.

"Do this for me, Liam, and I'll show you a fighting trick a Sioux warrior taught me. Then Renny'll never get close enough to your nose again to do any damage."

"Promise?"

"Promise."

The boy looked up at Garret for long seconds, his babe-soft brow crinkling in bemusement. "Know what,

Mr. MacQuade?" he said at last. "I wish you could be our da. Stay with us all the time in Texas forever an' ever."

Garret felt as if the kid had punched him in the gut.

Nothing lasts forever, he wanted to tell the boy, but he couldn't get the words past the tightness in his throat.

Instead he said gruffly, "Go on now." And watched as the boy stumped away on the crutch the two of them had painted with bright dragon patterns one rainy, dismal day.

Garret started up the hill.

I wish you would stay forever. . . .

Hadn't the child Garret said the same thing to Kennisaw on countless times when the frontiersman had wandered past Stormy Ridge, only to wander away again when his feet got restless? Hadn't he said the same thing to his father the day they had first driven their aged wagon up to the rise that was to be their home? He had run to the edge of a nearby cliff and had called down that they would be there forever, the words echoing back at him as if the spirit of the wilderness had given its blessing.

The cliffs, the cabin, the timber, and MacQuades on MacQuade land forever . . .

He was the only one left alive of those who had celebrated on that wonderful night while Kennisaw's fiddle had sung to the moon, Lily MacQuade's feet whirling in a dance that had drawn an indulgent smile from Garret's stoic father. Even Tom MacQuade had been drawn into the festive spirit, one big boot stomping in time while he watched his wife with loving eyes.

That night, when Garret was supposed to be asleep under the wagon, he had lain awake watching the stars appear. He had listened to his parents' voices rising and falling, alive with dreams meant to be shared only in the privacy of their big feather bed.

Garret had heard his mother's teasing, his father's laughter, and he had known that they were kissing when their voices at last fell silent. It had been so damn comforting, knowing they were there together. It had seemed that nothing bad could ever touch them.

But the ugliness, the pain had been lurking about the cliff's face even then, waiting. Just as Meggie's fever had waited on the edge of Ashleen's bright laughter the night they had made love.

He had nearly crested the hill when he saw her. He froze. She was bent over Meggie, her golden hair tangled over the child's narrow chest, her face buried in shaking hands as sobs racked her.

A low, strangled sound ripped from Garret's throat, denial rending him with merciless claws. He ran to Ashleen, falling on his knees beside her, sweeping her hard against him.

Her arms twined around his neck, her sobs seeming to reverberate through Garret's whole being.

"Jesus, God, Ash, I'm sorry . . . so damn sorry . . ."

"No . . . no, Garret, you don't understand. The fever —it's broken. She—she's going to be all right."

Garret couldn't breathe, his heart seeming ready to hammer its way from his chest. He pulled away from Ash, his hand curving gently over Meggie's chest. The child's delicate ribs rose and fell, her breath soft and warm on his hand.

"She's sleeping," he said in a choked voice, his finger-tips skimming the child's cool, sweat-dewed brow. "She's sleeping."

Laughter—tearful, wonderful laughter—was bubbling from Ashleen's pale lips, the eyes that had been dull with exhaustion and worry snapping now with a joy so deep it seemed to drench the world in sunshine.

With a sound that was pure relief Garret's mouth sought Ashleen's, kissing her as if to draw life from her, hope, to touch the angels who seemed ever to be battling on her side.

She clung to him, half sobbing, half laughing, all loving, and in that single moment Garret knew the piercing sweet joy his own parents must have shared.

"I love you, lady." He couldn't seem to say the words

enough, the sound of them on his tongue only making him hunger all the more for the light they spawned in Ashleen's crystal-blue eyes. "I love you so damn much."

As if from a distance he heard the sound of running feet and turned with Ashleen still in his arms to see Liam limping up the hill as fast as he could go, Shevonne running toward them, her skirts flying behind her, Renny outdistancing both of them. His eyes were round with stark terror.

"She's dead, isn't she?" Renny was crying. "She died 'cause of me."

"No, she's alive!" Ashleen pulled from Garret's arms to catch Renny in the fiercest of hugs. "She'll be down at the wagon in no time."

It seemed to take a moment for the boy to draw the words in. He shook his head, relief and regret flooding his animated features. It was as if the days of pent-up torment suddenly grew too heavy for him to bear, and he dissolved into choked sobs, clinging to Ashleen desperately, pleadingly.

"I—I'm sorry, Sister Ash, 'bout callin' her names," he sniffled. "'Bout everything I said 'bout you and—"

"Quiet now. I'm sorry, too, sweeting." Ash smoothed her hand over the boy's tousled red hair, and Garret was stunned to feel a shiver of something like jealousy. "We'll all be together now," she said, her voice vibrant with gladness. "Together."

She opened her other arm to gather Liam and Shevonne close, their joyous babble rising all around her.

Garret stood a little ways away from them, feeling as if he were a child himself, his nose pressed to the glass jar of horehound drops in a local mercantile, able to see the sweetness tempting there, but never able to reach in and take it.

A strange emptiness knotted in his chest, and he turned, busying himself tidying up the lean-to as the children all sat near Meggie, their voices eager, laced with relief and a blind, innocent faith Garret knew he had never shared.

It seemed an eternity had passed before Ash noticed him gathering up the cloths with which she had bathed the child, the extra blankets, the soiled nightgowns.

"Garret, you don't need to bother with those," she said, and he thought she had never looked more beautiful than she did in the limp dress with her eyes shining. "Shevonne and I can wash them up."

"We won't be washing them," Garret said, scooping up a bright-hued quilt. "Everything she touched, everything you used will have to be burned."

"B-burned?" Ash stared in disbelief. "What in the world—"

"Kennisaw learned it from an old sawbones in Santa Fe—insisted that people with measles and smallpox and diphtheria—well, their things somehow carry the diseases to others. The old man swore you could become sick just from touching—"

"I never heard of such a thing! It's ridiculous! Even if the sickness was lurking in the blankets, if we wash them there should be no more problem. We'll take the things and scrub them with lye soap."

"No. None of you are to touch any of this." Garret knew his voice was hard, but he had seen what was left of a village that had disregarded the old buzzard's warnings. "It's better to be safe than have one of you take sick."

"You're really . . . really serious about this, aren't you? You mean to burn up the quilts and the cloths and—"

"Everything. Down to her damn hair ribbons."

Ash nibbled at her lip, bemused. "It seems such a horrible waste. But if you're certain . . ." She bent down to tug the pink bows from the ends of the child's frayed plaits. She added them to the growing pile in Garret's arms, then busied herself getting the child out of her flannel nightgown.

"Shevonne, run and get one of my nightdresses and a pair of sewing shears. I'll cut it off for her, then hem it later."

The girl dashed down the hill as Ashleen carefully unbuttoned the gown up the front. She was nearly to the topmost button when she ran into the raggamuffin doll yet clutched against the little girl's breast. With a loving smile Ash shifted the disreputable-looking plaything onto the blanket. Her knuckles brushed against Garret's scuffed boot, and she was suddenly aware of a crushing silence.

"Ashleen." There was reluctance in his voice, and implacable resolve. "The doll. I have to burn it, too."

Ash snatched the toy up as if it were a living thing. "No. Absolutely not. I don't care if you burn up every feather tick in the wagon, but not—not this doll. I won't have Meggie waking up to find it gone."

"She's lucky to be waking up at all. I won't have her getting sick again, or causing one of the others to take ill. We still have no idea what caused her fever."

"Exactly," Ashleen said, crushing the doll against her. "It may not have been anything like those sicknesses you mentioned. It may have just been spoiled food, or a—a bad chill. It could have been anything."

"Anything. And are you willing to risk *anything* happening to Renny or to Liam or to Shevonne? Is this doll so damn important you're willing to risk dying for it?" His voice was as hard, as unyielding as Ashleen had ever heard it, his eyes flinty with resolve. Her grip tightened on Meggie's beloved plaything, but the expression in that implacable face made her feel as much a child as the others—an unreasonable, stubborn one at that.

All Ashleen could see was Meggie in the dim light of the cottier's hut, clutching the doll as if it were her only shelter in a world gone mad. All she could see was Meggie's little fingers weaving flower crowns and making aprons out of leaves, caring for the bit of rags as tenderly as any mother could have.

The doll had come to represent so much more than just a toy to amuse the child, had come to mean even more than just a cherished belonging. When all those at the convent had shaken their heads and whispered that the child should be taken up to an asylum for the insane, Ashleen had held on to Meggie's responses to the doll, clinging to the hope that one day the love Meggie bore it would somehow be set free. Free to be showered upon people who could love her back.

The child had made such astonishing strides before she had gotten sick—responding to Garret, trailing after him like a small, sad-eyed puppy. Hope that had begun to fade had burst into full flower, and Ashleen had assured herself time and time again that it was only a matter of patience, of waiting.

"Garret, please," she said. "She has come so far. I'm afraid—"

"I'm damn scared, too. Afraid that someone else is going to get sick. That we're going to be stranded out here. Do you know what happens to wagon trains when sickness strikes? When everyone is taken with fever? Unless there is someone well enough to take care of the sick ones, they slowly starve to death. Or else it's Indians, or predators. What would happen if you and I died, Ashleen? Tell me. How do you think Renny and the little ones would survive? Hell, they wouldn't even know which direction to go."

Ash felt tears sting her eyes, shudders working through her at the stark picture his words were painting. "We could—could wash the doll out with lye soap. Tuck it away somewhere until we see—"

"See what? Whether someone dies? For Christ's sake, woman, what do you want me to do? Stick it in my damn bedroll and wait to catch the blasted fever? If anything in this lean-to could carry Meggie's sickness, it's this damned doll. And you know it."

Gunmetal hard, and just as unyielding, Garret's eyes bored into hers.

"You can't let 'im take the doll!" Renny's agitated voice cut in. "Sister Ash, you can't! I'll stick it in my shirt. Don't care if I get sick! Just don't—don't let him burn it!"

Anger welled up in Ashleen's chest, hardening there

with tears of hurt. "Renny," she said at last, "I don't have any other choice."

At her words the boy gave a cry of anguish, turning and running back to the wagon. Ash saw the returning Shevonne stop him, heard him spill out his pain, his fury. The girl stared, and Ashleen could see the disbelief in her eyes.

Scalding tears welled over Ashleen's lashes, tears infinitely different from those of joy she had shed in Garret's arms. It was grossly unfair, this anger directed at the man standing so still before her. But she had no strength to stop it.

Biting down on her lip to stifle a sob, she jammed the plaything into his chest. "Here. Burn it," Ash choked out, her own eyes spitting accusation. "After all, it's nothing but a clump of rags. Nothing but the only . . . only thing this little girl has ever been able to love. Except maybe you."

Garret flinched as if she had struck him, a stricken look entering those steady gray eyes. "Ashleen, you have to know I don't want to do this."

"But you will, won't you, Garret? Just like you forced yourself to play guide on this journey. Just like you'll ride away when we reach Stormy Ridge."

"Damn it, Ash—" he started to protest, dragging one hand wearily through his thick, dark hair.

"Do it, damn you! Quick! Before she wakes up! Before she knows"—her voice broke on a heart-wrenching sob—"blast it all to hell, Garret, just do it!"

A knife seemed to twist deep in his gut. He wanted to reason with her, beg her to understand. Wanted to love away her anguish.

He could only turn and walk away, more alone than he'd ever been in his life.

17

Ashleen stared out over the horizon, wondering when the world had suddenly grown so bleak. The sun-seared prairie stretched out endlessly before the lumbering wagon, the faint tracks in the dirt spewing up dust devils beneath the oxen's plodding feet. The sun blazed above, a glare that burned at Ashleen's eyelids despite her sunbonnet.

A fine layer of grit seemed to cling to every fold of her dress, but even that discomfort didn't eat at her spirits as much as the solemnity that had wreathed the faces of the children. They had been that way for three days now, ever since that fateful afternoon when the smoke from Garret's bonfire had stained the cerulean sky, seeming to carry away with it the last vestiges of happiness and hope.

The children plodded alongside the wagon as stolidly as the oxen, keeping pace, yet no longer darting off to examine wildflowers or cunning little lizards scuttling along the rocks. They never complained, never bickered, never shouted, their silent reproach more galling than shrieked accusations. All the while Meggie wandered, her little arms empty, her eyes filled with an expression so lost it broke Ashleen's heart.

Her eyes burned, raw from countless tears shed into her pillow each night when the others were asleep.

Hopelessness embraced her in unfeeling arms as the memory of that single magical night with Garret taunted her.

It was as if she had betrayed them all—Garret, the children, herself. As if they all somehow blamed her—Renny, Shevonne, and Liam for surrendering Meggie's doll to the flames; Garret for her anger toward something he could not control.

But no one blamed Ashleen more fiercely than herself. She had been wrong.

Wrong to challenge Garret in front of the children.

Wrong to make him appear the villain.

Now that the shock of Meggie's illness had receded, now that time had slowly melted the biting edge of her temper, Ashleen was able to admit to herself that Garret had had no choice but to get rid of the doll.

Get rid of it despite her anger, despite the children's tears, despite the knowledge that he would be devastating the little girl he had come to love.

Love.

Ashleen sucked in a painful, shuddering breath. No, there could be no doubt that Garret MacQuade loved little Meggie as much as she did. For though he had never spoken the words, Ashleen had seen the agony in his face as he had watched the child's suffering, had seen the self-loathing that seemed to hang over Garret's handsome features like the grimmest of shrouds.

Ash tried to swallow past the knot that never seemed to leave her throat, her gaze shifting to where Garret sat sentinel astride his horse, staring off into the endless sweep of wilderness.

Not once since he had gone off alone to feed things into the flames had she seen him pull forth his drawing supplies, to capture with lightning strokes some scene of pristine beauty or stunning power. Not once had she seen him smile or heard that low, engaging chuckle. Not once had she caught his eyes upon her with that sweet, wild heat she had come to crave.

At every meal he rode dutifully into camp, providing

them with fresh killed game or edible roots or berries. Sometimes he had even prepared the outlandish foods, concocting astonishingly tasty meals that would have been a great relief from their monotonous diet if anyone among them had the least appetite.

He had sat upon the same crate, toying with his food until Ashleen wanted to snap at him as if he were Liam. And when, each time he came there, an even sadder, more solemn Meggie walked slowly to sit at his feet, Ashleen saw a hurt in him, a sadness that rivaled her own.

Never did he acknowledge the rift between himself and the children, or between the two of them. He only spent the days wandering as far ahead of the wagon as possible, stoic, silent.

When Ashleen had dared question him he had informed her in the most clipped of accents that he was riding so far afield to search for Indian sign. He didn't expect trouble, but it never hurt to be aware. At worst, he assured her, the braves might be tempted to run off with their horses, but God knew they couldn't spare even one. Garret's eyes had flickered to Cooley, and Ashleen had sensed that he was resolved to protect Renny's beloved gelding—the most likely target of any marauding braves.

So Garret had ridden day after day, disappearing for nearly an hour at a time, only to return as detached from her as if the night of the storm had never happened. If he had seen anything in his rovings, he never spoke of it, nor did he ever speak of the ostracism that was obviously tearing him apart.

Ash ached for him, ached for them all, her stomach feeling raw from the gnawings of guilt. As she watched him Garret's head turned toward her for an instant, and she could feel the longing in him, the silent suffering as agonizing as Meggie's own. But as if to hide his pain from her, from himself, Garret spurred the paint over a rill, vanishing into a clump of scrub timber that darkened the hillside like a bruise. Ashleen gritted her teeth, hating the sensation that swept over her as he disappeared, the wagon seeming suddenly vulnerable against the vastness of the prairie.

Wearily Ash flicked the bullwhip over the lead ox, the animal tossing its wicked-looking horns before settling in once again to pull against the heavy yoke.

She had seen the prairie serene as Eden, had seen its fury in the midst of storm. But today there was a brooding about the land stretching out around her, a quiet laced with menace that made her search the horizon for something that wasn't there.

Ash tried to brush away the vague stirrings of unease, feeling foolish as she continued to scan the countryside. It was as if she could feel someone watching her—as if she could taste a tang of danger in the thick, hot air, a danger she'd not felt since that day in West Port when she had made Cain Garvey stumble.

No. That was a worse Banbury tale than even Liam could conjure—outlaws tracking a lone woman and four children to avenge themselves for being tripped. It was just that she was so tired and hot, and it had been so long since anyone had smiled.

Ash sighed. More likely it was the ever-present grumbling of her own conscience that was making her so unsettled. Maybe it was time that she confront the wrong she had done Garret, the wrong she had done the children. Maybe it was time she attempted to make amends.

Resolved, she called to Renny, asking the boy to take the oxen for a while. With an aura of long suffering he climbed into the seat, taking the bullwhip in hand.

Ashleen went to the water barrel, drawing out a clean handkerchief and dipping it in what little remained of their supply. Garret had promised that they would reach water today and replenish the barrels, and Ashleen knew that no one would be more grateful than the sun-broiled oxen. Despite her aversion to the beasts she could almost feel sorry for them in the relentless heat.

She swabbed away as much of the trail grime from her face as she could, scrubbing away as well the traces of her all-too-frequent tears. Tucking the damp kerchief into the pocket of her dove-gray dress, she took one last look around the wagon.

Liam and Shevonne were still trudging along side by side, Meggie wandering about a hundred yards in front of the wagon. Her feet were lost in the hardy grass pushing forth from the strip of prairie between the ruts carved by innumerable wagon wheels. Her tiny sunbonnet was angled down toward the road as if she were still searching, ever searching for the beloved toy that had disappeared.

No matter how many times Ashleen had tried to explain what had happened to the doll, the little girl had never ceased her hopeless quest.

"Watch the little ones," Ashleen called up to Renny as she untied Cooley from the back of the wagon. "I'm going up to talk to Mr. MacQuade."

Renny didn't even respond but only stared at the far ox as if he wouldn't care if it dragged the whole wagon over the edge of a cliff.

Sighing, Ashleen swung up on the gelding's bare back, taking the leather reins in her hand. Her skirts bunched up around her thighs, but despite the scandalous length of leg displayed she hadn't the will to tug the cloth down as the faintest of breezes cooled her skin through the thin fabric of her pantalettes. Savoring even that slight comfort, she gigged Cooley into a trot. She raised her hand in salute as she passed the children, but they didn't even bother to ask where she was going. They didn't seem to care.

That would change, Ashleen resolved. Today. As soon as she made things right with Garret she would do so with the little ones as well.

Leaning forward, she urged her mount into a smooth lope, the prairie grass beneath her blurring, the horse's momentum cooling her face, making her hair fly back behind her. She reined in as she crested the hillock where Garret had disappeared, her eyes searching for the paint. She saw the gelding, a splash of roan and white, beneath a scrawny growth of cottonwood a hundred yards from where the wagon trail cut around rim of the hill. Garret was yet in the saddle, staring past the dusty ruts to where a creek burbled its welcome, waiting, just waiting for the wagon to come into view.

Ashleen could only be glad that the oxen's plodding pace would give her a little time, for if she had maintained even the slightest of doubts about apologizing to the man who sat astride the horse, this single glimpse of him would have driven those doubts from her mind.

He had dragged his hat from his head, the blazing sun merciless, exposing to her every line of that beloved, rugged face. Deep lines framed that sensitive, sensual mouth, that square, stubborn jaw. Dark brows shadowed eyes that were gray pools of regret.

There was a hunger in him, as deep, as searing as the hunger he had revealed to her when he had plunged deep into her body, making them one. But this was a hunger of the spirit, a hunger for the love, the acceptance, the warmth he had just begun to taste in the warm circle of the campsite before it had been snatched away.

No, not snatched away, Ashleen thought, her heart twisting. He had given it freely in exchange for the safety of those he had loved.

And she had been selfish enough to take it.

Swallowing hard, she set Cooley at a walk, winding down the hill toward Garret.

At the sound of the hoofbeats he looked up at her, and she could see naked longing before his face fell into its accustomed blank mask.

"You should be back at the wagon." Terse. Flat. The words held none of the warmth she had come to love.

"Renny's driving the oxen," she said as she dismounted, ground-tying her horse. "And as for the littler children, they're dragging about so slow there's not a chance of one of them getting into mischief."

Garret made no move to dismount. He only looked away, his lips thinning.

Ashleen forced a mockery of a laugh. "I swear, it's

getting so I'm hungry for just one little squabble between the lot of them. A lizard down Shevonne's back, someone snitching from the sugar stores. I wouldn't even mind so much if Renny gave Liam a bloody nose. At least they'd be talking."

Garret stared off into the distance. "They'll talk. They're just damned tired."

The thought that he would weave excuses for them all made guilt sluice through Ashleen. She drew a bracing breath. "No. They're not tired. They're behaving badly. But then, I can hardly blame them."

Garret's chest rumbled with a laugh edged with bitterness, but before he could speak Ashleen rushed on.

"I can hardly blame them for behaving so badly, considering how I've been behaving myself." The last words were soft, tinged with humility, and Garret's head whipped around, his eyes capturing hers.

"You've been fine," he said, rolling the brim of his hat between restless fingers. "You had every right to be angry."

"Angry because you cared so wonderfully for the children while Meggie was sick? Angry because you were always there for me, when I was terrified I was going to lose her? Or angry because you had the courage to do what had to be done to safeguard the other children, when I could not?"

His eyes widened as he regarded her, disbelieving, a residue of hurt still clinging to his features. With a muttered curse he swung down from the paint, but instead of coming toward Ashleen he stalked a few steps away, putting what seemed a world of painful distance between them. "Ashleen," he said at last, "you've done right fine by these young'uns. You would have—"

"Destroyed Meggie's doll? I don't think I could have, Garret. It would've been like . . . I don't know . . . like destroying a part of her soul. I know that sounds ridiculous—"

"No. It doesn't." His voice was so low she scarcely heard it.

She lay one hand on the sleeve of his shirt, felt the rigid muscles beneath the soft fabric. "Garret, no matter how much Meggie loved that doll, it wasn't worth dying for. I just wanted you to know that I'm sorry. For getting so angry with you, in front of the children. For making them think it was your fault somehow. I'm going to talk to them as soon as we make camp. Tell them—"

"No."

She watched him, stunned as he pressed the heel of his hand against his brow, his eyes drifting closed.

"Wh-what do you mean, no? Garret, I—"

"It's better this way, Ashleen. Better that they . . . well, that they don't get too"—he hesitated, his cheeks darkening—"too fond of me."

"I don't understand."

He crushed the brim of his hat so fiercely that Ash almost expected the thick material to tear. "Liam was getting right fond of me while you were nursing Meggie. Even Shevonne." His mouth twisted, bitter. "Renny'd still as soon spit in my eye as look at me, but the other three—I think maybe it's better if they don't get too used to—to having me around."

Ashleen felt a cold lump of dread sink deep in her stomach. "I see."

Garret paced away, avoiding her eyes. "We've both always known I'd have to ride out for good someday. Go off to find new things to draw, send back east." He scuffed the toe of his boot in the dust. "Could hardly do that tied to a patch of land."

Or a wife and children, Ash thought with a swift stab of sadness. She leaned against Cooley's warm withers, feeling drained, lost. Garret was ripping her heart out one word at a time, and yet even she, who searched for rainbows as tirelessly as Meggie searched for her doll, could hear the finality in Garret's voice, could see the stark resolve in those beloved features.

"Fact is, I've been doing a lot of thinking the past few days," he went on. "I'm behind hand with the commission I was working on before we met in West Port, and the newspaper I've been drawing for lately has about as much patience as that boy of yours. I've been thinking it might be better for everyone if we veer out of our way when we get to Three Forks. The next settlement is about forty miles from there. We could find you a new wagon guide, and I could—"

"Ride away forever." Ashleen closed her eyes, a sudden strange image taunting her—the image of the golden chalice upon the window ledge at St. Michael's, the sun glowing along its jeweled rim. If God had meant to devise some punishment for her great sin, no hell full of fire and brimstone could have cut her so deeply. She couldn't stifle a soft sound, rife with pain.

"Ash." Garret's voice was laced with torment. "I'm just trying to do what's best for everyone."

A shiver of anger worked through her, her chin jutting up, stubborn despite her anguish. "Like hell you are, Garret MacQuade."

He stared, stunned, his lips parting at the sound of her words. "Ash, listen to me—"

"I've heard enough to make me sick to my stomach already. I knew you had a nasty temper. I knew you were moody, and so blasted sullen sometimes you reminded me of Renny. But I never realized before that you were a coward."

His mouth thinned, his eyes darting away from her face. He jammed his hands in his pockets. "Maybe I am. Hell, I never told you different."

"No. You only told me you loved me."

"That was an accident." Garret's voice was low, strangled.

"An accident? Like spilling one of your paint pots, or breaking a piece of harness? Are you telling me that everything that happened between us the night we were together was a mistake?"

"I hurt you. I should have stopped things before they got out of hand."

"As I remember, there were two of us in the lean-to that night. I *chose* to come to you."

Garret gave a harsh laugh. "You were a little girl chasing after some dream you'd spun. Looking for some hero off taming dragons. I wanted to be that man for you, Ashleen. Wanted it so damn bad. But don't you see, I can't be. The dragons have already won."

"Only if you let them." Ashleen felt the faintest stirrings of hope as she heard the misery in his voice, the stark, soul-deep need. "Only if you run away. From me. From this." She reached out, taking his hands in hers. She stood on tiptoe, brushing his stiff lips with her own. His face twisted as if she had inflicted some excruciating agony upon him.

"For God's sake, Ash, don't."

"You can't stop me, Garret. Can't stop this. I know you love me. Give it a chance. Give us a chance. What we shared that night is rarer, more magical than any enchantment I could have dreamed of. Because it was real. I could feel it. In you. In me. Magic." She trailed her fingers down his rigid jaw, her eyes pleading, her throat tight.

"Don't you see, lady? That's why I have to go. It hurts too much. It scares the living hell out of me."

"What? Needing me? Wanting me?"

"Loving you. After my family was murdered I swore I'd never let myself hurt like that again. A part of me died the day I buried them. I killed it, Ashleen. On purpose. Because it was better to be alone forever than to leave myself open to so much pain again."

"You don't believe that, Garret. Not anymore. I saw you with Meggie. With the other children. And when you touched me—"

"When I touched you, Ashleen, I wanted you more than I've ever wanted anything in my whole damn life. But look at you. Look at you." He trailed his knuckles down her throat, took her hand in his, and turned it slowly against his palm. Her fingers looked slender, pale, dwarfed by his strong hand.

"My mother was like you—eyes always shining, laughing, teasing. She could never walk past without her reaching out to give me a hug or muss up my hair or drop a kiss on the top of my head."

"She must have loved you so much."

"Ma loved everyone. Hell, she even had a fox that would come and eat straight out of her hand. But most of all she loved my father."

Ash waited, sensing in Garret an awakening, a revelation of things he had kept hidden far too long.

"Her name was Lily, and she put me in mind of one," he said. "She was sweet-smelling and beautiful, her face always turned up to the sun. Kennisaw—and me, too, as I got older—we worried about her working so hard all the time. Pa always said she was strong as a little French horse. But even then I knew he only claimed that because he felt guilty as sin for dragging her away from her family, her friends, and all the fancy parties in Boston to grub on some dirt farm in Texas."

"Maybe she was glad to leave it all behind. Glad to follow him wherever his dreams led."

"I think she was happy enough. Hell, she didn't see the dirt and the bugs or feel the heat any more than you do. She didn't know she was working herself to a shade, or that her dresses were faded and worn."

"Are you saying your father didn't take care of her well enough? Didn't provide—"

"He would've strung her a necklace out of stars if she'd asked for 'em. And he would have laid down his life for her." Garret stopped, grief carving deep in his face. "In the end he did. I can still hear her screaming his name, clawing at that bastard Garvey, trying to get to Pa. I think he would've sacrificed even Beth and me to hold Ma again just one more time."

"You were lucky to grow up in the midst of so much love," Ash said. "My mother never laughed, and my father . . . when he did, it was usually because he's been guzzling Padraic O'Hearn's poteen."

"But don't you see? It only made it worse in the end.

The way they loved each other—it made them suffer. Garvey shot Pa, and while he was still alive the bastard gunned down my mother before his eyes."

Ashleen reached up to frame Garret's lean face in her hands, those features, so beloved, wavering before eyes brimming with tears. "Even if some fairy had shown your mother the future in some mystical pool, she would have followed your father gladly. I would, Garret. Follow you."

"Ashleen—"

"I would rather die. Rather both of us die the way your parents did than to walk alone forever in a living death without you. Whatever time we have is precious. I want to wake up every morning in your arms. I want to give you sons and daughters with mist-gray eyes and hair like spun midnight. I want to trace a baby's lips with my fingertips and smile because that tiny mouth is just like yours." She ran her thumb across lips trembling with emotion, heard a strangled sound rise in Garret's throat at her caress.

"And when I'm an old woman, in a cabin no longer echoing with children's laughter, I want to sit, quiet, as twilight lingers, and hold on to your hand."

Tears spilled free of her lashes, trickled down her cheeks. With a groan Garret pulled her into his embrace, his lips closing over hers, hungry, desperate.

She wanted to fill him with all the love he had denied himself through a score of barren years, wanted to draw away the brutal curtain of memories spun of the Garveys' violence and leave him with images of the beauty—that treasured, rare beauty—of the love his parents had shared. A love worth any risk.

Her hands delved back into his long, silky hair. Her mouth opened under his, her tongue tasting him, trying to gift him with hope.

His heartbeat thundered against her breasts, his passion, heady, raging through her like the fiercest storm. She could feel the need in him—his arousal hard against her thigh, his hands roving her back, her buttocks,

226

sounds of pain, sounds of need rumbling in his chest. It was as if he wanted to devour her very soul, to carry it with him always. And she would have given it to him. Gladly. To drive away the haunting in that bewitchingly handsome face for just a little while.

Shudders rippled through him, his hands shaking, his mouth seeking, and as her lips tracked fiercely across his cheeks, along his jaw, she tasted salt born not of sweat, but of sorrow.

"I love you, Ash . . . God help me, I do." The words were wrenched from him, his hands almost hurting her in their desperate questings. "But I can't . . . can't . . ."

Ash was drowning in his body, in the feel of him, in the sound of his voice, was drowning in the way his mouth was moving against her skin. The thundering of his heart seemed to fill the very core of her, seemed to expand to fill the whole prairie.

She could feel it, hear it, rushing down upon them.

She wanted to plunge deeper still into the passion he offered, and she would have, but a scream split the air.

Fear surged through her as she sprang away from Garret, both of them wheeling toward the strip of road below.

In a split second Ashleen's heart froze, terror such as she'd never known lancing through her as the vision branded itself in her mind—oxen crashing wildly along the road, the wagon careening at a breakneck pace over ruts and stones. Bestial horns tossed as a terrified Renny shrieked commands, trying to stop them, turn them from their path.

Shevonne and Liam ran in the wagon's wake, screaming as the vehicle plunged onward. But fifty yards ahead of the lethal, slashing hooves a tiny yellow sunbonnet was visible above the prairie grass. Meggie stood paralyzed in raw horror as death charged toward her with huge, tossing horns.

*A*sh screamed, grabbing at Cooley's reins, but the skittish horse bolted back in fear, tearing across the hillside.

The gelding's coat blurred and was lost in a splash of roan and white as something streaked by. Garret. He was plastered low over the paint's neck, the horse flying down the hill at a mind-numbing pace. But if the beast had been born of the Apocalypse, he could never have outrun the crushing death charging toward the helpless little girl.

"God . . . please, God," Ashleen begged as Garret's horse plunged toward the child, the huge oxen closing in at the same time. Sweet God, they would both be crushed.

Ash saw Garret leaning over the side of his horse, saw that strong arm reach toward Meggie.

There was a horrible neighing sound, and Ash screamed as the paint stumbled and went down.

Dust swirled up, nightmarish, as wagon, oxen, horseman, and child disappeared, a sickening sound of hooves striking flesh driving like a knife into Ashleen's stomach.

She ran down the hill crazed, terrified, as the wagon plunged past. Hooves splashed into water, and before the dust could clear the stampeding animals slowed. The wagon tipped crazily, then righted itself as the beasts sloshed to a halt, sucking greedily at the water before them.

Nettles tore at Ashleen's skirts as she ran stumbling down the hillside.

The paint stood a dozen yards from the track, two still, lifeless forms crumpled nearby like broken dolls. Dead, sweet God, they had to be dead . . . no one could survive . . .

At that instant Meggie stirred, a low, keening sound tearing from her throat as she crawled toward the man sprawled so still nearby her.

Ash reached them just as Shevonne and Renny did. She tried to scoop up the little girl, but the child fought desperately, clawing to get to Garret. Relief that the child was safe surged through Ash, only to be drowned in sick horror as she flung herself to her knees beside Garret's limp, lifeless form. He lay facedown in the turf, his body curled as if in a futile effort to protect himself, but his arms flung outward toward the place where Meggie had lain.

"He threw her out of the way," Liam said in a small voice as Ashleen searched for a pulse. "Then the oxen . . . they stomped . . . over him."

Ash felt her stomach lurch at the horrible image the boy's words had conjured, heard running footsteps as Renny dashed toward them.

"Sister Ash . . . I couldn't . . . couldn't stop them. The oxen." Renny's terrified voice raked her nerves. "Please, God, don't let him be dead."

Dead . . .

"He's not dead . . . I won't let him be." The words were a desperate litany as she bent over those shoulders that were so broad, so strong. "Damn you, Garret MacQuade, don't you dare die on me."

"I didn't mean to—to hurt him!" Renny cried frantically. "I didn't mean—"

Hysteria welled up inside her and was suddenly crushed as her fingers felt a shallow throbbing at the base of Garret's throat.

Alive. He was alive.

"Garret." She almost sobbed his name as she gently rolled him over, stroking the tangled dark hair away from his face. "Shevonne, get some blankets. Some water. Run, now!" Ash ordered. In what seemed a heartbeat the child was back, thrusting a cool cloth into her hand. Ash stroked it over Garret's gray face, whispering to him, pleading with him to awake. "Please, love . . . Garret . . . please be all right."

She gritted her teeth to stifle a sob when he didn't respond—not even the flicker of an eyelash, the twitch of his lips showing that he had heard her at all.

Surrendering the cloth to Shevonne, Ash moved to his side, searching for some sign of the injury that had driven him into unconsciousness. Deftly, carefully her hands stroked Garret's arms, legs, her lips forming prayers that she would find nothing broken.

Breath hissed through her teeth as she probed his left ankle through the soft leather boot and felt already a telltale swelling. Low, grating, a weak groan breached Garret's lips, his mouth whitening in pain. Merciful heavens, was the bone broken?

"What—what's wrong with him? Sister Ash—"

She raised her gaze to Renny's grimy, tear-streaked face, the boy's desperation seeming to prickle along her own nerve ends.

"I'm not sure." Ash tried to keep her voice calm. "His boot. We have to get it off."

Renny grasped the dusty leather, half crazed with the need to aid her. "I'll pull it—"

"No!" she shrieked, then she stopped herself. "We'll have to—to cut it off."

"Cut it?"

She felt along Garret's waist and found the leather sheath encasing the bone-handled knife she had seen there so often. The blade glistened in the sunlight. Sharp. Deadly.

"Renny, you'll have to hold him still," she said, her hand trembling. "I don't want to cut him."

The boy nodded. Sucking in a deep breath, Ashleen slid the blade beneath the leather and worked to slit the tough hide.

Garret shuddered and moaned, but Renny held him, pinning his shoulders to the ground.

It seemed to take forever, but at last the boot fell away, revealing what lay beneath it. Already the ankle was twice its normal size, the swelling making her queasy.

Steeling herself, Ashleen peeled back the wool stocking encasing it. Suffused with purple, the skin strained against the swelling. Slowly Ash probed the leg, sliding her fingers downward toward Garret's foot. Sounds of pain ripped from his lips, the knowledge that she was hurting him making her eyes sting. But there was no horrible lump of bone where it shouldn't be, no sign of anything misaligned or broken.

"It's only sprained," Ash said, as much to herself as to the frantic boy beside her. "We'll have to wrap it." Grabbing the edge of her petticoat, she ripped strips from the hem, carefully binding up the injured ankle.

When she lay it gently back on the ground, Garret seemed to settle a little, but she felt more uneasy than ever, her eyes skimming over him, her brow crinkled with puzzlement. Painful as the sprain must have been, could it have the power to drive a man as oak-tough, as stubborn as Garret to lose consciousness?

"There must be something else . . . something hurting him," she said aloud, dread a snake coiling deep inside her. Her hands shook as she raised them to the buttons of his torn shirt and slipped the small disks through the buttonholes.

Garret's eyes clenched shut more tightly, his mouth twisting in a grimace of agony.

Hastily Ash unfastened the garment and spread it wide. What she saw made her sick. A mass of darkening splotches stained Garret's whole chest, gashes oozing blood. Ash could see the massive beasts in her mind, feel their hooves slamming against Garret's flesh. Mother of God, how had he lived through such brutal punishment?

Or was he dying even now? Bleeding to death from wounds so deep inside him, no one could staunch the flow?

A whimper from Renny made her look up, her fear reflected in the boy's green eyes. "I didn't—didn't mean to," the child sobbed. "Didn't want him to die."

"Renny," she croaked, panic crushing her throat, "I—"

"Not . . . fault . . ." The faintest of sounds slammed Ashleen into silence. She stared down, hopeful, helpless, into Garret's face. Thick lashes stirred against his cheeks. His mouth twitched as if trying to form words.

"Garret," she pleaded, stroking back his hair, one hand capturing his, desperate. "Garret, what—"

"Renny"—Garret squeezed out the words, each one agony—"not . . . your fault, boy."

"Mr. MacQuade!" Sobs shook the boy's lanky frame. "I'm sorry! I was mean . . . so mean. But I didn't want to hurt you."

"Know that." Gray eyes fluttered open. Garret swallowed hard. Sweat beaded his brow at the effort it cost him to speak. "If . . . hadn't . . . been such good . . . driver . . . all been . . . killed."

"They ran away!" Renny shrilled, burying his face in his hands. "I couldn't turn them!"

Ashleen felt Garret's muscles tighten, saw his face twist in anguish as he drew his fingers from her grasp. Slowly, painfully, he raised his hand. The fingers that could wield a paintbrush with such skill trembled, and Ashleen's heart wrenched at the memory of how those same fingers had stroked so reverently, so tenderly across her bare skin. How they had deftly, comfortingly smoothed cool cloths over Meggie's fevered brow. Now they curved around Renny's hand, urging it away from a face red with tears of misery, guilt.

Renny choked out a sob, his own eyes opening as Garret's hand enfolded his and carried it down to rest against a beard-stubbled cheek.

"Don't . . . cry, boy." He whispered the words, lashes

drifting down to rest against pale cheeks. "Don't want you . . . to be afraid."

The fingers loosened their grip about Renny's wiry hand, but the boy clung to them, crying, as Garret slipped again into unconsciousness.

Ashleen's eyes filled at the sight of Renny's anguish, Garret's understanding, its poignancy mingling with an insidious sense of foreboding.

"Is he dead, Sister Ash?" Liam asked, low, tremulous.

"No!" Ash snapped, then she forced her voice to gentle. "He just—just needs some time. To rest. To heal."

"But what'll we do without him?" Shevonne snuffled. "What if Indians come, or outlaws?"

Dread prickled along Ash's skin, circling around the lone wagon like a vulture drifting above its prey with diabolical patience, waiting, waiting . . .

She raised her head to peer around her, the wilderness sprawling out like an endless sea, so vast, so unforgiving, it seemed almost a living adversary.

"We'll just have to do the best we can."

Ash caught her lip between her teeth and trailed her fingertips down Garret's face, so drained of color, drained almost of life.

Do the best we can, the prairie seemed to jeer at her.

And pray God that it's enough, she thought.

Cain Garvey glared at the fallen gray gelding, fury suffusing his trail-grimed features. The breath wheezed through the exhausted horse's foam-rimed mouth, its nostrils gaping crimson holes as it struggled to draw life into its shuddering body. But it was too late. And Cain would be damned if he'd waste water on an animal who had dared go to ground out in the middle of nowhere.

Eli stood behind him, and Cain could feel the stupid fool's dull eyes peering at him with that whipped-dog look he despised. "I told you we shoulda rested him," Eli said, hunkering down to run his hand over the horse's flank. "Told you he wasn't gonna make it."

"Why the hell should I listen to a half-wit like you? It was the damn horse—it had a weak heart, or—"

"You 'most rode him to death, Cain. Now we got to stop."

Eli straightened, stomping over to his own mount. Cain wheeled to see his brother unfastening the canteen tied to the saddle. He removed the cork, swishing the meager contents around, listening. Pacing toward the horse's head, Eli cupped one hand. "Here, Blue." His voice was soothing. "Easy, Blue."

"Hellfire!" Cain roared, driving the toe of his boot hard into Eli's hand, knocking the battered canteen from his grasp. The container clattered to the ground, a dark, damp stain spreading on the dust beneath it.

"What the blazes'd you do that for?" Eli yelped, jumping up, grabbing his bruised hand. "I was only tryin' to—"

"You was wasting water!" Cain roared. "I'll not have it—"

"You're the one that poured it on the ground! Damn it, Cain, least we can do is let Blue rest easy for whatever time be left—"

A nasty smile curled Cain's lips, the frustration that had eaten at him these past days on the trail at last channeling into an infinitely satisfying outlet. He looked from his brother to the sweat-soaked horse.

"You're right, Eli," he said, his fingers moving surreptitiously to his gun. His brother's face turned up to his in stunned amazement, that slack idiot's mouth gaping, wet, disgusting, in what was almost a smile. "I'm right? Cain, did you say I'm right?"

"Yeah, Eli. We'll make damn certain the worthless carcass rests easy." With a sharp surge of pleasure Cain whipped the pistol out, leveling it at the animal's head. A shot cracked out.

Eli sprawled backward as blood spread over the animal's temple and oozed into the dirt below. "You had no call to do that!" he roared, scrambling to his feet. Huge fists were clenched into weapons as deadly as any gun, eyes, usually dull, seething now with the lethal fury of a wounded grizzly.

Cain bit back the sneering reply he'd meant to fling at his brother and took a step away from that violent face.

Murderer. Eli had earned that title a dozen times over before he'd grown his first beard, and when Eli was in the heat of the rages that deepened half-wit into madman, Cain suspected the oaf could gut his own brother with the big knife he carried. But later, once the rage cooled, Cain knew full well that Eli would squeeze out copious tears of regret. He never intended to see Eli slobbering that way over his corpse.

Scorn and arrogance rose up to mingle with the wariness in Cain, but he managed to form his lips into the most conciliatory of expressions.

"Whoa, Eli, wait a minute before you get all riled. I'm sorry about the horse. Swear to hell I am. It's just that I'm fair crazy with needin' to get my hands on MacQuade. The gold. And you . . . I know what you been doin' under your blankets at night, thinkin' about getting under that pretty woman's skirts."

The fury in Eli's face diffused, dull red flushing up his neck. The hulk looked guilty as a schoolboy, except for the lust-filled curl to lips glistening with spittle.

"You don't s'posed to be watchin' me, Cain. Got no call to—"

"Damn it, Eli, don't you see? None of that matters. Soon as we find 'em you won't have to be diddlin' yourself under no blankets. We can't be more'n two weeks behind 'em. Ain't got no time to nurse along lazy horses!"

Eli blew his nose into his hand, scrubbing it on the stiff leg of his buckskins. "Well, you're s'posed to be the smart one! You tell me how the devil do you plan t' go chasin' after MacQuade with no horse at all."

Cain stalked over to Eli's winded black. "We'll ride double till we find another one. Maybe we can plug some

Indian buck out ridin', or there might be some damn dirt-grubber with a farm. We'll put them outa their misery, too."

"I'm not gonna run my horse int' the ground, Cain. I'm not." Eli's lip thrust out, eyes glittering with rekindled anger.

Cain's voice dropped low, wheedling. "Do what you're told, Eli, and maybe, just maybe, I'll let you do the killin'. Would you like that?"

Anger shifted to sullenness, Eli swiping one hand across his mouth. "Will it be a man? A man like Pa?" Eli's fingers reached up to the side of his head. Shaggy hair covered the skin, but Cain knew full well what his brother was touching—the thick, aged scar that had been there ever since their father, Bull Garvey, had driven an axe handle against five-year-old Eli's head.

Hell only knew how many times Cain had been tempted to finish the job for the old man. But that had been before Eli had proved himself so useful—before Cain had managed to maneuver a ten-year-old Eli into burying that same axe's blade in their drunken father's chest.

Cain smiled, remembering.

"It'll be a man mean as a snake, Eli," Cain said. "Just like Pa. And then, then we'll ride like hell and find you that woman."

Eli regarded the black for long minutes, then swung up into the saddle and extended his hand.

Pain.

It surged through Garret in white-hot waves, tearing at him with the diabolical glee of a blood-lusting Comanche. Knives of sensation seemed to slice beneath his skin, flaying away his sanity one layer at a time.

He shifted, restless, unable to open his eyes, unable to see. Dark . . . it was so damn dark. As if he were buried alive.

He tried to grope with numb fingers, to discern where he was, but his arm slipped from the flat plane into emptiness. Sick horror drove its fist into his stomach, and he dragged his arm from the void, clutching it close to his body as the terror swirled him away. Away to the last time he had felt that yawning nothingness as he had plunged over the cliff's edge on MacQuade land. Away to the living nightmare that had walked inside him for twenty years.

Faces spun in nauseating circles before him: Ma stricken, terrified, Pa blazing with courage, desperation, Beth helpless, caught fast in the jaws of the relentless horror only children can know. And the Garveys—Cain's devil face, Eli's broad, dull one, etched with an animal brutality that would have turned any sane man's stomach.

Garret moaned, battling to claw the images from his mind, struggling to lose himself again in the chasm of his pain—even that hell far preferable to the one now consuming him. But whatever demon held him in its clutches only tightened its sharp talons, dragging him deeper, ever deeper into the prisons of his own tortured memory until the stark child terror enfolded him like a living thing, filling his mouth with the taste of death.

Pa.

He sprawled battered and bloody upon the ground, crimson smearing his face as Ma clung to him, sobbing. His hands were bound before him, the leather thongs biting so deep into the flesh his fingers were purpling. His eye was swollen shut, his lip split from where the butt of Cain Garvey's pistol had slammed into his face again and again, until even Tom MacQuade's stubborn pride and oak-tough strength couldn't keep his knees from buckling. Dirt clung to the oozing wounds, the crimson staining the blue calico apron Ma wore, the apron that had been Pa's gift to her when last he'd gone to town.

Desperate and half-crazed with terror, Garret struggled against arms that held him, Eli Garvey's sour breath hot against his neck.

"The gold, MacQuade. Where is it?" Cain hissed, drawing back his gun to strike again.

"You're mad, Garvey. Insane," Pa gasped out. "Look

at this place—can barely scrape by. There is no damn gold."

"You and I both know better, MacQuade. You tell us where you stashed those strongboxes, an' me an' Eli here'll be on our way. That pretty wife of yours can tend those wounds, and nobody else'll get hurt."

"Like hell. Seen animals like you before. Murdering bastards . . . kill us anyway."

Garret screamed as Garvey slammed his boot into Tom MacQuade's midsection. Pa gave a grunt of pain, a horrible sob tearing from Ma's throat.

"Stop it!" she screamed, struggling vainly to shield her husband. "For the love of God, stop!"

"God don't love you anymore, woman," Cain chortled with evil glee, "but 'pears that my brother Eli sure do."

Garret wanted to retch. The man who held him captive had kept one arm locked around Garret's chest, the outlaw's rasping breath and harsh grunting sounds hinting at mysteries Garret sensed somehow defiled the mother he adored. "Don't you talk to my ma that way," Garret screeched, struggling to get loose, "or I'll—"

"Garret!" Anguish, fear, and helplessness raked stark claws across his father's rugged features, laying open a side of Tom MacQuade Garret had never seen before—a vulnerability, a core-deep love that the stoic man had kept so carefully hidden.

"Garvey, you touch my wife, and I swear to God, I'll kill you an inch at a time."

"I'm pure shakin' in my boots, MacQuade," Cain snarled with an ugly laugh. "But you know, that puts me in mind of a solution to our little problem here. See, we could go on like this till you was dead—me beatin' on you. You bein' stubborn. Hell, my arms is already gettin' right tired." Cain holstered his gun and fingered the steel hilt of the knife shoved in his belt. "Maybe we can get that pretty woman o' yours to see things our way."

"Garvey." There was warning in Tom MacQuade's face, lethal, killing fury. "Don't."

Ma was clinging to Pa, her face so white, so still, those laughing, beautiful eyes brimming with terror.

"Go 'way!" Beth's voice, shrill and frightened, cried out. "Go 'way! Leave us alone!"

"'Fraid we can't do that, girlie." Eli's voice was odd, almost soothing. "Till your pa decides to be more obligin'."

"Oh, but he will be. He'll crawl through live coals on his belly if I tell him to, once I got my hands on his woman."

Garret cried out, kicking savagely at Eli as Cain grasped a handful of Lily MacQuade's dark hair and yanked her to her feet.

"Lily—" Anguish, agony so deep in his father's voice it scarred Garret's soul forever.

Tom MacQuade struggled valiantly to shove himself upright, but a savage boot to the side of his face sent him crashing back to the turf.

A groan tore from his chest, his arms shaking as he struggled to right himself, his eyes bleary, fighting unconsciousness. "Damn it, Garvey . . . tell you . . ." Tom MacQuade tried to stagger to his feet. "Tell you what want to know if . . . just . . . let her go."

At that instant Garvey pressed the knife blade to Lily's soft breast.

"No!" Garret shrieked. With all his strength he slammed his head back into Eli Garvey's face, the horrendous sound of breaking cartilage and roared oaths ripping through him. He tore from the huge man's grasp just as Tom MacQuade launched himself at Cain.

In that instant Garret knew his father wanted to drive the outlaw over the rim of the cliff a dozen yards away, to carry both himself and Garvey to their deaths. But the outlaw had already flung Lily to the ground, the knife flying from his hand as he grabbed for his gun. In a heartbeat Garret had the knife in his palm, and he wheeled to his father's attacker, but before he could charge pistol fire shattered the air, crimson blossoming on his father's chest. Tom MacQuade took two more staggering steps, desperate, but another shot rang out, sending him crashing to the ground.

"Pa!" Garret screamed, flinging himself onto Cain Garvey's back, the knife slashing in frenzied grief and terror. The blade bit flesh, cleaving the outlaw's face, then his hand as Garvey groped for the knife, but Garret clung, fighting for his very life.

"Run! Beth! Ma!" He shrilled as their horror-stricken faces whirled before his eyes.

An animal roar sounded in his ears as huge hands closed about his throat, ripping him away from Cain. With a bellow of rage Eli Garvey flung him to the ground, those dull-beast eyes darkening with crazed rage as they fell upon the slashed countenance of his brother.

Garret tried to scramble backward, but fury made the bulky man swift, as dangerous as a wounded bear. He charged, jerking Garret high. With an inhuman scream Eli hurled him through the air.

Garret waited for the crushing blow of the earth striking him, waited for the bone-jarring impact. His arm struck a hard, stony rim, the bone snapping, but that hideous sensation was lost in a far more horrifying one as he plunged down into hellish emptiness, falling, falling.

His body slammed into something hard, the ledge halfway down the cliff's face. Agony speared through every pore of his body, the pain magnified by his mother's screaming and Beth's tormented cries.

They filled his head until he felt it would burst, until he thought he'd go mad.

His head exploded once, twice, with the sound of gunfire, and then there was only silence.

19

*T*he demons were stalking him again.

Ashleen could feel them as if her own flesh were being torn by their red-hot pincers. For four days Garret had been at their mercy. For four days she had watched, helpless.

Hell.

Now she knew the full meaning of that dreaded word.

She shoved herself to a sitting position upon the feather mattress where she had kept her vigil, close enough to touch him, to hear his faintest moan, feel his slightest movement. Dashing the tumbled curls from sleep-rimmed eyes, she peered down for the millionth time at the man lying beside her.

Moonlight filtered in through the opening in the canvas, skating merciless fingers of silver across Garret's face, cleaving away the defenses he had so carefully erected around himself, paring down to the horrible scars he had kept hidden for twenty years.

Time and time again as Garret had drifted in and out of consciousness she had caught hoarse whispers, words born of delirium painting for her the most merciless of images.

She had thought Kennisaw Jones's horrific tale on the journey to West Port had revealed the full depth of what

Garret had suffered the day his family had died. But awful as the old man's story had been, it held little more realism than one of Sir Alibad's tales when compared to the raspings of Garret's anguished voice—a whiskey-warm man's voice breaking with the terror, the grief, the shattering torment of the child he had been.

Ash smoothed her fingertips over his sweat-beaded brow, crooning to him as if he were Liam in the grips of some awful nightmare. But no such soothings would ever be able to drive away the hauntings so stark upon Garret's face, the fear, the guilt, the despair that this physical suffering had laid bare within him.

"N-no." His lips battled to form the plea. "Don't hurt . . ."

"I'm not going to let them hurt you, love." Ash pressed a kiss to his temple, her heart breaking. "I promise."

"Ma . . . Beth . . . they shot . . . shot Ma . . . shot them . . . all."

Ash huddled close, holding him, loving him so fiercely she would have given her life to spare him such pain. "It was a long time ago, sweeting. It's over now. Over."

"N-no . . . never over . . . never be over . . ."

A shudder worked through him, and he crushed her so hard against him she could feel the erratic hammering of his heart, feel the bindings she had wrapped around his injured ribs. He had held her thus a dozen times, as if she were his anchor in some secret storm. And she could only hope and pray that she had somehow helped him.

"Garret, I love you," she said against his hair. "I love you so much."

"Love . . . you . . ."

She felt him stiffen, draw back but a whisper. His lashes fluttered, opened, revealing eyes reddened with tears he had shed while lost in consuming blackness. Tears she would never allow him to know she had shared.

He stared at her long seconds, then shook his head as if trying to clear it. A ragged sound tore from his throat. "Ash . . ."

Her name. Her eyes stung, that sound the sweetest she'd ever heard.

"Ash, h-hold me."

"Forever, if you want me to."

"Couldn't . . . help them . . . Ma . . . Beth . . ."

"I know, love, I know."

"The Garveys . . . killed them. Threw me . . . over cliff. I fell . . ."

Ashleen's stomach churned at the image his words wove for her—Garret, her beloved Garret, being flung to what might have been his death—Garret screaming, falling, slamming into a ledge that had shattered his arm but saved his life.

Three days, Kennisaw had said, Garret lay there on a slab of rock barely three feet wide. No food. No water. Caught in the excruciating torture of fighting to live, knowing those he loved had died.

Kennisaw Jones had cried when he had told Ashleen of riding up to the MacQuade cabin after the massacre. Now she cried with him.

"Garret. I'm so sorry. Sorry you lost them. Sorry you were hurt . . . afraid . . ."

He shifted, and relief warred with pain as the mantle of nightmare drifted away from his features, leaving behind an even more devastating shadow of reality. He tried to sit upright and managed to jam one shoulder against the wagon box, arching his head back against one wood brace. His lips whitened, his face tinged green with what Ashleen recognized as nausea.

She lunged for a bucket, but he stopped her, his hand clammy on her forearm, his voice shaking.

"No. I'm all right. I . . . I am."

Ashleen stared into those wolf-gray eyes and doubted he'd ever be all right again. He let his lids drift shut, and when he opened them again Ash could discern a lurking shadow of embarrassment.

"I'm sorry." He said the words low, dragging his hands away from her, moving until a sliver of white feather tick was between them. She had held his hand for endless hours, had slept curled next to his lean, hard body. Yet this sudden break of contact reminded her of the wrenching sensation she had felt when Ireland had vanished into the mists of her memory forever.

Ashleen bent to retrieve a tin mug of water she kept near the bed and offered it to him, silent, waiting.

He took it, lifted it to his lips, swallowed. He winced, then set the mug into her palm, taking the greatest of care not to touch her. "Have I been . . . I mean, I've been making a fool of myself, haven't I? Babbling about—about what happened at Stormy Ridge."

Ashleen struggled to keep her voice soothing, sensing in Garret both raw emotions and badly stung pride. "You were half dead when we got you into the wagon. You were entitled to babble."

"Hell." Garret bit out the pithy oath, burying his face in his hands. "It was . . . the nightmare. Always have it when I'm hurt . . . or angry . . . or not strong."

Ashleen thought of Moira Kearny's fever-bloated face, of closing her friend's eyes the last time. "Some things stay with you forever," Ash said, her fingers clenching with the need to reach out to Garret, touch him. "Horrible things, hurtful things. But the beautiful and the good can also remain."

Garret gave a weak, bitter laugh. "Not when they're drowned out by guilt, Ash. Not when it isn't over. The Garveys are still out there. Murdering. Like they murdered Pa and Ma and Beth. Murdered Kennisaw."

She had waited so long for Garret's eyes to clear, waited so long for him to actually speak to her, to know what he was saying. Now she wanted to lay her fingertips against his lips, to silence him. She could sense where his thoughts were leading him, and it terrified her. "Maybe you should rest now, not talk. You must be—be tired."

"Tired? Hell, yes, I'm tired. Tired of dragging the guilt around with me day after day. Tired of the nightmares. While I was lying on that ledge I tried to die. Wanted to die. There was no way up the damn cliff face. Would've been too sheer to climb even if my arm hadn't been useless. I remember lying there hour after hour, listening. Wolves came. I could hear them snarling, fighting over . . . over the bodies. I could see vultures circling, knew that as soon as I was too weak to fight they'd be coming for me as well. So many times I nearly threw myself down the rest of the way."

He leaned his forehead against his arm, his face hidden by the fall of his longish dark hair. "I was crazy with grief. Was in so much pain. God, I wanted to die so damn bad. Wanted to be with Ma and Beth. Wanted to tell Pa . . . tell him I was sorry for all the hurt that had been between us. Wanted to tell him I was sorry I could never seem to be the son he had needed, wanted."

"You were everything any father could have wanted, Garret. I know he'd be proud . . . so proud if he could see you now."

Garret's lips curved in the most bittersweet of smiles, sorrow and regret lining his face as he raised it to meet her eyes. "The only thing that kept me clinging to that damn ledge was the memory of Cain Garvey's face. Eli Garvey's face. And the thought of taking Pa's gun and blasting them until there was nothing left."

Ash bit her lip, shuddering at the image, yet understanding Garret's thirst for it.

He raked his hand back through his hair, then curved one arm about his ribs, as if to ease the incessant ache that must still be throbbing within him. He was silent a long time. She waited.

"Three days had passed when I heard the hoofbeats. Riders. Hell, I didn't know if they were Comanche, Kiowa, or the Garveys come back to finish the job. I lay there so still, so weak, the sound seeming almost like a dream. Then I heard him. Kennisaw. I'd never heard a sound like that, before—a keening, scalp-prickling, horrible sound, as if someone had cut out his heart.

"There were other voices, too, angry voices, outraged voices. I could hear them, hear some of them retching in the dirt. I must have cried, moaned, I don't know. Next thing I knew, I heard someone shouting that I was on the ledge. That I might be alive."

"Thank God. Thank God you were."

"I didn't want to be alive. Didn't want to see . . ." His voice broke, and so did Ashleen's heart.

"What happened?" she urged softly, sensing that this was a cleansing for him, a baring of festering wounds to a sunlight that might heal them.

"There were about a dozen soldiers—later I found out they'd been sent by Sam Houston. They lowered Kennisaw down with a rope, pulled me up in his arms. The yard . . . I'll never forget . . . forget the stench of death. The blood. It all seemed so impossible, Ash. Like a bad dream. Outlaws. Gold. They'd been fighting the War for Independence in Texas for, God, I don't know how long. Kennisaw had spun tales about it every time he'd come to Stormy Ridge. It had all seemed so wonderful, so packed with heroes and adventure, courage and all the things a twelve-year-old boy hungers for. But none of it had ever seemed real until I saw the soldiers clustered around our yard, staring at the strongboxes laying in the dirt.

"Whatever had been in those boxes was gone. All I could remember was my mother pleading with Garvey, my father telling him to look around the place, see that we were barely scraping by. Where the hell had it come from?"

Ashleen hesitated, seeing in her mind's eye Kennisaw Jones's battered face, hearing that voice, so anguished, baring guilt that had eaten at him for twenty years. Was it fair to spill that knowledge to Garret? Would that revelation be a kindness to him, or one more cruelty?

Tell him I'm sorry, Kennisaw's voice echoed in Ashleen's head. Ask . . . forgive me . . .

She drew in a steadying breath and peered up into Garret's tortured eyes. "It was Kennisaw," she said softly.

"What the hell?" Garret demanded, incredulous.

Ash twined her fingers together, searching for the right words. "When we were trying to find you . . . on the way from St. Joe to West Port, Kennisaw told me. About what happened to your parents. About the gold."

"All this time you knew—about Ma and Pa and Beth. About what happened. You knew?"

Ash nodded.

"Damn that old bastard to hell! Why the devil didn't you say anything? Let me know that—"

"That Kennisaw had exposed a part of you you had fought so hard to keep hidden? If you had suspected I knew about your parents, about what you had suffered, would you ever have left West Port with us? Would my telling you have served any purpose except hurting you further when you had already suffered enough?"

"So all that time you sat there looking so damn sad, looking at me with those damn angel eyes, you were pitying me? Feeling sorry for me? Poor Garret, poor blasted little boy, as lost as any of the strays you've gathered up." He glared at her, his eyes silver fire. "That's what I was to you, Ash? Just another stray?"

"You were a man I was falling in love with, even when I didn't want to. You were the most sensitive, loving, gentle man I had ever known. Yes, I hurt for you. Cried for you. Ached for you. But I never pitied you."

"Hell, it must've been rich, watching me struggle to—to tell you—tell you about what had happened."

Ash winced, stung by his words, but she met his gaze levelly. "You know that's not true."

"Son of a bitch!" Garret slammed his knotted fist against the feather tick, his face a mask of pain and humiliation. "Well, since Kennisaw saw fit to tell you everything about me, maybe you could let me know what other goddamn secrets the old bastard spilled. That way I won't have to go through the torture of trying to tell you myself."

"Garret—"

"Damn it to hell, woman, do you know how hard it

was for me? To talk about it? To tell you? I've never told another soul—Christ, I wouldn't even let Kennisaw speak of it, because it hurt so much."

"You trusted me." Ash's eyes stung, her voice trembled. "It was the greatest gift you could have given me."

"Was it?" Garret sneered. "Then why didn't you trust me? Tell me—"

"I will. Everything." Ash pressed her fingertips to her eyes. "I just didn't want to hurt you."

"Well, you did, lady. Hurt me like hell."

And I'm going to hurt you far worse, Ash thought numbly.

"It was Kennisaw," she began, "Kennisaw who put the gold on your family's land."

"Kennisaw?" Garret gaped at her, disbelieving. "That's insane. He was lucky if he had enough to buy a jug of rotgut. Where the blazes would he get gold?" But when he saw the solemn expression in those sky-shaded eyes, a sick stirring began in his stomach, and he felt a sudden urge to stop up his ears like Liam or Shevonne.

"Kennisaw claimed he'd been on a mission for Sam Houston," she said softly. "They had waylaid a caravan of Santa Ana's men and discovered the pack animals' burdens were stuffed with gold. Houston needed it for cannon, ammunition, guns, but he couldn't spare enough men to get the money east to buy supplies. He decided to try to sneak the money through with a party of three men, men who could melt into the night—disappear, if need be. Men who wouldn't attract the attention of Mexican troops or the less savory members of Houston's own."

"You're telling me that Sam Houston sent a king's ransom in gold across Texas in Kennisaw's hands?"

"Kennisaw's. And two other gunmen. Firepower, in case they should be threatened."

Garret knew in that instant, the truth slamming into his gut like a cudgel. Betrayal churned deep, and he felt the blood drain from his face. "The Garveys."

Ashleen nodded.

"Why? Why the hell would Kennisaw bring animals like those down on Ma and Beth? He loved Ma—hell, sometimes I think he was more in love with her than Pa was. Why would he dump the gold on our land and then leave us to the mercy of those murdering bastards?"

"He didn't think you'd be in danger. The Garveys were going to doublecross him. He knew it. He took the gold and ran."

"Why didn't he run to goddamn Sam Houston—let him be shot to death, left to the wolves. Why—"

"The pack horses were so loaded down, Kennisaw knew they couldn't outrun the Garveys forever. Kennisaw dumped the gold on your pa's land, hid it, and rode for help. He never suspected the Garveys would track him to Stormy Ridge."

"You're telling me my pa let him do that?" Garret's head reeled. It was impossible. Tom MacQuade had hated war of any kind. Countless arguments about patriotism and duty rang through Garret's mind, memories of how Tom had told him to let some other bloodthirsty fool throw away his life over ideals. He'd just stay on his own land and grow corn. "No," Garret said. "I can't believe—"

"Your father didn't know," Ash interrupted softly. "Kennisaw thought it would be safer for all of you that way."

"Safer!" Garret raged. "For God's sake, if Pa had known, had been able to give them the gold, maybe they would have left Ma and Beth alone. Let them live."

Yet even before he looked into Ashleen's wide, pain-filled eyes he knew in his soul that Garvey would have killed them anyway and laughed while he pulled the trigger.

"He should've told Pa. At least we could've been ready. Waiting for the bastards when they rode in. As it was, Ma practically asked them to supper. Thought they were travelers—needed home-cooked food. I can still remember the way she was smiling up at them, all pretty and sunshiny, when they pulled their damn guns."

Garret's fist clenched so tightly the tendons threatened to snap.

"Damn it, why didn't he tell me? Why didn't he ever tell me? Twenty years I shared a fire with that bastard. Trusted him. Twenty years he looked me straight in the face and lied."

He wanted to see outrage in Ashleen's face, wanted her to share his fury at Kennisaw Jones. But she only stared, sorrowful, at the fingers clasped in her lap. "I think he wanted to tell you," she said, "but he was afraid."

"Afraid?"

"Afraid that you would hate him. That he would lose you. If what you say is true—that Kennisaw loved your mother and Beth, that he was your father's closest friend—" Garret felt her draw in a deep breath, sensed she was searching for words that wouldn't wound him. But it was too late. She already had. "Garret, you were all he had left. And he . . . he was the only one who could take care of you. If you had known the truth—"

"I would've hated him. I hate him now."

"You might wish you did, Garret, but you don't. There's no hate in you."

"He betrayed us. Led my family to the slaughter—"

"I'm not condoning what Kennisaw did. It was wrong. No one knew that better than he. When you were telling me about the day he found you, you said it was as if . . . as if someone had torn his heart out. I think Kennisaw had done so himself."

"He lied. Damn it, he lied. To me. To Pa."

"Kennisaw wanted to make it right with you. Before he died he begged me to tell you what had happened. He wanted to tell you himself. I think that was what kept him holding on so long, wanting to ask your forgiveness."

"If it was so all-fired important to him, why didn't you tell me as soon as we met? You knew all along I was torn up with grief over a man who had killed my family sure as if he'd pulled the trigger. Why didn't you tell me the truth?"

Her eyes glistened overbright, her voice wobbling, just a whisper. "What good would it have served, Garret? It wouldn't have changed what happened. Wouldn't have brought your parents back to life. Wouldn't have given you back your sister. All it would have done was steal away the only thing the Garveys left to you that day—Kennisaw."

Even through his own pain Garret could hear the anguish in her voice, and he hated it, hated hurting anyone so vulnerable, so infinitely sweet.

But when she raised her gaze to his it was strength that shimmered in those summer-sky eyes, strength and love, and so much understanding he loathed himself.

"Damn it, Ash. Damn it to hell." It was an apology. The closest he could come to one.

Silence fell. Long minutes fraught with pain. Kennisaw had betrayed him. Betrayed his mother. His father. Kennisaw had lied. But it wasn't Ashleen's fault. Any more than the happenings on Stormy Ridge had been little Beth's.

Wearily Garret dragged limp fingers through his hair, arching his head back to rest against the wagon bow. It had all happened so long ago. A lifetime ago. Why couldn't he lay it to rest?

Because it's not over . . . will never be over, a voice whispered inside him.

Until Cain and Eli Garvey are dead.

Garret's jaw hardened, his gaze sweeping the cozy confines of the dimly lit wagon, the shadowy, sleeping forms of Renny and Liam, Shevonne and little Meggie. Slowly he turned his eyes again to the face of the woman beside him. The woman who had taken the cold gnawing deep inside of him and made him warm again. The woman who had surrounded him with laughter, with love, who had terrified him with the depths of emotion she had stirred within his zealously guarded heart.

He let his eyes drift shut and saw painted in his imagination the cabin at Stormy Ridge, bustling again with activity, hard work, laughter, love. He could see Ashleen at the fireplace stirring a pot of stew while the little ones played about her skirts. He could hear the shouts and laughter as Renny and Shevonne scampered barefoot through the rich, fresh-turned fields. He could feel Meggie's hand slipping trustingly into his, clinging, so sweet, so warm, to his fingers.

And late at night he could picture Ashleen in his arms, so eager, so willing, he would never be cold again.

The vision was fragile. So infinitely precious he expected it to shatter. It was more than he'd ever dared hope for. He wanted it, wanted her, more than he'd ever wanted anything in his life.

He shifted toward her, a deep ache in his ribs reminding him of how close he had come to losing her forever. The thought of her stranded on the prairie, at the mercy of Indians, animals, outlaws, made his skin crawl, his whole body trembling with the hideous sensation of helplessness. Unable to stop himself, he reached out to pull her hand into his. Her fingers were chilled, shaking, and in the faint glow of the lamp Garret could see her lips quivering, her whole face shadowed with the pain of loving him, seeing him hurt.

He traced one thumb over the rosy curve of her lower lip, petal-soft, moist, agonizingly sweet. And he knew there could be no more secrets, no more denial between them.

"Ashleen, I love you." The words were simple. So terrifying.

"Garret, I love you, too. So much, I—"

"No, Ash," he said, laying his fingers against her lips to stop her. "Hear me out."

She stilled, and he sensed he had somehow hurt her again. He knew that if they spent the lifetime he dreamed of together, he would hurt her many times. He could only vow to bring her joy as well.

"I'm not very good at this, lady. This loving. It seems

to come so easy to you. But it'll never be easy for me, Ashleen. It will always scare the hell out of me."

"But you are good at loving me. Loving the children. Better than you can ever know. Liam worships the ground you walk on, and so does Shevonne. And Meggie . . . she trailed after you like a puppy dog before . . ."

She faltered, both remembering with stark clarity the day Meggie had ceased doing anything at all, save scour the ground for the doll she had lost. Ashleen flushed and fell silent.

Garret curved a finger under her chin and raised her face to his. Her eyes glistened with tears, shimmered with love, but the man he saw reflected in those eyes was woven as deeply of fantasies as the knight whose adventures she had spun night after night by the campfire. He wasn't any damn knight errant, wasn't some hero from one of her ancient Gaelic tales. But he wished to hell he could be. For her.

Sweat dampened his palms, and he felt as awkward, as clumsy as a boy with his first woman. Yet wasn't she the first? The first who had touched his heart?

"Ash, I don't know how to . . . to say pretty words a woman wants to hear. Don't know how to tell you how I feel. It's too painful, Ash. Too frightening. I should ride away, lady, and never come back. Should let you find some good, steady man with no goddamn temper. Someone who deserves a woman like you."

"I don't want anyone but you."

"Well, you damn well should. I'll make your life pure hell. Stomping around and yelling. And when I'm painting—God, what a son of a bitch I can be."

Her knuckles brushed butterfly-soft across his cheek, and she looked at him with so much tenderness he melted inside. "Garret MacQuade, you're the closest thing to heaven I've ever found. I love you. Even when you're stubborn and domineering and temperamental, and so . . . so very gentle . . ." Her voice broke, a tear spilling from her lashes to trek in a crystal path down her cheek.

"Well, then there's no blasted help for it," Garret said between gritted teeth. "Damn it to hell, woman, you're going to have to marry me."

"M-marry you?" She couldn't have looked more stunned if she'd just been struck by lightning.

"What the hell else can we do? We can't go living in sin in front of all these young'uns. And with the way I want you all the time . . . well, there'll probably be a dozen more before we're through."

"B-but your painting . . . you said you couldn't do it if you were tied to a patch of ground—"

"There are a million pictures to be painted on MacQuade land. And when I run out of those, I've got a million more in my memory—I don't need to see an eagle soaring to paint it anymore. I feel it now—that wild sweet freedom whenever I kiss you. I want to feel that way forever, Mary Ashleen O'Shea. If you'll have me."

"I'll have you, Garret." She choked, her whole face alight with love. He wanted to bury himself in it forever. Wanted to heal. She flung her arms around his neck, and he groaned as pain shot through him, but when she tried to draw away he held her fast against him, stroking her hair, the pain in his bruised ribs but a whisper in comparison to the precious ache of love in his heart.

She was crying, and he loved her for it, loved the feel of the joy thrumming through her. She raised her face to his, capturing his cheeks in her soft palms. "I want at least a dozen of your children, Garret MacQuade. I want them, want you, so much."

Garret's throat constricted. "I don't know what kind of a father I'll make. But I'll always be there for you, for the little ones. There's an old mission three days ride from Stormy Ridge. As soon as I come back I'll go there, bring a priest, and—"

"Come back?" The words sounded hollow, echoing through him. The eyes that had glowed with love were suddenly clouded, the lips that had been so eager stilled.

Garret felt something knot in his stomach, but he met her gaze levelly, his voice quiet. "Ashleen, I want to build a new life with you," he said. "To do that, I have to close the door forever on the old one."

He saw the flicker of fear in her eyes, saw the swift flash of denial. "You mean you have to finish your commission? Paint?"

"I have to kill Cain and Eli Garvey."

In the lamplight her face waxed as pale as the thin lawn nightgown clinging to her breasts. She stared at him, a frightened ghost, looking achingly young, vulnerable. "No."

"Ash, I have to. Don't you see?"

"See? No. No, I don't!" There was fire in her voice. "You say that you love me. Love the children. That you want a life with us. And with the next breath you're ready to fling that all away on some . . . some vengeance quest that could get you killed."

"I'm a good shot, Ash."

"I'll have Renny carve that into your tombstone! I'm sure it will give the little ones great comfort."

"Damn it, Ashleen, I have to do this. Don't you understand? The Garveys killed my parents. Murdered Kennisaw. What if someday . . . someday they came after you?"

"I hardly think they'd trouble themselves to trek halfway across the country after me just because I tripped them. We'll never see them again, Garret."

"You can't know that for certain, lady. But even if we don't see them again, Ash, somebody will." Garret grabbed her upper arms, forcing her to meet his gaze. "Don't you see, lady? Somewhere there is a little farm with children playing—just like ours. Maybe their pa has just sold some livestock. Maybe they've got a herd of horses that's their pride and joy. Or heirlooms, jewels their ma brought from back east. Or maybe their ma is just beautiful, like you are."

His gaze skated with agonizing love over her features, his memory haunting him with images of that face brutalized, battered, as his mother's had been. "Ash, their ma—she won't be beautiful anymore after the Garveys ride in."

He felt her shudder, hated himself for forcing her to look into the ugliness, the evil that threatened them, surrounded the Garveys wherever they went.

But she only peered up at him, her eyes heartbreakingly steady. "It's not your place to judge them, Garret—to be judge and jury and executioner all in one. I saw what they did to Kennisaw. We can set the Rangers on their trail, bring them to justice—"

"Justice?" Garret scoffed. "There is no justice when lawmen get hungry to gorge themselves on an outlaw's gold. Why do you think the Garveys didn't hang for murdering my family? Why do you think the law let those bastards live? They caged them up in their damn jail so there would be time to try to pry information out of the murdering scum—so that your precious lawmen could find the gold that cost Ma and Pa and Beth their lives."

"But maybe the Garveys gave them the gold to get free. Maybe it's gone now. If Cain and Eli went on trial for Kennisaw's death—"

"No, Ash. When the Garveys didn't hang, Kennisaw went wild. Three times he tried to break into the jail to kill them himself. The last time, the sergeant put a bullet in Kennisaw's leg and told him that if he tried to get to the Garveys again, he'd shoot to kill. Kennisaw took his chances with the law and lost. I won't make that mistake again."

There was something in her face that chilled him—stark disappointment, a kind of uncomprehending anguish. It was as if she were staring at his face for the first time without the mask she had woven of fancy, without the hero guise she had draped across his shoulders.

"You're telling me you're going to ride out alone, leaving us behind, so that you can gun down two men in cold blood."

Garret gave a harsh laugh. "Don't you see, Ash? They're dangerous. Evil. Killing them is no different than gunning down a rabid dog. They're animals."

"And they're going to turn you into one as well."

"For Christ's sake, woman, have you heard anything I've said? About what happened to my family? About Kennisaw? Don't you understand—"

"I'll never understand."

"Damn it, Ashleen—"

She turned away, sliding from the feather tick, the lamplight painting her flesh a soft rose beneath her nightgown. She grabbed up a dressing gown, slipping it over her arms.

"Where the hell are you going?" Garret demanded, feeling a sharp sting of unease.

"Out to look at the stars," she said, her voice strained, quiet. "To try to understand why you would leave us."

"Damn it, I don't want to! I have to, Ashleen."

"Do you? Or is this just one more way of running from what you feel? Running from me? The children? If the Garveys shoot you, you won't have to be afraid anymore, will you, Garret?"

He felt as if she'd slammed a fence rail into his gut. "That's not fair."

"Fair?" She whirled on him, all anger and anguish, tears spilling from her lashes. "Was it fair for you to say you love me? Ask me to marry you? You dangled all my dreams in front of me, let me touch them, then you snatched them away by saying you're going off to hunt down the Garveys. What did you expect me to do, Garret? What did you expect me to say? Good luck? Good hunting? Have a nice journey? Maybe I should pack up a parcel of food for you and check to see that your gun is loaded."

"Stop it, Ashleen."

"No, I won't stop it any more than you will! Damn you, Garret MacQuade! Damn you to hell!"

Razor-sharp chains seemed to clench about his chest, driving out hope, leaving stark despair.

"Where do you think I've been these past twenty years, lady?" he said softly. "Until you."

20

Garret sat on the wagon seat, his muscles aching from the effort it took to brace himself against the incessant rocking. Twice in the weeks that had followed his confrontation with Ashleen he had tried to mount his paint gelding, to ride.

He had wanted to escape the haven of canvas and wood, patchwork quilts and children's shy smiles. But the unrelenting pain in his side had forced him day after day to face the grinding reality of what he stood to lose if Cain or Eli Garvey's aim held true.

This time it was Ashleen who rode off ahead, her sunbonnet dangling down her back, her golden curls bare to the sun. It was as if she were trying to soak the sunshine into her very skin, the brightness, the light that had ever been her very nature a prisoner now of shadow.

A shadow of Garret's making.

Ever since the wagon had pulled out of West Port Garret had felt a sick dread at the thought of seeing Stormy Ridge again. He had regarded that certainty the same way he had looked upon Kennisaw the day the old man had wrenched the lance from Garret's shoulder.

Painful. Inevitable.

But now, as the oxen strained to pull their burden up the winding, overgrown road Garret had traveled a lifetime ago, he felt only a gut-deep sense of relief.

It would be over soon. Over.

This first painful sight of his parents' crumbled dreams.

This spirit-numbing waiting for the time he would have to tell Ashleen good-bye. He had promised to stay long enough for Meggie's saint's day two days hence. Already his gift to the little girl lay safely tucked in the folds of his bedroll. He would share this one celebration with them all, as if they were a family. His family.

Then he would ride away.

Only for a little while, Garret vowed to himself grimly. Not forever.

Why, then, did it seem so damn final every time he looked into those eyes that had broken the defenses about his heart?

Why did memories of Ashleen mingle with the echoes of faded laughter, the eager cries of Beth and Ma as they had dashed ahead to the piece of land Tom MacQuade had claimed for his own? Garret tried to banish the sense of forboding that had settled over him like a shroud. It was as if his mother and Beth were whispering in the wind, as if they were warning him . . .

Some things are too precious, too rare to risk losing.

That's why I have to go, Garret wanted to shout. To keep Ashleen and the children safe.

Yet weren't they in more danger from marauding Indians, and animals, and outlaws? From the dangers that might lurk just outside their own door? Weren't they in more danger from snakebite or storm or sickness than from two men who were probably halfway to Santa Fe by now?

No. His mouth set in a grim line as he watched the breezes riffle Ashleen's skirts against Cooley's glossy sides. If Cain Garvey suspected for an instant that Ashleen had had something to do with Kennisaw's disappearance, the bastard would hunt her down with all the cunning savagery of a stalking grizzly.

Garret had faced a dozen evil men in his life. Most times he'd parted company over the smoking barrel of his gun. But never had he confronted anyone who engendered in him the sense of soulless evil that had struck him the first time he had stared into Cain Garvey's eyes.

The road veered to the left, and the oxen turned, revealing a length of the trail that had been hidden by scrub timber. Behind the scraggly branches a shadowy form clung to the rise. Though it was still obscured by distance, in his mind's eye Garret could see the rough-hewn logs he and Pa had felled, could see every notch carved out by Pa's axe blade, could see the chinking of mud and grass that Ma and Beth had used to stuff any cracks in the cabin's walls.

Home.

He had spent the last twenty years trying to forget what this land looked like, trying to forget the strong lines of the cabin they had built together that summer of 1823. But suddenly he hungered for a glimpse of it—hungered to walk through the door Ma had kept propped open to let in the fresh breezes. Hungered to climb the loft ladder to where he'd dreamed as a child. Hungered to look up into the branches of the tree that had been his favorite place to doze and sketch.

A lump formed in Garret's throat as he remembered the day he and Beth had bolted up that final length of road, how Pa had swung Ma up in his arms in a rare show of exuberance, his voice gruff with tenderness as she had smiled down into his eyes.

"It's ours, Lil, all ours. You'll watch your grandchildren grow strong here, and their children's children. There'll be MacQuades on this land as long as this cliff still stands."

Ma had cried at those words. She had always cried when her joy became too great to hold. And Pa had held her against his shirtfront as he spun dreams for them—a common man's dreams of green fields and generous milch cows, of fattened pigs and chickens squawking, enough so all the MacQuades could gorge themselves on good food and self-reliance.

Even then Garret had not understood such tame dreams, his own already caught up in paintings so wonderful they would last for a thousand years. Yet now, as he listened to Shevonne and Liam chattering as they ran on ahead, as he watched Renny walking protectively beside little Meggie, he understood how beautiful simple dreams could be.

He cracked the bullwhip above the oxen's backs, urging them to greater efforts as he squinted, straining to see. But as the wagon rounded the last bend it was not the cabin his gaze fell upon, but rather Ashleen waiting for him on a hillock nearby.

She had swung down from Cooley, the gelding's reins trailing from one hand. Dark shadows clung like bruises beneath eyes filled with sadness, a testament to nights scarce of sleep, days weighed down with the silence between them. Wounded, vulnerable, she had watched him as the days passed, her face filled with fragile hope, as if waiting for him to come to her, to make things right.

He was trying to—Christ, at what a cost! Trying to make things right so that they could share the forever she so wanted. But he knew now that Ashleen would never understand that. That she could only see that he was leaving them, with murder in his heart.

Yet now she was regarding him with a quiet, soft sadness. Despite his eagerness to get to the cabin Garret commanded the oxen to halt, his hungry gaze caressing the pale curves of Ashleen's face.

Her voice was low, tentative when she spoke. "Sister Agatha always said beginnings should never be wasted."

Garret reached out his fingers, his heart seeming to burst as she put hers into his grasp. He helped her up into the wagon box, tying Cooley off to a wooden bow. When he slid back into the seat beside her, her face was angled away from him, but he could see a telltale droplet of moisture clinging to her lashes.

He set the wagon into motion; then, wordlessly, he curved his hand about Ashleen's slender fingers.

The tangle of branches obscuring their view thinned,

then broke into an unsullied sweep of cerulean sky as the team drew the wagon into the clearing where Tom MacQuade had built his home so long ago.

Garret's eyes devoured the patch of land—the cabin, built to last for generations, stood as if merely waiting for its mistress to return. A few wood shingles were missing from the slope of roof, while sprays of eager saplings had begun their relentless encroachment upon the land he and Pa had battled to clear.

The tree that had been struck by lightning had died at last, its massive trunk toppled in some storm that had finally emerged the victor. Yet the fence rails around his mother's garden still stood, as if the ground itself was impatient to be reclaimed. The sod stable rose like a miniature hill a little to the west. The well, its wooden cover only a little rotted by the elements, still beckoned those who thirsted.

Even the root cellar where Ma had stored all her precious preserves stood undistrubed—so much so that Garret was tempted to go down into its cool, musty depths to see if Lily MacQuade's shiny glass jars packed with berries and vegetables and sour green pickles were still stacked with loving precision upon her shelves.

Tranquil . . . it all seemed so tranquil. Like some sentimental artist's portrayal of perfect serenity. Only the small graveyard tucked away in a grove of poplars stood witness to what had happened in this clearing so long ago. Only that and the shattered fence rail along the cliff's rocky ledge.

Steeling himself, Garret forced his eyes toward the site where Eli Garvey had hurled him in rage. Meggie, her pink dress making her look tiny, delicate, was wandering near the splintered rail, still eternally searching.

"Meggie! Get away from there! Damn it, girl, do you want to fall off?" Garret felt Ashleen start beside him at his harsh words, saw the other children freeze in their delighted explorations and wheel to gape at him.

Meggie peered at him across the expanse of grass, her eyes stricken, as if he'd just split the sky with thunder.

Muttering a curse under his breath, Garret climbed gingerly down from the wagon seat and crossed to the little girl. Taking care with his ribs, he hunkered down and looked into those wide, hurt eyes.

"I'm sorry, sweetheart," he said, tucking a wisp of hair straggling across her cheek back behind one ear. "It's just that . . . that when I was a little boy I fell there, and—" Garret faltered, looking down at Meggie's small, grubby hands.

And when they dragged me back up, I wished that I had died.

Clearing his throat, Garret pushed himself to his feet. He stalked to the rear of the wagon, digging through the wooden chest where the tools were stored. He rummaged around until he found an axe, then strode over to a thick sapling, slamming the blade into its trunk. Pain shuddered through him at the impact, yet he drew back the axe again and again until the tree trembled, teetered, fell.

Garret could feel them all watching him—the children, Ashleen—could feel their confusion. But how could he explain to them the clawing terror the gap in that fence symbolized to him, and how he had felt when the child he so loved had wandered near its gaping jaws?

It seemed an eternity before he lodged the fresh-cut rail into place, as if it were a wood bolt barring a gateway to hell. When he turned away from the fence, his face damp with sweat, his side aching from the exertion, he was surprised to see the children still watching him. Yet he was not at all surprised to find Ashleen regarding him with quiet understanding.

He felt his cheeks heat. "There. Now you won't— won't have to worry about any of the children straying too close."

"No. It's safe now." Simple words. Yet they were threaded through with compassion, tenderness, pain. And Garret suspected she knew every fear he had suffered since he had laid his eyes upon the broken rail, suspected that she knew the shameful child terror he had not been able to quell.

Would he ever grow used to it? The way she could peer into his soul, see things he had ever battled to hide? Would he ever grow comfortable feeling as if she knew him, maybe far, far better than he had ever known himself?

It didn't matter. She was in his blood, as much a part of him now as his hand or his heart.

He cleared his throat, tearing his gaze away from her, shifting it to the quiet children. "Well, what the devil are you waiting for? I know damn well you nosy little gudgeons can't wait to see the loft."

"The loft?" Liam echoed, eyes wide. "You mean . . . there's a loft?"

"Yeah. And you're going to sleep in it," Garret said with forced lightness. "You don't think I'm going to let you sleep down near me any longer, do you? Kept me up all night with your snoring these past few weeks."

"I don't either snore!" Liam said, but he grinned as he turned to Renny. "You hear that, Ren? A loft! It'll be like sleeping in the sky!"

Echoes . . . it was as if Garret was lost in echoings of the past. Beth had said almost those same words the day Pa had pegged up the last rung of the loft's ladder. Grudgingly Garret had let her climb up first, but he hadn't regretted it when she had spun in a whirl of calico skirts and hair ribbons, her arms flung wide as if to embrace them all. "Garret! Garret! It'll be like sleeping with angels!"

Garret watched as Shevonne and Liam, Renny, and even Meggie spilled into the cabin door. He heard sounds of delight, squeals of discovery. Every muscle in his body tensed as he realized that there could be no more putting off the moment he dreaded. He felt Ashleen's arm slip into his, and he looked down at her, grateful for the warmth of her, the strength in her, thanking God for the miracle of finding her.

She waited, giving him as much time as he needed to ready himself. And when he started toward the doorway she kept pace beside him, her very presence more comforting than any words could be.

As he stepped into the cool, dim interior his heart lurched, the familiar walls seeming to close around him as his mother's arms had so long ago. The precious glass windows his father had given his mother for Christmas their second year on Stormy Ridge were grimy, yet all save one astonishingly whole, letting the boldest rays of sunlight filter through to the dusting of leaves and twigs scattered across the plank floor.

Garret remembered how glad Beth had been when he and Pa had laid the last board, covering the old dirt floor. "Now I'll be able to tell when I'm done sweeping," she had cried, brandishing the willow-twig broom. Neither he nor Beth had ever been able to see the sense in brushing away the dirt when there was only the ground beneath.

Garret's throat constricted as his eyes adjusted to the dimmer light, his gaze roving over his mother's curtains, now tattered ribbons stirring in the faint drafts, and over the stone hearth that had once been warm with her laughter. Some animal had torn apart the ticking of his parent's feather mattress to make a nest, but the thick posts of the bedstead hewn by Tom MacQuade's axe still stood tall. Garret walked slowly to trace his fingers over the carving at the top of the headboard. His parents' initials, and the year they had arrived in Texas.

His fingers froze as realization jolted him. This would be his bed now. The bed he would share with his wife. New babes born of the love they shared would be conceived in this bed, and he would carry them out in his arms to show Meggie and Shevonne, Renny and Liam their tiny brothers and sisters.

Life would begin here—new life, not only of the golden-curled children that were now just whisperings in his dreams, but life for himself. Beginnings.

Beginnings that could be snatched away forever by the blast of a single gun.

He braced one hand on the wood, leaning his face against his arm. He heard the sound of footfalls beside him and felt a feathering touch upon his hair.

Ashleen. Save for holding his hand in the wagon a little while past, she hadn't touched him since their argument. Now the feel of her was bittersweet, filled with promise, pain.

He turned, and in her hand he saw a scrap of paper, yellowed, faded, its edges crumbling.

It was the picture of his family Kennisaw had preserved, the picture Garret had drawn of them all when he'd been a child, blissfully unaware of how fleeting, how precious such moments could be.

"I saved this that night in West Port when you stormed off. Couldn't bear to throw it away," she said. "I thought you might want to hang this on the wall now, so that when you come back—" Her voice cracked, breaking Garret's heart. With a groan he crushed her in his arms, kissing her with a desperation that reverberated through them both.

"I will come back, Ashleen," he vowed into the cascade of her hair. "I swear to God I will."

He felt a shudder work through her as she strained him closer against her breasts. But she didn't speak, couldn't speak, her silence echoing inside him with the insidious chill of foreboding.

Candlelight glossed the fresh-scrubbed floor, the fire crackling on the hearth wreathing the room in a cozy glow. The window panes glistened like a bright Wicklow stream, while the goods that had been packed in the wagon so long were tucked about the cabin, giving it an aura of hominess that seeped into Ashleen's tired arms, filling her with a hollow sense of satisfaction.

Hours ago the giggles and whisperings of the children had stopped drifting down from the night-dark loft, blanketing the room below in silence as she had bustled about, setting the last of the things to rights.

A lantern had glowed through the open door of the stable since nightfall, Garret busy bracing the walls so that the livestock could spend the night safe from the wolves whose mournful howls drifted upon the wind.

Renny had been determined to help him with the work, the fragile new bond between the two agonizingly precious, tentative. Ashleen had practically been forced to drag the boy away by the scruff of his neck when it was time for bed, only Garret's promise that he would teach Renny how to shoot his rifle sometime the next day inducing the boy to trudge after Ashleen into the cabin.

She should feel relieved, what with their hard-won truce. Should feel glad that the boy was finally beginning to trust Garret's gruff affection and her love for the boy. But she could only think of what Renny's face would look like when he realized that Garret was riding away.

Wearily Ashleen emptied the washbasin where she had scrubbed the grime from each of the children in turn hours ago. She filled the container again with water drawn from the well. Clear, soothing, she splashed it upon her dirt-grimed face, scrubbing away the last traces of her battle with dirt and leaves and flyaway feathers that had been scattered about the cabin.

She dabbed at her cheeks with a towel, her eyes turning longingly to the plump new feather bed Shevonne and Renny had helped her settle upon the big bedstead hours before. Quilts were spread across it now, broken rainbows of color over crisp ironed sheets.

She had not made love with Garret since Meggie had taken ill, had scarcely touched him since the night he had rent her very soul by confessing he was going after the Garveys. She had never paid heed to walls other people constructed around their hearts, had always barged through them, heedless, as if they were nothing but mist.

Now she felt the pressing weight of walls of her own.

Going to the chest Garret had shoved beneath one window, she withdrew a fresh nightgown. Shedding her clothes, she let it slide in soft waves down her body. She fingered the ribbon that tied it primly at her throat, remembering the desire that had smoldered in Garret's silvery eyes the night he had stripped the gown from her, the way his hands had felt, eager, loving, driving her to madness.

She glanced out the window toward the stable and was surprised to see that the lantern light was gone. Instead it glowed upon the hill, casting shadows over the three homemade crosses that marked the MacQuade dead. She could see Garret there, a shadowy figure alone in the vast emptiness of night.

Alone except for ghosts he had never laid to rest.

Ash turned to peer into the small, cracked looking glass Liam had hung over the basin, and the face staring back at her was pale, sorrowful, afraid. Afraid of losing him forever to one of the Garveys' guns.

But if they didn't have forever, at least there was this night. One night alive with need.

Barefoot, she stole out of the door, the cool night nipping beneath the hem of her nightgown, the breeze whispering through the trees kissing color into her cheeks.

As she ascended toward the tiny burial ground she could see Garret more clearly. His back was braced against the trunk of a tree; one knee was bent, his elbow resting atop it. Sometime while he had been working he had caught his hair back at the nape of his neck with a leather thong.

The dark masses were pulled away from his lean cheekbones, revealing every plane, every curve of his face, a study in strength and sensitivity, raw animal power and heart-wrenching vulnerability.

Ashleen wanted to go to him, to draw his head down onto the soft pillow of her breasts. She wanted to stroke his hair and kiss him and tell him that everything was going to work out. Instead she let her gaze sweep the tiny grove. Moonlight glowed on the weathered crosses, the silvery rays picking out crude lettering carved in a childish hand. A lump knotted in Ashleen's throat as she read the single word on the marker nearest her. *Pa.*

She could see Garret's child hand clutching the knife, carving the letters, tears streaming down his cheeks. She could feel the sense of abandonment that must have streaked through him, could feel his anger, his agony, the question that must have torn him apart. *Why?*

"It's beautiful here," she said softly, wanting to break through the vast circle of his aloneness. "So peaceful. So quiet."

He didn't turn to look at her. "Ma loved it here. Sometimes she'd pack dinner in a basket, and we'd come up here to eat. Beth and I would play hide and seek. I always let her find me."

"If I had had a big brother, I would have wanted him to be like you."

Garret gave a soft, bittersweet laugh. "Beth thought I was Daniel Boone and Davy Crockett all rolled into one. Thought I could do anything. When the Garveys came she cried out for me. But I couldn't help her, Ash. Hell, I would've given my life, and gladly, to spare her."

"I know."

"When Kennisaw dragged me up the cliff ledge, when I saw what—what was left of Ma and Pa . . . and—and Beth, I passed out. Went all feverish, delirious. For a time Kennisaw thought I'd lost my mind. I'd scream and sob and fight anyone who tried to touch me. Wouldn't eat. I wanted to be with Ma and Beth. Wanted to die. He wouldn't let me, Ash."

Hand trembling, she reached out, stroking his spun-midnight hair.

"Finally I guess he couldn't stand it any longer. He scooped me up into his arms and carried me up onto this hill with the dirt all fresh and turned from the burying. Told me I owed my pa and ma better than what I was giving them. I was Tom MacQuade's son. A MacQuade. I owed it to Beth and my parents to grow up strong, make them proud. I owed it to them to live."

Ashleen cringed at the vision of the battered, heartbroken boy he had been. Tears dampened her cheeks for Garret, and for the desperate Kennisaw, who must have been half crazed watching the boy he so loved waste away.

"Kennisaw laid me down, leaned me against this tree, and put a knife in my hand. There were sticks of wood he'd cut, three crosses, lying by me. He asked me if he'd need another one."

Garret reached back, kneading the muscles at the back of his neck. "I thought about ending it. Taking the knife and plunging it deep. Knew it would be over, then, the pain, the grief, the loneliness. I held the knife ready, crying, but Kennisaw's words kept echoing back to me. I owed my family more than that. I was Tom MacQuade's son." His voice broke on a bittersweet laugh. "Christ knows, Pa had no tolerance for weakness. And killing myself—in his eyes, that would've been the most unforgivable cowardice of all. I hated Pa then. Hated Kennisaw for making me go on when I didn't want to, when I couldn't stand the pain of it."

He let his hand fall again to his knee, his voice low, racked with remembered grief. "After a while I picked up the crosses Kennisaw had made, and I started carving. Beth's name, Ma, Pa. It was hard as hell with one arm in a splint, but I didn't stop till I'd finished them all." He stared up at the moon through the tree's tangled branches.

"We had to stay at Stormy Ridge three more weeks, until I was strong enough to travel. I never came up here again until now." He was silent a moment, then he turned his grief-lined face to hers. "I miss them, Ash," he said in a tight voice. "I miss them so damned much."

Ash put her arms around him, feeling his anguish, old wounds raked open to the night. "Don't you see, Garret? They'll always be with you. Here." She pressed her palm to his heart, felt its precious beating. "Like I will be." Her eyes stinging, her heart aching, she pressed a kiss to his temple. "I miss you, Garret. What we have together. Come to bed."

He pulled away from her, eyes still stark with pain flooding with anguished love. She took his hand in hers and led him down to the cabin, to the warmth of patchwork quilts and children's sleepy sighs, and to the life in her arms.

21

*S*unlight streamed over the hillside, the sounds of children's laughter rippling through the trees. At dawn they had poured out into the fields, reveling with joyous abandon in exploring the place that was to become their home.

Only Garret and Ashleen had been subdued, each moment bittersweet because they knew that when the next dawn melted away Garret, too, would vanish, would ride out, maybe never to return.

Garret sat upon the slope of the roof, the new shingles he had used to replace those torn away by time showing as bright as a patch on a little boy's breeches. The hammer he had used had hung limp in his hands for almost an hour, but he hadn't been able to tear himself away from the sight of the little ones frolicking about.

There was still a dizzying amount of work to be done to get the place in shape, but Ashleen had insisted that the children be given a day free of anything but pure enjoyment. She had claimed it was in honor of little Meggie's saint's day, but Garret knew better.

She had wanted to give the children a day to remember. Maybe their last with him.

Garret tugged at the sweat-damp cloth of the shirt Ashleen had mended for him at first light, his chest burning with the thought of leaving them. He had wanted to talk to her about it, had wanted to talk to the little ones, but Ash had been adamant that he wait until the celebration was finished that night.

It would be better that way. He knew it. But it was so damn hard. Time and time again, whenever little ones had passed him, he had reached out to touch them— rumple Renny's hair, caress Shevonne's cheek, give Liam a fierce hug. He had wanted to scoop up Meggie as well, to bury his face in her sweet little-girl hair and hold on as if he would never let her go.

But the progress the child had made before she had gotten sick had disappeared. Maybe it hadn't really been there at all.

Garret winced at the thought of her once he was gone. He wondered if she would wander about, searching for him as she had for the doll. He had hoped to God he could fill up one hole in her life before he left, and he knew now it was safe to do so. Yet when he spurred the paint down the wagon track tomorrow, would he be leaving another gaping void to add to the silent misery in the little girl's eyes?

A flash of blue pinafore caught his gaze, and he saw the child disappearing yet again into the root cellar's door. Musty, cool, Garret could remember the allure it had held for Beth so long ago. Huge, fat pumpkins had been chairs and tables in a make-believe house; garlands of dried peppers and onions had served as crown jewels. The whole place had smelled spicy-good, the light from the open door setting the dust motes to shimmering like fairy dust.

It had been Beth's secret place, and Garret had rarely intruded there. Everyone needed a place to belong.

Thank God he had finally found his.

He closed his eyes, remembering the night he had spent in Ashleen's arms, the pleasure, the pain, intensi- fied by the knowledge that it might be the last time they would touch each other, love each other.

She had given of herself so freely, fiercely, demanding he do the same. And he had. He had loved her until they were breathless, exhausted. Then he had loved her again. At last they lay, their bodies twined, their arms clinging, awake until the first birdsong heralded the new day.

A flutter of white caught Garret's eye, and he looked down into the yard to see Ashleen, her skirts rippling in the breeze, an apron bound about her slender waist. There was a smear of flour on her nose and a haunting sadness in her eyes he knew he alone could see.

"Renny! Liam! You, too, Shevonne and Meggie-mine!" She called out. "Supper's ready!"

Garret's lips twisted in a taut smile as he watched the children scramble out of the woods, a frond of grass sticking out of Renny's red hair, a bird's nest balanced in Liam's hand, while Shevonne came decorously out of a break in the pines, not a strand of white-blond hair out of place.

Garret felt a tight sense of loss in his chest as he drank in the sight of them, only Ashleen's voice breaking through his musings.

"You, too, mister," she called, the smile she shot him overbright. "The saint's day dinner is growing cold, and Shevonne has been driving me mad begging to let Meggie open her gifts."

Jamming the handle of the hammer into his waistband, Garret made his way down the roof, swinging onto the oaken ladder he had found in the stable.

"You go to hell for lying, woman, just the same as stealing. You know damn well you've been worse than the little ones, poring over the store of packages you have stuffed up on the mantel."

"I know what every one of those packages is," she said with forced indignation.

"Except for the one I added this morning."

A smile played about her lips. A real smile, made more beautiful still by the blush tinting her cheeks as Meggie emerged from the root cellar and wandered toward the cabin. "I'll never forgive you, Garret MacQuade, for tying the leather thongs around it so tight. Couldn't even peek."

Garret leapt from the last rung onto the ground and slipped his arm around her. "Well, in a few moments you'll be out of your misery, lady."

The words fell out before he could stop them, and he felt her stiffen, then lean against his side, her head tucked in the crook of his shoulder. He pressed his lips to the crown of her head, breathed in the scent of cinnamon and wildflowers that clung to her glossy curls. Then he guided her slowly toward the cabin's door.

Mayhem reigned within—a racketing of shouts, arguments, Shevonne's shrill cry greeting them the moment they entered the room.

"Renny snitched frosting off Meggie's cake," Shevonne tattled, "and Liam stuck that bird nest in his bed! It's probably full of bugs and—"

"Enough, Shevonne," Ashleen chided, firm yet gentle as she went to the table Garret had set up earlier using crates and boards, with empty kegs as stools.

A silver-paper crown sat at the head of the table, each tin plate nested in a wreath of flowers. A chipped stoneware pitcher held a riot of blossoms, while a cluster of oddly shaped packages had been stacked near Meggie's place.

Garret took up the crown and walked over to the child, who stood regarding the proceedings with huge, dark eyes. He hunkered down to peer into her face. "Who do you think all these presents are for, sweetheart?" he said, unable to stop himself from tracing his finger down her small chin. "Must all be for me."

"No! They are not!" the other children squabbled, Liam chortling with glee.

"Do you know any little girl who might like to open 'em?" Garret asked, as if Meggie had replied. "They're fit for a princess, and I just happen to know where to find one." He took the crown and settled it on Meggie's dark curls. She stared at him, so solemn, so quiet. He would have sold his soul to the devil just to see her smile.

Instead he patted the keg that was to be her seat, gesturing to the presents.

"C'mon, Meggie, open 'em!" Liam shrilled.

"Open mine! Mine first!" Shevonne ordered, snatching up a small, soft package and thrusting it into Meggie's hand.

"Let her pick for herself!" Renny objected, his chin tipping at a dangerous angle. "It's *her* day, Shevonne."

"Stop it, all of you!" Ashleen broke in, laughing. "She could've opened them all in the time you've spent arguing! Give her a chance."

With a few more grumblings the children gave way, each prodding Meggie as eagerly as if the gift was their own. After a moment Meggie began to open their offerings.

The first was a fine square of lawn hemmed into a handkerchief. Crocheted lace worked by Shevonne's hand edged the fabric, a lopsided letter M embroidered in one corner. There was a jumping jack Renny had carved out of wood. The little man suspended by strings between two sticks would jump and dance and turn somersaults when the sticks were squeezed together. Liam had strung a necklace out of bright-colored buttons, while Ashleen's gift to the child was a woolen stuffed cat she had worked out of a pair of Renny's stockings.

Simple gifts, made with love, they brought back memories to Garret of Christmas mornings he and Beth had rushed to see what Father Christmas had left them.

At last there was only his gift on the table. He picked it up and knelt down beside the little girl. "Meggie, I would've given this to you sooner," he said, "if I hadn't gotten hurt. If I'd known . . . known it was safe."

Slipping out his knife, he snapped the thongs, then put the buckskin-wrapped gift in the child's small hands. Slowly Meggie unfolded the soft bit of hide, revealing what lay beneath.

He heard Ashleen's soft cry and the children's gasps as Meggie stared, transfixed, at faded yarn hair and a raggedy cloth face whose features had been loved away long ago.

"That's Meggie's doll." Shevonne glared at him, accusing. "You said you had to burn it up."

"Yeah, or she'd get sick!" Renny added, his eyes stormy. "She's been lookin' all over—"

"I know." Garret felt heat steal along his cheekbones as he glanced at Ashleen's stunned expression. "I just . . . I couldn't do it. Decided to keep it in my bedroll, see if—if I got sick."

Hell, he was babbling. How could he explain that he'd stood over the fire almost an hour, the doll in his hands? How could he tell them how hard he'd tried to add the doll to the flames, telling himself it was for the good of them all? And those days when they had all shunned him as if he were Judas the Betrayer—Christ, how he'd wanted to tell them that he was doing his best to restore Meggie's treasure to her as soon as he was able.

Three weeks. He'd promised himself he'd wait three weeks to see if he took sick. He'd cursed himself for a fool time and time again as he'd waited for the chills of fever to overtake him. And after the accident, hell, he had been in so damn much pain, he wouldn't have been able to tell if he'd been dying of goddamn cholera.

But as the days had passed, and he had healed, he'd begun to hope that maybe Ashleen had been right—that whatever Meggie had suffered from didn't cling like an invisible poison to the plaything the child loved so fiercely.

"You never told me," Ashleen's soft voice broke in. "Never told any of us."

"Didn't want to raise anyone's hopes in case things didn't work out. Thought Meggie could've worked through some of her grieving, not have to start afresh if I had to destroy it in the end."

He knelt down beside the child, brushing her cheek tentatively with his fingers. There were tears on the little girl's face, her lips trembling.

Garret's gut clenched. "I want you to know I took real good care of her for you, Meggie-girl," he said in a strained voice. "Kept it safe."

A sound came from the child's lips, so soft that Garret thought he'd imagined it. Whatever he had been going to say died in his throat as Meggie turned her lost-angel face up to his, those melting dark eyes shimmering with tears.

She reached up, pressing her soft hand against Garret's beard-stubbled jaw.

"Th-thank you." Her rosy lips struggled to form the word. "Thank you, Mr. God."

"M-Meggie? Sweet Christ, Meggie?" he choked out. He grabbed the little girl up in his arms, whirling her around. A ragged sound, half sob, half laughter, rose inside him and burst free.

The other children crowded around, whooping and hugging one another while Ashleen stood with tears streaming down her cheeks.

"Ash, did you hear her?" Garret called out. "Did you?"

"Tight," Meggie's muffled protest sounded against Garret's chest. "Too tight, Mr. God."

"Meggie, don't be a gudgeon! He ain't God," Renny began, but Ash quickly hushed him to silence.

"Renny's right. I'm not God, baby." Garret sank onto a keg, cuddling the little girl in his arms.

"Are so God. Said yourself."

Garret had the grace to flush. "You probably heard me . . . well, swearing, darlin'. It's a bad habit I've been trying to break."

Pink lips pursed into a pout, her delicate dark brows crinkling together. "Said *am God* when you 'frew 'way the rockin' chair. You said so. You did." Her lip trembled, and Garret could feel her stiffen.

An odd sensation swept through him, as though he were wandering on a river at thawing, waiting to plunge through dark ice. He was afraid, afraid of saying the wrong thing, of somehow jeopardizing this precious gift.

"That was a mistake, sweetheart. Tell her, Ash."

"Garret, don't you see?" Ash breathed, sinking down beside them, feathering her hand across Meggie's dark hair. "That's why—why she followed you, why she looked at you that way. As if she were expecting miracles."

"Well, I don't have any to give." Garret felt the urge to thrust Meggie into her arms, then quelled it. "I'm not—hell, I don't even think I believe in . . . in . . ."

Ashleen smiled at him, a smile that could light the way for a blind man. "You're holding a miracle in your arms, Garret MacQuade," she said. "Believe."

Garret angled his head to look down into Meggie's small face, awash with innocence, adoration. But no comfort took root inside him. Instead he felt himself tumbling again into a dark chasm of dread that seemed to engulf him, suffocate him.

He tightened his hold about the little girl, as if somehow to shield her from the insidious claws of the fates—savage, evil fates that had ripped from his arms another little girl twenty years ago, a little girl who had looked at him with the same unconditional love, the same blinding trust as the child he now held in his arms.

The first rays of sunlight teased at Ashleen's pink-calico curtains, the frying hotcakes and sizzling venison on the hearth filling the cabin with tantalizing scents of morning. Flowers still stood in the pitcher, the petals only a little faded since the night before, and clean tin plates glowed mellow silver.

Even the faces around the table were the same as those who had celebrated not only Meggie's saint's day, but the day she had again joined in the world of childish chattering and sweet laughter.

Liam and Renny were stuffed into clean clothes, their hair slicked down by wet combs; Shevonne and Meggie's braids were plaited to perfection, bright ribbons on the ends. Their best pinafores were smoothed in starched, ruffled perfection over their good dresses. But the faces scrubbed to a Sabbath day shine were so crestfallen, Garret couldn't raise his eyes from his plate.

"Mr. MacQuade, you can't—can't be leavin' us," Liam whispered with a telltale sniffle. "You can't be."

"Always knew he would," Renny snapped out, belligerence a meager shielding for the hurt the boy was feeling. "Our mas left us, and our pas, and all our folks. Why should he be any different?"

"Renny—" Ashleen's taut chiding was cut off by Shevonne's shrill cry.

"Shut up, Renny!" the girl demanded, her voice thick with tears. "Just shut up!"

"Well, didn't I tell you he'd leave?" Renny snarled. "Didn't I—"

"I'm not leaving forever," Garret said, forcing himself to confront the pain in their faces. He would rather have taken a beating. "Just for a little while."

"Where you goin', Mr. God?" Meggie's tremulous question was a knife thrust to his heart. "Up to heaven?"

"No, dammit, I—" I have to kill the Garveys, Garret wanted to yell. I have to find some way to protect you—like I couldn't protect Ma or Pa or Beth. He battled to steady his voice. "I have some business to attend to."

"See, Renny, it's paintin' stuff. Business." Liam bristled.

"Yeah, like my ma had business with that fancy man she run off with. *She* claimed she'd come back, too, but I never saw anything but her backside walkin' away from me. She didn't even look back."

There was a shuffling sound as Ashleen wheeled, turning her back on them, and Garret could see her shoulders quiver with stifled sobs. He wanted to go to her, stop her hurting, but there was nothing he could do but ride away.

"Renny," he said quietly, "all of you . . . I'll be counting the minutes until I can come back to you. I don't know what happened with your parents. Can't pretend to understand it. But this much I can tell you: Hell, I love you. Each one of you. And"—he paused, swallowed hard—"when I come back, well . . . I'd be real proud if you'd let me be your pa."

"Pa?" Liam's mouth rounded into an awed circle. "You wanna be our—"

There was a horrible crash as Renny leapt up from his keg, one booted foot slamming into it, sending it crashing to the floor. "Stop it! Just stop makin' promises you ain't gonna keep," the boy cried, his thin shoulders heaving. "It's mean, Mr. MacQuade. Mean! I never had a pa an' always—always wanted—" A most unmanly sob broke from Renny's lips. "Just go away if you've a mind to! And quit—quit lyin'."

He spun away, bolting out the door. Shevonne's face crumpled, and she whirled up as well, scaling the loft ladder. Garret winced as he heard a soft thud, the child flinging herself on her feather tick, giving way to a flood of tears.

But the worst torment of all was looking at the faces of the two children who remained at the table. Liam's impish features were solemn as he rummaged for the crutch they had painted those long, worry-laden days when they had feared for Meggie's life. His fingers closed around the dragons decking the carved stick of wood, and he climbed to his feet. "I'm gonna go be quiet near Renny for a while," he said. "Like you told me to when Meggie was sick."

Garret felt something knot in his throat. "That'd be real nice, boy," he said, then he reached out his arms. Liam flung himself into Garret's embrace, and Garret could feel the child shaking, could feel how badly the boy wanted to believe in happily-ever-afters and forevers with a pa of his own.

Gritting his teeth, Garret smoothed his hand over the warm golden silk of the boy's hair. "You take care of—of Sister Ash now," Garret said against the child's curls. "Promise me."

"If—if you're gonna be our pa, can—can we call Sister Ash our ma now?" Liam raised a tear-streaked face to look into Garret's eyes.

Ashleen's voice, strained, filled with grief and fear and

longing, whispered, "I'd like that, Liam. I'd like that very much."

Garret closed his eyes as Liam pulled away, heard the rhythmic thump of his crutch across the floor. Silence. It crushed his chest until he couldn't breathe, his mind roiling.

How can you do this, MacQuade? How can you leave them?

A tugging at his sleeve forced Garret to look down into a small angel face, wisps of dark hair pulling free from braids to curl about pink cheeks. He had thought he understood pain, guilt, remorse when Renny and Shevonne and Liam had fled the room. He had thought he understood how it felt to have one's heart ripped from one's chest when he had held Ashleen in his arms last night.

But now, as he stared down into Meggie Kearny's eyes, the emotions he had suffered increased a thousandfold.

Trust. Unquestioning faith. They shone beneath the thick fall of her lashes. "You're goin' away, Mr. God," she said, slipping one hand in the pocket of her pinafore. "Sir Abbledybab in Sister Ash's story went 'way, too. You gonna be slayin' dragons?"

Garret thought of the Garveys' evil faces, savage eyes. "In a way I guess I am, Meggie-girl."

She seemed to consider this. "Don't s'pose you got a 'chanting harp."

Garret traced her cheek with one fingertip. "Not many enchanted harps out on the prairie, sweetheart."

"No, but there's lots an' lots o' magic rocks out in my see-crud castle. Maybe you could take one of them with you while you're dragon hunting."

Her face was so earnest, those big eyes so solemn, Garret gave her a wan smile. "I'd be obliged, Meggie. Much obliged."

Her brow crinkled as she rummaged around in her pocket, then, with a triumphant nod, extracted a lumpy bundle bound up in the handkerchief Shevonne had given her the night before. "I put the prettiest rock in here," Meggie told him. "Tied it up all safe."

"I don't want to take your present, sweetheart," Garret said, starting to untie the knotted handkerchief. But Meggie reached out her small hand, stopping him.

"It'll keep the magic all inside," she whispered. "Then when the dragons come you can let it out an' it'll dee-feet them."

Garret curved his fingers around the hard object encased in the soft square of lawn. He tucked the talisman in his shirt pocket. "Thank you, sweetheart," he said. "I'm sure I'll use it often." But it was not the warding off of scaly monsters or even the Garveys he was thinking of, but rather other dragons—of doubt, of fear, of loneliness—that he knew would stalk him when he left Ashleen and the children behind.

Satisfied, the little girl reached up to bracket Garret's face with her hands. "You better go now, Mr. God," she said, her lips pursing. "The dragons are waitin'."

Garret hugged her tight, feeling the precious warmth of her, the sweet child scent of soap and innocence clinging to her skin. "I love you, Meggie-girl," he said hoarsely.

"Come back quick, Mr. God. Everyone'll stop cryin' when you do."

With that, the girl released him and turned to skip out the door into the dew-wet grass.

It was as if she had taken all the light with her, shadows clinging about the silent room. Claws of regret, of resolve tore at Garret's chest as he raised his gaze to the quiet figure who stood staring out the cabin window, her back ramrod straight, her golden hair kissed by the sun. He couldn't see her face, didn't need to. It was branded on his very soul—every delicate ivory curve, every angel-sweet smile, every twinkle of mischief and joy that had sparkled in those summer-sky eyes.

Christ, where could he begin? How could he tell her how much he loved her, how much he hated leaving her, even for a little while? He groped for the words but knew the quest was hopeless. "Ash, I—"

"Don't, Garret, don't—don't say anything. We've said it all a hundred times since that night in the wagon. There's nothing that can change the way I feel. Or the fact that you believe you have to go."

He raked agitated fingers through his hair, wanting to yell, to curse, to grab her and make love to her until they both forgot any world existed beyond this cabin, beyond their fields and the children Garret loved as if they were born of his own blood.

But painful as it was, Ashleen was right. In the end, nothing would change. He would still go. She would still let him.

He sighed, levering himself to his feet, wishing there was some way to make this easier on them both. But there was no way to ease this pain that was like ripping his goddamn soul out; there was no way to tell her good-bye.

Wordlessly he crossed to where she stood. "Damn it to hell, lady, I love you," he choked out.

She spun around, her tear-streaked face and pain-filled eyes searing themselves in Garret's heart forever. "Don't you dare die on me, Garret MacQuade!" she cried, beating on his chest with small fists. "Don't you dare!"

Garret caught her in his arms, crushed her against his chest. He could feel the passion in her, the love; and for the first time since the day Kennisaw Jones had pulled him up the cliff's ledge, he wanted to live—*forever*.

"I'm coming back to you, lady," he said, kissing her cheek, her temple, her lips. "You're going to spend the rest of your life fighting with me, making love to me, building a life with me. The devil himself couldn't keep me away."

He closed his eyes, wanting to cling to the beauty in her, the life in her, but it was Cain Garvey's face that rose in his mind, his eyes twin pits of evil, beckoning, ever beckoning him into hell.

22

*T*he Jesuit mission of San Fernando graced the valley like an old woman, careworn, weathered, yet beautifully serene. Garret reined in his horse and stared down at the tiny building that had served as a beacon of holiness in the rugged Texas hills since the last of the conquistadors had faded into legend.

He could remember his mother speaking of the priests there with a kind of wistful longing, remembered her spinning tales for Beth and him of the grand cathedrals and churches to be found back east. She had gone there, docile, devout, before Tom MacQuade had made her love him. Then she had closed the cathedrals and the comforting words of the priests into pages of her memory, sacrificing them as she had her sisters and her mother and her friends, sacrificing all she had known to follow the man she loved.

There had been times on Stormy Ridge Garret could remember her hinting to his father how wondrous it would be to have one of the wandering priests call at the farm, but Tom MacQuade had always had crops to plant or harvest, fields to clear, fences to repair. Any journey away from the farm had been consumed with gathering supplies or buying livestock at the town a week's journey in the opposite direction.

Never once in the years they had lived on Stormy Ridge had they seen one of the holy men who lived at the mission. Never once had Lily MacQuade knelt at Mass or received absolution—not that the gentle, laughing mother Garret remembered could have any sins to confess.

Hell, Garret doubted the holy men at San Fernando had even known Stormy Ridge existed, or the faith-hungry woman with the loving, bright eyes.

Until the day one had said words over her grave.

It had been a gesture of love from Kennisaw Jones, who had ordered one of the soldiers to fetch up a priest. Lily would've wanted it, Jones had said over and over. But Garret had often thought his mother would have taken a deal more comfort if either his father or Jones had brought her a priest while she was still alive.

That was why he had come here now.

Garret removed his hat and raked his fingers through sweat-damp hair. Before he'd ridden away from the cabin, away from the disconsolate children and Ashleen's sad eyes, he had vowed he would offer her at least this small comfort before he rode off on the vengeance trail. He would forge for her what fragile link with faith the wilderness would allow.

Feeling awkward, Garret dismounted outside the heavy wooden gate and fingered the brim of his hat, trying to frame what he was going to say once the portal swung open. He could remember his father's vague grumblings regarding the intolerance he'd faced from the priests when he had spirited his Lily away. What would the holy man say to Garret's own plea?

How did one explain a relationship such as he had with Ashleen to a priest who no doubt saw the world in dark and light, heaven and hell, sin and innocence?

I love her, want to marry her—hell, I've felt married to her since the night we made love. . . .

But I might be dead soon . . . either murdered or murderer.

Garret stared at the heavy iron bars strengthening the gate and cursed low. It was none of the man's damn business what had happened between him and Ash. The priest could just blasted well spout words from his little book and make his hand signs and raise his eyes to heaven to make their union legal and be done with it. For not even God himself could make Ashleen O'Shea any more Garret's wife than she already was. In his heart. In his soul. Forever.

If only he had told her that. Just once.

Garret started at the sound of creaking hinges and was surprised to see the thick portal swinging slowly open. Chin thrusting out with belligerence, Garret glared at the slice of the courtyard beyond the opening door revealed to him, and at the brown-robed figure who stood gratingly serene in the aperture.

A face that seemed to have caved in upon itself through the years, so wrinkled and weathered it was, rose above stooped shoulders. Snowy-white hair, impossibly thick, cascaded about skin dark as cinnamon bark. A hawklike nose still curved with a hint of pride between bushy white brows. Only the eyes in that face were young— vital, bright as yet, and full of tranquility and insurmountable strength.

Garret started, suddenly realizing how transfixed he had been by that aged visage. His cheeks burned.

"I am Father Dominic. May I be of service to you, my son?" The priest's voice was low, soothing as a mountain stream.

"No. I mean yes. I . . . I suppose so." Garret could have bitten his tongue off.

The old priest smiled. "Perhaps, my son, you might come in and quench your thirst with water from our well while you decide whether or not we can help you."

Garret bristled, feeling the fool, but as the old man motioned him to enter the flower-laden courtyard Garret grudgingly did as he was bid. The priest had settled him in a pool of shade beneath a gnarled tree and had slipped a mug of deliciously chill water into Garret's hand before Garret mustered the will to speak again.

"Father Dominic, I'm not here about me. There's a woman."

The old man linked twisted fingers loosely together and regarded him, silent. Garret was beset by twinges of guilt that reminded him of a thousand childish pranks, waiting for punishments to be doled out. He swore under his breath and gulped down a draught of the cool water.

"Blast it, I have to marry her!" he blazed defensively into the older man's impassive face. "I *need* to marry her. Hell, I want you to . . . son of a bitch!" He slammed his fist against a stone bench.

"You love her, no?"

Garret grimaced, his lips tipping in a wan smile. "I love her so much it hurts like hell."

"Is good to love so much. When the woman, she loves you back."

Garret's voice was hushed with the wonder of it. "She loves me back. I don't know why, but she does."

The old priest beamed, revealing a gap between his even white teeth that reminded Garret of Liam. "Then we will marry you." He rummaged around, checking a voluminous pocket. "We go now."

"No," Garret said hastily. "Not now. I have—have some business to take care of first." He was unable to meet the old man's eyes. "I want you to go to her, go to Ashleen in two months time. I should be back by then. If I am, you can marry us. If I'm not . . ." The very thought caused him the most excruciating pain. "If I'm not, Father Dominic, she'll need—need comfort."

"You are going somewhere that there is much danger?" The priest's eyes flicked to the tied-down gun slung low on Garret's hip.

"Yes." Garret fingered the butt of his pistol, unable to stifle a sigh.

"I hope it is worth it to you, my son, this dangerous quest. I am sure it is not to your lady."

Garret remembered Ashleen's pleadings, her ragings,

her stormy tears, and he remembered the resignation in her face that had burned inside him.

The priest was watching him, and Garret had the uncanny sensation that the old man could peel away layers of defenses as magically as Ashleen could, to see what lay beneath. Garret was sick and tired of people burrowing into corners of his heart that were secret, private; he was tired of that damn empathetic, knowing expression.

With a brusque motion he set the mug down on the bench and levered himself to his feet. "Ashleen is on a farm called Stormy Ridge about three days travel northeast of here. She—"

"Stormy Ridge? Is that not . . . not the MacQuade place? Was it not so long ago?"

Garret's lips thinned. "It was my father's place. I've come back."

"You. You are the boy . . . Garret. I remember."

The priest's eyes darkened with sorrow, one aged hand drifting onto Garret's shoulder as if he were still only a child. Garret would have knocked it away, but it felt strangely comforting. He had been so distraught when Kennisaw's priest had come, he had no memory of his face or features. But he knew instinctively that this was the man who had ridden onto the farm on the back of a donkey; he felt an unwelcome bond between himself and this man who was a stranger.

"I have prayed many times for you, Garret MacQuade. You and your mother and father and sister. I have never forgotten."

"I've tried to," Garret confessed. "I never could."
Unable to bear the priest's light touch another moment, Garret turned and paced toward the wall, examining the twisted vines crawling heavenward as if they held the secrets of the universe.

"You'll go to her," he said at last. "To Ashleen."

"I swear by all that is holy."

Garret swallowed hard, his eyes blurring as he stared down at his boot toes. "Thank you."

Again came that feather-light touch of Father Dominic's gnarled fingers, as if in benediction, again that sweetly stealing sense of peace.

The priest's voice sounded again, this time brusque, yet still infinitely warm. "You will sit now, for a little while, Garret MacQuade," he said. "Let me fill your stomach before you ride off on your journey."

Garret started to go with the old man, but Father Dominic held up one hand. "Wait here. Drink in the sunshine and the silence. I find this grotto nourishes me in a way Father Andrew's stew never could."

Garret nodded, sinking down onto the bench again, suddenly glad of the quiet, the solitude, glad of this moment to gather bits of Father Dominic's peace to carry with him on the trail.

Yet instead of the peace the old priest had promised, it was as if ghosts slipped from the shadows of the vined wall in Father Dominic's absence, the aged man's words setting up a gentle haunting that ate at Garret's soul.

He could see his mother, Beth, Pa, could see Kennisaw, his face torn by an inner hell Garret could only now understand. He could taste Renny's stark betrayal, touch Liam's fear, feel Meggie's unquestioning faith. And he could feel Ashleen's love as well, feel her loneliness, her terror, lying like a stone upon his heart.

I hope your quest is worth the risk to you. . . . Father Dominic's words seemed to echo through the little walled garden.

Muscles tensing at the subtle reproach, Garret slipped his hand into the pocket of his buckskins, his fingers closing about Meggie's gift to him. Slowly he withdrew the little talisman, rubbing his thumb across the awkwardly stitched lace as if to draw from it some of the warmth, some of the peace he had felt during that brief time he had spent in the circle of Ashleen's love.

Meggie had bade him unleash the parcel's magic to ward off dragons. And never had he felt their presence more strongly than he did now. With a tightness in his throat Garret unfastened the knot and spread the fabric open.

His fingers froze, his heart slamming to his boots as he stared down at the object glowing in his hand.

Magic. Since time began there had been men held captive by the magic in the thing now glinting in Garret's palm—men who had sold their soul to touch it, take it, men who had lost everything in a mad quest to possess it.

Gold.

Where in God's name could the child have found such a thing on MacQuade land? Impossible. It was impossible.

"Sweet Christ." The oath breached Garret's lips, and he dropped the nugget as if it had burned him, his mind filling with images of shattered strongboxes, blood, death—Garvey's fists smashing again and again into his father's face. He could hear Ashleen's voice as she gave him Kennisaw's message, as she told him about the treasure—a treasure Garret had assumed had fallen into the Garvey's hands.

Gold. Santa Ana's gold.

From the first Garret had thought Kennisaw's murder had been one of vengeance, payment for countless years rotting behind prison bars. Never had he suspected that Kennisaw might be the key to finding riches beyond imagining.

Riches that must still be hidden away somewhere on Stormy Ridge.

"My son?" The priest's voice startled Garret, and he spun, his heart thundering in his chest, raw fear tearing through him. "What is it?"

"Gold. The gold the Garveys murdered my parents for. Murdered Kennisaw for. It's there. On the farm. God in heaven, how could I have been so stupid?" Garret demanded, feeling panic jolt through him.

Scarcely realizing he did so, Garret scooped up the nugget and jammed it in his pocket. He dashed to where his horse was tethered and unfastened the reins. "Father,

I have to—to go. Ride." Garret flung the reins over the gelding's neck and swung up into the saddle. "Those bastards will be tracking the only person left alive who they think might know where the gold is. They'll be tracking me."

"Your lady, they will find her?"

"No! Damn it to hell, no!" He wheeled the paint and spurred it through the gates. The wind ripped his hat from his head, but he scarcely noticed. All he could see was Ashleen's face, so sad, so loving, the children so fragile, innocent, trusting.

Vulnerable.

Because he had left them.

"No!" The denial tore from him as he leaned low over his horse's neck, the vision of Ash and the little ones torturing him, submerging him in agony.

Three days. He had been gone three days—and the weeks on the trail had stretched so damn long, what with Meggie sick, him injured. A goddamn blind man could have followed their trail. Could have found them by now.

Pain and desperation slashed through him, giving him no quarter as Ashleen's beloved features melted into an image of starkest evil, hands stretching toward her as if from hell itself—hands red with the blood of everyone Garret had ever dared to love.

23

Ashleen flexed tired fingers upon the rough handle of the hoe, scarcely noticing the stinging of blisters that had long since broken.

Five days now she had struggled to immerse herself in work—brutal, physical, back-breaking work that would leave her exhausted when at last she crawled into the big bed. Work she had hoped would make her so numb she wouldn't feel the yawning emptiness where Garret had lain beside her those few precious nights. Work that she had hoped would drive back the suffocating waves of loneliness, the sense of doom that had crowded around her ever since she had watched him ride away.

Yet no matter how she had slaved over the patch of ground that was to become her garden, no matter how much she had thrown herself into bringing the farm back to its former state, she had not been able to free herself from the chains of dread that bound her. And she had spent night after night staring into the darkness, waiting.

For what? she demanded of herself inwardly for the thousandth time. It would be months before Garret would return, if he ever did. He would have to pick up the Garveys' trail somewhere, then follow them God knew where. She would drive herself insane with this worry, make herself sick. Already the children were regarding her with concern, as if they, too, were waiting.

Renny had been trying vainly to match her task for task as she worked; Shevonne had been sullen, resentful that her well-ordered life was being disturbed; Liam had wandered around as if lost, while Meggie had retreated more and more often into the "secret place" that seemed to give her so much comfort.

Ashleen knew that she should be the one to comfort the child, comfort all of them, soothe away their fears as she had so many times before. But even for them she had not been able to bestir herself from this ever-darkening gloom that threatened to consume her. Finally this morning she had thrust pails into Liam's and Shevonne's hands, put Meggie in their charge, and shooed them off to pick the berries ripening in a patch along the trailside. Only Renny had refused to be shunted off, his mouth set with a stubbornness Ashleen knew better than to challenge.

She had hoped at least to distract the smaller children from her depression, but they had been subdued even as they had trudged off into the sunshine, their silence echoing through her.

Even the songbirds that had ever darted through the trees had gone quiet, as if poised on the brink of something Ashleen found frightening.

Her gaze roved to the stand of trees that had seemed to wrap about the clearing like a comforter when Garret had been by her side, trees that now appeared almost sinister, as if jeering spirits hid amongst them, knowing how she suffered, knowing Garret's fate.

She wanted to scream at the relentless blue of the sky, wanted to curse Garret, wanted to plead with him again. Why hadn't she stopped him? Done everything, anything in her power to keep him with her?

Why hadn't he stayed?

The sound of a footstep beside her forced her to shove back her agonized musings to meet Renny's troubled gaze.

"Your hand." He said accusingly, pointing to her palm. "It's bleeding again."

She tried to muster a wan smile. "It's nothing. I hardly feel it."

"You'll feel it all right if it gets all festery. Mr. MacQuade"—she could see the boy almost choke on the word—"he'd be cussing a blue streak if he saw you."

Ashleen felt a knife blade of loving twist in her heart—for the boy, so earnest before her, for the man she feared she might never see again.

She ran her fingertip over the abrasion, thinking of how glorious it would be to have Garret bending over her, searing her ears with swear words to mask his very real concern. She'd never known how tender blasphemy could be before he'd come into her life.

"You're right, Ren," she said with a sigh. "I won't be any good to anyone if I can't work. Maybe I'll go to the well, soak this, and bandage it before—"

"Sister Ash! Sister Ash!" the sound of Liam's cries made her turn to see the three children racing pell mell toward her, their buckets spilling berries, their eyes alight.

"Somebody's comin', Sister Ash!" the boy cried, breathless, his bright-painted crutch all but skidding out from beneath him in his haste.

"Maybe it's Mr. God," Meggie chimed in. "Told him t' come an' make you stop cryin'."

"It's not his horse, goosey," Shevonne sniffed. "It couldn't be—"

But in spite of the girl's words, Ashleen found herself running to where the trail split the clusters of trees. Shielding her eyes with her hand, she squinted against the rays of the sun, trying to focus upon the figure just visible on the strip of road.

The roan coat of the horse blurred before her eyes, but there were no familiar splashes of white upon the animal and the man astride it rode with none of Garret's pantherlike ease.

Ashleen swiped her hand across her eyes as the rider plunged through a pool of shadow. Horror jolted through to the very core of her being. She had seen that face in nightmares, the scarred visage, soulless eyes, lips pulled back in an evil sneer over teeth that made one think of animals feasting on flesh.

Garvey. Merciful God, it was Cain Garvey. His brother couldn't be far behind.

Ash wheeled, feeling as if she were going to be sick as she screamed at the children. "Renny, the gun! Get the gun! The rest of you hide! For the love of God—"

For an instant the lot of them stood as if rooted to the ground, then, spurred by the raw terror in her voice, they sprang into motion. Shevonne caught up Meggie's hand, the berry pails crashing to the ground, spilling. Liam dashed toward the stand of trees a few paces behind the girls, while Renny darted toward the cabin door.

Ashleen scooped up the hoe, the only weapon she had to buy the children time. She had thought she understood the depths of horror, but at that instant Meggie screamed, Liam sobbed.

She whirled to see something spring out of the brush, dull-eyed, slavering, a giant beast that only remotely resembled a man. His arms were locked about Meggie, the child seeming so fragile, so delicate in his crushing grasp, it seemed that she would shatter.

"Don't hurt her! Let her go!" Shevonne's and Liam's shrieks tore at Ashleen's heart, the two of them pounding on the mountain of a man with their small fists, their blows as ineffectual against Eli Garvey as the batting of a butterfly's wings.

At the same instant Renny veered from his path toward the cabin and flung himself at Eli.

Ashleen charged toward Garvey as well, the hoe in her hand, desperation sluicing through her. As if startled, the big man flung out one arm, his eyes confused as one huge fist clipped Renny in the temple. Ashleen cried out as the boy fell, his head slamming against the hard ground with a sickening thud.

There was an impossible sound of something like regret from Garvey, his slack mouth gaping wide as he stared at the boy.

Still. Renny lay there so still, his face deathly pale as a trickle of blood rolled down his temple.

Ash shrieked, turning on Eli like a mother lion, raging, terrified. There was a thundering behind her, as if the earth itself shook with her fury. Dust swirled in choking waves, with massive equine haunches and blade-sharp hooves slashing inches from Ash's side. A shot rang out, shattering the children's shrieks, tearing a scream from Ashleen's throat. She felt a cruel hand knot in the fall of her hair, yanking her head back against a bony shoulder. The hoe flew from her grasp, leaving her defenseless, more vulnerable than she'd ever been in her life.

Her cheek pressed against the beard-stubbled face of her captor, and she felt the hard ridge of Cain Garvey's scar.

"Shut up, all of you," he hissed, pressing the hot barrel of his pistol against Ashleen's temple, "or the next bullet blasts a hole clear through yer ma's face."

Ashleen's heart wrenched as the little ones' sobs subsided into whimpers. Shevonne had dashed over to where Renny had fallen, dropping to her knees by his side, while Liam fell back from Eli's huge bulk and Meggie went still in the big man's arms.

"Don't shoot her. Pl-please, mister, don't—" Liam begged, scooting away from the Garveys, his face streaked with tears.

"Well, whether we do or whether we don't don't depend on me none, boy," Cain sneered, his lips twisting in a devil's smile. "That all depends on the man she's been entertainin' these weeks past a-tween her thighs."

Ashleen tried not to retch from the helplessness and hopelessness raking her with ruthless claws. "G-Garret's not here," she choked out, trying to think of some way, any way to protect the terrified children. "He rode out days ago. Looking for you."

"Shoulda stayed put. Woulda found us, hey, Eli?" Cain sneered. "But then, how do we know MacQuade ain't waitin' for you in some mudhole somewheres, sweet thing? His pants on fire, an' his hands all hot—"

"Cain." Eli's voice was wavery, his face oddly stricken. "The boy—he—I hurt him."

"He got in the way, dammit. Took a bump on the head. It's nothin', Eli! For God's sake, you done good. He woulda just done somethin' stupid, an' we woulda had t' kill him."

A shudder went through the big man, his eyes still fixed on the boy's crumpled frame. Ash struggled against Cain Garvey's grasp, desperate to get to Renny, but the outlaw held her pinned, helpless. She could only be grateful Shevonne was holding the boy, his head pillowed on her lap, her eyes fiercely protective despite her fear.

"Don't stand there like a half-wit, Eli!" Cain snapped. "We gotta find MacQuade. Get the gold. Damn it—"

"He . . . he's breathin' . . . the boy's breathin', Cain."

Cain cursed, low, savage. "Now, if this lady wants him t' keep on breathin', she'd best tell us where MacQuade's holed up."

"He's not—not here," Ash said. "I swear it."

"Mebbe we'll see 'bout that." He jammed the pistol harder against her temple. "MacQuade!" he yelled. "You see this? We got your boy. Got your woman! Got her just like we had yer ma an' yer sister! I'm gonna kill her, MacQuade, less'n you come out! Give ye a count o' three."

"He ain't here!" Liam cried desperately.

"He's not! We promise!" Shevonne cried.

"One," Garvey bellowed in Ashleen's ear. "Two. Three."

Something jerked her hair, almost breaking her neck as Garvey yanked her head back. The pistol barrel tore away from her skin, the weapon discharging.

Ash's knees buckled, and she waited for the sharp burn of pain as she tumbled into the void of death, but Garvey held the weapon in one outstretched arm, only powder smoke singing her eyes and her nostrils, the pistol having been yanked away from her at the last moment.

Hysterical sobs rose from the children, Ashleen's fury racing wild. She fought to wrench free, managed to elude

Garvey's arm. His fist, savage, brutal, cracked into the side of her head, sending her crashing to the ground. She slammed into the dirt, the breath driven from her lungs.

"That was smart, woman," Garvey said. "Real smart. Tellin' us the truth."

"Mr. God's comin' back!" Meggie screamed, her tiny face flushed with terror. "He's comin' back an' shootin' you!"

"No, he ain't, girl," Eli slurred.

A shudder of relief worked through Ashleen as she saw the huge man put Meggie down, but those unsettling dull eyes still studied her as if she were an intriguing doll.

"You don't have to worry 'bout him hurtin' ye no more now." The man swiped his hand across his damp mouth. "I'm gonna kill 'im for you."

"No! Can't kill Mr. God!" Meggie stormed. "Magic! He gots magic!"

"Well, it's gonna take more than magic to keep him alive once we get hold of him." Cain cast a contemptuous glare at the tiny child, then turned his attention to Ashleen. "But for now, woman, you know you been keepin' my brother here up nights with wantin' you."

Bile rose in Ashleen's throat, and she shoved herself to a sitting position, terror all but paralyzing her as she stared into the lust-filled face of Eli Garvey.

"Yes, ma'am, my brother, he been doin' some wicked things to himself under his blankets at night—that pretty face o' yours just dancin' in his mind. I promised him once we found you, well, you an' Eli could do a little entertainin' of your own."

The huge man had turned his attention from Meggie, his face suffusing with ugly color. "Cain promised me," he said licking wet lips. "Some entertainin'."

Ashleen closed her eyes against the horror of it, her fists clenching at the memory of Garret's tender caresses, her stomach pitching at the thought of Shevonne and Meggie and Liam being subjected to witnessing the atrocities the Garveys had planned for her.

She blinked back tears, not too proud to beg. "Please,"

she whispered. "Do—do whatever you want to me, but please, for God's sake, don't . . . don't let the children . . . see it."

Cain sneered, one hand groping at her breast. "Be an education for 'em, lady. Mebbe we'll even let these boys o' yers take a turn after Eli's done."

"No! Sister Ash! No!" Liam shrilled, hysterical, scrambling over to cling to her arm. Cain cursed, backhanding the boy, sending him flying. Ashleen flung herself to protect the child as Cain drew his hand back again, but something stopped it in midswing. Garvey cursed, and Ashleen looked up to see Eli towering over his brother, one meaty hand locked about Cain's wrist.

"No hurtin' kids. You promised." Fury simmered in Eli Garvey's eyes.

"Let go of me, you ass! I—" Cain started to swear, looking into Eli's face. Ashleen saw a subtle shift, as if even this scar-faced monster of a man feared his brother.

"Please." She turned her gaze on Eli. "If you don't—don't want to hurt the children, don't let them see—lock them away where they won't have to . . ."

For a moment Ashleen thought her plea had been futile. Then Shevonne's whimper made Eli wince. "Where? Where can I put 'em where they ain't gonna get hurt?"

Desperate, Ashleen tried to think of somewhere without windows where they wouldn't have to endure her suffering. Somewhere there was a chance they might be able to get away, run. The root cellar rose in her mind—one of the projects there had been no time for, the wood door half rotted, the hinges loose. Rickety enough so Renny might be able to burst free once he regained consciousness, free after this horror was over.

Ash swallowed hard, fearing it might also become the children's grave. "The—the root cellar. Shevonne! Take Meggie and Liam into the root cellar."

"No! Not—not leaving you!" Liam wailed, clinging to her, his tears dampening her sleeve.

"Go, Liam! Now!" Ash gave him a fierce shake, afraid that Cain Garvey would grow impatient, change his mind. She hated herself as his eyes widened with stark betrayal. The child scrambled back, stunned. "Liam, go!"

With a shuddering sob the child crawled to his crutch and levered himself painfully to his feet. Eli started toward Renny's limp form, obviously intending to scoop the boy up in his arms, but Cain stopped him.

"No. Leave the boy here less'n yer lady friend needs a little encouragin'. The brat's out cold anyway. Ain't gonna see nothin' fer a week the way you slammed him, Eli."

"Don't say that, Cain! Blast it, don't—"

There was real distress in Eli Garvey's voice, a distress that stunned Ash. But instead of defying his brother, the big man only herded the other children toward the cellar, glowering.

Ashleen closed her eyes as the sounds of the children's crying faded, the thud of the root cellar door being jammed shut drowning out their sobs as surely as the closing of a casket's lid.

She opened her eyes to see all traces of humanity again banished from Eli's face, the huge man lumbering toward her, his eyes fixed on her breasts. She had thought —almost hoped—that Renny's injury had somehow unsettled the man, but if anything it gave his face a brittle glaze of madness, his eyes wild, drool running from the corner of his mouth.

Ash cast a last glance at Renny. The boy had moved just a little. She prayed he wouldn't wake until the Garveys had finished with her. She closed her eyes, remembering Garret when she had come to him that magical night, remembering his touch, his kiss, so tender, loving. Gone now. Forever.

"I put 'em away like you said," Eli told her, his fingers fumbling at the buttons of his trousers. "You got to do what I want now. Stand up, pretty lady, and let me see what you got under that there dress."

Ashleen couldn't stop herself from shrinking back. She glanced at the hoe, gauging her chances of reaching it, using it against the two men. It was hopeless, pitted against a gun and enough brute strength to crack her neck at will. And there was Renny sprawled on the ground, defenseless, seeming littler somehow, more a child than he had in months. She dared not do anything that might put the boy in further jeopardy.

She started at a swishing sound as Cain pulled a bowie knife from his boot top, the wicked blade glinting blue in the sun, his eyes flicking to Renny with unholy glee. "You an' Eli had an agreement, slut. You wouldn't be thinkin' on goin' back on it, would you? Mebbe we should wake this boy o' yers up after all."

"No! No, please . . ." Ashleen forced herself to her feet, her numb fingers unfastening her bodice. The fragile white fabric of her chemise lay beneath, and she tugged at the pink ribbons binding it together, the strip of bare flesh between widening, feeling somehow soiled beneath Eli Garvey's gaze.

Eli licked his lips, his fingers closing about the lacy chemise edge, pulling it to the side until her breast was naked.

"Damn, yer pretty, woman. Real pretty, ain't she, Cai—"

At that instant the world exploded, gunfire blazing.

"What the hell—"

Eli spun toward the sound, and Ash screamed as the man stumbled back, his chest a mass of crimson, eyes wild with pain. She wheeled to catch a glimpse of feral bronzed features, cold gray eyes alight with murder.

Garret. Sweet God, he was on the roof. His feet were braced wide on the shingled slope, guns spitting fire.

For a frozen instant she thought he was a mirage, a vision conjured of her own anguished terror. But no mere chimera could have such hate in his eyes, such killing fury. Such desperate, desperate love.

She took a running step toward him as the weapon fired again, a guttural sound coming from behind her. Cain Garvey staggered, and she sobbed in relief, certain the outlaw had met his brother's fate. But somehow the man righted himself, his hand knotting in her skirts, dragging her back into hell.

Something wet and sticky dampened her shoulder, the stench of blood filling her nostrils as Garvey used her body as a shield. A knife blade bit into the tender flesh at her throat, a stinging cut appearing where her pulse beat.

"Put down the gun, MacQuade."

"No, Garret . . . don't . . . don't . . ."

"Your brother's bleeding to death, Garvey, if he's not dead already. And so are you."

Cain cast a contemptuous glance down at Eli, then flashed it back to Garret. "Don't brag on your aim, MacQuade. I've had worse cuts off'n women clawin' beneath me. As for Eli, you saved me the trouble o' wasting an ounce o' lead. He's had his uses, but he's got a powerful wicked temper, an' he's been gettin' t' be a bit of a burden. Couldn't afford t' carry him forever."

Cold. The man's voice was so cold, calculating, evil, a devil's voice jeering from the pit of hell.

"Soon as Santa Ana's gold was in my hands, I was gonna kill him anyways. As it is, I can just concentrate on havin' my fun now with your little lady."

"Cut her and I'll kill you, Garvey—an inch at a time."

"You'd have t' get hold o' me first. And I don't think you'll do that, MacQuade. Not if you have to blast your way through your slut's body to get to me. Remember what I did to your mama, boy? You thought you could save her, too."

A muscle ticked in Garret's jaw, his whole body taut, his hands rock-steady on his guns. "Let the woman go." Ash sensed he was judging the odds of being able to drill a bullet through Garvey's skull without missing and hitting her. It was as if Garvey knew that, too. Knew Garret would never risk it. He chortled, his breath hot against her cheek.

"Where ye think I should start carvin', MacQuade? Her face? Like you done to me? Ain't got much use for her face anyway, do ye, MacQuade? No, it's the rest o' her yer hungry for."

"Garvey, I'm warning you. Don't—"

"You ain't in no position to be givin' orders. No, sirree, you ain't."

Ash drew in a shuddery breath as Garvey skimmed the blade up the curve of her jaw, laying its razor-sharp edge against her left cheek.

"How you think this lady's gonna look with her face all laid open? How you think she's gonna look with her face so slashed up you won't even be able t' look at her, let alone touch her, boy?"

Ash's breath hissed between her teeth as he pressed the blade a whisper harder.

She heard Garret curse.

"Put the gun down, MacQuade, or the woman bleeds."

Ashleen saw Garret warring with himself and knew he must be thinking his weapons were their only chance. If he surrendered them, he and the children would die as well.

"Don't do it, Garret! The little ones—they need—" She gritted her teeth as Garvey made the knife tip bite flesh, a slight burning stinging her cheek. She felt a warm droplet of blood gather and trickle down.

"Stop it, Garvey! Goddamn it!" Garret took a step toward them, his voice threaded through with desperation, hopelessness, raw fury. "The gun's down, damn it. It's down." Slowly he lowered the pistols, his eyes locking with Ashleen's. She could feel the pain in him, the despair, the crushing guilt.

"Garret, don't—"

"Damn it, I can't let him—let him cut you, lady." She saw Garret's eyes slide closed for a second. "I can't—"

"MacQuade, yer bringin' tears t' my eyes. Now drop them guns and get down off that roof. Slow like. Real slow."

The thud of the guns hitting the dirt was like a death knell, and Ash felt tears stream down her cheeks as she watched Garret make his way toward the roof's edge.

"That's right, MacQuade. Do it slow an' easy, an' I might kill your woman quick, 'stead of long an' lingerin' like when we've tended t' our business. Spent some time with the Comanch', ye know, an' learned . . . hell, I learned how t' draw out pain like a fiddle player tightenin' a string. Ye could ask yer friend Kennisaw how damn good I am at dishin' out pure agonies, 'ceptin' he was coward enough t' die of 'em.''

Ash saw a muscle tick in Garret's jaw, felt the rage building in him, lava-hot, just beneath the surface. She knew Garvey was trying to bait him into doing something rash, something foolish.

Somehow Garret managed to cling to what small rein he held on his temper.

"Let her go, Garvey," he said levelly. "It's me you want."

Cain barked a laugh. "An' I could flay yer skin off a layer at a time, an' you wouldn't tell me the sky's blue, would ye, MacQuade? Naw, yer jest like yer pa. Stubborn as hell."

"I'll give you what you want, Garvey. If you let Ashleen and the children go. Give them a good head start, and—"

"You think I'm stupid, MacQuade? I ain't Eli—ain't a damn half-wit. I let her go, you'll jest grit yer teeth an' let me kill ye any way I want. Ye won't even give me the pleasure o' hearin' ye scream. Naw, sir. You got anythin' to say 'bout the gold, boy, you'd best do it now. I been sharpenin' this knife for three nights jest waitin' t' get hold o' yer woman. An' I'm gettin' real jittery, boy. Yep. Jest real anxious t' see her bleed."

"Damn it, I told you, I have—have what you want. The gold."

Ashleen felt panic roiling within her, knowing that Garret was wagering their lives upon a lie—a lie that would further infuriate the animal who held her in its grasp.

"Prove it." Garvey snarled. "Here."

Ashleen held her breath, certain that his fury would break free, but Garret's voice was cool, deceptively calm, threaded through with danger.

"There's a nugget of pure ore in my pocket right now, Garvey," he said, stopping inches from the roof's edge.

"Yeah, right next to your palm gun."

"You know damn well I wouldn't shoot with Ashleen in front of you. You want me to prove I know where the gold is. I'm willing to do it."

Garvey shifted the knife, the point digging into the soft flesh under Ashleen's chin. "All right, MacQuade. But mebbe we'll up the stakes a little. One false move an' I'll slit her throat an' be done with it. Understand?"

With excruciating care Garret slipped his hand into his pocket, Ashleen's heart threatening to beat its way out of her chest. A thousand prayers roiled inside her, her mind whirling as she struggled desperately to figure out what wild plan Garret had conjured up, what crazed move he was going to make in an attempt to save her.

But he only met Cain Garvey's gaze, drawing his knotted fist from the pocket, his face impassive, eyes death cold.

"Throw that down here, whatever the hell it is. Now," Garvey commanded.

With agonizing slowness Garret opened his fingers, casting an object into the dirt.

Her eyes fixed upon it, locking on the thing Garret had thrown at the same instant Cain's did. She felt the outlaw stiffen, heard his bellow of triumph as the sunlight glistened upon a chunk of gold as big as Meggie's fist. His grasp on her loosened, the knife slipping inches away from her flesh.

"G-gold," Ashleen choked out, stunned. "Merciful God, it's—"

"Ash!" Garret's cry of warning made her start, tearing against Garvey's grasp. In that frozen heartbeat she knew what Garret wanted her to do, and she dived instinctively against the outlaw's arms.

Greed and gold lust mingled to slow Cain's reflexes as Garret launched himself from the edge of the rooftop.

The knife scraped across Ashleen's shoulder, and she felt blood well in its wake as she pulled free, just as Garret slammed full-length into Garvey.

She heard Garret grunt in pain, saw the knife glisten-

ing with fresh blood—his blood—the two men locked in
death grips, battling viciously, their faces contorted in
masks of fury and hate that had spanned twenty years.

Ash scrambled toward Garret's guns, her fingers closing about one, bringing it to bear, but even had she been
a crack shot there was no way she could fire as the two
battled over the knife.

"G-Garret—get away from him. The gun—I have—"

Garret's eyes shifted for a heartbeat.

That was all Garvey needed.

With a bloodcurdling cry of triumph the man drove
the knife down. At the last instant Garret attempted to
lunge out of its path, but even his lightning reflexes
couldn't save him entirely.

A low groan ripped from his throat as the knife
plunged into his thigh, the force driving him to his knees.
Lips pulled back in ghoulish pleasure, Cain wrenched at
the blade, tearing a cry from Garret as he battled to grasp
the knife hilt.

At that instant Ashleen fired. The bullet blazed past
Garvey, the outlaw wheeling on her with a hellish glare.
She levered back the hammer, but before she could fire
something lashed out from behind her. She spun to see a
white-faced Renny, his fingers clasped around the handle
of the hoe.

Barely able to stay on his feet, the boy struck at Cain,
the hoe biting into Garvey's shoulder. Garvey staggered,
blood seeping from a wound in one arm.

The man slammed his fist into the boy's stomach,
driving him back as Garvey reached for his own gun.
Ash's heart stopped as she heard Renny cry out. She saw
Garret rip the knife free of his flesh and hurl himself at
Cain.

Death. It groped for him with skeletal fingers as
Garvey took aim.

Suddenly a movement caught Ashleen's eye. Eli
Garvey reared up like some creature spawned of hell,
blood dribbling from his mouth, his eyes glazed. Ash
screamed as he grabbed Garret by the throat, certain he

was going to kill him, but the man yanked Garret upward, hurling him out of the way as though he were Meggie's rag doll. Garret cracked into the fence rail an arm's length from the cliff's edge and struggled to gain his knees.

"Eli! What the hell—Kill MacQuade! Kill him!"

"You hurt . . . boy, Cain . . . hurt . . . promised not . . ."

"What are you? Crazy? He was gonna kill me, Eli!"

"You were gonna kill . . . me . . . heard you . . ." Eli slurred, staggering closer, ever closer. "Have to . . . kill you 'stead."

Cain turned his gun on his brother and fired, the bullet slamming into Eli's shoulder. The man faltered, then righted himself, staggering inexorably forward.

Garvey's pistol fired again, and blood blossomed on Eli's leg.

Cain backed toward the fence bordering the cliff, pulling his trigger yet again. This time the click of an empty chamber seemed to shatter the clearing. Cain's eyes widened, mouth twisting in very real terror as his back slammed up against the fence rail.

"Stop, Eli! Damn it, I'm your brother! Don't—"

"You made me kill them," Eli almost sobbed. "The pretty lady. The little girl—made me."

"Don't be a fool! Eli! Stop—"

"Don't have to do what you say no more, Cain . . . dead . . . we'll both be . . ."

The huge man stumbled, but his hands reached out, curving around Cain's throat.

A strangled sound came from the smaller man as Cain clawed at Eli's face. Ashleen stared in horror at the tears coursing down Eli's cheeks, sobs coming from the man's crimson-stained chest.

With a soul-chilling cry Eli threw his weight against his brother, the fence splintering with a sickening crack.

Ash screamed as the two men teetered on the brink of the cliff, then hurtled down, down into the relentless arms of death.

24

*F*or a heartbeat Ashleen stood frozen, eerie silence blanketing the clearing with an aura of unreality, as if nothing so horrible could have happened in this oasis of serenity, of warmth, of love.

Ash saw Garret struggling to rise, heard the shuffling of Renny trying to right himself.

Then she was in Garret's arms, crushed against him in a desperate, half-crazed embrace.

"You're safe, Ash . . . sweet Jesus, you're safe," he repeated over and over again in a hoarse voice. She felt the warmth of his tears against her cheek, his hands roving restlessly up and down her back as if to draw in the very essence of her, to assure himself that she was indeed alive and well.

"I'm fine, Garret, but you . . . you're hurt. Your leg—"

"The devil with my leg!"

She succumbed to a shivery sob, and the full impact of her terror crashed down about her. "Oh, God, Garret . . . Eli . . . he was going to—to—"

"He didn't. Damn it, Ash, he didn't."

"But he was going to—to rape me in front of the children. Was going to . . ." She buried her face in his chest, glorying in the warmth of him, the steady thrumming of his heart. Life. It was infinitely precious in the wake of having it all but swept away.

"Couldn't believe it when—when I looked up and saw you on that roof. Like a miracle."

"It was a miracle, Ash." Garret pulled away, catching her face in his hands. "Sweet Jesus, a miracle. I was coming up the western rise when I saw the strange horse, and I thought maybe . . . maybe it was Garvey. Thank God I'd left the ladder up against the back of the house the day . . . the day I was working up there. It was the only thing that gave me a chance to get the drop on them."

"You going to be all right, Mr. MacQuade?" Renny's voice broke in, shaken but—thankfully—strong.

They turned to see the boy's pale face, his freckles stark against his skin as he stared down at where blood welled from Garret's thigh, staining his buckskins a dark red.

"Yes, boy," Garret said, rumpling the boy's fiery hair. "I'm going to be just fine, thanks to you. Going after Garvey with that hoe was one of the stupidest moves I've ever seen"—Ash could see the boy squirm, but Garret's voice softened just a whisper as he went on—"it was also one of the bravest." His voice wavered, and he gave Renny a fierce hug. "I'm proud as hell of you, boy. But if you ever try anything like that again, I'm going to tan your backside till you can't sit for a month of Sundays!"

"Yes, sir." The words were the essence of obedience, but Renny's eyes were shining with shy pride and adulation for the man he had fought so hard to hate.

Ash felt her throat swell shut with the joy of it, hastening to busy herself with other things as she tore off her calico apron, bending down to staunch the flow of blood from Garret's leg. But he brushed her hands away, taking the piece of cloth and knotting it carelessly about the wound.

"It's all right, Ash. I swear it. Just tell me about the children. Where the hell are they?"

"They're in the root cellar. Eli locked them in before . . . he touched me."

With astonishing speed Garret limped toward the building and ripped the door open. Ashleen could hear one of the children scream, could hear Liam's sob as Garret plunged through into the dim room beyond.

"M-Mr. MacQuade!" Liam shrilled, flinging himself against Garret. Shevonne, her face streaked with grime and tears, rushed past them both to hurl herself against Renny. Awkward, yet obviously pleased, Renny patted her on the back, his face reddening.

"R-Renny! You're alive!"

"Was till you started chokin' me," he said sheepishly, but Ashleen could see his lips tipping in a shy smile.

Her heart wrenched as Garret caught Liam tight in his arms and buried his face in the child's curls.

"M-Mr. MacQuade, I was so scared. . . ."

"Thought we'd agreed you were going to call me Pa."

"P-Pa. Thought you'd . . . never come."

"Told 'em you'd come." Meggie's voice cut through their stammerings. Everyone turned to look at the little girl standing in the shadows, her arms crossed over her small chest. "It was the magic."

Garret released Liam slowly, carefully, easing down onto his good knee to bring himself eye level with the little girl. He reached out, taking the child's small hands in his.

"It was the magic that brought me back, angel." His voice broke, and he swept the child against him, holding her, the love in those gray eyes piercing through to Ashleen's very soul.

"Magic?" Ashleen echoed.

"Meggie's magic rock. She gave it to me before I left to ward off dragons. When I opened its wrapping I saw the nugget. I knew that the Garveys had never found the gold. That it was still somewhere on Stormy Ridge." His mouth went grim. "And I knew those bastards would come stalking."

A shudder worked through him. "Damn it, Ashleen, I was so scared . . . that I'd be too late. That those animals had already hurt you, the children. I was out of my mind thinking of what they might be doing to you, wondering if you were still alive."

"Did you slayed the dragons, Mr.—*Pa?*" Meggie's voice. Impatient. It broke through his tormented words.

"Yes, baby," Garret assured her, kissing her tumbled hair. "The—the dragons are gone."

"Shevonne said they were out-laweds, not dragons. That more of 'em might come. But I tol' her not to worry."

"No, Meggie, love. I'll always be here from now on. Taking care of all of you—"

"'Course you will." Meggie reached up to pat Garret's dark silk hair, and it was as if with that childish caress she were wiping away a lifetime of pain. "An' I got 'nough magic to last for a million years."

She pulled away and went to the side of the cellar, tugging at a piece of the sod wall. It fell away, revealing a space behind it. Light from the doorway spilled in, a mellow glow filling the secret niche. Ashleen went to it, sinking down on her knees. She reached in, her hand closing about something hard, odd-shaped. Gold.

"Garret, the whole space is filled with it," she gasped, stunned.

"It had to have been Pa. Pa who hid it here." Garret's voice held love, pain. "He must've seen Kennisaw when the old buzzard dumped the strongboxes. He must've taken the gold out of 'em. Buried it down here for safekeeping. That day . . . when the Garveys rode in, Ash, I remember Pa was coming out of the root cellar. I remember . . ."

"But why didn't he tell the Garveys from the first if he knew—"

"He knew from the beginning the bastards wouldn't leave any of us alive after they got their hands on the treasure. Wouldn't leave any witnesses to identify them. I think he was trying to play for time . . . find some way out." A shudder racked him. "He wasn't as lucky as we were, lady."

"Holy Mother MacCree!" Renny's astonished cry made them start, and they turned to see that the boy had scooted over to peer into the niche, his eyes round. He clapped a hand over his mouth. "Holy . . . Sister Ash, there's enough there to—to make us rich!"

"We're already rich, boy. Richer than I'd ever dreamed." Garret moved to look as well, dragging out a huge nugget, holding it in his hand.

"You could build a castle with all that gold," Liam said, awed. "A real castle. Bet you could even build a dragon if you wanted to."

"Don't be a goose, Liam," Shevonne broke in sharply, but then her voice softened, tinged with uncertainty. "The cabin's better than any old castle anyway. It's got a loft and . . . and a fireplace, and—and now it's got a real pa and ma."

"And children." Garret curved his arm about Shevonne's knees, drawing the child against his side. "My children."

Ashleen felt something burst inside her, the pain, the terror, a thousand gnawing doubts that had eaten at her conscience since the day she had fled the convent seeming to melt away, leaving behind the shimmering wonder of dreams turned real.

Grimacing with pain, Garret forced himself back to his feet, and he turned to where Ashleen stood, his wolf-gray eyes alight with tenderness, love.

"With this I could buy you anything you wanted, lady. Fine gowns, carriages. You'd never have to do without."

"I agree with Shevonne. There aren't any lofts in castles, Garret, and as for carriages . . . I'd rather watch the stars from the back of the wagon. With you."

Callused fingers traced her cheek, and Ashleen turned to press a kiss into Garret's palm.

His hands trembled as he paused and curved his fingers about her face as if it was wrought of angel mist.

"Then what would you say if we bundled all this gold up and sent it off to Ireland? To that Sister Agatha you loved so much? There's enough here to pay for a chalice, lady. And food for a hell of a lot of orphans." His voice was soft, so gentle, it branded itself forever on Ashleen's heart.

Her throat constricted with love, eyes blurring with tears. "I'd like that. I'd like it very much."

There was a tug at Garret's sleeve, and they looked down into Meggie's troubled features. "But the magic, Pa. Will it go away?"

With one strong arm Garret swooped the little girl into their embrace as Ashleen drew Liam, Shevonne, even Renny into a warm, wondrous hug.

"No, Meggie mine," Garret said, his voice breaking. His gaze caught Ashleen's and held it, and there were tears in those wolf-gray eyes. "The magic is here. Forever."